MORE TO IT

C.J. REGINA

MILTON & HUGO L.L.C.
4407 Park Ave., Suite 5
Union City, NJ 07087, USA

Website: *www. miltonandhugo.com*
Hotline: *1- 888-778-0033*
Email: *info@miltonandhugo.com*

Ordering Information:
Quantity sales. Special discounts are granted to corporations, associations, and other organizations. For more information on these discounts, please reach out to the publisher using the contact information provided above.

Library of Congress Control Number:	2024910438	
ISBN-13:	979-8-89285-151-0	[Paperback Edition]
	979-8-89285-231-9	[Hardback Edition]
	979-8-89285-152-7	[Digital Edition]

Rev. date: 07/10/2024

Special thanks to:

My Parents ("I love you forever")
My Brother and soon-to-be Sister-in-law, Joe and Katie (Boo and Earl)
My Grandparents
The Curtes
The Pluchinos
The Marascias and Danny
The Becks
The Insalacos
Kate D. (and Macy)
Christine S. (and Trixie)
Adrina R.
Adam and Saneesh
Jessica "Creampuff"
Sam C.
My Bros: Anthony, Jon, and James
Everyone at T2T Wrestling
The staff and students of Port Richmond High School
Model and Talent Management/John Casablancas
Miss M and Family
Mr. Mike
Gabby
My fur babies: Nala, LC, Boscoe, and Nikko

Those who tried to bring me down but ultimately made me better and stronger.

Everyone who's ever helped me back up on my journey to this point, even when I didn't ask for or wanted it.

Chapter 1

New Year, New Faces

There's an old saying that goes "You can't judge a book by its cover." As cliché as it is, there's a lot of truth to that saying; what may seem like a delicious meal on a menu could have a bitter and resentful taste to it. But that can also work the other way around—what appears to be one thing might be something entirely different. Or, at least, was something entirely different. Whatever the case may be, it's easy to pass judgment on anything. Or anyone. But taking enough time to get to know somebody can change your whole perception, and who knows? You could even have a larger-than-life impact on them.

The year was 2016: the *Ghostbusters* reboot was the most political topic in the middle of a presidential election, the celebrity death toll was rising at an unprecedented rate, the infamous "Curse of the Billy Goat" was being broken, and the Summer of *Pokémon GO* had come to an end. You know that feeling when you wake up on the first day of the new school year? When the harsh reality of knowing you can't wake up on your free will anymore and having to start working again sinks in? Then there's that feeling in your gut that reminds you you're starting something familiar but new, almost like a whole new adventure is beginning. Some people's adventures are more exciting than others, but this one is something truly special.

It all started at Meadows Forest High School, Staten Island, New York. It was the middle of September. Teachers were resuming their jobs, and the students were dreadful, already missing their vacation. At least most of them were, but some didn't mind as much. It sounds odd, yes, but that's also the word so many used to describe one particular girl: Paige Hetfield.

If you were to ask anybody about her, they would all describe her the same way: "Yeah, she's that odd girl who always sits in the front of class and never talks to anyone." Okay, not everybody said it exactly like that, but you get the idea. Outside of that, she was beautiful, had a gifted intelligence, frequently got straight As, and maintained a decent social status. But that's all the majority of the student body knew about her. She was never much of a sociable person, often keeping to herself; was rarely spotted at any school events; would always spend her lunch period in the library; and was the kind of person who preferred to stay indoors on a weekend. She never had her mind on romance, and even if she got asked out, she always said no.

The only people she would ever hang out with were her three friends: Morgan Chambers, Amy Brookes, and Jennifer Owens. They were all very close, but even they didn't know everything about Paige. Was it shyness, lack of interest, preference to concentration on her work, or something else? There was a lot of mystery to her, and nobody was able to crack it.

Monday, 8:00 AM

It was the second week of the year. Paige entered her Monday homeroom English class with her headphones in and sat down at her desk by her best friend, Morgan Chambers.

Morgan snuck her head in close enough to hear what she's listening to.

"Hmm, Kelly Clarkson. Fancy," Morgan said.

Paige snapped out of the trance she's in took her bud out and giggled. "A little personal space, please?"

"I had to get your attention somehow."

"I can see how saying 'hello Paige' was too complicated." She chuckled.

"So you do anything special this weekend?" Paige asked.

"Well, my family went to the beach on Saturday, where I saw this fat guy lying down on his blanket, and then this seagull came swooping down, stole his bag of chips, and when he saw it, he tried to stand up, but he couldn't." Morgan cracked up while telling her story. "He looked like a turtle on the back of its shell. It was amazing."

Paige slightly giggled. "You're sick, you know that?"

"Like you're any healthier than me." Both girls shared a laugh. "So what'd you do this weekend?" Morgan asked. "Wait wait wait, lemme take a guess! You were playing either *Rise of the Tomb Raider* or *No Man's Sky* on PS4. Or both."

"Wrong," Paige defensively replied.

"Xbox One." Paige didn't reply. "Score!"

"I hate you so much."

"Aw, come on, baby, you don't mean that. You know you love me," Morgan said as she cradled her head and pinched her cheeks.

"Will you cut that out?" Paige demanded while chuckling.

Morgan obliged and chuckled. "Seriously though, I love gaming as much as you, but it's nice to switch it up once in a while. You rarely ever go out."

"I've told you a dozen times—I don't need to go out to have a good time, and besides, you know I tutor on weekends too."

"Yeah. Because clearly that's more fun than going out and getting some action," Morgan sarcastically said while making suggestive gestures with her hands.

"Oh my god, Morgan!" Paige exclaimed with wide eyes.

"I'm just saying, a girl as pretty as you can have any guy she wants."

"Well, I don't want 'any guy' right now. I just wanna focus on me and me only."

Morgan sighed. "Sometimes I just don't get you, Paige."

The bell rang, and more students began crowding the classroom. Most of the faces were ones they'd seen since the class started; but a new face caught their attention, an older-looking, tall, muscular tattooed guy, dressed primarily in black with a gold necklace: Steven Jacobs. Or as he's made himself known: Steven Axl.

They'd seen him around their school, ever so briefly, and had heard his name brought up a lot; but they'd never shared a class with him.

Steven noticed the two staring at him. "Can I help you with something?" he asked rudely.

Paige and Morgan didn't reply.

"All right, I see how it is." Steven walked to the back of the class and sat down, putting his feet on the desk.

"Isn't that Steven Axl?" Paige whispered to Morgan.

"Yeah," Morgan whispered back.

"Isn't he a senior?"

"He's supposed to be. But I heard he got left back."

"Seriously? I mean, I guess I shouldn't be surprised but still."

"I just thought that was a rumor, like the one about him killing a dog and making a rug out of it."

"What!?"

"That's just what I heard. I didn't believe it, but now I'm not so sure."

Paige was disturbed at that idea. "I always hoped I never came across that guy."

"I don't know. I feel kinda like I just discovered Bigfoot. Now we get to observe the phenomenon," Morgan said enthusiastically.

"I feel like I should call the cops."

Before Morgan could respond, their teacher, Mrs. Curtis, finally entered before the late bell. Unbeknownst to every other student in the school—excluding her friends who promised to keep it a secret—Mrs. Curtis was actually Paige's mom. Paige thought it would be embarrassing if word got out that her teacher was family, so Paige decided to go by her stepfather's maiden name. Her mom respected this and swore she would keep it confidential.

Mrs. Curtis set her coffee down and addressed her students. "All right, class, I know it's Monday and you'd all rather be in bed, but I need some cooperation. Please complete the Do Now on the board."

The class proceeded to do exactly that. Paige took a brief second to look back at Steven. Steven noticed from the corner of his eyes and turned his head to face her. She looked back down at her binder quickly and pretended nothing happened. Steven dismissed it and sighed as he looked back down at his phone.

If there was anybody in the school more mysterious than Paige, it was Steven Axl. Even less was known about him, and he was far less gregarious. He intimidated a lot of people, but that only made them

more curious about him; and even though she knew better than to get involved with people like this, Paige was one of them.

Chapter 2

Friendly Little Encounter

Dismissal Time

Paige and Morgan left the school and headed to the parking lot where they met up with their other friend, Amy Brookes.

"Sup, bitch!" Morgan shouted at Amy.

Amy turned around to greet them. "Hey, ladies!" She and Morgan hugged tightly. She then hugged Paige who was less stiff.

"Hey, Amy. Did you get your nose pierced?" Paige asked.

"Yeah, just got it last Friday at the mall."

"That's hot! Finally, all of us have rocks in our bodies!" Morgan said with enthusiasm.

"Speaking of which, where's Jenn?" Paige asked.

"Yeah, she's our ride," Morgan said.

"She went to get a soda from the vending machine," Amy answered.

"Eww, why? Those are disgusting. I don't think they're even real sodas. I think somebody just cut some fruit in half, rubbed it on their sweaty bodies, squeezed it into a can, and started selling it with a soda label," Morgan ranted.

The two stared at her, weirded out.

"That's actually not too far off. Why?" Paige asked Amy.

"I guess somebody has to like it, and we all know how selective she is with what she likes," Amy answered, and they both agreed.

"Anyway, how'd the date with Zack go?" Paige asked.

"It was okay. I don't think there's gonna be another one though," Amy answered.

"What happened?" Morgan asked.

"I don't know. We just didn't click that well. We didn't have anything in common, didn't have any conversations that went on for more than a minute, and I just felt no spark," Amy explained.

"Seriously? When he asked you out a week ago, you swore he'd be your soulmate," Paige replied.

"I know what I said. He's really cute, but now that I actually got to know him, something wasn't right. He tried to kiss me good night, but I didn't want to," Amy said.

"Aw. Well, that's a shame," Morgan said.

"I'm sorry to hear that. I know this is the fourth time this year," Paige said sincerely and rubbed her shoulder.

Amy touched where Paige's hand was. "It's okay. If I get into a relationship, I want it to be for the long run. I'll know it when I feel it."

"If anything, I feel more bad for him. Anybody would be lucky to be dating you," Morgan assured her.

Amy smiled. "Thanks, Morgan. You may be weird, but you always know what to say."

Amy hugged Morgan who warmly embraced her back.

Amy checked her phone. "I'll be right back. I'm gonna see where Jenn is." She walked off to call Jenn.

Morgan swooned as she watched her walk off.

"I heard that," Paige said with a grin.

"No, you didn't. I didn't hear it. Whatever it was," Morgan dismissed her.

"Morgan, you've obsessed with her for almost a year now. Just tell her how you feel."

"What would the point be? She's clearly not into girls."

"So then you have nothing to lose." Morgan looked down. "I'm telling you, you'll feel better if you just get it out."

Morgan leaned against a car. "Opening up is harder than you might think, Paige. It's not just something you can forget about. If you ever felt like this about someone, you'd know how scary it is."

Paige chuckled. "Since when you afraid of anything?"

"Don't judge me, Miss Perfect. I—"

Morgan was cut off when she heard somebody shout, "HEY!"

They both looked over where they heard the voice and saw a familiar face walk over, Steven Axl.

"Get your ass off my car!"

Morgan did exactly that. "All right all right, don't take your PMS rage out on me," Morgan replied.

"Morgan, shhh!" Paige panicked.

"You wanna say that to my face?" Axl challenged Morgan.

Morgan, refusing to be intimidated, went back to reply but was stopped by Paige.

"No, she doesn't. We're so sorry. We didn't know it was yours," Paige said with a nervous smile.

"It's true," Morgan said. "If I knew that, I would've used my keys to carve my name on it."

Paige's eyes widened, certain that death was just upon them.

"Ah yeah? How 'bout I carve my name on your face?" he threatened. "And while I'm at it, how 'bout I break the glasses on yours?" He turned his attention to Paige who's frozen with fear, while Morgan stood her ground.

"How 'bout a counteroffer?"

The three of them turned to face the source of the sound and finally saw Amy following behind the large muscular frame of their retrieved friend, Jenn Owens.

Jenn stepped in front of them and got up close to Steven. "You back away from my friends right now before I smash your head through your windshield and stick your keys into your dick hole!"

Steven had a stare down with the taller girl, not fazed by her remark.

At that moment, Steven's friend Jason Kennedy came up and pushed him back.

"He'll take you up on that offer," Jason said.

"Get outta the way, Jason!" Steven demanded.

"Dude, just relax!" he said sternly. "It ain't worth it. Plus, we gotta pick up Lisa."

Steven took a deep breath. "Consider yourselves lucky, ladies!" he said, pointing at them.

"Believe me, I do," Paige mumbled to herself, still petrified.

Steven turned around to get into his car.

Jason looked back to address the four girls. "Sorry about that. I swear he's not always like this. He's just a little on edge."

"A little?" Morgan questioned him, with an incensed tone.

"You get my point. Seriously though, sorry for all the trouble."

"Well, I'm just glad no blood was spilled," Amy said. "Thanks for setting him straight."

"Don't mention it. I was afraid for a second your friend here was gonna break him. She looks like she could," Jason referred to Jenn.

"Thanks for noticing," Jenn said apathetically.

"Of course, I mean that in a good way. 'Cause I gotta say, you're not so bad to look at either…" Jason said with a smirk.

"Get in your buddy's car, and drive away," Jenn ordered.

"Yeah okay, okay. Have a nice day. See you all around." Jason tried and failed to sound casual as he got into the passenger seat. "Probably." Jason closed the door.

The two drove off.

Paige forced Morgan to turn around and face her. "Are you nuts? You almost got us killed!"

"Aw come on, he wouldn't have actually killed us," Morgan bluffed.

"He would've made you wish you were dead!" Amy said with concern.

"Well, JO always tells us that these kinds of people can smell your fear, and when they confront you, ya can't let them." Morgan justified herself.

"That doesn't mean you go around picking fights!" Jenn told her.

"Maybe so, but at least we can say we survived an encounter with Steven Axl," Morgan said.

"You have some serious issues," Jenn said.

"'We're all mad here.'—Cheshire Cat. Copyright *Alice in Wonderland* by Lewis Carroll," Morgan replied.

"Ah geez." Paige rubbed her temple. "Thanks for saving us, Jenn."

"No prob. To Morgan's credit, it's always fun to get in on some exciting action," Jenn said.

"Well, that's enough excitement for me for one day," Paige said, still feeling the effect.

"It's all right," Amy said, comforting Paige. "Our friendly little encounter is over. Let's go out for some ices," she requested.

"Sweet," Morgan said.

Paige took a brief breather. "Yeah. I could use one right now."

The four proceeded to get into Jenn's car.

"Oh and by the way, Morgan, *Alice in Wonderland* is in the public domain. Nobody has a copyright on it," Paige corrected her.

"I stand by my word," Morgan replied.

The four exited the parking lot and drove off, hoping to just forget about that "friendly little encounter" they just had.

Chapter 3

The Assignment

Three Days Later

Paige was still shaken up from the confrontation with Steven a few days ago. Any sort of conflict completely stressed her out, whether minor or major, and this one she experienced forced her into a disturbed state of mind. She already didn't like to draw attention to herself, but now she's made even more of an effort to stay low. She was often the first to raise her hand to participate in class, but throughout the last week, she did none of that; she just wanted to forget about what happened that past Monday. It turned out it's not so easy when you're forced to see the same face every morning. Even just catching a glimpse of him or hearing his name startled her.

It also didn't help that Steven was incredibly outspoken in class. It seemed like anything he thought, he would say it out loud without any hesitation. He often disrupted class by calling out loud, questioning what his teachers said, or attempting to start arguments with students and even threatening to fight them. He had little to no interest in his lessons, and all the days he would spend in detention seemed to just encourage him to rebel harder. With all this in mind, it wasn't hard to see why he had to repeat the eleventh grade.

Paige knew better than to stay away from him out of principle, but now she avoided him out of fear. She just wanted to get through the rest of her life without anything to do with this guy. Thus far, she had succeeded in her efforts; but little did she know, it was about become impossible . . .

First Period, Dismissal

The bell rang, and first period had been let out.

"Sweetie?" her mother, Catherine, called; and Paige turned around to face her. "Could I see you for a minute?"

Paige closed the door and approached her desk. "What's up, Mom?"

"Well, first of all, I've noticed you've been quieter than you usually are. Is everything okay?"

"Yeah. Yeah, everything is okay, just readjusting to the new year, that's all." Paige tried to reassure her.

"You sure?" she asked Paige, who nodded yes. "O-kay. So I'll get straight to the point. Now, I need you to just bear with me for a second."

"I hate sentences that begin with that," Paige replied.

"I know. Just hear me out. I don't know if you've noticed, but the student that just joined our class, Steven Jacobs, has been . . . a little disruptive."

"That's an understatement. Why did he get transferred here anyway? Out of every class in this school, why'd he have to come into yours?"

"No special reason. Some classes were just overstocked, and he was one of the few to go. Happens all the time."

"You must feel so blessed," Paige said sarcastically.

"Anyway, my point being, he hasn't been doing very well so far in any of his classes."

"No surprise there."

"Please let me finish," Catherine appealed. "So I've talked to his other teachers about what to do to switch that around, and I suggested getting him some extra help on the weekends."

Paige's eyes winded when she started to realize what her mom's about to say.

"So I was hoping that you can take time on the weekends to tutor him."

"What?" Paige asked, horrified. "No way!"

"Sweetheart, please think about this."

"Why me? Why should I have to look after that lunatic?" Paige's voice rose slightly.

"Because you're one of the brightest students in school, and I'm not just saying that because I'm your mother. And besides that, you've helped a lot of students turn their grades around. You've turned plenty of F students into A students."

"But none of them looked like they could rip out my intestines!" Paige remarked.

"Oh, come on now. I'll admit he's been a handful, but that's a bit of an exaggeration."

"Do you know he killed a dog?"

"What?"

"I only heard that, but now I totally believe it's true!" Paige exclaimed.

"All right, calm down. Just breathe." She paused as Paige took a few deep breaths. "Look, I understand your lack of enthusiasm. But I really think that you could make a difference and help him pass the eleventh grade."

Paige said nothing, silenced by her own fear.

"Just please think of giving it a chance for at least a marking period, and if it doesn't work out, we'll search for somebody else to help him. But if it does work out, I'm hoping you could keep it going for the rest of the semester. The end of winter break at best." Catherine tried assuring her, but just the idea of spending the whole semester with this guy appalled her even more. "And you'll get extra credit in all your classes."

Paige nervously thought it over. "I really don't think this is a good idea."

"Well, you never know what'll happen unless you take the risk. And if the risk doesn't pay off, it's always important to remember: Failure starts with an F but is followed by an A."

"Please don't use that on me."

"Too late. And you may be surprised what could come of it. You might even make friends with him. It happened when you were helping Amy with earth science."

"Yeah, because Morgan pushed me into convincing her to hang out with us."

"Why?"

"Because she really wanted to get to know her better."

"And now you're all inseparable."

"Well, I don't think Steven and I will get along so well," Paige said before looking down.

Catherine leaned back on her chair. "You said the exact same thing about Richard."

Paige moved her eyes up to stare at her mom. She thought about what she just said before sighing in defeat.

"All right. I'll see what I can do."

"That's my girl!" Catherine said excitedly. "So we'll set everything up, and you kids can start this Saturday."

Paige begrudgingly nodded. "May I go now?"

"Of course." Her mother handed her a late note. "Thank you for being so understanding. You're such a terrific kid."

"Thank you." Paige walked out and closed the door.

Paige mouthed to herself, "What did I just do?" before proceeding to her next class.

Chapter 4

Video Chat

Later That Evening

Paige was in her room having a video call with Morgan, Amy, and Jenn.

"YOU WHAT?" Amy asked.

"Yeah, turns out I can bench-press two hundred pounds," Jenn said.

"Wicked! Watch out, Ronda Rousey, here comes Jenn Owens!" Morgan exclaimed.

"Show off those arms, girl!" Amy requested.

Jenn flexed as demanded.

"All right, check out those weapons!"

"Whoo! I'm swooning!" Morgan said.

"I'm sorry, Paige, you were saying something?" Jenn said.

"Yeah. Long story short, starting Saturday I'm gonna be tutoring Steven Axl," Paige simply put it.

"WHAT!" the three said in unison.

They all gave each other weirded-out looks.

"That was weird, right?" Amy asked.

"Yeah, that was weird," Morgan said.

"Abnormal," Jenn reassured them.

"Hmm-hmm. Moving on, *you're tutoring Axl? What are you thinking!*" Amy asked, practically interrogating.

"Oh, trust me, I'm not exactly stoked about this," Paige said.

"So then why are you doing this?" Amy asked.

"A combination of an extra credit promise and because my mom thinks I can change him," Paige answered.

15

"Well, Paige, when you put it like that, it sounds like your mom wants to get you killed," Morgan said, causing Paige to gulp.

"Yeah, what'd you do? Use her credit card without permission?" Jenn asked.

"Guys, can we be a little more sincere? She's clearly upset," Amy said.

"I'm not upset. Just nervous, worried, nauseous, overall scared for my life," Paige listed.

"All right, listen, just calm down. You're usually the positive-thinking one, so just try to keep that mindset," Jenn said.

"How? What if I piss him off? You know what conflict does to me!" Paige spoke.

"We know. We've seen how shook you've been all week," Morgan said.

Paige started to tighten up her body, and she noticeably started sweating.

"Just remain calm, and at least try to not act so intimidated. That's what people like him want," Jenn said.

"You always say that, but how am I gonna know that works?" Paige asked.

"I live in Brooklyn. I know how to handle these kinds of people. Trust me, girl," Jenn said.

"And you got good people skills, though you hardly ever show 'em. Just apply those to him," Morgan said.

"Except after Monday, I can't even think about him without feeling like I'm gonna die of a heart attack. Like right now, I feel like I'm about to explode. How can I even talk to him?" Paige said.

"You're smart. You'll figure something out," Jenn said.

"Just get through this and you never have to speak to him again," Morgan said.

Paige tried to loosen up a bit.

"I still think this is a bad idea, but if you're really gonna go through with it, then best of luck," Amy said.

"Thanks, guys. I'm gonna need it."

"Anything we can do for now?" Amy asked.

"I think I'm just gonna go to bed," Paige answered.

"You sure?" Amy asked.

"Yeah. Good night, girls."

Paige disconnected right as they're saying their goodbyes and stared at the open tabs and programs on her screen, before turning her head to look out her bedroom window onto the empty, dimly lit borough of Staten Island, where the rain was pouring at a heavy rate. She stayed there for about half a minute before she walked away from her personal work area and crumpled onto her bed. Her face was engulfed by her pillow as she's internally panicking.

Chapter 5

First Session

Saturday, Twilight

The day of the first tutoring session had come. Paige's mom talked to Steven about getting a tutor, and he was as stoked about the idea as Paige was. I mean, let's be honest, the weekends should be a temporary escape from schoolwork. Despite his reluctance, he agreed to the sessions and set it up for it to be at his house, much to the dismay of Paige. Being up close to him was scary enough; now she had to be in his home. She couldn't begin to imagine what the rest of his family would be like. She was beyond nervous but knew there was no turning back now. She just tried to heave her friend's advice, as well as what her mom told her: remain calm.

The sun was starting to set. Paige's stepdad, Richard, was driving her to Steven's—his house was about ten minutes away from theirs. Her heart was beating faster with every passing street corner, knowing how much closer she was to meeting her fate.

They pulled up to the house. She was expecting some sort of run-down, poorly constructed house with a chain-link fence, but to her surprise, it was much nicer than she thought. It was about three stories, had a big backyard with a big tree planted that had a swing chained to it, and had a big colorful garden. She was unsure if her dad put in the right address. But this was indeed Steven's house; the moment of truth had come.

"All right, we're here," Richard said.

Paige didn't respond. She just sat there to herself for a few seconds, taking in this surprise.

"You okay, kid?" Richard asked.

Paige took a deep breath. "Yeah. I'm fine," she responded.

"Well, I'll be at the coffee shop up the street, and I'll get you around seven. But if anything happens, or if you feel uncomfortable, just gimme a call and I'll be back here in a snap," her stepfather told her.

Paige slightly smiled and nodded yes. "Thanks, Dad."

Paige grabbed her book bag and opened the door.

"I love you," Richard said.

"You too," Paige responded and closed the door.

Her dad drove off.

Paige turned around and proceeded to Steven's house.

I can't believe I'm doing this, Paige said to herself.

She walked up the steps and rang the doorbell.

She waited for about seven or eight seconds, observing the house and front lawn, before finally hearing the doorknob turn.

The wooden door opened; she turned forward and looked up, expecting to see Steven, but he wasn't there. She then looked down where she spotted a little blonde girl wearing a colorful outfit.

"Oh. Sorry. Hello." Paige awkwardly waved to the child, lightly chuckling.

"Hi," the girl said, smiling at her. "Mom! There's a girl at the door!" she called.

A woman about only an inch taller than Paige, dressed business casual, came to open the second door that's made of glass. At first, the handle didn't turn, so she had to aggressively jiggle it around until finally getting it to cooperate. She finally opened it and greeted Paige with a smile, trying to be casual.

"I'm so sorry. Sometimes this door just gets stuck." She uncomfortably laughed. "Hi. You must be Steven's tutor." She spoke, still smiling.

Paige looked slightly confused and surprised. "Uh, yes, I am," she answered.

"Great, come in," she invited her. Paige walked in, still unsure of what to make of this. "Just make yourself at home," the lady said as she closed the door.

Paige took a moment to observe the house and found it's just as nice on the inside as it was on the outside.

"Right. Um, I'm Paige," she said, extending her hand.

The lady shook her hand back. "Beautiful name. Call me Samantha."

"It's… nice to meet you." Paige put on a smile.

"Hi, Paige, I'm Lisa," the smaller girl greeted her.

Paige hunched over. "Hi, Lisa."

"You're really pretty," Lisa complimented her.

"Thank you. So are you."

Lisa smiled big at her. "Thanks."

Suddenly she heard some rapid footsteps. She turned her head and saw a Rottweiler approaching her. The dog sniffed her out as she's saying hello and then stood on its hind legs to lick her face.

Paige let out an "oh" sound and started giggling.

"Boscoe! Down, boy. Down," Samantha said. The dog obeyed her and let out two barks. "Easy, baby. Easy. I am so sorry. Again," she apologized as she got the dog under control.

"No, it's okay," Paige said, wiping her face, and started petting him. "He's an affectionate one." She giggled.

"His name is Boscoe," Lisa said, joining her in petting him. "My dad found him at his job, and we brought him home."

"Aww, aren't we a lucky scamp?" Paige said to Boscoe.

"Do you have a dog?" Samantha asked.

"No. I'd love to get one though," Paige said.

Needless to say, this was not nearly close to what she was expecting. As relieved as she was, she was just as much confused.

"So, uh, where's Steven?" Paige asked.

"He's upstairs in his room. Lisa, could you take her upstairs and show her where to go?" Samantha asked the small girl.

"Okay. Come on, Paige."

Paige followed her behind as they headed upstairs.

"I like your shirt," Lisa said, noticing her *Avatar: The Last Airbender* tee.

"Thank you. You watch *Avatar*?" Paige asked.

"Oh my god, I *love* it! Is it not the greatest show ever?" Lisa said with great enthusiasm.

"Hard to argue with that," Paige said with a laugh.

"How hot is Zuko?" Lisa asked.

Paige laughed at her remark. "He's pretty cute, I'll admit."

"Seriously!" Lisa remarked.

The two finally arrived at Steven's closed door.

Lisa knocked on it. "Steven, your tutor's here!" she shouted.

The door opened. Steven was wearing a sleeveless Korn shirt that showed off more of his tattoos, along with the same gold necklace he always wore to school. He looked up from Lisa to see the girl standing next to her.

"Ah great. You," he nonchalantly said.

"Steven, this is Paige. You've met her?" Lisa asked.

"Kinda. We have English together, and we parked next to each other on Monday," Steven told her as he's looking at Paige with a passive-aggressive expression.

"That's cool. Well, have fun," Lisa said.

"Nice meeting you, Lisa," Paige said.

"You too, Paige," she said back. "Steven, Mom says to leave your door open when we have company."

"I know, I know—I heard her the first hundred and three times. Just run along. Go draw or something," Steven told her.

"You know what? I will, and it's gonna be awesome. I might even post it on Instagram! Or Tumblr!" Lisa replied before walking away.

"You do that!" Steven replied, annoyed. "You just gonna stand there? Or are you coming in?" he asked Paige.

Paige projected an uncomfortable chuckle before stepping into his room. She looked around and saw a bunch of metal-band posters hung up and some laundry on the floor, and she can hear grunge music blasting. This was more what she was expecting, but she was more eased up after meeting his family. She felt like she was in a safer environment now, so she let her guard down. There was still a rather tense presence in the air, but Paige decided she would just act casual.

"So . . . Your sister's really cute," Paige said, nervous.

"She's definitely something," Steven said, clearly not wanting to make small talk.

A few seconds of awkward silence followed as Steven walked over to his computer desk and sat down. He gestured toward Paige to sit down, which she did.

"Your mom seems nice," Paige said, giving a half smile.

"All right, look, whatever your name was, this ain't a blind date; so let's just get this over with," Steven told her.

"It's Paige."

"I don't care."

"Okay then. Um, I guess we can start with English."

"Whatever. I don't get the point of it though. I'm never visiting Paris."

"Uh, that's actually not what this class us about; and France is actually its own country, not a part of England—"

"Oh, I'm sorry, I thought you were teaching me English, not geology," Steven interrupted her.

"Geology is the study of the physical structures of Earth and its history—"

"Okay, one thing at a time, Einstein. I'm not trying to get into college," Steven interrupted her again.

"Okay okay, sorry," she apologized, feeling more offended than fearful.

Paige proceeded with the session the best she could, but it was just as difficult as she thought it would be. She wasn't going to dare start any kind of debate with him, or anything that could repeat the incident from earlier that week. He was just as uncooperative, outspoken, vulgar, and fractious as he was at school, maybe more so. Her patience was becoming thinner; she started becoming less afraid of him and more aggravated with him. How could someone like this come from a family that seemed so warm and welcoming?

An Hour and a Half Later

"Okay. I think we made a little bit of progress," Paige said.

"I think I just wasted my time. I could be out right now getting my dick sucked, but instead, I had to learn about how Americans killed each other over owning black people. Not to mention from a fourteen-year-old," Steven ranted.

"Fifteen-year-old," Paige corrected him.

"Did I ask you?"

Paige said nothing in return. She started to pack up her stuff.

"You know, I'm curious. How the hell do you get through all this learning crap without wanting to blow your brains out?" he asked.

Paige didn't respond.

"Nah, come on, you were trying to make small talk an hour ago. What's your secret?"

Paige sighed, not looking at him. "There is no secret. I've just always liked learning."

"Uh-huh. There are millions of things you could do with your time, and you spend it doing brainy stuff. That's kinda sad."

Paige started to get offended and fed up with his attitude.

"For the record, there's a lot more to me than just 'brainy stuff,'" Paige said, still not making direct contact.

"Like what?"

Before Paige can respond, she got a message from her dad letting her know he's outside.

Paige let out a sigh of relief. "I gotta go. We'll pick this up tomorrow."

"Pff. Whatever." Steven turned around to face his computer.

Paige packed up and started to leave the room. She turned around to catch a glimpse of Steven with a look of resentment on her face that went completely unnoticed. She then shook her head and just walked out the door.

Chapter 6

Call from Morgan

Later That Same Evening

Paige returned home and went up to her room. She put her bag down and sat on her bed with her head down. She thought back on everything Steven did and said during their session. She felt a variety of emotions: disrespected, annoyed, disgusted, embarrassed, but, above all, confused. The rest of his family was nothing at all like him; it was like that "One of These Things Is Not Like the Other" bit on *Sesame Street*. So what was going on with him?

She almost wanted to feel sympathetic; but anytime she did, she just thought about what a jerk he was to her, in the parking lot and tonight. But the core memory now wasn't the parking lot fiasco; now it was the discussion they had right before she left, which was replaying over and over in her head . . .

"There are millions of things you could do with your time, and you spend it doing brainy stuff. That's kinda sad."

"For the record, there's a lot more to me than just 'brainy stuff.'"

"Like what?"

That last line especially stuck with her. She looked at herself in her bedroom's mirror for a good couple of seconds with a frown on her face. She then collapsed onto her bed and stared at the ceiling for a while.

The monotony was broken up by her phone going off: Morgan was calling.

Paige rubbed her eyes and answered, "Hello?"

"Hey, you're not dead! Awesome!" Morgan said. "So how'd it go?"

Paige sighed. "Well, it went about as bad as I thought it would, but it also wasn't what I was expecting either," she explained.

"What does that mean?"

"Well, I met the rest of his family, and it was so bizarre. I was expecting them to be something out of *Sons of Anarchy*."

"I've never watched that show."

"Not the point. They were more like a family you'd see on the Disney Channel."

"For real?"

"Yeah. He has a sister, his mom was really nice, and apparently the dog rumor was... a bit exaggerated. They were all so polite and made me feel comfortable around them—much more than he ever did. These are the sort of people you'd never associate with him," Paige explained.

Morgan was confused. "Are you sure that he didn't chloroform you, tie you up in a dark room, burn you repeatedly with a cigarette, piss all over you, and threaten to kill you if you told anybody about it before letting you go; and this is just a cover-up?" she asked.

Paige was disturbed by that visual. "No. But thank you so much for making me think of that sick scenario."

"So you're serious?"

"Yeah." She sat up and was on the edge of her bed. "Don't get me wrong, he was just as much an ass as you'd imagine, but I didn't even feel scared this time. Just . . . confused. He has all this, and for whatever reason he acts like an ungrateful prick. Seeing all that, it made me look at him differently. Now he just seems like less of a brute and more like just some jerk."

"Well, clearly there's something more to this guy than everybody lets on. You should try and figure out what it is."

"Ha! I can barely even talk without him saying something rude. How am I supposed to get him to be open about his 'feelings' that I'm not convinced he has?"

"I don't know, man. You're the one with the 4.0 GPA. Put that brain of yours to good use."

Paige sighed. "This is gonna end badly. I just know it."

"And while you're at it, stick up for yourself. Don't let him make you feel as bad as he already did."

"That's not the kind of person I am, Morgan."

"Why not?"

"Because…"

"Because what? Why are you so afraid to fight back?"

"I just don't like to! Okay?" Paige palmed her face and let out a breath. "It's complicated." She stroked her hair backward.

"So then what are you gonna do?"

"I don't know. The only thing that's certain is I can't stand this guy, but I'm just gonna have to find a way to pull his grades that he doesn't care about up. So I guess I'll just got to suck it up until it's over and find some method that works. If not, then I'll just have to do something I've never done before and back out of this."

"Well, whatever you decide to do, just be strong about it. You're way tougher than you give yourself credit. I know for a fact that you're tougher than him."

Paige nodded. "I'll do what I can. Thanks for checking on me, by the way."

"Anytime, babe."

Paige lightly laughed. "All right, I'm gonna let you go. Talk to you later."

"Peace out."

The two hung up.

Paige sat up and took another long look in the mirror. A lot was running through her mind: what Morgan said, what her mom said, what Steven said, about his family, about what could've possibly happened that made him how he was, and about the struggle that this had now become for her. There was a lot to think about, but for now, her mission was to find a way to cooperate with a guy who'd antagonized her, to be a stronger person than he was. She was going to prepare for the worst to come, the best to come, or anything in between to the extent of her ability. And who knows? Perhaps she might learn a little something herself.

Chapter 7

Second Chance

The Next Day

Paige arrived on time for the second meeting with Steven. She went up to the front door and knocked on it.

This time, she's greeted by a muscular man with a tattoo on his forearm.

"Hey, stranger, you lost?" he asked her.

"Uh, no," she replied.

"Bruce, that's Steven's tutor. Let her in," Samantha called from the kitchen across the room.

"All righty then." He vigorously pulled the door before getting it to open. "Sorry, sometimes this door gets stuck."

Paige nodded her head. "You don't say."

"Yeah. Should probably get it fixed one of these days. Anyway, please enter." He stepped aside to let her in. "Name's Bruce."

"I'm Paige."

"So I've heard. How you doing?"

"All right, I guess. Is Steven here?"

"Nah, he went out with his pal Jason. He should be back soon."

"Okay," Paige said, slightly disappointed and thinking to herself, *Already off to a great start.*

"Until then, are you hungry? We have some extra pasta," Samantha offered.

"It's okay. I don't wanna be a burden." Paige politely turned her down.

"No, not at all. Have a seat," Samantha offered.

Paige reconsidered. "I guess I could eat."

"That's the spirit!" Bruce said.

Paige sat down at the table.

"Hi, Lisa," Paige said.

"Hey, Paige. What's up?" Lisa replied.

"Nothing new since yesterday."

"I see. Did you help Steven get any smarter?" Lisa asked.

"I'm doing my best," Paige answered.

"Yeah, he's a pretty tough learner, ain't he?" Bruce said.

"That's one way to put it," Paige said.

At that point, Boscoe walked around the table and got between Paige and Bruce.

"Oh, hey, Boscoe. How are you, baby?" she happily said while petting him as he licked the palm of her hand.

"He seems happy to see you," Bruce commented.

"He loves her. He loves everybody," Lisa said.

"I see that," Paige commented. "Lisa said you found him at work?" she asked Bruce.

"Yeah. My crew and I were doing some construction on I-278, and we found this little guy as a puppy, all by himself under the highway as skinny as a twig. I took him to the vet and was gonna bring him to the shelter, but Lisa begged for us to keep him."

"Guilty as charged. I knew he couldn't say no to me." Lisa smiled innocently.

"You're both lucky I ain't made of stone," Bruce said.

As much as Paige was enjoying this conversation, it didn't cut down on her distracting thoughts about Steven. He wasn't learning any of his behaviors from his father either, so what was going on?

Samantha sat down shortly after, and they began to eat. Eight minutes passed before Paige started to get concerned.

"Where is he?" Paige asked, beginning to lose her patience.

"I don't know. I thought he'd be back by now," Samantha answered. "I'm so sorry. I understand your frustration."

"No. It's okay."

By this point, Paige's curiosity got the best of her, and she decided to delve deeper.

"So, um, if you don't mind me asking, was Steven always like this?" she asked, sounding as respectful as she could muster.

"What do you mean?" Bruce asked back.

"Well, you know, was he always struggling with his work this much? And was he always this... Oh gosh, how do I put this? Um, independent?" Paige blurted out, trying not to offend anybody.

"I get it." Bruce spoke out.

"I'll admit he can be a bit perverse. It's just that he's dealing with a lot of stress and feels that he needs to keep to himself," Samantha answered.

"His grades aren't always what we hoped they would be, but he did fine enough, I guess. Somewhere down the line, I suppose he just got discouraged and gave up," Bruce further explained.

"But he's got a good heart. He takes really good care of Lisa," Samantha said.

Paige wasn't sure what to make of this. It only sparked more confusion.

"I'm just trying to understand why—" Paige began.

At that moment, the door swung open, and Steven had finally arrived.

"Yo," he carelessly inaugurated before tossing his jacket onto the couch.

Finally, Paige said to herself. She got up and walked to greet him.

"Oh joy, Einstein's back," he sarcastically said.

"Yeah, you and I were supposed to start ten minutes ago," Paige stated.

"Better late than never. Or in this case, better never than ever," Steven remarked, which was met by a huff from Paige.

"Steven, we're going to see a movie, so you're in charge of Morgan and Boscoe until we get back."

"Yay, tripling my workload," Steven grouched.

"Chill out, ya grump. I'll hang out in my room with Boscoe and won't bother you, crazy kids," Lisa teased him.

"You sure, Lisa? You won't need anything?" Samantha asked.

"Yeah, he usually takes a nap around this time anyway. I'll probably just watch some YouTube," Lisa said.

"Perfect. All right, be good, guys." Samantha bade their children farewell by hugging Lisa and kissing her cheek and then rubbing Steven's back and got no reaction. "It was great seeing you, Paige." She hugged her too on the way out.

"Thank you. You too," Paige responded, surprised.

"Nice meeting you, stranger. Take care of our kids," Bruce joked.

Paige laughed. "I'll try. Nice meeting you too."

Their parents finally left.

"Welp, I'll be in my room if you need me, big bro," Lisa told him. "Come on, Boscoe!" Boscoe ran over and followed her upstairs to her room.

"So you thought getting along with them would change my opinion of you?" Steven questioned.

"No, I'm getting along with them because they're sweet people. It's called 'being friendly.' You should give it a shot sometime," Paige responded.

"Aaahh, your mouth got bigger since yesterday, didn't it?" he said as he got closer to her face to be imposing.

"A lot can change in a day. Let's see if your attitude can do the same."

Paige was clearly less daunted by him, much to his surprise. Getting a little more insight on him and the pep talk from Morgan yesterday gave her some more confidence and comfort around him. She still had the parking lot incident in the back of her head, but the more and more accustomed she got, the less she saw him as the guy who threatened her; now she just saw him as a pretentious rebel. She realized that Jenn was right; all these people want is satisfaction, so she wasn't going to give it to him. Let's just hope that means the session will go better.

Fifty Minutes Later

"One more time: tell me the quadratic formula," Paige said.

Steven tried to rephrase it but kept getting it wrong, saying a different formula or just spewing gibberish.

"Okay." Paige started to get impatient. "Please, pay attention this time. X equals –b, plus *or* minus, the square root, of b squared, minus 4ac, over 2a," she explained.

"Ugh. I still have no idea what you're talking about." Steven raised his voice.

"If you paid attention, you would," Paige said.

"It isn't physically possible to pay attention to algebra. What even is algebra anyway?"

"The study of mathematical symbols and how to manipulate them. Now if you could please—"

"It was a figure of speech. I don't care!"

"I could tell. Maybe if you did, you'd be in twelfth grade, and I wouldn't be here!"

Steven got an aggravated look on his face. "You've got an answer for everything, do you? Well, answer me this: where'd this sudden backbone come from? Every day this week you were too scared to look in my direction, and now you're acting like a dominatrix. When'd you become Joan of Arc?"

"Well, at least you know who Joan of Arc is. That's the most impressive knowledge you've displayed all night," she responded.

"Answer the question, smart-mouth!" He got up out of his seat.

She's about to retaliate but quickly realized how confrontational she's becoming. As much as she wanted to stick up for herself, she just couldn't allow herself to do so. She instead turned away from his face and calmed down.

"I'm only trying to help."

"Well, you're not doing a very good job."

"Just gonna ignore that," she said after inhaling.

"Oh, now all of a sudden you got nothing? What's with you? The switch on the back of your neck change modes or something?"

Paige just remained in silence, listening to him trash-talk her.

"Yeah. Not so tough now, huh? You got so much knowledge in that brain there wasn't room for a nerve? If you're so smart, Einstein, why you wasting your time with me? Is this your best shot at any human interaction? You getting tired of those Bratz dolls? Do you really have nothing else better to do with your time?"

31

Paige got more and more incensed with every passing insult; her face heated up, and her vision became blurry from the tears forming in her eyes.

"Ha! I figured. You're even more sad than I thought."

She finally turned to face him, stood up from the chair, and then…

Slap!

Steven fell backward with his chair and hit the floor hard. He slowly got to one knee, holding the back of his head in pain.

He groaned. "You stupid—" Steven began, still on one knee.

"SHUT UP!" she yelled at him.

He looked up at her in shock and surprise.

"For once in your life, shut the fuck up! If you think I'm thrilled about taking time out of my life to help your lazy ass, you're wrong! All week long, I haven't even been able to sleep because of you!" A single tear ran down her face. "I didn't just do this for me. After seeing how sweet your family was, I thought there was something more to you. I almost felt sorry for you. I felt like maybe you weren't a complete ass, and if I could help you, maybe you'd turn your life around just a little bit. But clearly that's not gonna happen. Because you are the most stubborn, selfish, narcissistic, egotistical jackass I have ever had the misfortune of associating with!" She raised her voice as more tears started to shed. "I didn't understand how someone like you could come from a family so warm and caring, but I get it now. You're just insecure. This whole rebel-without-a-cause act you're putting on, that's all it is—an act! You walk around like you own the place, making people fear you, hook up with any girl who throws themselves at your feet no matter how shallow they are, so you can compensate for your lack of self-esteem! Well, let me tell you this: I am done with you! You can repeat eleventh grade all you want, because in a few months from now, you'll just be a distant memory to me!"

Paige stared deeply into the eyes of Steven, who's overwhelmed by what she just said. Her face was boiling red and soaked with tears.

"You say there's nothing more to me …Well, there's ever less to you!" she whispered up close to him.

She turned away from him, lifted her glasses up, and wiped her tears on her wrist.

Steven just sat there taking in everything she just said, still holding on to the back of his head with an unreadable look on his face.

She packed up her stuff and just walked out the door, not looking back at him.

Steven slowly got up and began to walk over to her with his arm raised out. Before he can touch her, she closed the door on him.

She started to walk down the stairs dialing her phone and called Jenn to come get her.

Steven's hand was on the door. He kept it there for a few seconds before bringing it up to the cheek she slapped, and just stood there, completely lost in his thoughts.

Nobody had ever stood up to Steven like that. He was always the one who would put others in their place, but now he was on the other end, and by Paige Hetfield of all people. Who would've ever thought that such a silent girl would be so outspoken? That somebody who seemed so sweet could be so assertive? Paige was looking to find out something about Steven, but instead, she found out something about herself.

Chapter 8

Aftermath

Paige and Jenn met up with Morgan and Amy at a donut joint. Paige wasn't in the mood to talk about what happened, but Jenn wasn't going to take no for an answer.

They ordered a dozen donuts, but Paige didn't have much of an appetite. She just sat back with her head tilted down, arms folded, and barely engaged.

"We're not going anywhere until you spill your guts," Jenn said.

Paige gave no answer.

"None of us are your mom. That ain't gonna work on us," Morgan added.

"Paige, please. We're just trying to help," Amy said.

"If you wanna help, drop it and take me home," Paige demanded.

"Don't be like that," Amy said. "Paige, you can tell us. We never keep secrets from each other."

"Not as far as you know," Paige said.

"Huh?" Amy asked.

"Don't ask me. Ask Morgan," Paige said.

"PAIGE!" Morgan panicked.

"What?" Amy asked.

Jenn looked at Morgan, who lightly chuckled.

"Okay okay, let's not make this about me." Morgan tried to dismiss the conversation.

"You want me to tell her?" Paige said to Morgan.

"I know you're upset, but don't you do that to me!" Morgan pleaded.

34

"Do what?" Amy asked.

"Ah boy," Jenn commented.

Morgan took a glance at Amy and stared at her for a few seconds. "Look, we're talking about you, Paige. What happened? What did Axl do?"

"Nothing! He didn't do anything! I'm serious. There's nothing to talk about!" Paige said, slightly raising her voice.

"It sure doesn't sound like 'nothing,'" Morgan said.

"Would you just get the fuck off my case?" Paige loudly dictated, getting the attention of the small number of people in the joint.

Her friends stared at her, surprised by her remarks. None of them had ever heard her use the f-word before.

Paige put her hands to her face and slumped.

"Where the hell did that come from?" Morgan asked, trying to be sincere.

"I don't know," Paige said, on the verge of tears again.

The other three did their best to comfort her.

"Paige. What did he do?" Amy asked.

"It's not what he did," Paige answered.

"What do you mean?" Amy asked again.

Paige released a deep exhale. "Ever since I was little, people used to treat me differently. They'd either talk to me like I'm some kind of alien; or they'd hurt me because of how I look, how I act, or how I talk."

"What are you talking about? I've never seen anybody treat you badly," Morgan questioned.

"Neither have we," Amy said, pointing back and forth between her and Jenn.

"Yeah, but you guys haven't known me that long. Growing up, my mom and dad couldn't afford to send me to school. So my mom taught me everything I know in between working as a substitute."

"Yeah, we know that," Morgan said as the other two nodded along. "What about tonight though?"

Paige sighed. "Well, because of that, I didn't have a lot of friends. The only kids I knew were the ones who lived in our apartment complex. But none of them would play with me, talk to me, or ever invite me over; and the ones who did talk to me would just pick on me. They'd

35

call me names, push me to the ground, pull my hair, steal my shoes, my toys—anything they could do to make me cry. They all hurt me somehow. But some…"

She turned herself away from the three and moved the side of her hair to reveal a scar, left from a large cut that had to be stitched closed on the right side of her head.

"Hurt me more than others."

The three were surprised and saddened by seeing this scar.

She nodded yes and turned back around as another single tear slid down her face.

Amy handed her a napkin to wipe it off.

"And when I lost my dad, I sank even lower. I felt like whatever god was above just loved fucking with me. I became so overwhelmed with emotion that I just wanted to die!" she whimpered. "It wasn't until I started going to public school and met you guys that I started gaining any sort of morale, or when people started being nice to me. It's great to finally be accepted, but I felt like you three were all I needed. Everything these past few years made me feel like I was finally past all that." Paige slowly, barely cracked a smile. But it faded away much faster than it developed. "But tonight …something happened to me."

"What did you do?" Jenn asked, worried.

"Please tell me you didn't do anything stupid," Amy asked even more anxiously.

Paige collected her thoughts before continuing. "All weekend, he's acted obnoxious and has been talking down to me. He just brought back all these nasty feelings, ones I haven't felt in years." Her voice cracked in between her certain words. "It was like . . . like he helped something I've kept dormant for years break free. I just lost control of myself, and then . . ."

"And then . . . ?" Morgan asked.

Paige took a big gulp, remembering her actions. "I slapped him." She pulled at her hair.

"Oh my god!" Amy said, her jaw dropping.

"You're kidding!" Jenn added.

"I really wish I was," Paige said.

"Whoa," Morgan said. "Then what happened?"

"Well, I told him how much of a jerk he was and that I was finished with him. Then I just left," Paige said, sounding uneasy.

"Damn. Who knew Miranda Paige Curtis was such a badass!" Morgan said.

"Well now, I'm gonna be dead!" Paige cried out.

"No, you're not!" Amy said.

"Yes, I am. He's gonna hunt me down and hurt me ten times worse!" Paige said hysterically.

"Look at me," Jenn instructed her. Paige turned her head to face her, but her eyes were directed at her lap. "Look at me!" she repeated, slightly louder, causing Paige to make eye contact. "He's not gonna get you. If he even *thinks* about you, he's gonna deal with me!"

"And me! And Amy!" Morgan said, putting her arm around her.

"Wait, what?" Amy asked.

"You don't gotta be afraid of that asshole. He or any other asshole won't ever do anything like what that asshole did to you again," Morgan added, referring to her scar. "You've got real friends now, and we'll always have your back."

Paige's eyes panned over all three of them before she took a deep breath. "Thanks, guys." She wiped more tears. "But you know? I gotta admit, it felt good giving him what he deserves. It's weird, but I feel like that needed to happen." She slightly grinned.

"Somebody had to do it. I just can't believe it was you," Amy said.

"And I'm glad you finally stood up for yourself," Jenn said. "You still wanna leave?" she asked.

"Well, I love you guys, but yeah. Can you take me home?" Paige asked.

"Of course. Let's go, you little killer," Jenn joked as she and Paige stood up.

"Can I have your donut?" Morgan said.

"No!" Paige said as she picked it off the table.

"Fine, I hate glazed anyway!"

"That's a lie. You love them," Amy commented.

"I know. I just ain't gonna mess with Ripley here," she referred to Paige, being met with laughter from Amy.

"All right," Paige said, feeling embarrassed. "Night, guys."

"See you tomorrow!" Amy said.

"What she said," Morgan added.

The two exited, leaving Amy and Morgan alone.

"You can take your arm off me now," Amy said.

"Oh yeah, sorry," Morgan replied with an awkward giggle and did such.

Amy chuckled with her, before an awkward silence followed.

"So what did Paige mean by 'ask Morgan'?"

"Huh?" Morgan asked nervously.

"I don't know, it sounded like she was gonna reveal something before you flipped out."

Nervous laugh. "Uh, she was just upset. I don't know what she was talking about." She checked her phone. "Whoa, the bus is gonna be here in two minutes. We should probably go wait by the stop."

She got up, and Amy followed behind, putting her hand on her shoulder.

"Morgan!" Morgan turned to face her. "I know you're hiding something. Just tell me. Please."

Morgan looked deep into her limpid eyes. She never realized how beautiful she really was until she got this close up to her.

Morgan took a deep breath in an attempt to lower her speeding heart rate. "I can't do this anymore. I'm just gonna say it. Amy, I…"

Amy's eyes widened.

"I lied when I said I liked that dress you wore to my birthday party," Morgan lied.

"What?" Amy asked, confused.

"Yeah. You usually have good style, but that was hideous. It looked like it was made of dead Smurfs that were born prematurely. Sorry, but it's been killing me for months." She gave an overly exaggerated smile.

Amy continued to give her a confused look. "Fine, you don't wanna tell me? Don't tell me." Amy walked around her to leave. "See you outside," she said before walking out the door.

Morgan breathed a sigh of relief. She then looked over, noticing a young boy with a tablet, perplexedly staring at her.

"I actually loved how it looked on her. That was a lie," she said, smiling to the child as he continued looking weirded out.

She looked at his screen. "Ooh, *Minecraft*. Good game. Have fun." She walked off, leaving the child dumbfounded.

Meanwhile

Steven was reflecting on what just transpired, completely motionless. He just sat there at his computer desk, staring out the window, with her handprint still imprinted on his face, pondering. He had gotten into a lot of fights before; he'd heard people talk down to him behind his back or to his face and never let any of it bother him. But something about this encounter got him thinking. A few days prior, he had this poor girl trembling in fear of him, and tonight it was like someone else took over her body. He wasn't sure what to take away from this, but for once, he didn't feel angry or even vengeful; just confused.

Suddenly, his curiosity about her sparked, like how hers did prior about him. Anybody who knew Paige saw her as a smart, sweet, shy, selectively social tomboy who hated conflict. True, he didn't know her as well as others did; he didn't even "meet her" until a week ago, but just from a general impression, he never would've expected anything like this out of her. So where did that come from? How could someone who seemed so fragile be so bellicose?

Lisa entered the room and saw her brother in a deep state of concentration.

"Steven? Are you okay?" she asked from across the room, concerned.

"Yeah, I'm all right, kiddo."

"What happened?"

"Don't worry about it."

"Fine. I'll just wait for Mom and Dad to come back and let them handle it," she bluffed, beginning to leave.

"Don't you dare do that!" he responded.

"Then..." She picked the chair that's still lying on the floor back up and sat in it alongside him with her arms folded. "Start talking, big bro," she finished, leaning back with a grin.

Steven sighed in defeat, knowing he had no other choice. "How much of that did you hear?" he asked.

"Everything after that thud on the floor," she answered.

"Ah geez. Whatever you do, don't tell Sam and Bruce," he dictated her.

She zipped her mouth shut and threw away the invisible key. He rolled his eyes at her perkiness.

"What do you think of her?" he asked.

"She's really cool. I don't see what your problem with her is."

"Well, for one thing, it's embarrassing to be taught by someone younger than you, so that doesn't help. But..." He stopped to touch the handprint on his face. "After tonight, I don't know what to think."

"Go on..."

"I mean, I felt like I just saw a totally different person. It was like she got possessed or something. She was really pissed off. Even more than you were when you were eight and I knocked over that one Lego set."

"I remember that—I got so mad I kicked you in the balls and Mom and Dad put the pieces away."

"Yeah, and to make up for it, I spent the whole day helping you rebuild it."

"Hmm-hmm. You and your crotch should thank God I kept the instructions."

"Ditto." The two shared a snicker. "But yeah, this is kinda like that. I don't know why, but something about what she said tonight... struck a nerve with me."

"That wasn't the only thing that struck you," Lisa joked.

"My point being..." he began, slightly aggravated, "I really hurt her feelings, and I think I gotta fix this."

"Since when do you care about how other people feel or fixing problems? You don't even know her name," she pointed out.

"I don't know. I shouldn't care, but tonight I felt something that I haven't felt in a while. Not since... Never mind."

"Since what?"

"It's not important. It's really hard to explain. Honestly, I'm not even sure why I'm telling you this."

"Because you've been sharing your secrets with me since before I could talk, and because you don't want anybody to see you as a softie."

"I am not a softie!" he defended himself.

"Not as far as Mom and Dad or anybody outside this house is concerned." She smirked.

"Ha ha, cute," he sarcastically responded.

"I am, aren't I?" she said, fluttering her eyes with a big smile. "I will say this though: you've brought a lot of girls into this house, and this is the only one I've seen more than once, or whose name I caught. So that's a step-up for you."

"Not the point!" he said, embarrassed.

"Whatever. So what are you gonna do?"

"I don't know. I'm not even sure how I'm gonna be able to talk to her after all that," he confessed, unsure of himself.

"Well, for your sake, I hope you think of something. 'Cause I don't know if you realize this, but at the rate you're going, you and I are gonna be in the eleventh grade together," she humorously reminded him.

"Ah Christ, seriously?" he asked, annoyed.

"Just thought you could use a boost," she said, feeling smug.

"Ah yeah? Well, don't worry about that, 'cause I'll make sure you don't make it out of sixth grade alive!"

"You don't have the guts, ya big softie!" she said before she poked his nose, making a "boop."

"Don't tempt me, kid. You know I'll do it someday." He attempted to sound threatening.

"Sure sure. If you need any more encouragement, I'll be down the hall," she said as she exited the room.

He shook his head with a slight grin, amused by her actions. He then sat down on his bed and got lost in his thoughts again.

Steven had a lot to think about. He found himself determined to uncover whatever this girl was suppressing. But Lisa brought up an even greater point; not only was his future on the line—he also had a lot of making up to do for probably the only person who could help him. So whether to satisfy his own curiosity, to ensure he had a future, or out of guilt, he knew something had to be done.

Steven picked up his phone and dialed a number.

The call was answered.

"Yo, Jason. Listen, man, I need your help with something ...Yeah yeah, I know, I've never asked for help before, but this is serious ..." Sigh. "Will you help me or not? ...Good!"

Chapter 9

All or Nothing

The Next Day

Paige remained on her guard all day, anticipating when Steven would come after her. She came to school in a hoodie, kept it up whenever she was out in the hallway, and stayed by her friend's side; or if they weren't around, she'd follow close by another random kid—doing her best to stay out of sight. But fortunately for her, he was absent from their first-period class, and her friends assured her that they hadn't seen him either. She felt a little safer knowing he seemingly wasn't around that day, but her mind was still on him nonetheless, and she remained vigilant. It might not be today, but she knew he was coming for her, and she wouldn't have the upper hand this time.

Dismissal

The crew met up and were walking back to Jenn's car when they suddenly spotted somebody familiar.

Steven was standing in front of her car with Jason. The handprint from Paige's slap was still partly visible. Steven had a reputation for cutting school a lot, and he must've done that on this day too, but there he was, scouting the farthest point of the parking lot. They then spotted the girls coming toward them.

"Oh my god!" Amy exclaimed.

Paige gasped when she saw the two of them. She tried to run away but found herself wrapped up in Morgan's arms. She squirmed to break free but to no avail.

"It's okay, it's okay. Just look tough. Channel what you felt last night," Morgan said, trying to amp her up.

"That wasn't something I can replicate! I'm gonna die!" Paige freaked out.

"Chill out, all of you!" Jenn said. She looked over at the two and cracked her knuckles. "Just stay behind me."

The other three followed behind as she walked toward them.

Steven began to take steps toward them but was cut off by Jenn giving a "stop" signal with her hand.

"Not a step closer, punk!" Jenn said.

Steven stopped in his tracks. He put both his hands up, meaning no harm. "I'm not here to start anything."

"You expect us to believe that?" Amy asked.

"I know you have no reason to believe me but—" Steven began.

"Glad you agree!" Morgan said, still clinging to Paige who's completely stressed out.

"Look, I just wanna talk," he tried to explain.

"Just hear him out," Jason added.

"Sorry, Ms. Hetfield is not taking interviews right now, so get out of here," Morgan demanded.

"I come in peace. I swear, I don't wanna hurt anybody." Steven tried to be sincere.

"Yeah, and rats aren't carrying diseases. I held back last week, but I won't hesitate this time!" Jenn threatened and put her fist up.

"That means get lost, M. Shadows!" Morgan shouted.

Steven sighed deeply before looking in Paige's direction.

"Please . . .," he asked her. Paige took a step back from him. "Just give me a few minutes of your time . . . I promise, I won't hurt you."

"Just go away. This is too much, and you're wasting your time," Amy said.

"Paige, listen," Jason began, gaining the girls' attention. "I'll admit that Steven can be a hard-ass, and he does have a bad habit of saying stupid shit and doing even stupider shit. He's also somewhat ungrateful, deranged, assertive, and is terrible at parallel parking—" he listed.

"Dude!" Steven interjected.

"But with all that said, he's not as bad a dude as he makes himself out to be. I wouldn't be his friend otherwise," Jason tried to testify.

"Don't listen to him, Paige. His loyalty lies with Axl. He probably instructed him on what to say," Morgan told her.

"He didn't set me up. I swear," Jason defended himself. "Just give him a chance to talk."

The rest of the girls looked at Paige, waiting for a response—certain that they knew what her answer would be.

Paige stared into Steven's eyes before she took a large inhale and exhale.

"I'll give you five minutes," she stated.

"WHAT?" her friends and Jason all said in unison.

Steven turned his head to him.

"I mean, uh… seriously?" Jason asked.

"Are you fucking kidding me right now?" Amy asked.

"No. I wanna hear this," Paige answered with a more bitter expression. She saw this vulnerability the night before, and it eased her.

Her friends all looked at her, skeptical.

"And you're sure about this?" Amy asked and was met with a nod from Paige.

"Yeah. In fact, everybody else leave," she said with confidence.

"But, Paige—" Jenn began in a stern tone.

"I'll be fine, Jenn. Trust me," Paige assured her.

"Ugh. Fine. But we'll be watching from a distance." She went right up into Steven's face. "So one wrong move and you die," she threatened.

"You have my word," Steven responded, maintaining his composure.

"You!" Jenn pointed to Jason. "You're coming with us."

"Ooh, I like a take-charge type of woman," Jason said in a flirtatious way.

Jenn shot him an unamused look, to which he just smirked.

"Come on, ladies." Jenn leaned over to Paige. "Just say the word and I'll rip his ass inside out," she whispered, and Paige nodded.

"And I'll be sure to film it," Morgan whispered before she finally let her go. "Remember, look tough," she whispered again.

Amy patted her on the shoulder and kept it there for three seconds before they all walked off.

"Don't blow this, man," Jason told him before going toward the girls' direction.

A moment of silence occurred between the two of them.

"Your five minutes start now. Go." She crossed her arms and gave him an uptight look.

"All right, I'll just cut to the chase." Deep breath. "I'm sorry."

"For…?"

"For the way I acted, what I said about you, being so impatient, and not giving you a chance to teach me anything."

"If you're trying to convince me to keep tutoring you, I already told you. I don't care if you're held back again."

"Nor should you."

"Just get to the point. You're coming on four minutes," she sassed.

"All right, the thing is…" He sighed. "I feel like that was something I needed to hear." Paige raised an eyebrow. "I've been in plenty of fights, and I've heard a lot of bad things said about me, but nothing like what you said. Usually I'd be angry, and I would wanna hurt you, but I don't know." He paused. "Something about what happened opened my eyes. When you left my house, I thought about how mad you were and what you told me, and… I realized how much of an asshole I really am."

Paige relaxed a little bit and stopped squinting.

"And I guess I… Now I really want to start making some changes to that …and the best first step I feel would be to… to make things up to you."

Paige was surprised by what she was hearing. Was this really the same person who was insulting her less than twenty-four hours ago? Or was he just trying to dupe her? He sounded sincere, enough so that she was undecided on what to think. Even debating on if she should honor his request. But why would she after all of that? Nobody changes their entire morale that quickly.

"How would I know if you mean that or not?" she said, maintaining her sternness.

"How can I prove it?"

She turned her head away, put her hand on her chin, and thought about that. She got an idea and turned back to him with a wide smirk.

"All right. Here's the deal."

"Shoot."

"This Friday, we have our first vocabulary test. It'll consist of twenty words, and Mrs. Curtis is going to be giving us five of them every day this week. I just thought I should share that considering you apparently cut today."

"Yeah yeah, we established I do stupid shit. Continue," Steven said.

"Anyway, because I'm generous, I'll give you one more chance."

"For real?" She nodded yes. "What's the catch?"

"Every day this week, you and I will stay after school and study them in the library. And if you can pass the test on Friday, I'll keep tutoring you. If you fail, then I'm finished wasting my time, and the two of us will be strangers who share one class from that point forward."

"Wait a minute. What if somebody sees us together?"

"They won't. There's a room in the front area behind a closed door we'll use, and even then, nobody's ever in the library after dismissal. It'll be like we're in purgatory."

"You're sure of that?"

"You think I want to be seen with you? I wouldn't be arranging it like this if I wasn't. Unless you don't think it's worth the risk. If so, then say it now."

Deep exhale. "All right, I'll do it," Steven said.

"Hold on. When you take this test, not only do you have to pass— you need to get a hundred percent."

"WHAT!?" Steven panicked.

"If you're serious about this, I expect to see three digits on that test. Then, I'll believe all of this. Hell, maybe the two of us can be friends, and you can start to 'make things up.'"

Steven groaned.

"Your choice, big boy." She extended her hand. "Deal?"

Realizing he has no other choice, he replied, "Deal."

He shook her hand.

"Oh, and one more little thing."

"What now?"

She pulled her hand away and took out her phone and began typing. "I want you to admit that you're a stupid, selfish, egocentric, irresponsible, psychopath, who thinks the world revolves around him, but in reality, he's just a small footnote in the evolution of humanity that desperately needs the help of a sad little girl, who's way smarter than him." she said, looking up from her phone to finish that statement with a look of poise.

Steven looked bewildered by what she just said. "Wow. Forget what I said about you not having any nerve. I'm actually impressed. I never expected such spunk from you."

"Even fragile glass can kill if you handle it the wrong way." She finished typing. "Now say it." She held her phone up to his face.

"You have got to be kidding me," he protested.

"Nope. Unless you wanna call this off," she bluffed.

He palmed his face with one hand. "Jesus Christ," he mumbled to himself before reading.

"I'm a stupid, selfish, egocentric, irresponsible psychopath, who thinks the world revolves around him, but in reality, I'm just a small footnote in the evolution of humanity, and I desperately need the help of a sad little girl, who's way smarter than me." he begrudgingly recited.

"Why, thank you, sir." She grinned.

"Now do we have a deal?" he asked, somewhat irritated.

"Oh, we already had a deal. I just wanted to enjoy this brief moment of superiority." She laughed to herself.

"What the—are you seriou—" he began before being cut off.

"Times up! Now back off!" Jenn said, stepping in front of Paige, followed by Amy and Morgan.

Jason came up to Steven's side.

Steven took a breather. "Sure. I got out everything I had to say anyway."

"Good talk, Jacobs. I think we've really come a long way since last week," Paige boldly proclaimed.

"Yeah, no blood was drawn, no tears were shed, and no piss was leaked. That's definitely a sign of progress," Jason said.

"Good. Now get out of my sight!" Jenn said.

"All right, we'll go. Not because you told us to, but because I don't like being at this school," Steven stated. "Come on, let's beat it," he said to Jason.

Jason nodded. "We should do this again sometime." He turned his face to Jenn. "Anytime." He winked at her.

"Keep walking," Jenn replied as they walked off.

"Yeah, keep going! You guys got a bunch of tattoos? Ooh, well, we got a Jenn!" Morgan shouted.

Amy grabbed Morgan by the shoulders and pulled her close to where her back was up against her chest and her head was between her head and her shoulders.

"Morgan, let it go." Amy pleaded.

"Hold me tighter." she whispered with her eyes closed.

"What?" Amy asked.

"What?" Morgan asked.

"Never mind." Amy let go. "So what did he want?" she asked Paige.

"Well, he practically begged me to give him one last shot at tutoring, and we came to a little compromise," Paige explained.

"So you're gonna do it again?" Amy asked, alarmed.

"Relax, Amy. I've practically got this guy by the balls. I'm safe from harm."

"How do you know that?" Jenn asked.

"Because he's the one with everything to lose," Paige gloated.

"Damn. I knew my pep talk would help, but I didn't think I'd inspire you this much." Morgan said with pride.

Paige chuckled. "I can always count on you, Morgan." She patted her on the shoulder to humor her.

Could the seeds of trust have just been planted? Or is this just the beginning of the end? Will an unlikely friendship bloom? Or was it never meant to be?

Chapter 10

Progress

This week had a lot of writing on the wall; not only could this be his only chance of turning his grades around, but it could be his only chance to show Paige he was serious about turning his attitude around. He felt somewhat dirty stooping this low. He was always in control of everybody he encountered, and now he was dependent on someone who under normal circumstances should be lower on the totem pole. But reluctance and all, he knew what he needed to do.

Steven entered through the front doorway of the school library. Just as Paige said, nobody was there aside from a librarian who was stacking some newly delivered books. This made Steven feel slightly more relaxed knowing nobody would have to find out; how embarrassing would it be for the biggest rebel in school to be seen after school learning something, let alone from somebody younger than him?

He looked around until he spotted another door on the same walling, which led to the secluded room she told him about. It was a small room, with two rows of tables lined up against each other with about two dozen chairs seated on both sides of each of them, and a storage closet right by the door. Not the most luxurious area in the school, but it was the most private.

He looked to the right and spotted her on the farthest part of the room, seated in the first chair up against the wall. Paige looked up from her phone and saw him coming toward her.

"Well, you're on time. That's a good start," she greeted him.

"What can I say? When I want to, I can be a productive guy," he replied.

"And you know the meaning of the word 'productive' and used it properly in a sentence. I'm impressed."

"Okay," he began as he's sitting down. "If we're gonna do this, it'll be a lot easier if you don't tease me. This is already degrading enough."

"All right all right, let's lay down some ground rules," she proposed.

Steven nodded and agreed. "What do you have in mind?"

"First off: I'll stop teasing you, if you agree not to tease me."

"Easy."

"Second: neither of us will raise our voices or hit the other person."

"Fair enough. I'm looking to keep this on the down-low anyway."

"Don't freak out. Like I said, nobody comes in here during this time of day. It's virtually deserted."

"Well, just to be safe. Third: if anybody sees us in here, I was picking on you."

"Fine by me. Do you want me to fake cry too?" She playfully quivered her lips.

"If you could, that'd be great."

"Whatever. Fourth: you won't ask any questions, unless it relates to the work or you're asked first."

He nodded yes.

"Great, so let's get started." She opened her binder and flipped to her English section. "You copied the notes from today, right?"

"Well, I didn't want to, but…" He turned the pages of his binder to the same notes. Then he turned the book around for her to read. "There ya go."

She looked impressed. "Good. Then you shouldn't have a problem remembering what these words mean."

"All right, fine. It's only five words. Shouldn't be that tough."

"Ten."

"Huh?"

"Ten words. You cut yesterday, remember? So you missed the first five words."

Steven realized she's right. "Crap."

"It's fine. I've got you covered." She turned to yesterday's notes. "Just be sure to get the rest of them tomorrow and Thursday. It's gonna be twenty words overall."

Sigh. "This is gonna be the end of me."

"With that attitude, it will. Now come on, try and be more positive about this. Failure starts with an F but is followed by an A."

Steven looked at her with a face that said, "The fuck did you say?" "That sounded dumb."

"There's that attitude again. Keep that up and nothing will follow that F."

"I can think of a couple of things that follow F."

"Ah-ah-ah. Remember our ground rules."

Steven rolled his eyes. "All right, I'll go along with it."

The pair proceeded with their tutoring session, this time in a more collected and cooperative manner. They didn't have much of a conversation during this time—not a casual one—but at the very least they were able to work together without igniting a war. Paige did her best to help him memorize the growing number of vocabulary words they received every day, using the same tricks her mother used to teach her when she was homeschooled, in the hopes that they'd stay with him, in spite of her disdain toward him. Fortunately, he was making more of an effort to remember them, and he obeyed the ground rules that they set. Over the course of three days, Paige was pleasantly surprised by how smooth this was going and began to ease up around him without feelings of fear, resentment, or dominance. At first, she didn't buy what he said the Monday prior, but she was starting to believe he was serious. That maybe his family was telling the truth about him. Maybe there was more to him than she thought.

Thursday, 2:49 PM

"Okay, let's try this one last time." Paige picked up a stack of index cards with the vocabulary words on them and proceeded to read them one at a time.

"'Photophobia'?" Paige asked.

"Fear of lights," Steven answered.

"Good. 'Sciophobia'?"

"Fear of shadows."

"Yes. Okay, 'Electrophobia'?"

"Electricity."

"Right. 'Scotophobia'?"

"The dark."

"Good, good. 'Thermophobia'?"

"Heat."

She nodded yes. "'Chemiaphobia'?"

"Cold."

"Yes! So far so good. 'Ornithophobia'?"

"Birds."

"Yep. 'Ailurophobia'?"

"Cats."

"Yes. 'Cynophobia'?"

"Dogs."

"Correct. 'Atychiphobia'?"

"Failure."

"Right. Halfway there. 'Claustrophobia'?"

"Tight spaces."

"Yes. 'Gamophobia'?"

"Marriage."

"Right. 'Herpetophobia'?"

"Reptiles."

She nodded yes. "'Ophidiophobia'?"

"Snakes."

"Hmm-hmm. 'Philophobia'?"

"Love."

"Yep. 'Pteromerhanophobia'?"

"Flying."

"Yes."

"Wow, that's a long word."

"I know. 'Xenophobia'?"

"Foreign things."

"Close enough. 'Pathophobia'?"

"Diseases."

"Good! 'Coulrophobia'?"

"Clowns."

"Excellent! And 'Hydrophobia'?"

"Water!"

"Perfect!" Paige said with great enthusiasm.

"Whoo! I'm the man!" he said, pounding his chest.

"All right. Twenty out of twenty, not too bad."

"Not too bad? I fucking murdered this bitch!" Paige can't help but chuckle at his excitement.

"Well, don't celebrate just yet, big boy. You still have to pass tomorrow's test. Plus, you still have a longer road to the honor roll."

"Whoa, ease up, Einstein. I ain't running for Jesus. I'm just gonna graduate out of this government babysitting service, buy a motorcycle, ride off Satan's Island, and never come back," Steven specified.

Paige nodded, slightly amused at his plans. "Well, if you keep doing what you've been doing this week, you just might accomplish that, Lao Tzu," Paige responded.

"Hey, who you callin' 'soup'?" Steven asked, prompting Paige to shake her head.

"Okay, well, on that note, we're just about done here. All I can do now is just wish you luck tomorrow," Paige said as she got out of her seat to pack up her stuff.

Steven nodded and looked down. "Well, listen." Paige shifted her attention to him. Steven looked up and met her eyes. "For what it's worth, you're actually a… pretty cool chick. And with that said, even if I don't pass and this is our last session, I do appreciate you wasting your time to try and help me. Even after… you know, what went down. Which again, I'm sorry about that. I really am sorry. I was so sure you wouldn't give me a second chance after the way I treated you, but you did, and I'm glad you did… So thank you."

Paige stared at him, surprised by the sincerity of his words.

"I don't get it."

"Get what?"

Paige sat back down. "One minute you're impatient, raising your voice and hurting people, or threatening to hurt people. The next you're

cooperative, calm, showing gratitude, and saying all these nice things…
What's up?"

"I don't know. You're the one who called me 'insecure' and that I was
all just 'an act.' You tell me what you think it is up," he replied.

"No no, it's just, when I said that, I was just angry and trying to hurt
you like you hurt me. But it's true, you make yourself out to everybody
like you're this bad guy, but I don't feel like I'm talking to that guy,"
Paige explained.

Steven thought about what she was saying. "Let's just say a long time
ago, I learned the hard way what happens when you show vulnerability.
It's a merciless world out there, and as far as I'm concerned, it's either
you can walk towards the king's throne or get walked all over by others
seeking power," Steven explained.

"But that doesn't make sense to me. Your neighborhood, your house,
your parents, Lisa, nothing about it seems like a person living this kind
of lifestyle would come from that," Paige said.

"All right, well, answer me this. You're always sheltering yourself
from people. You don't talk to or hang out with anybody except for your
little entourage. You're practically the quietest girl in this school, and
all week you've pretty much been the exact opposite of that. You don't
show it, but you've made it clear to me that you have personality and a
backbone. Not to mention the people you do hang out with don't seem
like the kind of people you'd be pictured with. At least, not the you that
everybody else sees. So why hide it?" Steven asked.

Paige began to feel pressure on her. She touched the back of her
head where her scar was and scratched around it casually enough to not
draw attention to it.

"I just . . . don't really have much interest, that's all."

"Why? Why can't you just let loose and be this version of yourself?
Let it show. Go out and have fun, get drunk with strangers, smoke
weed, make out with somebody, stay up 'til 3:00 or 4:00 AM. Live your
life a little bit. Nobody else is gonna do it for you."

"Because…" Paige stopped herself. "Because I've just been really
focused on my work. I don't really spend much of my free time doing
that sort of stuff. Besides, I have three really good friends. That's all I
need."

"Well, no offense, and I know I already said this, but that sounds really boring. 'Oh, I have to work.' So what?" he asked. "Listen, you've been throwing away your valuable time giving me lectures, so now let me return the favor. Get away from it for a while. Take time for yourself, even if it's just a day. Lie to get out of work if you have to. I don't care. Just something. If they don't feel it, it doesn't hurt."

Paige was silent, completely invested in his "lecture."

Steven took a breath. "I'm not telling you this to make you feel bad. I'm just saying, there's more to life than this. A lot more. You really wanna spend the rest of yours teaching a bunch of idiots and lowlives like me about how Ben Franklin flew a kite in a thunderstorm?" he asked.

"No. Of course not," Paige said. Steven stared intensely at her, waiting to hear more of her defense argument. "I just, I just want to take everything a step at a time and do what I need to do. Even if it means putting off what I want." Paige looked away and released a deep exhale.

Steven took in what she just said and lightly nodded. "I guess I get that," Steven said before he realized how dejected she looked. "But could you just answer me one more quick question?" Paige turned her head back toward him with a frown on her face. Steven picked up one of the index cards. "Who the hell has a fear of lights?"

"What?"

"I mean, I can understand snakes, water, the dark. I could even understand birds, but what person is ever like 'No! Get me out of the light! I'm terrified of the light!'?"

Paige's frown quickly turned into a smile, and she chuckled through her teeth. "That's your big takeaway from this session?" she asked.

"I'm sorry, but that's been bugging me since we learned that word today. All I could think was some guy seeing a sun and being like 'AH! THE SUN!'" He hid under the table. "'Let me know when it's gone!'"

Paige was surprised by his sudden animated act and covered her mouth with her hands, trying not to burst out laughing.

Steven came out from under the table. "Like, who does that?"

Paige regained her composure. "Again, that's really what's staying with you after all this?"

56

"Nah. Whenever Lisa's upset, I always do this sort of stuff to make her laugh."

"Pff. I'm not eleven. I don't need people to make asses of themselves for a laugh."

"But you're laughing, aren't you?"

"Only because I wasn't expecting that."

"Would you have preferred I tickle you?"

"Please don't."

"Ha. That's what Lisa always says." Paige chuckled. "Seriously though, I don't get how somebody can be scared of light," he questioned.

"I don't know. Maybe a light bulb blew up in their face or something."

"Or maybe they're vampires!"

"HA. Where have you been? Don't you know vampires sparkle when they're exposed to light?" Paige joked.

"Uh-huh. Also, if your mothers have the same name, that's enough to stop hating somebody."

The two shared a brief laugh before the room went quiet.

"Um…" Steven looked at the time on his phone: 3:02. "Whoa, look at the time!"

Paige looked at her own phone. "Oh shoot, yeah. I told my dad to come get me at three, and I can't keep him waiting." Paige gave a nervous chuckle.

"You are absolutely right!" The two quickly packed up their stuff and stood up. "So uh, I'll go around back. You go to the front entrance?"

"Sounds good." Paige chuckled nervously again.

"Great. So I'll see you tomorrow."

"You shall!" The two walked off in different directions and exited the library.

After they stepped out of their respective door to the hallway, the two expressed the exact same thought:

"What the hell just happened?" they both said out loud before walking off, lost in their thoughts.

Chapter 11

The Start of a Major Turn...?

Friday

Today was the day that would decide the future of Steven and Paige's… rather interesting relationship. Throughout the week, they made the most of their brief but beneficial tutoring sessions; and going into this vocabulary test, both of them seemed sanguine. Paige was rarely one to struggle when it came to tests. Even if she did, she would still pull out a passing grade, but she was even more optimistic about Steven. Steven was feeling confident himself; for the first time in his life, he was determined to pass with flying colors, to prove to Paige he was serious about wanting to change. The only people who knew about their sessions were Morgan, Amy, Jenn, Jason, and their parents. Aside from that, they successfully kept this a secret from everyone else. They both had reputations to keep up and didn't want anybody to begin associating them both as friends—or more. But amidst all of that, they both couldn't get their minds off yesterday. It's been nearly two weeks since the first time they met, and in that time, they'd gone from hating each other to making each other laugh. They were slowly but surely starting to feel more comfortable being around each other. This was all either of them could think about for the past day, and it kept lingering in their heads into the following day. But as of now, they had to just shrug it off as tough as it was and focus on this test ahead of them. A test of not only their lexicons, but a test of Steven's solemnity.

Paige was sitting at her desk, staring down at her desk until a familiar pair of hands placed themselves down on it. She looked up and saw Morgan smiling at her.

"Good to see you're still alive," Morgan joked.

"Do you have to say that every day?" Paige asked.

"As long as you're…" Morgan looked around to see if anyone was listening. She leaned in to whisper, "Alone with Alice Cooper, yes."

Paige let out a sigh.

Morgan took a seat next to her. "Seriously though, how's that going?"

"To be honest, it's… actually been going pretty well."

"You think he's gonna pass this test."

Paige nodded her head. "Yeah, I think he's got this."

"I really hope so."

"Hmm-hmm, and why is that?" Paige asked with an entertained look.

"Because you've already exposed this guy. We've now seen he has weaknesses. Keep it up and we'll have him on his knees with a leash!" she said with a sinister enthusiasm.

Paige shook her head, amused by her comments. "We had a deal. I'll only keep tutoring him if he passes this test."

"So what? Forget about binding deals. Think about the power!" she said, clenching her fist.

"Ah man," Paige replied. "Relax, I'm not trying to make him my slave. I'm just doing my job." She turned away to face the front of the room.

"Come on, after all the things he said to you, you owe it to yourself to make him suffer." Paige didn't reply. "You're really gonna go soft on him now?"

"Listen, it's really early. I don't wanna talk about this," Paige said, trying to end the conversation.

Morgan looked confused. "What happened to 'I've practically got this guy by the balls'? Wasn't this whole thing about humiliating him?"

"Yeah, it was…"

"But now…?"

"I don't know. I just figured holding on to a grudge probably isn't worth the energy."

"What kind of 'tutoring' are you guys doing?"

"What's that supposed to mean?"

"Come on, you're not that naive."

"All right, why don't you—"

Before she can finish, she noticed Steven walk into the room and eased up. Morgan turned to look at him.

Steven didn't notice the duo looking at him. As he walked by them on the way to his desk, Paige looked away from him. He noticed Morgan staring at him and turned his head to face her.

"What do you want?" he asked, giving her the familiar attitude that everybody knew him for.

"Oh nothing. Nothing at all." Morgan grinned, unfazed by his tone.

Steven looked agitated at her and walked away to sit at his desk.

Morgan smirked. Remembering how soft he was four days ago, she now found his tough-guy attitude humorous.

Shortly afterward, Mrs. Curtis entered the classroom, and the rest of the students took their seats.

"Good morning, class. I trust that you're all ready for today's test." She took out copies of the test from her folder and gave them to the students in the front row to pass them back. "Take out a sheet of loose-leaf for the sentence part, and please write your name on both sheets. Any tests I see with no name on it will be unmarked and given an automatic zero."

As she's explaining all this, Paige took her test sheet and handed a set of other copies back to the students behind her. While she did this, she stole a glance at Steven. He looked up to grab his copy, noticed she's looking at him, and looked back toward her. She quickly looked away back to her test, and Steven maintained his gaze at her for a brief second before looking down at his copy.

"Keep the noise down to a minimum, and I hope I don't catch any of you cheating. If I do, I won't stop you, but don't expect a good grade." Mrs. Curtis sat down at her desk. "With that said, you all have thirty minutes to complete it, so good luck. You may begin now."

The students started to take their test.

Morgan leaned in to whisper something to Paige. "We're gonna talk about this later."

Paige replied with a "Shh."

Morgan then went back to taking the test.

Paige, as per usual, was the first person to finish. She went up to hand the sheets to her mother. Mrs. Curtis took them & then gestured for her to come closer so she could tell her something.

"Could you stay after class for a few minutes?" she whispered.

Paige nodded and then returned to her desk.

She took another glance at Steven, who was very focused on his test, before she sat back down and went into her thoughts.

8:48 AM

The bell rang. All the students had handed in their tests and proceeded to their next class—except for Paige, and Morgan who stood by her side.

As Steven was walking to the front of the room from his desk all the way in the back, Mrs. Curtis stopped him.

"Steven?" His attention shifted to her. "Could you stay for a minute?"

He rolled his eyes and walked over to where Paige and Morgan were.

"Morgan, you don't have to be here," Mrs. Curtis said.

"Come on, I wanna see this!" Morgan whined.

"Morgan, I appreciate the enthusiasm, but please go to your next class," Mrs. Curtis said.

Morgan looked at both Paige and Steven. "Ugh. Fine! But I want a full report from you, Paige!"

"Sure, whatever. Just go," Paige said.

Morgan exited the class.

"Bless her heart," Mrs. Curtis said.

"All right, enough of her. What are we doing?" Steven asked.

"Well, I won't waste too much of your time. Steven, I graded your test, and I think the both of you will be happy with the results."

She smiled as she slid his test paper across her desk for the two to see his grade: 105 percent.

The duo's eyes widened when they saw the grade.

"Oh my god! You did it!" Paige excitedly said.

"No shit," he said with barely an enthusiasm as he nodded his head, trying not to sound interested.

"You even got the extra credit question!" Paige said.

He shrugged. "I go above and beyond the call of duty."

"Obviously," Paige said with a mixture of sarcasm and cheeriness.

"I have to say, I am very proud of you both. I'm glad to see the tutoring is going well so far," Mrs. Curtis said.

"Eh, I'll give credit where it's due. She should take a lot of these teachers' jobs," Steven complimented Paige.

"I'll take that as your way of saying, 'Thank you, Paige, my lord and savior,'" Paige replied with a broad smile.

Steven just nodded and agreed, refusing to show too much gratitude.

"It's okay, Steven, you don't need to show it. I know how excited you are on the inside," Mrs. Curtis joked.

"Yeah yeah. Can I go now?" Steven asked.

"Yes, you may," Mrs. Curtis answered as she handed him a late note. Steven took his test and walked out the door, paying no mind to either of them.

"You should be proud of yourself, sweetie," Mrs. Curtis said.

"Actually, I am. I really helped that guy get a good grade. To be honest, I do feel accomplished," Paige admitted.

"I knew you'd be able to fix him."

"Okay, let's not get too ahead of ourselves, Mom. It was just a vocabulary test. I wouldn't exactly call this 'fixing him.'"

"I know, but you've already done more than you thought you could. If you apply yourself, you could really kick-start a major turnaround in his life."

"Well, I'll keep doing what I can, but I can't promise anything," Paige said, trying to act like she's unsure of what's being told to her.

"I know you will. I'm sure it already hasn't been easy, but just remember our homeschool motto."

"I know. 'Failure starts with an F but is followed by an A.'"

"That's my girl. All right, you should really get to your next class. I'll see you tonight," she said, handing another late note to her daughter.

"Thanks, Mom. You too."

Paige collected her stuff and left the classroom.

Chapter 12

A Deal's a Deal

Paige had a lot to think about for the rest of the day—what her mother told her, Steven passing the test, what happened between them yesterday, and where the future of whatever you want to call this thing between them went from here. He kept his word to her, so she knew now she had to hold up her end of the deal and keep being his tutor. A week ago, she would've been dreading it out of fear, but now, she wasn't so sure how to feel. After getting to know his family and seeing a side of him she never considered, or how he brought out a part of her she never thought she had, now it was like they could speak to each other in a way nobody else could, even if not deliberately. Something was different. But what?

Dismissal

Paige was speed-walking down the hallway, ready to exit the building. But she came to a fork in the road—her friends.

"Paige!" Amy called, getting her attention.

She kept walking, and the trio followed behind her.

"There you are. We've been looking for you all day," Amy said.

"Well, here I am," she replied, still moving.

"Wait." She stopped at Amy's response. "How are things?"

"Good. I suppose. What's there to be not good?" Paige turned away and started walking again.

"Then why are you in such a rush?" Jenn asked.

"I'm not in a rush."

"Really? 'Cause it seems like you're trying to get away from us," Morgan said.

"I don't know. Keep up with my pace," she said, picking up her speed.

Morgan caught up to her. "Then where were you during sixth? I faked a period to get out of history and go look for you in the library, but you weren't there. So now, I went to the bathroom and wasted a tampon to make it look convincing for no reason whatsoever," Morgan said in an irritable tone.

"Why are you answering questions I don't want to ask?"

"You know how uncomfortable this feels. I don't need to document it!" she exclaimed, pointing to her crotch.

"All right, horror stories aside, how come you weren't there?" Jenn asserted.

"I'm sorry, guys, I skipped lunch and snuck off to the auditorium to get an early start on my homework," Paige explained, still not looking at any of them.

"And what about all our texts you've been ignoring?" Jenn asked.

"I didn't want to be distracted," Paige replied.

"Paige!" Amy stepped in front of her before she can go out the front door of the school. "What's with you?"

"Noth—" Paige began.

"And don't say 'Nothing.'" Morgan cut her off and moved to Amy's side. "Paige, you've been acting weird all week. We just wanna talk."

"Yeah, you haven't been the same since Sunday. We all feel like you're becoming distant from us. You sure nothing's going on?" Amy continued.

"I'm fine, really! Right now, I just need to find Steven," Paige said as she walked through Morgan and Amy out the doorway.

The three ceased their motions and watched her walk away, leaving them with looks of confusion/concern.

"Okay, now I *know* he drugged her," Morgan said.

"He didn't drug her! But something's up with those two, and I'm gonna beat the answers out of him!" Jenn walked toward Paige in an aggressive manner.

"Oh god, Paige, wait up!" Amy chased after them with Morgan following her lead.

—◆—

Paige walked into the parking lot, looked around, and spotted Steven by his car with Jason.

Paige started to walk toward them and caught Jason's attention, who noticed the other girls were following behind.

"Aw, son of a Bieber," Jason exclaimed.

Steven turned around and saw her standing there. "What up, Einstein?" he asked.

"Good question! Why don't you answer that for us, Axl?" Jenn walked up behind Paige.

"What are you doing to my friend?" Morgan walked up behind her.

"Whoa whoa, I didn't do nothin'!" Steven put his hands up as he defended himself.

"Bullshit!" Jenn exclaimed as she started to march toward him, but Paige stopped her.

"Guys!" Paige shouted, taking her friends by surprise. "Relax. I got this," she assured them.

She turned around to face Steven and Jason again and walked up to them. Jenn tried to step forward, but Amy grabbed her wrist to stop her. Morgan then grabbed Amy by the wrist and was met by a "Don't touch me" expression. Morgan quickly let go, crossed her arms, and turned her attention back to Paige.

Paige stopped in front of Steven. A few awkward seconds of silence materialized before she spoke.

"Hi."

"Sup?" Steven replied.

"You know, we really need to stop meeting like this," Jason said out of nowhere.

"Shut up," Steven told him.

"Just saying," Jason whispered.

"Seriously, what's so important you brought in the cavalry?" Steven asked.

"I didn't bring them by choice," she said as she shifted her focus to them. "But that's beside the point. I never got to say this before you stormed off . . . I'm impressed," Paige admitted.

"That I'm not as stupid as you thought I was?" Steven asked.

"No. That you actually kept your word. I'll admit, I didn't think you were serious, but you've shown me you are teachable."

"So you're still gonna tutor me?"

"We had a deal, didn't we?" Paige smiled.

Steven was about to crack a smile but remembered there were people around him and went back to acting like a brute. "Well"—cough—"just don't go stupid on me, squirt!"

Paige nodded her head, catching on to his shtick, and just rolled with it. "Don't worry, I've had my shots. I won't catch it from you." She nodded.

"Oh! Shit!" Morgan said, prompting Amy to cover her mouth with her hand.

"Don't encourage her!" she whispered.

"This just got interesting," Jenn said.

"Hehehe, cute. Any other wiseass remarks?" Steven replied, stepping in closer to her.

"Nah, I'm done," she replied with a smirk.

"And so are we. Let's go, Jason. I wanna get to the Barclays Center as soon as possible."

"Couldn't agree more," Jason said.

"You jerks going to the Breaking Benjamin concert?" Jenn asked.

"As a matter of fact, yes. Are you? Maybe we'll bump into each other," Jason replied before giving her a few blinks.

"Yeah, but you better hope we don't, 'cause I'll punch some more holes in your face," Jenn said.

"Beats having to pay somebody to do it," Jason said, touching his lower lip ring.

"Jason, let's go!" Steven ordered.

"Welp, good chat, ladies. Hopefully next time we meet, it'll be under better circumstances," Jason said, getting into Steven's car.

The pair drove off, leaving the four where they stood.

Paige watched the car disappear from her view and walked back to her friends.

"That was weird, right? This, this thing that just happened, whatever it was?" Amy asked.

"Told you I got this," Paige said, holding on to her smirk.

Morgan finally got Amy's hand off her mouth. "Okay, as awesome as that was, it still didn't answer anything."

"Just forget about it," Paige said.

"No way! I said we were gonna talk about this later. Now it's later. We're gonna talk about this," Morgan demanded.

"I agree. We wanna know what's up with you two, and we wanna know now," Amy added.

Paige, realizing she was outnumbered, reluctantly agreed. "Jenn, take us somewhere to eat?" she requested, to which Jenn nodded and agreed.

All four of them piled into her car.

Later

The girls were at a Checkers and Rally's restaurant only a few blocks away from Meadows Forest High, having their own choices of food as they listened to Paige explain the whole story.

"You know we're talking about Steven Axl, right?" Amy said.

"It sounds crazy, I know, but I don't think he's the guy he makes himself out to be," Paige said.

"Steven Axl? The guy who got arrested for smashing a kid's head against a car window in ninth grade?" Amy spoke.

"I know who we're talking about, Amy. I never would've willingly made direct contact with him had my mom not rope me into this. But after everything that's happened this week, I don't feel so grim anymore," Paige said.

"He did pass our vocabulary test today," Morgan backed up.

"Yeah. But besides that, yesterday and today, I felt kind of, I don't know, comfortable around him," Paige further explained.

"I can't believe we're talking about the same person that threatened you both two weeks ago," Amy said.

"Me neither. A part of me is saying this is crazy, but there's this other part of me that's remembering something Morgan told me last Saturday, about there being more to him and how I should figure it out. I didn't want to dig that deep, but now, I feel like I need to. Now I really want to know what this guy's deal is," Paige explained.

"Finally, you've got the right mindset. Get close to him, earn his trust, get him to open the lock. Then, take whatever he's hiding and blackmail him with it! We'd have power over the toughest guy in school!" Morgan deviously envisioned.

"I told you already. I'm not gonna do that to him," Paige said.

"So what are you gonna do? You were really enjoying having power over him, and now you wanna be all buddy-buddy?" Amy asked.

"I don't know. It was nice at first having the mental advantage, but now seeing his softer side, it seems wrong. His parents told me he's got a good heart, and I feel like I'm starting to see it," Paige said.

"So wait, 'cause none of this is making sense to me. What exactly is your motivation? Are you trying to make friends with him 'cause you think he's a legit good person? Or are you just letting your curiosity get the better of you and just want to find what he's all about?" Jenn asked.

"Yes?" Paige answered.

The rest of her friends tried to comprehend everything they'd heard, unsure of what to tell her.

"Well, I can tell this is a lot for you to take in," Jenn said.

Paige nodded at her comment.

"It's a lot for me to take in," Morgan said.

"What do you guys think I should do?" Paige asked.

More silence followed the group.

"I say go for it," Morgan replied. The other three looked at her.

"Why? So she can fulfill your own wicked desires?" Amy said.

"No."

Amy and Jenn gave her looks that translated to "Come on now."

"Okay yes, but also, Paige, if you're really sure about this, then maybe this can be good for you," Morgan said.

"What do you mean?" Paige asked.

"I mean, after hearing all this, I just can't help but feel like you both came together for a reason. He brought out something in you,

you brought out something in him. You both already seem like semi-different people, so if this continues the way it is, who knows what'll come of it? And maybe he sees something in you that nobody else is seeing, and he wants to bring that out. The way I see it, you can both help each other become the best people you can be, to make the people you're both scared to be break free and share themselves with the world," Morgan speechified.

The others were blown away by what she said.

"Or I just overthought it," Morgan said.

"No, I think the moon child just said something profound," Jenn said.

"Are we sure this is the same Morgan who runs around revolving doors?" Amy asked.

"Does that bother you?" Morgan asked Amy.

"No. I just... had no idea you were so deep," Amy said and was met by a soft smile from Morgan.

"All right, let's keep the focus where it needs to be. Paige, forget what any of us say. This is your ballpark. So what do you think you should do?" Jenn asked.

Paige thought it over.

"Well, I already made a deal I need to keep to him, that much I know. As far as everything else goes, I'm just gonna keep this as casual as possible and see what happens. Maybe we'll become friends, maybe we won't; but as of now, I'm just his tutor," Paige said.

Morgan and Jenn agreed with her.

"Am I the only one who still thinks this is crazy?" Amy said.

"No. I ain't buying into this either. But I've never been one to question her judgment yet. So I trust her," Jenn said despite how badly she didn't want to.

"I'll be all right, Amy," Paige assured her.

Amy took a deep breath and reluctantly said, "I trust you too." To which Paige responded with a smile. "Just call us every night when you guys are done," Amy finished.

"Deal," Paige said, still smiling.

The group collectively agreed and resumed eating their meals.

"I still have that tampon in me." Morgan spoke up.

"Oh, for God's sake, why say it?" Jenn asked.

"Because I've been very uncomfortable for the last three hours, and I'm losing it."

"Why didn't you throw it away when we got here?" Amy asked.

"We all had a prior commitment to her."

"Okay, go to the bathroom right now," Jenn said.

"Eh, I don't like doing this in public," Morgan said.

"GO!" Paige demanded, feeling disgusted by this topic.

"All right all right, I'm going." Morgan stepped away from their table. "It's not even real," she said loud enough for them to hear.

"Ugh. Her voice is the last thing I'll hear before I die." Jenn favored her cranium.

"Give her a break. She's inappropriate, but she's always fun to be around," Amy defended Morgan.

"That's great. It's so nice you feel that way. I'm sure she'd love that you think that about her," Jenn responded.

"All right, I can tell you're heated. Let's all just finish our food," Amy said, taking a bite of her meal.

While these two were engaging, Paige thought to herself how Morgan was also good at getting the attention off her, whether that was her intent or not. Either way, Paige was relieved to be finished with this conversation finally. She just wanted to eat and enjoy this time with her friends before her duties resumed tomorrow.

Meanwhile

Steven was with Jason, driving in his car.

He had just told Jason all the details as to what'd been going on between him and Paige since Monday and how they'll continue to be working together.

"So what exactly are you two anyway?" Jason asked.

"I don't know, man. All I know is I'm lucky enough that I got her to keep up this damn tutoring thing."

"Well, let's not beat around the bush. You don't really care about passing eleventh grade. The whole reason you agreed to do this was 'cause you felt sorry for making her cry. Which I wanna note: in the five years I've known you, I have never seen you show pity on anybody."

Steven said nothing; he just shrugged and focused on driving.

"I mean, I've seen you get into fistfights, spill blood, fracture jaws, damage property—hell, I've lost count of how many girls you've hooked up with and never talked to again after one day. A week ago, you were the most hardcore person I knew, and then one girl hits you hard enough to shatter your armor and expose the soft flesh you apparently have? Why does this girl get your empathy? What makes her so special to you?" Jason interrogated him.

Steven got fed up listening to this and swerved off the road to illegally park by the curve, still gripping his steering wheel.

"I don't know!" Deep breath. "I don't know." He squeezed the wheel. "I just…" Sigh. "I can't shake this feeling off. There's something about her that I feel this weird connection to. I don't know what it is, but I can't remember a time when I ever felt anything like that. And I gotta know what that is." He pressed his hand against his face and let out a groan. "What's happening to me?"

Jason took a moment to let everything he'd heard sink in. "I'm sorry, dude. I didn't realize this was so personal."

"Whatever."

"Look, this whole thing is really weird to me, but if this is something you feel strongly about, then who am I to say otherwise? You do whatever you gots to do."

"Thanks. But I was gonna do it without your consent anyway."

Jason snickered. "Good," he said. "And hey, as long as you're gonna fuel your obsession, do you think you—"

"No, I'm not gonna convince her to hook you up with Owens," Steven cut him off.

"Oh, come on, man! That's messed up. You're not gonna help your best friend?"

"You know, you mock my 'obsession' with Einstein. Well, what's your obsession with her?"

"She's hot, man!"

"She clearly has no interest in you."

"Nah, she's just playing hard to get."

Steven put his fist to his face. "Why do I put up with you?"

"Because I'm your bro and you love me."

Steven rubbed his eyes at his response. "Anything else before we get the hell outta here?"

"Yeah, why did you decide to talk about this after you picked me up?" Lisa, who had been sitting in the back seat this whole time listening to their conversation, spoke up.

"Ah yeah, sorry about that, kiddo," Steven responded.

"It's fine. I wasn't complaining. I always love hearing these stories."

"Well, listen, just do me a favor and—" Steven began.

"Don't mention this to Mom and Dad, yada yada yada," Lisa cut him off and impersonated her big brother. "I got you."

"Good," Steven said and got back on the road.

"So, Lisa, where do you stand on this subject?" Jason asked, grinning.

"Well, I for one think it's cute that my big brother is finally brave enough to show his vulnerable side," Lisa said, also with a grin.

"Hey, I do not have vulnerabilities!" Steven defended.

"The past five minutes says otherwise," Lisa taunted.

"Yeah, dude, let's be real, you're slowly going from pop star Taylor Swift to country musician Taylor Swift," Jason said and shared a laugh with Lisa.

Steven groaned.

"She's the reason for the teardrops on my guitar, the only thing that keeps me wishing on a wishing star."

Lisa and Jason duetted and continued laughing.

"I hate both of you," Steven said.

Chapter 13

Where Do We Go From Here?

Saturday, Twilight

Richard was driving Paige to Steven's for the second weekend in a row. Not much was different, except Paige was much more comfortable this time. Steven kept his word and started to take this ordeal more seriously, as he showed yesterday when he got a passing grade. She started thinking maybe this could actually work. Maybe he wasn't as bad of a guy as he made himself out to be. Maybe Morgan was right about all of this happening for a reason. Her friends and her mother really opened her mind yesterday, giving her more assurance as she went into this weekend. However, she wondered if he had a similar mindset. Was he thinking as strongly as she was? Or was she just way too into her head? This was constantly running through her mind, but nevertheless, she had a job to do, and that's what her game plan was.

"So, Paige." Her father suddenly spoke up, breaking her trance.

"Huh? Uh, what?" she replied.

"Your mom tells me that you helped this guy get a hundred and five on your test yesterday. Is that right?" he asked.

"Um, yeah, I did," she replied.

"Well, look at my little prodigy. You must be proud of yourself!" he said, lightly punching her on the shoulder.

"Oh, it's not such a big deal," she shyly said.

"Everything you do is a big deal to me, especially when I see you helping people," he praised her.

"Thanks, Dad."

"You know, she told me a bit about this guy; and when she told me she was going to assign you to him, I really didn't like the idea."

"I can't say I blame you."

"I tried really hard to talk her out of it, but she was really certain that you could connect with this guy."

"You have no idea," she whispered to herself, not looking at him.

"It wasn't that I didn't have faith in you. It just sounded like he was a real thug, and I never want you getting wrapped up with the wrong people. But you know your mom. When she sets her mind on something, she's determined to fulfill it."

"Yeah, I know."

"With that said, so long as I've got you here—just between us—I'm still not entirely on board with this whole thing. But I guess you're doing something right, from what I've heard at least."

Paige shrugged her shoulders.

"Just tell me something. I've noticed you've been a little... on edge lately. Is anything bothering you?" he asked.

"No. Of course not." She chuckled. "I don't know what you're talking about," she said while she played with her ponytail, still not looking at him.

"You sure? You sure you're not telling me anything about this guy that'll warrant me breaking down his door and both his arms?"

"Dad!" She turned to face him. "There's nothing for you to worry about. I swear," Paige said.

Her father stared at her with a look that she knows means "Are you lying?" Richard was always very stern when it came to her meeting new people, especially boys. It always suffocated her when he got like this, but she knew deep down he just wanted to protect his girl.

"Look, I wasn't exactly too excited about this either. But it's not as bad as I thought it would be. He was tough to work with at first, but now we're starting to cooperate, and it's actually going pretty well. Trust me, you don't have to worry about him."

"I do trust you. I just want to make sure I can trust that you won't get too close to this guy. Boys his age are only after one thing."

"DAD!" she shouted, embarrassed.

"Sorry, I probably shouldn't have said that out loud."

"Dad, I can assure you, I would *never* date a guy like him. We're not even friends. I'm just his tutor, nothing more. As soon as he doesn't need me anymore, we're going back to being strangers."

Richard took a deep breath and finally pulled up to Steven's house.

"Just know that I'll be here as quick as I can if you need me."

"Dad, I'll be fine." She leaned in to kiss her dad's cheek. "I'll see you in two hours." She grabbed her bag and opened her door.

"I love you, baby girl."

"You too," she replied, closed the door, and headed through the walkway.

Richard was left skeptical by what she said. Even Paige was suspicious of what was really transpiring. She couldn't exactly call him a friend, but she didn't consider him an enemy either. A frenemy? At best? Whatever their connection was, that couldn't be her concern right now.

She knocked on the glass door, and it was answered by Lisa.

"Paige!" she excitedly greeted her.

"Hi, Lisa! How are you?" Paige replied, smiling at the girl.

"I'm good. Come in," Lisa advised.

Paige opened the door after having to tussle with it.

"Wow, this door really does suck."

"Hmm-hmm," Lisa agreed. "Steven! It's for you!" she shouted upstairs.

"Paige, great to see you again," Samantha greeted her.

"Thank you. You too," Paige replied.

Boscoe eagerly ran up to her and stood on his hind legs to lick her face.

"Boscoe! Oh, hello hello hello hello," she said as she's running her hands through his fur. The dog hopped down on all fours as Paige continued to pet him.

"So how's everything?" Samantha asked.

"Pretty good, I'd say. Where's Bruce?" she asked.

"Oh, they're doing some street paving over by Forest Avenue, and they needed him down there," Samantha explained.

"Ah yeah. Why bother though? They're gonna get destroyed again when winter comes, and we get all sorts of potholes."

Samantha chuckled. "That's what I said, but he just says what he always says: 'Don't care as long as we're rich.'"

Paige laughed. "Sounds like my friend Morgan. She's always talking about moving into a beach house in Jersey."

"That's the life I wanna live," Samantha said.

"It sounds nice, except she can't even walk past a Hot Topic without spending money," Paige said and shared a laugh with Samantha.

"I know what you mean." She looked over at Lisa who's sitting on the couch.

"Hey, I can't help it if they're always changing their inventory and acquiring things that suit my taste in fashion. Or how you and Dad always unsuccessfully resist the urge to tell me no," Lisa defended herself as she showed off some fresh new merch she just got from there.

Samantha shot her a mocking expression followed by a chuckle.

"Anyway, sugar doll, the meat loaf will be ready in a few minutes."

"Sweet! I'm just gonna touch this up real quick. I'll be there in a li'l bit," Lisa said.

"Okay," Samantha said, heading into the kitchen.

Paige walked over to the couch where Lisa was sitting to look at what she's doing. She saw Lisa's doing a drawing of one of the murals from *Kingdom Hearts*.

"Wow. Lisa, did you draw this?" Paige asked, amazed by her work.

"Yeah, do you like it?" Lisa asked.

"This is good. Really good," Paige praised her, taking a seat next to her.

"Really?" Lisa asked, smiling.

"Yeah, how'd you get to be so talented?"

"I've been taking art classes since I was in kindergarten. I love to draw."

"Well, it shows. I love all the attention to detail. It looks exactly like how it looks in the game."

"You play *Kingdom Hearts*?"

"Oh my god, I love *Kingdom Hearts*! It's one of my favorite series!"

"It's the best. Don't let anybody tell you otherwise!" Lisa proclaimed. "How stoked are you that we're finally getting *Kingdom Hearts III*?"

"Oh, they've been teasing that for years. Let's just face it, it's never coming out."

"No! I refuse to lose hope. That game will come out, or I'm gonna riot!" Lisa declared and was met with a laugh from Paige.

"I'm glad somebody still has hope." Paige then checked her phone to see Steven's two minutes behind schedule. "Oh, good god, does he always take this long?"

"Consistently. He's probably lifting weights or something. Just wait a li'l bit."

Paige sighed as she leaned her chin on her hand and petted Boscoe again.

Lisa looked up from her drawing. "Hey, can I ask you something?"

"Of course." Paige looked back at her.

"When you're done working with Steven, will you still come around?"

Paige's eyes expanded, and she monitored the eleven-year-old's expression. She just had this talk with her dad, and it was easy to answer him directly, but she wasn't sure what she could say to this sweet girl she had gotten along with so well. Her relationship with Steven may have been rocky, but she admittedly grew fond of the rest of his family, especially Lisa.

"Um… Well, Lisa, it's been great getting to know you and your family. But you see, this is kind of my job, and I'll have to do this with other people, so… I don't know if that's gonna happen."

"Why not?" Lisa asked. "You can still hang out with us."

"I know, but it's not that easy. I'm a really busy person. I have some other things I'll need to be doing soon. I just don't have that kind of time," Paige explained, wanting to let the younger girl down lightly. "I'm sorry."

Paige looked away from her, and Lisa felt disappointed.

A few seconds went by before Lisa spoke up again. "You know, Steven's not the guy he acts like." Paige looked back up at her, captivated by what she said. "He's better than that."

This whole situation kept getting more conflicting with every new dialogue.

Paige took a deep breath. "I know."

"Huh?" Lisa asked, surprised.

"Things weren't exactly solid between us at first, but I've been working with him all week, and now... I don't know what to think of him. It's strange, but something about your brother... struck a nerve with me," Paige admitted.

Lisa's eyes widened this time. "Funny, he told me the same thing about you."

"He did?" Paige asked. Lisa nodded. "What else did he tell you?"

Before Lisa could speak up, she heard a door slam upstairs and footsteps drawing near. They both turned their attention to the steps to see Steven with a towel, wiping the sweat off his face.

"Lisa, you called me?" He removed the towel from his face and saw Paige sitting next to her. "Oh good, you made it," he said with a smirk.

"So did you." Paige stood up. "You know? It's quite fascinating, even when you're at the place you're supposed to be, you're late." She returned a smirk, crossing her arms.

"Hey, you don't get these kinds of arms slouching around," Steven said, flexing his muscles.

"I guess not," she said, somewhat impressed by his physique. "But you know, if you put that much effort into other districts, you wouldn't need me here."

Before he can reply, Samantha reentered the moon.

"Lisa, your dinner's ready."

"Yay." Lisa stood up. "Have fun, you two," she teased, before exiting the room.

"Steven, I'll leave a piece for you and you can just heat it up later," Samantha said before she went back into the kitchen to join Lisa at the table.

"You do that," he exclaimed. "And you," he said to Paige before he stepped aside, "be my guest." He invited her upstairs.

"Why, thank you," she said as she started walking up the steps with Steven following behind. "Suddenly, this is like something out of *Beauty and the Beast*."

"Don't you dare start comparing me to cartoons."

"Fine. I'm just gonna say it's kind of funny when you think about it."

"I don't see the connection. You're delusional."

"Am I? Well, let's do a little recap. I offered up my freedom to a grouchy brute, except said grouchy brute doesn't immediately realize how much good this could be for him and keeps screwing up after the fact, because he can't help but continue to act domineering towards everybody. Meanwhile, this situation makes me feel imprisoned, except for the rest of the residence of the abode that give me a sense of being welcomed and safe, right up until the grouchy brute makes me run away, only to come searching for me once they realize what a fool they've been. Only when I see him completely vulnerable do I decide to come back and help him."

"I do *not* have vulnerabilities!" Steven cut her off.

"Then, as some more time passes and I become more coefficient with him, a mutual trust is formed, and then the grouchy brute starts acting more inviting, kind, and gentle." The duo entered Steven's room. "And on top of all of that, you just said, 'Be. My. Guest.' Yeah, clearly, I'm delusional," Paige finished.

Steven left the door slightly open behind him. "You gave that way more thought than it was worth."

She shrugged. "I love Disney movies."

"Yeah, I can tell," he said, referring to the *Lilo & Stitch* T-shirt she was wearing.

"Well, let's get back on track quick. We're about"—Paige checked her phone—"seven minutes behind schedule. I hope you didn't lose your mojo," she teased as she's setting up her stuff on Steven's desk.

"Same to you."

The two sat down and began the session.

—⁂—

From then on, everything seemed to be set in motion. The tension between Paige and Steven had lightened up, and the both of them were taking this arrangement a lot more seriously. As the month went by, Paige's teachings were having a noticeable influence on Steven's grades. He was doing significantly better in just about all his classes. They weren't all perfect like that first vocabulary test was, but they were a step-up from his D through F average, and at the rate he was going, he was sure to get decent grades throughout the semester. Their trust in each other helped them both as a teacher and student toward the end of the marking period, Paige even gave him her phone number to keep the flow going. Steven wasn't so sure he could handle doing homework by himself, but Paige had enough faith in him that he could do it without her. She still willingly shared her number anyway because you never know. They started communicating with each other more casually with every following session, and as the final week of marking period dawned upon them, they were well acquainted. It was still weird for a brief amount of time, especially whenever they thought back to how this started. Nonetheless, as it kept going, it drifted further from their thoughts; they both knew if they were going to keep working together, then they had to maintain peace, so they let it all be just a distant memory. When that was established, it became easier for them to cooperate, and to converse, to a point where they enjoyed talking to each other; and although they wouldn't admit it, they actually started looking forward to their sessions. They were less of a student and mentor, more than strangers, and no longer foes.

"Perhaps there's something there that wasn't there before."

Wednesday, October 19, 8:38 AM

It was the final day of the marking period, and report cards were given out; this would either make a parent's day better or make their child feel like shit. The report cards were given out toward the end of homeroom; the results of a month's worth of work would be unveiled, and for the team of Paige and Steven, this is where they'd know if all of that tutoring had paid off.

As per protocol, Mrs. Curtis handed out the report cards to their designated student and allowed the rest of the class to pass by until the bell.

Paige, as usual, received straight As.

Morgan noticed her friend's grades and said, "Oh, 'big shock,'" while making air quotes with her hands.

"It's not a big deal, really," Paige modestly said.

"To any average person it would be," Morgan said. "You wouldn't know looking down at us from your pedestal, Your Grace." She spoke in a bad British accent. The two shared a laugh.

"What about you? How'd you do?" Paige asked, looking over at Morgan's report card.

"Eh, let's see... 80, 70, 70, 86, 82"—snicker—"69, and a 90 in English." She leaned in toward Paige to whisper, "At least your mom loves me." The two laughed again. "Well, enough about me. How do you think Trace Cyrus did?" she whispered.

Paige snuck a subtle glance at Steven, who seemed to be paying no mind to his report card.

"He better have done well. I could've spent my weekends on something else, and I sacrificed them to lecture that guy. I hope it wasn't all for nothing," Paige whispered.

"Well, let's be honest, they were probably the most exciting weekends you ever had," Morgan stated.

Paige laughed sarcastically.

"I'm kidding. Lighten up." Morgan playfully shoved her. "Seriously though, any updates? You've been weirdly discreet about this."

"Well..." Paige took another look back at him. This time he's looking at his phone and didn't notice. She turned her attention back to Morgan. "I'll say this, he's not so tough to teach once you get through to him."

"That's not what I meant. Has any progress been made? Did you find out anything innermost?"

"No, I didn't 'find out anything innermost.' Although..." Morgan leaned in. "He is a lot easier to talk to now, and—"

"Wait, stop there!" Morgan cut her off.

"Seriously?"

"Yes, seriously. This is historic. This needs to be discussed at great length."

"I was just gonna say—"

"I know, but we don't have that time. The bell's gonna ring right about . . ."

A couple of seconds passed with no bell.

Paige was about to speak up, but the bell rang before she can.

"There it is," Morgan said.

The class began emptying out very quickly since most students got up to wait by the door.

The two girls stood up.

"Morgan, it's really not that crazy—"

"Shhhh," Morgan cut her off as she put her finger to her lips. "When the right time comes, we'll talk all about this, trust me." Morgan picked up her stuff from her desk and left with the rest of the class before Paige could reply.

"Dear God," Paige said, palming her face.

She turned around to pick up her stuff and saw Steven standing behind her chair.

"Oh. Hi," she said, surprised. "What are you doing?"

"Just chillin'. Nothing special. Later." He began to walk away casually.

"Wait," Paige said, stopping him in his track. "How'd you do?"

"All right. I guess."

"That doesn't answer my quest—"

"Bye." Steven walked away, avoiding further conversation, leaving Paige bewildered.

She collected her things and left the room.

Later

Paige went about her day like normal, but she couldn't help wondering what Steven was doing back in English. Why was he so quick to blow her off? She knew they agreed to keep it low, but that seemed particularly odd; he couldn't have at least told her his grades after all the work they'd done? If he was in such a hurry to get out of there, then why was he just standing behind her desk like that? How was any of that even being discreet? She had multiple questions but just gave the benefit of the doubt and put it off, deciding she'll ask him again later when nobody is around. Until…

She was on her lunch break and went back to the library, this time giving her friends notice in case they were looking for her again.

Paige was sitting on the floor between two rows of bookshelves, casually reading something she took off one of them, when she felt her phone vibrate.

She put the book down, pulled her phone out from her pocket, and saw a message from an unknown number, with a photo attached to it. She opened the text and saw the picture was a shot of a report card with no visible name.

She read the grades: 85, 81, 85, 85, 88, 80, 94.

She then read the other message that came with it: "Look in the front of your book bag."

Deducing where these texts were coming from, she did exactly that. She unzipped the front compartment of her bag and reached her hand inside. Immediately she felt something unfamiliar in there. She fished out a folded-up piece of paper, unraveled it, and saw it had a note written on it.

> Hey Einstein. I know we didn't start off strong, but I'm grateful that you gave me another chance. If I planned this out correctly, you're reading this after you saw my grades; otherwise, I'm confusing the hell out of you right now. Anyway, I want you to know that I never would've done this without you. Technically they're my grades, but you deserve all the credit for what's on that report card. I don't know what it is, but you have something that inspires me, that makes me want to be a better guy. Starting today, I'm going to keep my word to you, & I'm going to commit to that as best as I can. Let this note serve as a vow of that.
>
> Thank you. I really do owe you one.
>
> –Your Friend, Steven.

Paige smiled as she read this. She was genuinely touched by his words; if it was pencil to paper, then he had to have been serious. Reading him refer to himself as her friend would've been unheard of at the start of the year, but he did, in his own handwriting.

She looked at his text messages again and smiled even bigger rereading his grades. She wasn't feeling the same pride she often felt knowing that she had helped somebody do better in school; this was bigger than that. She felt happy. She felt like a promise was kept, and now she could fully trust him. Like she made a friend.

They were now far beyond strangers in the same class who had one hostile encounter. Now, they were closer. In a way, it felt right, like it was something they both needed. This phase of their bizarre relationship was over, and both were prepared to step forward, beyond tutor and student. But where do they go from here?

Chapter 14

Halloweekend Havoc Festival

Thing seemed to be going smoothly for Paige and Steven. As she promised her mother, Paige would continue tutoring Steven for the remainder of the semester. His report card grades proved that there was hope for him to learn and that she could trust him to progress—something that would've been unheard of a month ago. The rest of the week came and went with them not seeing much of each other since report cards were given out, only catching glimpses of each other in homeroom or in the hallway. Since it was the end of the marking period and homecoming, not much work had been done that week, so she didn't have to tutor him that weekend, and this meant even more time apart—they hadn't even texted or anything. Paige couldn't even meet up with her friends to talk about it. All three had their own plans that weekend. Morgan went out of town with her family to visit some relatives in Philadelphia, Jenn spent the weekend getting a new tattoo and getting another one touched up, and Amy had a gymnastics competition that Saturday plus a date on Sunday (it didn't work out well). This left Paige to do her typical activities: stay home to either watch some movies, catch up on anime, or play video games. Steven didn't have much else to do himself. He needed to watch Lisa because their parents weren't around. Meanwhile, his pal Jason went to an open-mic night and then to the movies the next one to see the second *Ouija* movie. He invited Steven to come but declined, not feeling up for it. Probably for the better though, because being given time for themselves after a month of sessions made the two of them realize how much they enjoyed each other's company. Sure it was tutoring, but at least it gave them something to do regularly, and with a friend.

Paige and her friends were at her house, this being the first time in a week that they got to hang out for a prolonged period. Needless to say, they had some catching up to do.

"Imagine somebody getting their penis forcibly ripped off, then their disembodied dick being shoved into his own mouth down his throat after being done with sex where it's covered in dried-up cum. That doesn't come close to describing this," Morgan explained.

"Okay, I really don't wanna hear any more of this," Amy said, disgusted.

"How did we even get on this subject?" Paige asked.

"Beats me. I was zoned out for like five minutes, up until I heard the word 'penis,'" Jenn added.

"Can we please talk about something else? Like tomorrow night?" Amy requested.

"That's right, tomorrow's Halloweekend Havoc," Jenn said.

"You mean the best party of the year!" Morgan excitedly said. "Man, am I hyped!"

"All right, so I'll pick you guys up between five and six, right?" Jenn asked.

"Works for me," Amy said, and Morgan nodded, agreeing.

The three turned their attention to Paige, waiting for her to answer.

"Uh, yeah, the festival—" Paige began.

"What? Are you trying to bail on us?" Jenn interrupted.

"You wouldn't!" Morgan exclaimed.

"I wasn't gonna say that," Paige defended herself.

"Then what were you gonna say?" Morgan asked.

"Well, I wasn't gonna say 'bail.'"

"Paige, are you seriously not gonna come with us?" Amy asked.

"Ugh. This is about Axl, isn't it?" Jenn accused her.

Paige started getting nervous. She already felt guilty about thinking this, and it's even harder to tell your friends no. So she said nothing and just slumped.

"I knew it," Jenn said, reading her face out.

"Come on, guys, you knew when I took this job it was gonna intervene with stuff like this," Paige defended herself.

"Yeah, but we've all done Halloweekend together for the last two years. You and I have gone together every year since sixth grade. Now you're just gonna throw it away like a vote for a third-party candidate?" Morgan interrogated her.

"Not to mention, you're dumping us for Axl?" Amy added.

"I know, and I'm sorry, guys, but I made a commitment, and I need to stay true to it," Paige said.

"What about your costume you sent away to have made over summer? The one you were really excited about, and when we asked you what it was, you said, 'You'll see in October'?" Morgan asked.

"Look, it's not like I want to do this," Paige said.

"Don't you now?" Jenn asked. "Do you 'not want to do this'?"

Paige again said nothing in return, just stared blankly at her.

"Paige, we're not trying to put any pressure on you, but you have been acting—how do I put this?—different since you've started spending time with Axl," Amy said.

"What do you mean? I haven't changed at all. I'm still the same girl," Paige defended herself.

"It's not that. You've been pretty quick to defend him, and at the same time, you're so vague when you talk about him. Is there… anything you're not telling us?" Amy asked.

"No. I'm just trying to help him pass eleventh grade. What's wrong with that?" Paige objected, beginning to sweat.

"There you go. You're doing it again," Amy said.

"You're not fooling anybody, girl," Jenn added.

"Okay, why do you even care? You all encouraged me to do this," Paige reminded them, beginning to feel agitated.

"Yeah, but when I said all that, I didn't think he'd miraculously start doing well, let alone pass," Amy stated.

"I've just been waiting for you to get some dirt on the guy to blackmail him with," Morgan said.

"And I've been waiting on your permission to kick his pretentious ass," Jenn added.

"Okay, guys, he isn't *that* bad—" Paige began.

"AHA!" Morgan cut her off, prompting Paige to then cover her mouth. "No no no, you ain't getting out. I said we were gonna talk about this at the right time, and that time is now!" she continued.

"You said that over a week ago," Paige said.

"My point exactly!" Morgan stated.

"Why is this even news? I already explained all that stuff," Paige said. Her vexation was growing.

"You said you felt comfortable around him, that he wasn't as much a hard-ass as he seemed, that you saw a good person in him, and that you wanted to see what his—quote, unquote—'deal' was," Morgan listed. "Is there anything you left out?"

Paige covered her head, still perspiring.

"Paige, just be honest with us, please," Amy said.

"What's up with you two?" Jenn asked, with a 'tude in her voice.

"Jenn!" Amy said.

"ALL RIGHT!" Paige suddenly exclaimed loudly, taking the other three by surprise.

They were used to her being the mellowest of the group and never heard her raise her voice like that. Granted she told them about her outburst against Steven, but they were now witnessing it firsthand, even if it was just a small dosage.

Paige regained her composure after a few huffs and puffs.

"I'm sorry. I love Halloweekend. I really don't wanna miss it. The thing is, I might not have known him as long as you three, but him and I have reached a point where we can trust each other. He's ...he's my friend. He kept his word to me, and now I have to do the same with him. I'm the only one who can help him, and if I just left him like that, what kind of friend would that make me if I jinxed his trust?" Paige speechified.

"Is that what this is? You think you gotta do this to prove your loyalty?" Jenn asked and was answered by a nod from Paige.

"Paige, correct me if I'm wrong, but wasn't he the one who came to you asking for a second chance? Wasn't he the one that made an agreement with you? And wasn't he the one that pulled out a hundred percent on a vocabulary test just to prove to you that he's changed?" Morgan asked.

"Hundred and five," Paige corrected.

"There ya go! All that after you bitch-slapped him, and you're worried about trust?" Morgan asked Paige, who didn't respond.

"Paige, I still don't feel good about this whole thing, but if you say you've reached that point with him, then you shouldn't have to prove anything. Besides, after all the progress you've both made, I think he can afford to miss one session," Amy said.

"What she said," Morgan agreed.

Paige stayed silent, feeling too overwhelmed by her own stress.

"You know what? Fuck whatever we say. It won't be the same without you there, but we'll respect whatever choice you make. So what do you wanna do, Paige?" Jenn asked.

Paige took her time to think this over. She's feeling too conflicted and afraid to decide what to do, and her friend's anxiousness for her to speak up wasn't making it easier. For her, the biggest factor was "What would Steven say?" and she thought hard about that. Until she remembered the conversation that they had in the library:

"You're always sheltering yourself from people... Why can't you just let loose and be this version of yourself? ...Live your life a little bit. Nobody else is gonna do it for you... 'Oh, I have to work.' So what? ...Get away from it for a while. Take time for yourself, even if it's just a day. Lie to get out of work if you have to. I don't care. Just something."

And with that, she came to a decision.

Her facial expression suddenly went from concern to resolute; and without saying anything to her friends, she stood up, walked away from the couch—exiting the circle they made up—pulled out her phone, scrolled through her contacts, and made a call.

"Samantha? ...Hi, it's Paige. ...I'm doing good. I'm just calling to let you know that I'm not gonna be around tomorrow. ...No, everything's okay. I'm just gonna be in Long Island all for my aunt's birthday. ...Uh-huh, so when you see Steven, could you let him know? ...Yeah, he told me about that. ...Okay great, so I'll see you all Sunday. ...Cool. Thank you, Samantha. ...You too."

She hung up and looked back to her friends who were all surprised.

"Weird, I thought you ladies would be more excited."

"Did I really just see that? Did you seriously just lie about a family birthday to get out of your job?" Amy asked, as she had Morgan wrapped around her arm, who claimed that the phone call was "too intense" and she "needed to cling on to something."

"Well, no. Just about the part where I said I was going to it. Her birthday really is tomorrow, and my parents actually are, but it's an adult-only thing anyway," Paige clarified.

"Nevertheless, you clearly made up an excuse to get out of tutoring," Jenn added. "I've been telling you to do that for years!" She stood up, walked over to her, picked her up from under her arms, and spun her around. "Our girl finally toughened up!"

"I never thought I'd see the day," Amy said. "I guess we're all going to Halloweekend!" She got up and gave Paige a tight hug.

The three then looked over to Morgan, awaiting her response, knowing she'd be ecstatic.

"His mom's name is Samantha?" Morgan said.

"Yeah," Paige answered with a confused look.

"Hmm, Samantha Axl. Sounds hot," she added.

"Morgan!" Amy spoke.

"Sorry, just had to get that out. *I'm so proud of you!*" she finally stated as she jumped out of her chair and clasped Paige. "I knew you had it in you. I just knew it!"

"And you don't feel bad about this?" Amy asked.

"No, I do. I hate lying to them, especially after how nice they've been to me. But hey, 'If they don't feel it, it doesn't hurt,'" she stated.

"Seems like a very confused moral, but who cares! Trick or treat, bitches!" Morgan exclaimed, and the group had their own little precelebration.

The Next Day, October 29, Dusk

Halloween weekend was in full effect, and the four girls were getting set for the best party of the year. Morgan went over to Paige's house so they could get ready together, while Jenn got to Amy's house early to prep with her—so Amy could do Jenn's makeup for her.

When they were finished, they got in Jenn's car and proceeded to Paige's house.

They both exited the car upon arrival and went up to the house. They rang the doorbell and called up to the open window that led to Paige's bedroom.

"Paige? Morgan? It's us!" Amy called.

"Come in, guys, door's open!" Paige called out from the window.

The two girls obliged. Amy went to the bathroom to touch up her makeup. Shortly later, Jenn looked toward the stairway and saw Morgan coming down.

She was dressed as Tifa Lockhart from *Final Fantasy VII*, complete with her black hair done to match her style.

"Sup, ladies."

Morgan turned to see only Jenn was in the room, wearing an all-black bloodstained blouse, skinny jeans with a pair of damaged knee-high black boots, a messy shoulder-length black wig, and a makeup scar across her cheek.

"Or sup, Jenn? Where's Amy?" she asked.

"In the bathroom touching up her face," she answered. "So you're—"

"Tifa, from *Final Fantasy*," she cut her off.

Jenn nodded. "That's what I thought."

"And you're... I have no idea what this is," Morgan blatantly said.

"Killer Kate."

"Who?"

"From *The Hateful Kate*."

"I don't know what that is," Morgan dryly said.

"Yes, you do. That Syfy Channel movie from last year?"

Morgan pondered. "Oh, you mean that movie about the zombie chick who starts killing all her ex-boyfriends?"

"No, you're thinking of *Dana of the Dead*. It's the one with the girl who controls a bunch of dogs to kill everybody who bullied her," Jenn summarized.

"Oh, *that's* what that was?"

"Yeah."

"Oh okay. Yeah, I never watched it," she lucidly stated again.

Jenn sighed. "Whatever."

"I like it though," Morgan complimented her costume.

"Ditto," Jenn returned the compliment.

"No, I'm Tifa."

Jenn shook her head. "Smart-ass."

"Wrong again," Morgan said before laughing at her own joke.

The bathroom door opened, and Morgan turned her head. Her jaw dropped when she saw Amy was dressed up as Harley Quinn as she appeared in *Suicide Squad*. Amy turned her attention toward Morgan and noticed her costume.

"Wow!" Amy walked over to Morgan, who's trying to control her urges. "Morgan, you look hot!"

"Uh—" Morgan tried to clear her throat. "Thanks. You look pretty hot yourself," Morgan said, doing her best to act natural and hide how turned on she was.

"Eh, it's not much. I'm sure I won't be the only one dressed like this," Amy shyly said.

"Well, none of them will look as good as you," Morgan complimented her. "Oh god, don't take that too serious!" she said, realizing what she just said.

"It's cool. Thank you. You're definitely gonna stand out yourself." Amy chuckled, and Morgan responded by smiling as she bit her lip.

Amy took out her phone. "Gimme a minute."

She walked to a corner of the room to get some selfies, unaware that Morgan was still admiring her.

The three suddenly heard a door close upstairs and drew their attention.

"Yo, Paige, you ready or what?" Jenn called up.

"I'm coming!" she called back.

Paige walked downstairs, dressed as Link from *The Legend of Zelda*. She had on a wig, pointy ears, and blue hooped earrings, complete with her own Hylian Shield and Master Sword in a sheath on a shoulder strap.

"There she is!" Morgan introduced her.

Amy gasped.

"Do I look okay?" Paige diffidently asked.

"You look awesome!" Amy answered.

"Geez, Paige, you don't have to make us all look bad," Jenn humorously said. "Just kidding. Kick-ass getup, girl."

"I would hope so. I spent a lot of money on this," Paige said.

"Show us the sword and shield," Morgan said.

Paige obeyed, removing the strap holding the shield from her body and pulling the sword out of the sheath.

"Nice!" Morgan said.

"It's nothing fancy. I just got these at Party City," Paige said.

"It doesn't matter. They really make the look," Amy assured her.

"Well, thanks. And hey, I love what you're all wearing too—Harley Quinn, Tifa, and, ooh, Killer Kate, nice," she listed.

"See, she gets it!" Jenn said to Morgan.

"Well, I'm sorry I'm not majored in the art of Syfy Channel Original Movies. I watch actual good stuff," Morgan fired back.

"You mean like Hallmark Christmas films?" Paige asked.

"Hey, lay off Hallmark. Lay. Off. Hallmark!" Morgan defended herself.

"All right, who cares? Let's get the fuck outta here," Jenn said.

"Agreed. Just give me a minute while I put my shield on and put the sword in its scabbard," Paige said.

"That's fine. I'll just start up my car," Jenn replied.

Jenn walked out of the house to her car while Paige went into the dining room to get her stuff together, leaving Morgan alone with Amy who's picking up her baseball bat.

"How can anybody not see the majesty of those movies?" Morgan asked out loud.

"I don't know," Amy answered. "But at least I can take comfort knowing I'm not the only one in this group that enjoys them."

"You watch Hallmark movies too?"

"Like you said, I don't know how anybody can't enjoy them."

"The only people who don't have never seen one."

"Oh my god, *finally* someone gets it!" Amy said before she hugged Morgan, catching her by surprise. She let her go and giggled. "Welp, let's get to it," she said before walking off.

Morgan bit her lip again as she blushed and then released a deep breath after watching Amy walk out the door.

Paige walked up behind to whisper to her, "Are you wet?"

"I almost was," Morgan whispered back.

"Wonderful. You're sitting by the door."

"Fine."

The two left the house and met Amy outside before they all went in Jenn's car and drove off.

6:30 PM, Nicotra's Ballroom/Halloweekend Havoc Festival

The group arrived at the festival, prepared for a fun-filled, worry-free night. They started off with their own little photo shoot in the venue's garden, and after that, they went inside to join the party.

Everywhere you went, you'd see teens, adults in various age ranges, and even a couple of children—drunk, high, sober, or on a sugar rush—all having fun in their own ways, and the occasional depressed person going through some sort of emotional episode. There was a dining hall where cooked foods and candies were being served, and in the main ballroom, there was a DJ playing music with some strobe lights going off. From left to right, top to bottom, the whole building had been decorated to make for a creepy/festive atmospheric party. What was there not to enjoy?

The girls made the most of the night however they could; Jenn was with Amy, taking advantage of the free food while Amy talked to a bunch of different guys, while Paige stayed with Morgan who was in the ballroom dancing like a drunken idiot despite being sober. Paige at first found it hard to get into the proper mood; she was happy to be there but couldn't shake off the anxiety she was feeling. In general, she could be uncomfortable being around this many people without her friends beside her. This time was different though; her conscience was making this Halloweekend Havoc less preferable than previous ones. As freeing as it feels to be excused from your obligations, you still could never brush away the guilt from not being there. She tried to not think about it, but something always reminded her of Steven; at one point the DJ was playing "For Whom the Bell Tolls," which made her think of a Metallica *Ride the Lightning* T-shirt he was wearing one day. Some partygoers were wearing outfits that matched his everyday style. She even saw one person was dressed as Albert Einstein—the nickname she was used to him calling her. She was sure he was excited about not having to learn anything, but how would he really feel if he found out where she went tonight? What would his parents think if they found out she lied to them after how generous they'd been to her? She tried covering up those feelings of treacherousness from her friends, but she thought about this a lot throughout the night, even while she was in the ballroom watching Morgan from the sidelines.

Morgan noticed Paige over there and motioned for her to join in, to which she was hesitant about. She was already shy as it was, so she would've done that regardless of how she was feeling, but Morgan wasn't gonna take no for an answer tonight—she knew what her friend needed. She mimicked like she was spinning a lasso, threw it at her, and squeezed it tight. She looked at her for a moment, but Paige was too bashful. Morgan then pulled her invisible rope upward until it was straight; knowing she wasn't going to give up on this, Paige smiled, moved in sync with Morgan's hands, and hopped toward her as if she's being pulled.

When she was within arm's reach, Morgan grabbed Paige and made her dance with her. Paige couldn't help but burst out in laughter, and the duo started moving on their own. Not long after, Amy and Jenn walked in and noticed them. Morgan invited them over. Amy immediately rushed over to them while Jenn moved at her own pace. Being surrounded by them helped Paige forget how she was feeling a minute ago. She may regret it later, but for now she was going to take Steven's advice: have fun and live life. It's what he would want her to do. ...Right?

9:00 PM

The girls were all sitting at one table in the dining hall, getting a break from the music.

"I don't know about you ladies, but I'd say this night has been a success," Morgan said.

"Well, we all look good; if this punch was spiked, it would've taken effect by now; and nobody's given me a reason to kill them, so I agree," Jenn said before taking a sip.

"And I got six guys' numbers, so I definitely feel accomplished," Amy bragged.

"Ah yeah—two Jared Leto Jokers, some dude in a Pikachu onesie, Obama, Deadpool, and a banana. That's quite the choice," Jenn said and shared a laugh with Amy, as Morgan tried to hide her seething jealousy. "Nah, for real, who you gonna go for first?"

"I don't know. Pikachu was cute, oh, but Obama had these little dimples. One of those Joker guys was hot, but the other one seemed really sweet. I don't even know what Deadpool looks like, but he had a sexy voice, and Banana Guy had this funny double entendre about bananas—"

"So, Paige!" Morgan interrupted her with a fake smile. "You haven't said anything in a while. How are you enjoying this shindig?"

"What? Oh yeah." Paige snapped out of her own thoughts. "Actually, and I'm being perfectly honest, I'm feeling pretty good," she confessed.

"I like hearing that. Aren't you glad you picked us over that pretentious twat?" Jenn asked.

"Jenn!" Amy said.

"Relax, it's okay," Paige assured her. "I mean, I still feel guilty. I've never liked lying or keeping secrets. Hell, I feel guilty having to hide the fact that my mom's my teacher. But I'll admit now that I'm here, I am glad I did this—is that bad?"

"How's that bad? For once, you did what you wanted to do, and you enjoyed yourself. So what if you told a fib? You ain't gonna get anywhere in life if you never stick up for yourself," Morgan replied. "Aren't I right?" she asked Amy and Jenn.

"She's not wrong," Amy answered.

"It's true. Take it from me," Jenn said.

"Hey, buddy, aren't I right?" she asked a random person wearing a hoodie with a *Purge*-themed mask.

They looked over at Paige, stared at her for a few seconds, and then walked away.

"Very profound," Morgan said.

"Yeah. …I'm starting to realize that now," Paige answered.

"Relax. This time tomorrow, you'll forget you ever felt bad at all," Jenn reassured her.

"Retweet," Morgan agreed.

Paige suddenly got a text message; she looked at her phone to see who it's from. Her eyes widened upon reading the notification: "Message from Steven."

"Uh, I'll be right back. I gotta take this," she said as she's getting up.

"Oh hey, as long as you're up, could you bring me back some mozzarella sticks?" Morgan asked her and was met by an annoyed look. "I'm kidding. Go do your thing." Paige chuckled and rolled her eyes as she walked out of the room.

"All right, guys, we need to talk," Amy started. "About her."

"What this time?" Jenn asked.

"I didn't want to say this last night, but all that stuff she said about how she hasn't changed—I don't buy it," Amy exclaimed.

"Ah man, Amy…" Jenn began.

"Come on, we all see it," Amy said.

"Yeah, she's got a little more spunk in her, and her self-esteem has gone up. What's wrong with that? It's not like she's turned into a complete bitch on us," Morgan said.

"No, she hasn't. I'm glad she's gained some confidence, but I just can't shake this feeling like …like we're only seeing the start of a drastic change in her. I don't know if that's a good thing or a bad thing, but I do know that Steven has something to do with it," Amy said.

"Amy, I don't like Axl any more than you. As a matter a fact, I hate his guts. But ultimately, anything she does is up to her. Who are we to tell her who to hit it off with or not?" Jenn said with disdain.

"I'm not saying we should do that, but doesn't this all come off as a little conspicuous? This was all just supposed to be a tutoring assignment she didn't even wanna do, with somebody she didn't like, and then she tries to convince herself that said somebody isn't so bad, refers to him as her friend, and now all of a sudden, it's going so well that she thought about blowing us off to go 'tutor him'? I don't know what they're doing when we're not around, but I got a hunch I wouldn't like it," Amy ranted.

"Whoa! I'm just gonna stop you right there. If you're really implying what I think you're implying, then you're even crazier than Morgan," Jenn said.

"I don't want to accuse her of anything, but she's showing all the signs. Trust me, I've dated guys like that before. I've said the same things about them she's been saying about him, and it always ended for different reasons, but each one was just as painful as the last. Only difference here is that he didn't even pretend to be a nice guy!" Amy backed up.

"Aims, settle down. I know Paige. She would never go for that Tommy Be Wanna-Lee. ...I mean—" She groaned. "You know what I meant. He doesn't even match her ideal type," Morgan reassured Amy.

"I hope you're right. She's just so pure and innocent. I'd hate to see her get hurt," Amy said.

"Don't you worry about that. If he hurts her at all, he'll never be able to hurt anyone again after I've dislocated every one of his fingers," Jenn stated, clenching her fist.

"And he could never please himself," Morgan added. The other two pairs of eyes grew wide at her comment. "What? When nobody else is doing it, somebody's got to. Otherwise, you'd just feel empty," she continued.

"You're fucking weird. Fucking weirdo." Jenn stood up and went toward the service tables.

"This is facts. You are weird," Amy said.

"She's just jealous," Morgan replied.

"Of what?"

"Something."

Meanwhile

Paige was standing up against the wall in the front corridor, well engaged with her conversation with Steven:

Steven: Yo Einstein how's it going?
Paige: I'm doing well. You?
Steven: Meh. I ain't dead so I guess decent.

Paige: Well, that's a relief lol. So, what's up?
Steven: Not much. So Samantha tells me your in Long Island?

Paige began to get nervous, fearing he'll catch on to her ruse.

Paige: You're*
Steven: Geez thanks so much you grammar Nazi.
Paige: (*shrug emoji*) Just doing my job.
Steven: Teeheehaha. 4 real though she said YOU'RE celebrating your cousins birthday or whatev?
Paige: My aunt, & yes.
Steven: Eh close enough. So how is that?

Sigh. *I'm too young for all this pressure*, she said to herself.

Paige: I mean, it's nothing too special, just with some relatives & some cousins, your typical family gathering.
Steven: So boring as fuck.
Paige: Yes. Lol no, it's always nice to see them.
Steven: Come on you don't gotta keep stuff from me you know you'd rather be at Halloweekend Havoc tonight.

Midway through typing her response, another costumed person walked up and leaned up against the wall next to her, distracted by their own phone. Paige took a glance at this person and realized it's the same one wearing the *Purge* mask that Morgan bothered a few minutes ago. As she resumed typing, the masked person looked over to her and didn't say a word, eventually recapturing her attention.

Paige looked up from her phone.

"Hi," she said, awkwardly waving and giving a smile. They nodded in response. "*The Purge*, nice." They remained silent. "I've only seen the first movie. I hear the new one is good though." They just gave her a shrug in response. "I'm sorry about my friend, by the way." She chuckled. "She's one of those 'live in the moment, act without discipline' kind of people, you know?" No response. "You don't care." She chuckled.

Paige finished her message and sent it.

> Paige: Don't remind me, I would kill to be there right now. I felt so bad blowing off my friends, & I got this awesome costume made for it. But I mean, it is how it is. But I could always wear it to ComicCon or something, & they'll be another one next year, so I'll be okay.

She looked back at the masked person. "Oh, don't mind me. I'm gonna go back in a little bit. I'm just talking to a friend."

Suddenly, she heard the person's phone vibrate. They took it out of their pocket and looked at the screen.

Paige gave an awkward laugh.

"That's funny. You get a text message right after I sent one." She chuckled. "So weird, right?" she said as the person was typing and hit send.

Very shortly after, Paige got another reply and read it off her lock screen.

> Steven: Yeah. That is funny.

Chapter 15

You Can Trust Me

"That's funny. You get a text message right after I sent one." She chuckled. "So weird, right?" she said as the person was typing and hit send.

Very shortly after, Paige got another reply and read it off her lock screen.

Steven: Yeah. That is funny.

Paige squinted at her screen, confused, before having an epiphany. She then slowly looked over to the masked person who's looking down at her.

They lifted their mask up to reveal their face.

"Sup, Einstein?"

"Steven!" Paige exclaimed with an expression of both surprise and fear. "Oh god! Uh, uh uh—" She cleared throat. "What a pleasant surprise!" she said, trying to put on an innocent smile, despite her heart beating faster than a speed date with Sonic the Hedgehog.

"You sure it's a pleasant one? 'Cause the way you're smiling is the same way Jason did when his dad noticed a crack in his car's taillight," Steven said with a smirk.

Paige tilted her head down, lifted her glasses, and rubbed her eyes with trembling hands. She quickly put her glasses back down and looked back up at him. "Okay, just let me explain. You see, I—"

"Said you were going to Long Island to celebrate your aunt's birthday so that you had an excuse not to tutor tonight and come to Halloweekend with your girly friends, except it isn't really her birthday

101

because the truth is this supposed 'aunt' doesn't even exist?" Steven finished for her.

Paige was silent for a second. "All the things you just said minus the second half."

"So then that makes two parties you've bailed on." He crossed his arms.

"Okay yes! Yes, I lied! I was hoping nobody would figure it out, but I had a strong feeling somebody would, and I still did it anyway. I went against all I stand for and betrayed whatever amount of trust I had—" Paige ranted in defeat as Steven tried to speak to her.

"Hey!" Steven cut her off. "Shut up." Paige hyperventilated. "What the hell do you mean 'betrayed trust'?" Paige froze up. "Tell me."

"It's just that we were finally starting to get along, and I figured if you found out about this that it might… jeopardize that," Paige confessed.

"Yeah?" Steven asked and was met with a nod. "Well, that's dumb."

"Huh?"

"You really thought I'd get pissed off about that?" Paige nodded. "Au contraire, my dear Watson, I'm proud of you," Steven said.

Paige was perplexed by his reaction. "Again, huh?"

"You, the most law-abiding citizen in the entire school, actually stuck up for herself and went up against authority. I mean, wow! When I told you to lie to get out of work, I was just overexaggerating, but you really did it!"

"Are you drunk?"

"No. I mean, okay, I have had a little bit, but I swear I'm not there yet."

"Oh, lovely," she sarcastically replied.

"Seriously though, it's cool. There's nothing wrong with doing something for yourself once in a while."

"So it doesn't bother you at all that I lied to get out of tonight's session?"

"Well, you doing that meant I got to go out on a Saturday night, come to this party, and get a break from learning anything. So nope."

Paige breathed and collected her thoughts, feeling a lot of guilt coming off her shoulders. "All right, that makes me feel a lot better."

"Hey, if it helps, you saved me the trouble of coming up with an excuse to bail. If you didn't lie to Samantha, I would've."

"Oh really?" Paige said with her hands on her hips and a raised eyebrow.

"Yep."

"And what kind of excuse would you have given?" She tilted her head to the side.

"I was gonna tell her that Jason's mom died."

"Oh, sweet Jesus. And what was your plan for after you said that?"

"Doesn't matter. Thanks to you I didn't need a phase two."

Paige rolled her eyes and giggled. "Well, then I guess this worked out. Just promise me you won't tell your parents about this."

"So long as you promise you won't tell them I brought Lisa here. They'd freak out if they knew she was at a party like this."

"You brought Lisa?"

"I did. If they ask, we're at her friend's house in Brooklyn."

"Great," she agreed. "So where is she?"

"I left her with Jason when I saw you were here. She's fine."

"I can tell."

"Good. What?"

She pointed behind him.

Steven turned around to see Lisa walking up to them, dressed as Katara from *Avatar: The Last Airbender*.

"Sup, big bro?" she casually asked. "Paige, you're here too?" she asked excitedly.

"Yeah, hi, Lisa. I love your costume," Paige complimented her.

"Thanks. Yours is awesome!" Lisa returned the compliment.

"Lisa, I told you to stay with Jason," Steven said.

"Actually, you told Jason to watch me. You never told me to do anything," she corrected him.

"Don't get smart with me. Where is he?" he asked.

"Would he by any chance be the zombie over there?" Paige asked, pointing at said zombie.

"You've gotta be shitting me. Yo, Jason!" he called from across the room, getting his attention.

Jason saw Lisa was with Steven. "Oh, thank God," he exclaimed loud enough for the three to hear.

"You serious, dude? This happens way too often than it should!"

"She ran through crowd of people. What was I supposed to do?" Jason defended himself.

"Don't let her do that!"

"All right, relax," Paige intervened. "Relax. She's fine. Nobody got hurt. It's not worth causing a scene. Just breathe," Paige told Steven.

Steven collected his thoughts and let out a sigh. "Fine."

Lisa saw her brother was tense and started to feel bad. "I'm sorry, guys, I was just feeling nosey," she apologized to both boys.

"It's cool, kid. Just try to make watching you easier," Jason requested.

"I can do that," Lisa agreed.

"You good, man?" Jason asked Steven.

"I'll be fine as long as no one causes me any more stress for the rest of the night," Steven answered.

"Sounds good to me," Paige agreed.

"Anyway, what are you doing here, Paige? Steven said you were in Long Island," Lisa asked.

"Yeah, I'll explain it to you tomorrow. I don't wanna get into all that again," Paige answered.

"Fair enough," Lisa said.

"Man, who knew somebody that constantly makes the honor roll was such a rebel?" Jason added.

"It's true. I have a secret double life that nobody knows about. I also sell crack and cocaine during after school hours," Paige said, playing along.

"Hmm, you know, now that you mention it, you look like you sold me an ounce of that stuff last March," Jason continued.

"So nice of you to remember. Now I know who to get rid of if I'm ratted out." She did a playful glare.

"Hmm, smart and cunning, just like Oprah."

The two shared a laugh.

Paige leaned down to say to Lisa, "Sorry you had to hear that, Lisa."

"Meh, I've heard worse," she replied.

"I'm sure you have," she said, turning her head to Steven who had a look of disdain.

Jason leaned over to whisper to Steven, "I like this one." He didn't reply. "You know what? I don't think we've actually met," Jason said to Paige.

"I mean, aside from three separate times at school, if you count that," Paige replied.

"Well, I don't. So…" He extended his hand to her. "Hi, I'm Jason. Jason Kennedy."

Paige shook his hands. "Paige Hetfield." She smiled.

"Nice to meet you, Paige."

"You too, Jason."

They both released their hands. "Hey, mind if I ask you about your friend Jenn?" Jason asked.

"Jenn? What about her?" Paige asked.

"Well, you know, what does she like? Is she into musicians? Is she single? Is she straight? Bi? Pan?" Jason listed.

"Why don't you ask her yourself?" Steven interrupted, looking off into the distance.

"Hey!"

Jason, Paige, and Lisa all turned to where the voice came from. It was from Jenn who's walking up to the group being followed by Amy.

"Shit! Lisa, get behind me," Steven commanded, to which she obliged.

"Oh god." Paige stepped in front of Jenn, making her stop in place. "Jenn, before this gets ugly, nothing's going on here. It's all good."

Jenn looked up from Paige and turned her attention to Steven and Jason.

"What are you two doing here?" Amy asked.

"Same reason she's here with you—just to have fun," Jason assured her.

"And why do I suspect I wouldn't like you guys' idea of 'fun'?" Jenn added.

"All right, listen. I get it. After everything that's happened, you girls have no reason to trust me. But if I really wanted to do something to her, don't you think I would've by now?" Steven asked them both.

Neither gave an answer; it was a good point. He took a deep breath before continuing. "I'm not gonna ask for you to change your opinions of me on the flip of a dime. I'm not a good person. I can't deny that. But even if none of you like me, at the very least, I ask if you can just give me a chance? Like she did?" he pleaded.

Amy was surprised by his words. She leaned over to speak to Jenn. "Did you just hear the same thing I heard?"

"Either I heard what you heard or that punch bowl was spiked after all," Jenn replied.

Steven and Jason looked at the two, unable to read their expressions.

"I... I don't know about this," Amy admitted.

"And I don't know how you manage to convert her, but I'm not gonna fall for it as easily," Jenn stated.

"Guys..." Paige spoke up. They both turned their heads to face her. "I know you don't believe him, but you said you trust my judgment," she reminded them. "If you mean that, please give him a chance," she implored them.

Amy and Jenn looked back at Steven.

"All right. If she believes you, then I'll buy this. For now," Amy consented.

Jenn sighed. "That was a low blow," she told Paige. "Fine," she hesitantly agreed.

Steven sensed a bad vibe from her response, knowing she still had some problems with him; but for the sake of everybody else, especially Paige, he sucked up his pride and simply nodded and agreed.

Paige smiled big, so happy to finally see a truce established between both parties.

"Hey, uh, correct me if I'm wrong, but weren't there four of you?" Jason asked them.

"Yep!" Morgan exclaimed, catching everybody's attention.

"How long were you standing there?" Paige asked.

"Three minutes," Morgan replied. "Came out of the bathroom in time to watch all this unfold. So no need to repeat the same peace offering to me. If Paige sees a good guy in you and you're serious about turning your attitude around, I'll gladly contribute to this treaty. That and because I haven't been this intrigued to see how a gathering of two parties goes since I watched *The Red Wedding*," she said, gradually walking closer to Steven until she's right up in his face.

Steven stared at her for a second. "Is this one for real?" he asked the trio.

Morgan looked behind him to see Lisa still behind his leg. "Who's the kid?"

"That's my sister," Steven answered.

"So this is the little sister we've heard so much about," Morgan said.

Lisa stepped out from behind her brother. "I guess so."

"So there really are two of them." Jenn spoke out.

"You must be Jenn," Lisa replied.

"Yeah. How do you know that?"

"Jason talks about you a lot. He said you were like those women in the UFC and that he'd let you put him in a choke-hold."

Jenn, Jason, and Paige's eyes all simultaneously expanded, while Amy gasped and covered her mouth. Morgan covered hers too, trying not to burst out laughing, and Steven just turned his head away from everyone.

Jenn scowled at Jason, whose zombie makeup was practically sweating off on account of embarrassment.

"You know what?" Jason spoke up loudly. "This makes me realize that most of us haven't been properly introduced! So uh, why don't we all use this opportunity to start over! Yeah, I like this idea. I'll go first." He cleared his throat and adjusted himself toward Paige's friend, offering his hand again. "Hiii, I'm Jason," he greeted, acting casual.

They each shot him a befuddled look, but one at a time they all gave in.

"I'm Amy." She accepted the handshake.

"Morgan." She waved. "I'm not touching that."

Amy wiped her hand on her shorts.

"You already know my name ...Jason," Jenn said with her arms folded.

"All right, good start so far," he said, putting his hand down.

"Well, as long as we're doing this, guys, this is Lisa. Lisa, this is Morgan, Jenn, and Amy," Paige introduced her.

"Nice to meet you all," Lisa said.

Amy leaned over to say, "Hello, Lisa. Your costume's so pretty."

"Thank you."

"What up, kid?" Morgan said.

"Nothing," Lisa answered.

"Yeah, story of my life."

Lisa turned her head to Jenn who still had her arms folded; Jenn just nodded her head hi, not saying anything. As innocent as this young girl appeared, she was still Steven's sister, and Jenn had no interest in getting along with anyone affiliated with him.

"Have you ever put somebody in a hospital?" Lisa asked.

"No. Although one time I hit someone so hard they had to get their tooth replaced," Jenn blatantly admitted.

"In a fight?"

"No," Jenn answered, leaving a second of silence.

"That's so cool!" The excitement in Lisa's reply took Jenn and the other two by surprise.

"I'm starting to see the resemblance," Amy whispered to Morgan, who nodded in agreement.

"And you all know Steven," Paige said, accompanied by an awkward chuckle. "Steven, I'd like for you to meet my friends: Jenn, Amy, and Morgan."

"Pleasure," Steven said, playing along.

"Oh, the pleasure is all ours." Morgan's tone was condescending.

"Morgan. I've heard a lot about you," Steven said.

"And I've heard such wonderful things about you too," Morgan said with a cocky grin.

Amy gulped. "Hello, Steven."

"Brookes, right?" Steven asked.

"Yeah. How'd you know my last name?" Amy asked.

"You're a popular topic amongst a bunch of idiots at school."

"Oh. You don't say," Amy said as she blushed.

"Not tough to see why." He flirtatiously smirked.

Her blush deepened. "Um, thank you," she said, biting her lip.

"Yeah, well, she's not going to settle for just anybody, so don't give her any ideas," Jenn interrupted.

"And Jenn Owens. I'm sure you and I will get along swimmingly," Steven said with a more casual smirk.

"We'll see," she said sternly.

"Great. Now that we all know each other, why don't we go back in and enjoy the rest of the party?" Morgan suggested.

"Actually, why don't we all go outside to the garden area?" Paige counterproposed.

"Why?" Steven asked.

"You know, just to hang out, get to know each other better away from all the craziness," Paige answered.

Steven thought it over. "Eh, why not?"

"I'm game," Morgan concurred.

"Great," Paige said.

The rest of them agreed, except for Jenn. "You all go. I'm gonna go out to the parking lot." She spoke.

"You okay, Jenn?" Amy asked.

"Yeah. I just need to get some air. I'll meet you in a bit," Jenn said, going out the front entrance.

"Should we do something?" Lisa asked.

"Nah, she's fine. She's just going out to smoke," Morgan said. "Now come on." She started walking toward the garden.

"Whatever," Steven said.

Everyone else followed her, except Jason who's still looking at the entrance, puzzled and concerned.

"Yo, Jason, if you're gonna tend to her, you gotta walk out the door!" Steven shouted to him from across the room before putting his mask back down and disappearing down the hall.

Parking Lot

Jenn was standing by her car having a cigarette when Jason walked up to her.

"Yo," he called out.

She said nothing and shot him another death glare.

He put up his hands. "Relax, just thought you could use some company."

"I don't. And if I did, certainly not yours," she shot back.

"All right, I get it. You don't like me very much, and I can see why. But I swear, I'm not a creeper, and I'm not here to try anything," he defended himself.

"As much as I find that hard to believe, that's not my biggest problem right now," she said before taking a smoke.

"So then, what is it?" he asked, being met without a response. "Come on, you clearly got something harsh on your mind you want to get out, so now's your chance. Be as cruel as you want," he invited.

She threw the cigarette on the ground and stomped it out before getting up close to him.

"I don't know what kind of tricks your buddy is playing on her, but I don't like it one bit. He might have earned Morgan and Amy's trust, but I'm not so easy to win over. Okay? I grew up in Brooklyn. I've dealt with a lot of scum that aren't much different from him, or you, for that matter. She can convince herself all she wants about these illusions she's having about Axl, but I see him for who he is, and who he is, is how he presents himself, and it pisses me off having to pretend I'm cool with this. The only reason I haven't done anything is because I gave Paige my word that I wouldn't, and I hate myself for that! But as much as I do, I'm going to keep that word and sit this out for as long as required because it's what she would want. So just remember this, ya vagina: if he makes her so much as shed a single tear, I'll spill a good ounce of his blood on the ground. Then, I'll do the same to you!" She brought her balled-up fist to his face, threatening him. "Got that?"

Jason stared at her with an alarmed expression. "Every last bit of it," he agreed with his hands in the air. She brought her fist down, maintaining her irate expression. "You know, I expected less than that, but then I remembered who I was talking to," he added.

She rolled her eyes before turning her back to him and folding her arms.

"Look, with all seriousness, I get where you're coming from. I'd be lying if I said he wasn't a hard-ass, that he's always pleasant to be around and that he was completely responsible."

"But let me guess, 'he's not such a bad guy.'" She mocked his voice.

"Actually, I was gonna share a story of this one thing involving sausages, firecrackers, and an old piano, but yeah, I was gonna get to that eventually."

"Well, I don't wanna hear it."

"That he's a nice guy or the thing involving sausages, firecrackers, and an old piano?"

"I just don't wanna hear anything from you," she clarified. "But I'm still going to, aren't I?"

"I'm just gonna say this: this is just as weird to me as it is to you." Jenn turned back around to face him, suddenly engrossed by what he said. "I mean, he has chicks throwing themselves at him all the time, and she's the first one who has a face that he remembers. Up until she came around, I've never even heard him say the word 'sorry,' or if he ever did, then I can't recall. So if it'll make you feel any better, I have no idea what it is, but she's apparently got something that he feels connected to, and it's brought out something in him I never would've guessed he had."

Jenn briefly absorbed what he said. "Not just him."

"Huh?"

"This whole thing has somewhat changed Paige in a noticeable way."

"That bad?"

"Honestly, no. She's been more open about her feelings, she's doing the things she wants to do, she stood up for herself for once, and I don't know. I guess she has gained more self-confidence."

"I'll say this—she's probably the only person who's ever struck him without getting struck back. That's quite the achievement."

"Yeah, it's like Sarah Connor destroying a Terminator."

They snickered. "Right down to the both of them becoming friends one movie later."

"I was actually gonna say that there's also a child he's looking out for."

"Yes!"

They both laughed.

Jenn realized what she's doing and snapped out of it.

"Dammit," she exclaimed and put her defenses back up.

"Problem?"

111

"I know what you're trying to do. Just 'cause those two are pals doesn't mean me and you are gonna be anything."

"No, I swear, I'm just trying to talk," he said.

"Ah yeah?" she replied, not believing his words. "Well, just thought I'd make that clear."

"You have," he clarified. "I swear, with all sincerity, I'm not trying to bring you down or anything. But it looks like all of us are going to have some kind of association from here on out. I know your friends aren't a hundred percent for this either, but they're still gonna try to get along with him. That's what Paige would want. So to make this easy for everybody, maybe the both of us can do the same and at least be friends." She crossed her arms. "Just, friends," he reassured her with some disappointment in his tone.

She sighed. "So long as those two are buds, I'll do my best to be patient with you. But when they cut ties, you and I cut ties."

Jason stiffly nodded. "You have a deal," he begrudgingly agreed. "But you know, if given the chance, I feel like we'd get along well."

"I doubt that."

"Ah, come on, just now you were enjoying our little banter, and you know it," he teased.

"I can't confirm or deny that."

"All right, fine, don't admit it."

"You just watch what you say, or I'll rip your tongue out."

"Gotcha," he agreed.

Jenn lit another cigarette.

"Ooh, could you spare one of those?" he asked. She gave him an annoyed look. "Please?" he asked again.

She handed him a bud, which he lit with his own lighter that he kept on his key chain for "emergencies."

"So... Killer Kate?" he asked, referring to her costume.

"Yeah," she replied. An awkward silence arose as both casually smoked their buds. "And you're a zombie *Family Guy* fan?"

"Nope. I'm just *Family Guy*."

She observed it again. "Oh, I get it. Dead."

"Exactly. This show died years ago, yet they keep going for some reason."

"Honestly, I never really got into that show to begin with."

"What?!"

"I mean, it had its moments. I just couldn't get into the show."

"How the hell could you not get into it?"

"It's way too unfocused. All the jokes are just a bunch of random segues into gags that have nothing to do with the story."

"Well, yeah, nowadays, that's pretty much all it is, but come on, the first few seasons were hysterical. Ever see the one where Brian owes Stewie money?"

"Yeah, the one where he beats him up two times."

"Yes! How can you not find that funny?"

"I said 'it had its moments,' but that's all everybody talks about, the cutaway jokes and a few random scenes. Aside from that, it always comes off like they're overcompensating for an inability to tell a narrative."

"You're breaking my heart here, ma'am."

"Just calling it like I see it."

"*Family Guy* was never about the narrative—it was about being shocking, scandalous, and breaking the barriers of social norm. To satirize how outrageous and cruel our society can be."

"Through a show about a baby bent on world domination who is sometimes gay but other times not?"

"Exactly. You're not supposed to take it that seriously."

"Didn't they once do an episode about abusive relationships?"

"Yes."

"A show with a talking baby and has a running gag about them abusing their daughter thought they were smart enough to talk about domestic abuse."

"We already established that the later seasons are bad, hence the idea of this costume."

"And I just never thought it was that good to begin with."

"You know? We both agree that it sucks now, and that's good enough for me."

"Whatever." They both took a smoke. "I actually did kind of like that one episode where Peter knocked out the TV satellite," she admitted.

"I love that one!"

"It at least had a plot."

"Trust me, if you thought they were lacking in plot, then you oughta see what they're doing now."

"I don't want to see."

"Smart decision. Just stick to the Syfy channel."

"Don't tell me what to do."

Jason chuckled, and Jenn can't help herself to share it.

The awkward silence returned.

"Listen, so long as I've got you in a decent mood, I'm sorry if I ever made you feel uncomfortable."

"I wouldn't say 'uncomfortable' so much as annoyed."

"Whatever it was, I'm sorry. I guess that approach doesn't work on everybody."

"It doesn't."

"Now I know for sure."

"Yeah. But I guess it's cool." The two shared a smile. "I suppose you're somewhat more decent than I assumed you'd be. Somewhat."

"Hmm. A compliment from the great JO. I hear those are rare." He grinned.

"Well, they're not common."

"Then consider me humbled."

"Yeah yeah. …So question."

"Yeeeees?"

"Why do you hang out with Axl?"

Jason's giddy mood shifted.

"What do you mean?"

"I mean, you're the only dude that's ever around him, not just at school—anywhere. And aside from the grungy emo look, I'm not gonna lie—I don't see any connection."

"Who you callin' 'emo'?"

"Answer my question first."

"I don't know. I guess because I actually took time to get to know him."

"Oh okay, that explains it," Jenn sarcastically replied.

"Look, we both like the same music. We laugh at the same things. We dress similar. In eighth grade, we fought over marrying the lead singer of Evanescence. I don't have any special reason." Jenn stared at him, unconvinced. "You know? It's boring as fuck out here. How's about we go back and join 'em?" he said before throwing his cigarette on the ground and stomping on it.

"Fine, be discreet all you want." Jenn disposed of her own cigarette. "Just remember, I'm watching you two," she reminded him before beginning to walk back to the hotel.

Jason cracked a small grin unbeknownst to her before following behind.

Hotel Garden

Paige, Morgan, Amy, Lisa, and Steven were all in one of the hotel's gazebos that would normally be rented out for weddings, just sitting there in silence. Even though they were on seemingly good terms, for their own reasons, they felt uncomfortable in these circumstances.

"So…" Amy eventually tried to start up a conversation. "Nice night for this, huh?"

"Yeah. I was thinking the same thing," Morgan added. "Look, the moon's almost full." She pointed to it.

"Wow! That's so pretty," Lisa added.

"Hey, Lisa, if it was a just a little more visible, you'd be able to bloodbend," Paige said and shared a laugh with the young girl.

"You're right," Lisa responded.

"Bloodbend?" Amy asked.

"It's an *Avatar* thing," Paige answered.

"It's when waterbenders can manipulate the blood in someone else's body to control them like a puppet," Lisa added.

Amy's skin crawled hearing that concept. "That sounds really disturbing."

"Much more than it sounds. It was considered so inhumane that in *Legend of Korra*, it was made illegal," Lisa replied.

"Ah, that's lame. If I had that power, to make anyone move however I want them to, I'd have a lot of fun with it," Morgan said, rubbing her palms together with a sadistic smile.

"I'm sure you would," Amy replied.

"Too bad you'd only be able to do it during a full moon," Steven reminded them.

"Not unless you're as skilled as Katara or Aang. Or Yukon and his sons. No spoilers," Lisa shushed herself.

"Regardless, it'd be awesome," Morgan said.

"Eh. Personally, I'd rather be able to shoot lightning," Steven said.

"Good luck. Only the most powerful firebenders are capable of shooting lightning," Paige said.

"Oh, you don't think I'd be able to do that?" Steven asked.

"At best, you'd be able to redirect it. Provided you don't blow up while doing so," Paige said.

Lisa laughed at her reply. "She's right, bro."

"Yeah? Well, she didn't exactly think I could pull up my grades either," he gloated.

"That happened because of me, thank you very much," Paige shot back.

"Don't nitpick," Steven exclaimed, to which Paige giggled.

Morgan and Amy shared a look, both astonished as they were witnessing their chemistry firsthand. Neither of them had ever seen Paige lighten up in a way like she's doing right now. This made them lower their barriers a little bit and feel more secure being around Steven.

"So yeah, it's beautiful out here tonight," Amy repeated. "This whole field is just really nice. I can see why somebody would wanna get married here."

Morgan gulped. "I feel ya. And the best part: since this is a hotel, you could immediately consummate the marriage."

"Morgan!" Amy playfully smacked her arm.

"Oh my god." Paige pressed her palm against her face.

"Lisa, ignore that," Steven demanded.

"Chill, bro, you always forget your room's right next to mine."

"Oh—Jesus Christ!" Steven exclaimed.

Amy covered her mouth, trying not to laugh, whereas Morgan didn't make any effort to fight it and burst out in hysteria.

Steven looked over his shoulder away from the girls and pulled his mask back down. Normally he would gloat about that and relish in it, but for some reason, this instance made him feel embarrassed.

116

"Hey. I think that was the first time he's ever had a color on him that wasn't black!" Morgan referred to him blushing before proceeding to laugh hysterically, and eventually Amy broke and joined her.

Paige looked up from her palms and over at Steven who's clearly bothered by what Lisa just said. She didn't know why, but hearing that bothered her too.

After Amy and Morgan laughed themselves out, Paige took the opportunity to get off this topic and the attention away from Steven.

"I, uh, I was actually at a family wedding here not that long ago."

"Was it nice?" Lisa asked.

"Yeah, it was really nice actually." Paige smiled as she reminisced.

"Eh, if you ask me, just because you love somebody, that doesn't me you should have to take a whole day away from people to rub it in their faces," Steven said.

"Well, that's a perspective," Morgan said.

"Just saying. Weddings are a big waste of time. Just slap on the ring and get on with your life."

"Well, you do you," Amy said. "I'd love to have a fancy wedding one day. I always dream of it being on a beautiful beach in Greece. Me and my husband taking pictures against their crystal blue water, having our first dance as the sun's just beginning to set, and then spending the rest of the week there for our honeymoon in a luxury resort in a Greek Village."

Morgan begrudgingly mustered a smile, listening to her enthusiasm.

"That does sound beautiful," Paige said.

"That sounds ungodly expensive," Lisa said.

"I'll worry about that when I get there," Amy said, still smiling.

"I admire that, Amy. Knowing for sure that you'd wanna make that kind of commitment," Paige said.

"What? You don't think you could?" Morgan asked.

"Not even that. I honestly just don't see myself ever getting married," Paige confessed.

"Why not?" Lisa asked.

"I don't know. I have a clear vision of where I wanna be years from now—going to college at a prestigious university, earning a bachelor's degree in literature, becoming a professor living in a big city, maybe

117

having a pet. I just never really saw marriage as part of that equation," Paige summarized.

"Well, who knows? Maybe something'll change overtime. You can never predict when somebody's gonna walk into your life and make you rethink everything you thought you knew," Morgan said.

"Screw that. You've got the right mindset. Marriage ain't nothing but a delusional foundation built on vows and promises they say they're gonna keep 'til death do us part' that turn out to be fake, and then they'll start counting the days for death to take either you or the one you swore you'd always love when you realize that they're a lying sack of shit!" Steven ranted.

A string of eerie silence and big expressions became perceptible at Steven's sudden outburst.

"I did not think I was gonna hear that tonight," Morgan said.

"Steven? Where'd that come from?" Paige asked.

Steven's clouded mind cleared up when he turned his head and met Paige's face. He saw the fret in her eyes and instantly recomposed himself.

"Never mind… N-nothing," he stated.

"Sure didn't sound like "n-nothing," Amy said.

"No really, I'm just thinking out loud. It's what I do," Steven said.

"Yeah, but that was… Umm…" Paige searched for the right words.

"Bitter? Hostile? Estranged?" Morgan asked.

"D. All of the above?" Amy asked.

"Yeah, sure," Paige answered. "What's wrong?"

"I'm cool. Just forget about it. Let's not ruin this night," Steven exclaimed.

"I'm just saying you don't have to—" Paige began.

"Wassup! Did we miss anything?" Jason abruptly joined them in the gazebo behind Jenn.

"Nope. Nothing at all, just talkin'," Steven said.

The rest wanted to speak up but decided to leave it alone and enjoy the evening.

"Whatevs," Jason replied. "Any of you girls got a beer?"

"If we did, it'd be making a journey through my bladder right about now?" Morgan replied.

"Welp, there goes my last chance," he responded.

"I tried telling you," Jenn said.

"What fun is a Halloween party if you can't get wasted? Help me out here, people. We might as well be in third grade!" he raved.

"Trust me, if I wasn't driving us all and knew you two were gonna be here, I would've stacked up," Jenn replied.

"I'll just interpret that as a compliment," Jason answered, making Jenn roll her eyes again.

"Well, I see you two are getting along." Amy spoke up.

"Oh yeah, we're like total besties now," Jason said with a huge grin.

"Immediate minus five points for using the term 'besties,'" Jenn said.

"Yeee-p," he said.

Suddenly, Alice Cooper's "He's Back (Man Behind the Mask)" began to play on the speakers.

"Oh shit! I love this song!" Jenn said.

"For real?" Jason asked. Jenn nodded her head in response. "So do I!"

"Really now?" Jenn indulged.

"Yeah, this was one of the first songs I taught myself how to play."

"Oh, so now you're a musician."

"Yeah, a guitarist specifically. I also sing."

"Oh. Well, you're not gonna start—"

He then proceeded to start singing the lyrics. Jenn mouthed, "Oh my god," and sat next to Amy and Morgan. He took the empty seat next to her, but she refused to look at him. But after really listening and hearing how decent his voice was, she lightened up, looked at him, and slowly started to crack a smile. Halfway through the first chorus, she joined him, and the two started a duet.

Paige, Morgan, and Amy were surprised seeing them bond, but in a good way. They were delighted to see Jenn ease up and enjoy herself.

Morgan suddenly started dancing in her seat and began shaking Amy by the shoulders, making her join. All Amy could do was grin and chuckle, allowing her to keep doing it.

Paige leaned back and laughed at this sight, happy to see these groups had finally established harmony.

She then turned to Steven and saw that he's still a little tense. She watched Lisa put her hand on her brother's knee; she always did this as a means of comforting him, but he didn't look back at his sister.

Paige then placed her hand on his shoulder.

He turned to her and pulled up his mask, and the two shared a caring smile. Lisa smiled along with them; he then placed his hand on his little sister's, maintaining his warm expression as he looked down at her. She was one of the rare people who'd ever seen her brother smile, but none of them were ever this authentic.

Unbeknownst to Steven, Paige kept smiling as she gazed at him— admiring his full sweet side.

The rest of the night went on, and this new conjoined group ended up having more fun than they could have anticipated. A few months ago, they were in a turf war; but from then on—through Paige and Steven—these inseparable groups were unified, becoming bigger, and more integral. Suddenly, it felt as if all prior tension had disappeared.

Chapter 16

Switching It Up

Things were going well for both Steven and Paige. With their respective friends learning to get along with each other and their tutoring sessions being met with positive results, it seemed like their friendship could really work. With that said, if word got around that any of them were affiliated, a lot of heads would turn, and rumors would surely spread throughout school; and they all had reputations to keep up. So they unanimously agreed to take the same pact that Steven and Paige made: to keep things on the low and that any relations with the opposite party would be a secret until they all graduated. At least by then they wouldn't have to worry about the entire school finding out. Most high school ties are cut after graduation, and people start worrying about more important things than dumbass gossip that doesn't directly affect them.

What was nice about Halloweekend is because they were all costumed up, they didn't have to worry about sticking out or being noticed. Outside of that, anytime they hung out as a unit was a rare one. Every so often they'd all chat over Skype or occasionally meet up at Morgan's, Amy's, or Jason's house to watch movies or play video games. On Thanksgiving weekend, they all went out to support Jason at an open-mic night; the girls would sit as a group while Steven went incognito a few tables away with Lisa—doing the same just for the fun of it. On another exceptional weekend, they went to support Amy in a gymnastics competition at another high school, under the same circumstances with Steven, Lisa, and this time Jason incognito away from them. Amy came in second place, but her performance still managed to help the team qualify for another competition during one weekend in mid-December. (Jason thought she didn't come in first because the other girl "had bigger tits." He was then met by a hard slap by Jenn.)

As strange as it felt at first, they all started warming up to each other, and there was much less fear about socializing. For Paige and Steven especially, it was refreshingly nice for them to be able to communicate with other people besides those they already did. It helped them both feel less irresolute about socializing this often, and they allowed themselves to ease up in their own different ways. Life suddenly seemed like it had more to offer than they thought.

Saturday, December 17, 9:00 AM

Paige had just gotten out of the shower, dressed, and put her hair up into her trademark ponytail. Shortly after, she received a request from Amy to join a Skype group chat. She was in White Plains for her gymnastics competition, calling to give the group another update on how it was going. Paige went to her computer desk and immediately answered the call after tightening her hair.

She entered to chat where Amy and Jenn were already talking.

"Hey, guys," Paige said.

"Sup, girl?" Jenn replied.

"Hi, Paige!" Amy responded, especially ecstatic.

"Ooh, sounds like the competition went well," Paige replied.

"Oh god, it was great! I'll wait for Morgan to come in before I talk about it."

"Aww. I'm sure she'll be happy knowing you waited for her," Jenn said.

"Huh?" Amy asked.

"Oh nothing," Jenn answered.

Morgan's screen name then popped up, alerting them.

"Oh, she's online now," Paige noticed.

"Sweet," Amy said, sending her a request to join.

Morgan entered the chat. She's still in her bed and wearing just a bra with her hair undone. "What's up, bitches!" She presented herself in a gravelly voice.

"Whoa! What happened to you?" Paige asked.

"Nothing. I just woke up five minutes ago, maybe four. Was up 'til like 2:00 AM binging the *Captain America* movies," Morgan replied.

"Ah, I get it. You can never fall asleep on Chris Evans," Amy swooned.

"Unless you're watching *Fantastic Four*," Jenn commented.

"He was in that?" Amy asked.

"Yeah, he was Johnny Storm," Paige answered.

"Don't worry, you're not missing much. They both suck ass," Morgan added.

"Thank you for the review, Morgan." Amy replied, nodding her head.

"Though to be fair, they're not as bad as that new one that came out last year," Jenn added.

"Regardless, thanks to good ol' Chris, you ladies get to witness Morgan Chambers"—Morgan flipped her hair, trying to be sexy—"all natural." She gave a wink.

"Ah yeah, I feel so privileged," Jenn said sarcastically.

"Moving on, tell us all about it, Amy." Paige changed the subject.

"Ah yeah, how's the gymnastic thing going?" Morgan asked.

"It's been great! For one thing, I qualified for the second portion of the event today," Amy began.

"That's great!" Paige said.

"Yeah, B!" Jenn said.

"As I knew you would," Morgan said.

"Well, let's not get too excited. I haven't won anything yet. Besides, a lot of these girls are incredible. There's this one who did a swing off the bar and landed a double backflip, and another girl who's like six feet tall that skinned the cat to sit up onto the bar and spin around. I've been trying to just skin the cat for the last year!" Amy recapped.

"All right all right, chill out. Rule number one in athletics: don't get too inside your head," Jenn cut her off.

"I know. I'm sorry. I'm just sore, tired, and nervous," Amy said.

"Don't be nervous. You'll do great. You always do," Paige reassured her. "Besides, isn't it an achievement that you made it this far at all?"

"It is. But you know, it'd just be nice to win." Amy chuckled.

"Well, if you don't, then those judges were either bought out or they don't recognize true talent. Because you're talented as fuck!" Morgan said, being met with a snicker from Amy.

"Thanks for the reassurance," Amy said.

"I'm always here for ya, bae. I'm your biggest fan," Morgan said, garnering a snicker from Amy. "And even if you don't, just know that you'll always be number one to me," she said in an affectionate tone.

Amy looked confused at the way she made that last remark.

"You mean us." Paige spoke up amidst the silence of the chat.

"Huh?" Morgan asked. "Uh, right-right." She nervously tittered. "You'll always be number one to us. Us—all of us! These two included. That's what I meant. To say," she finished.

"I get it. That's what I thought." Amy snickered. "Thank you, Morgan." Morgan nodded her head and bit her lower lip. "So enough about me. You guys have any plans for the weekend?"

"Nothin' special. Just gonna hit the gym," Jenn said.

"Well, I need to get my mom to take me to get my Christmas shopping done," Morgan answered.

"You waited 'til the last week before Christmas to shop?" Amy asked.

"I didn't want to. I've been very occupied," Morgan answered.

"Doing what? All I've ever seen you do is play PS4, rip the loose threads on your jeans, or lick the center out of every Oreo in the pack," Jenn listed.

"Exactly. I'm a completionist," Morgan responded.

Jenn shook her head. "How 'bout you, Paige? What's tutoring look like?" she asked.

"Uh, nothing new really. Just gonna help Steven brush up on some stuff before next week's finals," she answered.

"And then you're done, right? No more babysitting Edward Tattoo-Hands after this?" Morgan asked.

Paige didn't answer right away. "Oh yeah. After this week, we're on break, and then regents. ...I didn't think about that," she said, sounding a little desolate.

"Are you okay?" Amy asked.

"Yeah. I guess I just got used to this being a regular thing. I didn't even realize how quick these last few months went by," Paige answered.

"I can see how you would lose track. There's never a dull moment with him and Jason," Amy replied.

"Ain't that the truth? Jason especially," Jenn agreed.

"Aww, sounds like JO is warming up to Jason!" Morgan commented.

"No, I'm not!" Jenn defended.

"Yes, you are. Whenever we all hang out, you talk to him as much as Paige does with Steven," Morgan brought up.

"I'm just being nice for the sake of everybody involved. He means nothing to me. He's just some dude," Jenn said.

"You're a terrible liar."

"Hey? Morgan? Will you shut the fuck up?"

"I will. But you can't shut the voices in your head the fuck up."

"Jesus Christ, you're annoying."

"Hey, what'd Jesus ever do to you?"

"Jenn, lighten up. It's okay to be nice to people," Amy said.

"I don't need a lecture," Jenn defended herself.

"It's not a lecture. I'm just saying that there's nothing wrong with making friends besides us."

"Meh."

"Come on, you know deep down you want to," Morgan said.

"Morgan, please," Amy said.

"It's not that I don't want to. I choose not to. The more friends you have, the more drama comes into your life," Jenn said.

"Drama's good for you. It builds character and shows who your true friends are," Morgan said.

"Morgan!" Amy reiterated, and Morgan put her hands up. "Jenn, don't be embarrassed. You and Jason get along great. Surprisingly great."

"I said I'd give those two a chance. I never said I'd get attached to them. We may have a friendly little chat here and there, but they're not my friends. I've got you three. That's all I need and will ever need," Jenn stated.

"Whatever you say," Amy said. "So yeah, you're pretty much done after tomorrow, right, Paige?"

Paige didn't answer. She just stared down to her keyboard.

"Paige?" Amy called.

Paige broke out of her thoughts. "Uh, what? Sorry, I completely missed what you were talking about."

"Doesn't matter. What's got you distracted?" Jenn asked.

Paige took a few seconds before talking. "I, uh, was just thinking about how this isn't gonna be a regular thing for me anymore. How I'm not gonna be spending every weekend doing this anymore. With him," Paige said.

"I get it. It'll take time to readjust your priorities again," Amy said.

"Yeah, shame that you no longer have to sacrifice your weekend nights recapping what you're told five days a week," Jenn commented.

"Yeah. That sounds nicer than it is," Paige said.

"You're upset, aren't you?" Jenn spoke.

"I wouldn't say 'upset,'" Paige said. "I'd say I'm more…"

"Disappointed that you're not gonna see Steven every weekend now," Amy finished for her.

Paige didn't answer; her silence said enough.

"Well, what does it matter if you don't? If you're serious about whatever the hell this is, then that won't be an issue," Jenn said.

"Well, yeah but… How do I put this? I… You're right, it's stupid," Paige said.

"You sure there's nothing you wanna share? You can tell us," Amy said.

"No, it's fine. Jenn's right. It's not that big a deal. You know how I overthink things," Paige said, followed by some brief silence.

"May I say something?" Morgan said.

Amy chuckled. "Yes, Morgan."

"Good," Morgan said.

Everybody stopped talking, waiting for Morgan to speak up.

"Aren't you gonna say something?" Paige asked.

"Oh, I got nothing. I just wanted to make sure it was okay for me to talk," Morgan said.

Paige snickered. "Thank you. That really put a lot into perspective," she joked.

"Sorry," Morgan apologized.

126

"It's cool," Paige said. "You know what? I'm really hungry. I'm gonna get some breakfast. I'll talk to you guys later. Good luck today, Amy."

"Yeah, I'm actually gonna log out too. Call time is ten, so I might as well eat something myself," Amy said.

"Later, Paige. Kick ass, Amy," Jenn said.

"Good luck, Amy. You have my heart and soul—hopes and sup! Port. Sup-port! My hopes and support," Morgan said.

Amy gave a bewildered look. "Yeah. Thanks, girls. Uh, I'll call tonight to tell you all how it went. Have a nice day," Amy said.

Paige and Amy signed off, leaving Morgan and Jenn still in the chat.

"You know? You're terrible at keeping secrets," Jenn said.

"Wha-what do you mean?" Morgan asked.

"You think I haven't noticed? You're not very subtle in hiding your feelings for Amy."

Morgan blushed and let out a nervous titter. "What are you talking about, dude? I am super subtle."

"You're as 'super subtle' as Dan Schneider's foot fetish. You didn't even deny it."

Morgan's face quickly turned cherry red.

"Just count your blessings you always have Paige to cover your ass."

"Yeah, well, I can't help myself sometimes. I can barely think straight when I'm around her. It's like I was hypnotized so that whenever I hear her voice or see her face, I just go, 'Blugh blugh.'" Morgan made weird faces while saying more inane gibberish. "Blame her, not me."

"Well, I just saw my nightmares for the next five nights. But look, if you're not gonna be subtle, you might as well just tell her."

"And what would that do? It's not like she'd go out with me. She's not gay. It'd be like whispering to a deaf guy."

"Well, if you know it'll never happen, then why are you so hell-bent on this?"

"Because!" Morgan sighed. "Because..." She pressed her palm against her face.

"Morgan, I know you don't wanna hear this, but you gotta do one of two things: you either gotta get on with your life, or you gotta do something about it."

"Like what?"

"I don't know. And frankly, I'm the wrong person to ask. What do you think you should do?"

Morgan thought and let out a sigh. "I... I think I'm gonna log off now."

"I get it," Jenn said, nodding. "Try not to strain yourself there."

Morgan simply nodded back and lightly waved before disconnecting.

She flopped backward, her head hitting her pillows, and she just lay there with her laptop still on her lap, staring at the ceiling, lost in her thoughts.

Meanwhile

Paige was in her kitchen having breakfast with her parents, still thinking about her conversation with the girls, specifically about the future of her still relatively fresh relationship with Steven.

"Paige?" She's pulled out of her thoughts by her mom calling her name. "You okay, sweetheart?"

"Yeah. I'm okay. I just got off Skype with the girls, and one of them said something you might find inappropriate." Paige covered up.

"Knowing those three, you're probably right," Richard said, being met by a snicker from her mom.

"So, Paige, tomorrow is your last night of tutoring. You must be excited," Catherine said.

Her parents weren't aware of what was going on, and Paige certainly wasn't gonna risk her parents knowing how she'd been hanging out with someone whose permanent records read like lyrics to a Gorillaz song.

"Well, it'll be nice to have my weekends open again," Paige said, not looking up from her French toast.

"I'm sure. But I just want you to know that I'm proud of you."

"Oh, it's not that big a deal."

"It is a very big deal. In just a few months you brought him up from an F average to Cs, Bs, and As. That's something to take pride in."

Paige shrugged it off and smiled awkwardly, taking a bite.

"You don't gotta be so modest, kiddo. You made a moderate success out of a dumbass," Richard said.

"Richard!" Catherine exclaimed.

"Well, she did." Catherine shook her head at his comments and looked down at her plate, taking a bite. "Come on now. When I was working on that school, I heard a lot of teachers shit-talk the students. I know you're thinking it," Richard added as he sat up from his chair to bring his dish to the sink.

Catherine was rendered unable to resist snickering. "But yeah, you really did help Steven a great deal, Paige," she said.

"Well, we'll see how he does on the finals," Paige said.

"So long as he remembers everything else that he's learned, he'll do just fine."

"Easier said than done."

"You both will be fine," she assured her daughter, patting her hand.

"Hey, Catherine," Richard called out to his wife. "We're still on for today," he said, pointing to his phone.

"Oh, great," Catherine replied.

"What's today?" Paige asked.

"Oh, we're just going out to with the Gomez's this afternoon. We didn't tell you?" Catherine asked.

"No," Paige answered.

"Oh, I'm sorry. I almost swear I did," Catherine said.

"Well, looks like I won't be able to drive you tonight. Is that gonna be an issue?" Richard asked.

Paige was too busy chewing to answer right away. Suddenly, she got an idea before swallowing her food.

"No. No no no, I can just ask Jenn to give me a ride, and I guess I'll just take the bus home."

"Bus? I'm not so sure about that," Richard said apprehensively.

"Dad, I'll be fine. It's not like I'm traveling to the Bronx," Paige said.

"I'm just saying, there's a lot of trash in this borough," Richard said.

"Honey, don't get so paranoid. She's a smart girl. She knows what she's doing."

Richard sighed. "I don't know. I'm not even sure about Jenn driving her."

"You don't even trust me driving her."

"I'm gonna have to take public transportation on a regular basis at some point. Shouldn't I get a start somewhere?" Paige debated.

"Richard."

He thought it over.

"I want to be notified when you get on and off and when you make it home."

"No problem," Paige said.

"Great, everything's all settled. Paige, when you come home tonight, just heat up some chicken. And be careful," Catherine said.

"I will, Mom." Paige finished her food and got up to put her own plate away. "What time you two leaving?" she asked.

"I suppose we'll just get our things together after I'm finished eating and leave then," Catherine answered.

"And unless you need us for anything, we'll be home after ten," Richard added.

Paige put her plate in the sink and turned back to face them. "Good to know."

Twenty Minutes Later: Steven's House, Living Room

Steven was playing *Call of Duty: Black Ops III* on Xbox Live.

"All right, someone go check on the window by the gate. Make sure it's boarded up. ...Because I'm the farthest from there, I can't. ...Yeah, that's good. Cover him. ...Well, we told you not to waste your cash on the Mystery Crate yet! ...Yeah, and you got the teddy bear! ...It's fine. Just keep Cl0ckw0rkAngel alive. They gotta open the bridge. ...Yo, SIN-Claire, where are you? I need some backup. ...Shit. All right, I'm coming to you. ...It's good I can save you. ...No, no, you stay with Rachel_Stunner. We'll all meet up there. ...I said to stay with Angel! ...No, Angel has to stay alive! ...Yeah, now you're down 'cause you're dumb! Now I'm gonna die too, you idiot! ...I can't revive you. I'm surrounded! FUCK!"

Game Over

"'Cause you don't fucking listen to what I tell you! ...Ohhh, is that what your mommy says? Well, that's not what she said when I fucked her!" he screamed before discounting from the party room, slamming his controller on the couch, and removing his headset. "God! Learn how to play this fucking game!" he said out loud to himself.

130

He then heard his phone's ringtone.

"Grr. What now!" He angrily checked his lock screen and saw Paige's name. Upon realizing who it was, he took a second to regain his composure before he picked up.

"Yo!"

"Uh, hey, Steven. How are you?" Paige asked, sounding nervous.

"Uh, I guess fine. You all right?"

"Yeah, I'm totally all right." She giggled.

"Well, you called me, so this must be serious."

"It is. I mean, kinda. Sorta. Depends on the criteria of 'serious.'"

"Can't this wait 'til later for you to teach me new words?"

"Right, sorry. That's actually what I need to talk to you about."

Steven rolled his eyes, not wanting to deal with anything relatively school related this early (so a typical weekday mood.). But it was the last weekend of this, and clearly it was important, so he listened.

"What's the deal?"

"So, um…" she began. "Oh my gosh," she whispered to herself. "Uh, long story short: my parents are out right now, and they're not gonna be around to drop me off later. So…" Paige began to wonder if this was a bad idea. "You still there?"

"Never left."

"Oh. That's interesting. Anyway, uh…"

"Are you trying to tell me that you're not gonna make it tonight?"

"No. No, that's still happening. But I was just, maybe wondering, since I can't make it out to you, what if…" She huffed. "What if you… came to… m-me." She covered her mouth, panicking.

Steven sat up straight after hearing that last part. "What do you mean?"

"I mean, what if we do tonight, at… my house?" Paige asked as her hands quivered, barely able to keep her grip around her phone.

"You're… asking me, to come to your house tonight?"

"I mean, unless you can't, then that's fine! I can just take the bus to you, no problem at all! My parents gave me permission and everything!" she said, intermixed with a nervous chuckle.

"Hey, hey, Einstein, relax! Don't split an atom."

Paige breathed rapidly.

"So let me straighten this out. Your parents are gone for the day, leaving you without a ride. So your solution is you want me to drive up to your house, to tutor me?"

Paige didn't answer right away, still flustered. "Ye-yes."

"Are you just trying to get me alone?" he said with a smug smile and in a raspy tone of voice.

Paige's eyes widened. "NO! No no no no! Not like that at all! Absolutely not! If that's how it came across, it wasn't. I just-just—" Paige said, panicking even more, going back and forth between stuttering and laughing in between words.

"I'm kidding, I'm kidding! Calm down," he said, laughing to himself.

"You are such an ass!" Paige sassed.

"Guilty as charged." Steven finished laughing while Paige huffed. "Seriously though, if your only option is taking the bus, then yeah, let's do it?"

"Really?"

"Trust me, you do not wanna take the bus on a Saturday. They're all full of stoners and wannabe gangsters. I'm doing you a favor."

"Oh. Well, thank you. I guess. But are you sure you're okay with this?"

"Yeah, why the hell not? Switch things up a little bit."

"Exactly! Keep it interesting."

"Yeah, 'keep it interesting,' in the last two days."

Paige snickered. "Make that a smart-ass. So I guess same time as usual?"

"Five o'clock?"

"Yeah. Got a couple of things to brush up on, so seems best."

"Yay," he dryly said.

"So I'll just text you my address."

"You do that."

"Okay. I'll… talk to you later then."

"And you as well. Later."

"Bye."

Both hung up.

Paige let out a sigh of relief.

"Okay, so now this is happening," Steven said to himself.

"Sounds like you've got some fun plans tonight."

Steven looked over the couch to see Lisa, leaving their kitchen with a pack of Chips Ahoy!.

"For the love of—when did you get here?" he asked.

"Well, I started coming down while you were screaming at your game. I walked into the kitchen right as you answered your phone, spent the first minute of that call deciding what to take from the cabinet, and once I did, I opened the bag and stood here to listen to the rest," she said in a peppy manner.

He sighed. "Why do I ever bother repeating myself?" he said to himself. "Well, if you're looking to bug me later, I ain't gonna be around."

"Thanks for letting me know," Lisa joked as she started walking back.

"And while I'm gone, try finding something better to entertain yourself."

"Nothing is more entertaining than your life."

He looked at her with an unamused glance. "Someday you'll be great for cops to put a wire on."

"Yeah. Especially if they're looking to arrest you," she shot back before disappearing up the stairs.

Steven shook his head. "Anytime she's around is an event."

He checked his phone again and saw that Paige sent a message. He opened it to see her address.

He then got another message reading,

See you tonight. (*winking emoji*)

Steven slowly cracked a smile reading the second message.

Brooklyn, 10:58 AM

Jenn got off the bus with a gym bag.

"Every time. Every time there's gotta be either someone stoned off their ass or a wannabe gangster. I'll bet none of those idiots have even been to the "ghetto"," she said to herself.

She walked up to the Coliseum Gym—where she went every Saturday morning to workout.

After checking in, she went into the locker room to change into her gym wear. When she walked out, she was surprised to see a familiar face.

Jason was doing machine flies, and from the look of it, he had put on quite a sweat. Jenn was about to go up and say hi, but she stopped herself, questioning what she's doing. Why would she want him to know she was here? She's hesitant, but something in her gut convinced her to go through with it. What harm was there in saying hello?

While in the middle of a fly, Jason was clenching his eyes shut, struggling to finish what he started. He opened his eyes to see Jenn right in front of him and was so surprised that his arms swung back into starting position. After crashing, he briefly struggled to get out of it.

"Shit! Jenn! Uh…" He let himself up, regained his composure, and leaned his arm against the machine, flexing his bicep. "What's doin'?" he greeted, trying to sound suave.

"Well, I was just about to get my workout in."

"That's good. I was just in the middle of crushing one of my own."

"Yeah, it sure looked like it," she sarcastically replied. "So what are you doing in this gym?"

"Well, my regular gym on the Island apparently flooded, so I'm just using this for today."

"There weren't any other gyms you could've gone to?"

"There were, but they're all either crowded or just shitty. Plus, my dad said this was a great one to go to, so I figured why not?"

"Hey, it's your money to spend."

"So this your regular spot?"

"Yeah, and I should really get started right now. Enjoy yourself," Jenn said before beginning to walk away.

"Hey wait," Jason called, stopping her in her tracks. "What are you working on?"

"Upper body."

"Hey, that's perfect! We can do it together!" he proposed.

"I prefer working out by myself," she said before continuing to walk away.

"Ah, come on," he said, following her to the weight racks. "Experts say you exercise better when you've got others to motivate you."

"I know what they say, but I do better when I can concentrate."

"Don't be like that. One session with someone else ain't gonna hurt your progress." Jenn started to reconsider his proposal. "Come on, it'll be fun."

She thought it over.

"How's your conditioning?"

"I'd say pretty good."

"Well, hope you don't jinx yourself. Show me how much you can curl."

"All right!"

—⟋⟍—

Jason kept to Jenn's workout routine, which he found to be quite grueling. He had done these kinds of exercises a lot, but never to this level. Between the number of sets, the amount of weight, and how much she was pushing him, he wanted to die. His entire upper body felt lighter than a pillow, but he managed to get through it all without collapsing on the floor.

One Session Later

Over an hour had passed before they completed their workouts.

Jason was hunched over, breathing heavily and downing a bottle of water, or at least as much as he can catch that didn't spill onto the floor.

"How you feelin', protégé?" Jenn smirked after taking a sip from her own bottle.

Jason let out a large groan. "Excellent."

Jason stood up straight and felt pain in his shoulders and biceps.

"You were right. This was fun."

"Jesus Christ! This is… what you do every weekend?" he asked, breathing heavily.

"Yep. I thought you did the same deal," she said in a patronizing way.

"I do but …never to this level of extreme."

"Now you tell me."

"Though to be fair …I got a …little bit of an early start. …So …I didn't exactly …have a full tank," he said in between breaths.

"You were doing flies."

He nodded. "That's one whole extra exercise."

"Whatever you say. Come on, let's walk this off on the treadmill."

Jason took a deep breath before he followed her to the treadmills, where the two began walking at their own pace.

"So what's new?" Jason asked.

"Not much, just waiting for the rest of this year to end."

"Yeah, I feel that. Any holiday plans?"

"Aside from starting 2017 with a hangover, not really."

Jason snickered at her remark. "Been there. To me, that's how you know it'll be a good year."

"And what exactly gives you that impression?"

"I don't know, but it's a good excuse to drink until you forget you're around people."

"You need an excuse to do that?"

"Point taken." The two shared an agreeing glance. "And hey, after today, thanks to you I can have more than usual."

"That's not entirely how it works, but whatever makes you feel less guilty."

He shrugged. "Seriously though, now I can see where you get the physique from. How do you do this every week?"

"Not much to it really. Just gotta have a proper amount of endurance. After a while, you get used to it."

"Yeah, I get that part. I mean, what's the drive?"

"Drive?" she asked. "I guess once you do it one time, you just want to outdo yourself the second time. Then every next time going forward."

"I guess I relate. Whenever I learn a new song, I always want to up myself the next time and learn something more complicated. I can't tell you how many nights of sleep I lost to practicing."

"Hmm, that's rough. You should be like Green Day and just play the same three chords."

"That'd be nice. Sadly, when you're not famous you have to work harder."

"Well, based on what I saw today, you're way too stubborn to quit. Sooner or later, somebody will sign you to something just to shut you up."

"You have such a way with commending people, you know that?"

"Welp, take it or leave it."

Jason pretended to grab something she threw at him out of the air, put it in his pocket, and gave her a thumbs-up.

Jenn shook her head, admittedly amused by his antics.

She stopped the treadmill after seeing what time it was.

"Fuck. Listen, I should really go. I'm gonna miss the bus," she excused herself before heading back to the locker room.

Jason stopped his machine and followed her lead. "You took the bus here?"

"Yeah, and it leaves in less than ten minutes, so I gotta change now and wait for it—"

"Whoa whoa whoa—wait a minute, wait a minute." He stood in her way of the locker room's entrance, stopping her from going in. "Let me drive you."

Jenn was surprised by his offer.

"It's good. I can take care of myself," she refused.

"I know, but you don't wanna take the bus. It's freezing outside, and you're covered in sweat."

"I'll be fine. I'll just take a hot shower when I get back. Now get out of my way!"

"Come on, you know how Brooklyn traffic is. It'll be a lot faster this way."

"Look, you, I—"

"Jenn, please! For once in your life, let somebody help you."

Jenn was thrown off. Most people who spoke to her in that sort of tone would be gasping for air, and not in the way he was right now. But she held back, for she knew he was coming from a place that wanted to do well. She was still skeptical about whatever this was between them, but the more she thought about it, the more she realized this would be the better of the two options.

She let out a sigh. "Meet me at the front desk."

Jason smiled. "Glad to hear that," he said before finally standing aside to let her go in.

"You really are too stubborn to quit," she told him before disappearing behind the door.

A Few Minutes Later: Jason's Car

There was an awkward silence between the two, being filled only by the car radio playing Christmas songs that neither decided to do anything about.

Jenn was feeling humiliated; she always had an issue with relying on others, never wanting to come across in any way vulnerable. Jason could tell she wasn't very thrilled about riding with him and decided it'd be best to keep to himself. He was lucky to be on her good side, let alone spend this much time with her without any of their friends around, and he didn't want to risk screwing up a fresh friendship.

Jenn took her pullover sweatshirt off over her head, still wearing a zip-up hoodie underneath.

"You all right?" Jason asked.

"Yeah. Just a little warm," she said, unzipping her second hoodie.

"You can turn down the heat if you want," he suggested.

"It's fine. Don't worry about it," she sternly said before crossing her arms.

Jason turned his attention back to the road, not wanting to aggravate her any further.

He looked down at her sweatshirt that's lying on the floor.

"I like the sweatshirt. The Misfits. Nice," he said.

"Thanks," she said, not looking at him.

Jason gripped the steering wheel tighter, feeling a little tense. "Aren't they the name of the villains from *Jem and the Holograms*?" he joked, attempting to further the conversation.

She gave him a mystified look. "Why do you know that?" she asked.

"Why wouldn't I know that?" he dodged. He sensed Jenn was staring at him. "All right. When I was in middle school, I dated this girl who loved the cartoon. She had this whole collection of dolls that took up an entire corner of her room, it was crazy." Jenn, still with her arms folded, tapped her fingers on her biceps. "And I… might've seen the movie that came out last year," he embarrassingly confessed.

"Wwwww-wow," she responded.

"Just to laugh at how bad it was. I swear," he defended himself. "Which wasn't a problem, because I was the only one in the theater." He snickered to himself.

"I don't think that was 'cause of the movie," Jenn replied.

"Oh, ha ha. That's funny," he said sarcastically.

"You offered me a ride. You brought that on yourself."

Jason shrugged, as if to say, "Can't argue with that."

"Nah, for real. From what I saw in the trailers, I'm not surprised it sucked."

"It did. Sucked as hard as a porn star on a dick."

Jenn's eyes grew, and she turned her head away quickly to hide her visible smile and resist a chuckle.

She turned back around. "I'm sure it's not as good as the show."

"From what little I've seen of *Jem*, yeah, it isn't as good. Have you seen the show?" he asked.

"Actually, my parents used to watch it when I was younger, so I have seen a little bit. Not a whole lot, only enough to get the gist of what it was about and to have the theme song stuck in my head forever," she answered.

"Oh, you mean . . ."

"Don't you dare start—"

"Jem! Jem is truuuu-ly outrageous!" he started singing.

"Oh, fuck me!" She covered her face.

"Truly, truly, truly outrageous! Wh-o-o-oa, Jem! Jem! The music's contagious! Outrageous! Jem is my name! No one else is the same! Jem is my na-a-a-me!"

"I hate you."

"JEM!"

She rubbed her temple and looked up to see they're turning onto her block.

"Oh good, we're here," she said as Jason pulled up in front of her house.

"Nice digs," he commented.

"Meh, it's the same as all other houses on this block," she said, unbuckling her seat belt.

She got out of the car and opened the back door to get her gym bag. She glanced over to see Jason putting in directions back to Staten Island on his phone. "Yo," she said, prompting him to look over his shoulder at her. "Thanks. You know, for the ride. It was… nice of you," she told him.

"Don't mention it, and I'm sure I'll wake up tomorrow regretting this, but thanks for the workout."

"Sure thing. I know I was fucking with you earlier, but it was honestly kinda fun." The two shared a smile. "Well, I'll see you around," she said before taking her gym bag.

"You too. Stay warm."

"And you, take a long shower."

He snickered. "Don't have to tell me twice, Coach."

Jenn shut the door, and Jason watched her walk up the steps to her doorway. She unlocked the door and took one last look back at him. Though distant, they met eyes through the closed window. Jenn nodded her head to gesture another goodbye. Jason returned it with a two-finger salute. Jenn then entered her house and closed the door. Jason sat there for a moment before he began to drive away.

Paige's House

Paige was sitting on her couch, waiting for Steven to arrive. She grew a little anxious when she saw it was five o'clock on the dot. Sure enough, a few seconds later, she heard the doorbell ring; and she became more apprehensive. She faltered as she stood up and walked to the door.

"Quit being so weird. You know what you're doing," she whispered to herself. She fixed her posture and opened the door to see Steven standing there. "Steven. Hello." She gestured for him to come in.

"What's doin', kid?" he said, stepping inside.

"Kid?" she said before closing the door. "You're not even two years older than me, sir."

"You said you were born in 2001."

"I was."

"Ninety-nine." He pointed to himself.

"March, 2001. What's your birth month? I mean, you already told me, but answer my question anyway," she said, raising an eyebrow.

"August '99," he answered. "Shit," he muttered to himself, and Paige smirked at him. "Close enough. We doin' this or what?"

"Of course. Um …we'll just use my room, I guess."

"Your room, eh?" he said with a suggestive look.

"Shut up."

The two walked upstairs and entered Paige's room.

Steven began to take in the surroundings. "Very vibrant living space."

"Too bright for your liking?" she joked.

"Cute. Seriously, this is like three times bigger than mine."

"It's not too crazy. Besides, your house is huge."

"Yeah, but this is big enough to be its own apartment."

"All right, let's not exaggerate too much."

"Christ, you even have your own bathroom. I have to share one with Lisa. You know what it's like sharing a bathroom with a little girl?"

"No, not really. Although whenever Morgan sleeps over, she leaves her clothes all over the sink counter, and she always wakes me up while she's singing in the shower, so I guess I can kind of relate."

"Trust me, you can't," he responded.

Steven continued to observe the room and came to her tall seemingly full bookshelf. He picked up a paperback manga that's sitting on the edge of it and started to casually scroll through it while she set up her work area.

He got confused trying to read it. "Hey, uh, why does it feel like story is being told backwards?"

She turned away from her desk and saw that he's reading one of her volumes of *Fullmetal Alchemist*.

"Oh." She walked over to him. "You see, this is a manga. They're supposed to be read from the back cover to the front." She demonstrated. "See?"

He took it back and breezed it again in reverse. "Oo-hhh. Interesting. Why though?"

"It's a Japanese thing. They always write things out from right to left."

"That's stupid."

141

"Well, I'm sure if you showed a Japanese person how we do it they'd think it's stupid too."

"Meh." He closed the book. "So you've actually read all these?"

"Not all of it. I left this volume out so I could read it tonight. But I have read this whole row of comics, these manga series, uh, a couple of these autobiographies—oh." She took her copy of *The Fault in Our Stars* off the shelf. "This past summer, I finally read this."

"Ah yeah, that one."

"You read it?"

"No. But I saw that movie at least eight times."

"Eight? Wow, never would've guessed you were a John Green fan."

"I am now. Turns out that watching it with a chick will one hundred percent of the time result in a blow job." He grinned.

"Ohhh my god." She turned from him to put it back on the shelf, feeling nauseous.

"Hey, it isn't my fault that people dying of cancer is a big turn-on."

"I don't think that was it."

"I like to think it was."

She rolled her eyes at his remark. "Well, on that gross note, we should've gotten started by now, so let's get to that," she said, rushing him over to her desk.

He followed and took a seat next to her, and the session began.

Later

"X equals negative b, plus or minus the square root of b squared, minus 4ac over 2a," Steven recited the quadratic formula.

"Right on the mark," Paige said before turning to the next index card to read the next question. "What equation do you use to find the area of a circle?"

"A equals 2 pi r," he answered.

"Incorrect."

"What?"

"Again, 2 pi r is to find the circumference of a circle. To find the area, you use pi r squared," she explained.

"Fuck. You know what? This is—" he began.

"'This is stupid. When am I going to need to know this in real life?'" she finished for him.

Steven was stupefied for a second. "Yeah."

"To answer your question, I don't know. But as Mrs. Curtis always tells us, 'You never know.'"

"Teacher's pet."

"You would know what that's like."

"Shut up," they said in unison.

"Ha, I knew you'd say that too!" Paige said.

"Okay, stop doing that. It's weird and annoying."

"Sorry, but when you spend enough time with people, you start to pick up on their patterns—like Jane Goodall observing apes. It's too tempting to not make predictions."

"You sayin' I'm predictable?"

"Pal, at this point I can predict everything you'll say and do way too easily. I'm practically living in your head."

"Like hell you are. Quit that! Yeah, well, fuck you too!" they both said in unison.

"Fuck!" he exclaimed and stood up out of his chair as Paige laughed.

"Told you."

"Ah yeah?" he said with a sinister smile. "Well, can you see this coming?"

He wrapped his arms around her, picked her up from her chair, and pulled her in for a bear hug, before he started tickling her.

Paige gasped before she started to laugh uncontrollably. "Stop it! Put me down!" she cried out, trying to get out of his grip. He threw her onto her bed, knelt onto it, and continued to assault her. "Get off me! I'll kill you! I swear to God, I'll kill you!" she threatened, still laughing.

"Yeah? Could you predict this, Einstein? Could you?" Steven said as he's tickling her, chuckling to himself.

Paige got one of her arms free and grabbed one of her small pillows. She started repeatedly hitting him in the face until her let go. She reversed their positions, putting Steven on his back and straddling him, still laughing as she's hitting him with the pillow.

"Hey, no foreign objects!" he said in between taking hits to the face.

"Be quiet. I'm killing you!"

He grabbed both her wrists, and she struggled to get out of his grip. He pulled her downward, and both their heads bumped into each other's. They both registered the impact, still laughing.

They started to quiet down as both turned their heads forward. They stopped laughing as they met each other's gazes. Paige's glasses had fallen off her face as she was thrown onto the bed, so Steven was able to see her eyes unfiltered, and he was close enough that Paige could see his face clearly. They stayed where they were and just stared into each other's eyes, with their smiles never leaving their faces.

Eventually, the two snapped out of their trances and realized how they were positioned.

Paige gasped, crawled off him, and, from her bed, put her glasses back on and started fixing her hair.

Steven rolled off on the other side, straightening out his shirt and his necklace.

"Uhh, that, umm—" Steven cleared his throat. "I really shouldn't have, you know—"

"It's-it's okay," she said, giving off an awkward laugh and blushing like mad. "Just-just …glad my glasses didn't break," she added, continuing her nervous giggle.

"Yeah, that was lucky. Um …let's just… finish …what we were doing."

"Yes! Let's do that!"

Both returned to their chairs and looked down for a good amount of time before simultaneously looking up—shooting each other awkward grins.

"By the way…" Paige broke the silence. "Never do that to me again."

Steven playfully gestured like he's intimidated by her effort at spite. "By the way, you have a hard head."

"Oh, that's rich coming from you."

"Just saying, this big brain of yours is being kept behind some serious protection." He tapped his finger on the top of her head.

"Aw, big strong Steven Jacobs can't handle the power of a superior mind?" she teased, grabbing his bicep.

"Oh, you wanna go again?" He took his hand off her head and made a tickle motion. "Got more fight to put up?"

"Try it. See where this ends up," she threatened him with a pen.

"Shit, she's packing." He put his arms up. "Hey, it's cool, bro."

"That's what I thought." She smirked before cracking up.

Steven ended up giving a chuckle too.

"It's true. The pen is mightier than the sword," she said, grinning at him.

"Cute," they both said in unison.

Steven gave her a look of displeasure as she still grinned. He tried to hold it in, but her glee got the better of him, and he laughed.

"Let's just do this," Steven said.

"Yay."

Paige picked the index cards back up, and they shared another grin—one projecting more amusement this time—before they picked up where they left off.

7:59 PM

Despite what just occurred, whatever that was, they managed to complete the rest of their session and keep it casual enough. Steven had shown a lot of progress, much to Paige's delight.

"Area is pi r squared. Circumference is 2 pi r," he recited.

"Excellent!" she replied.

"Finally! I was losing my goddamn mind there," he exclaimed.

"You're not the only one," she agreed. "Okay, I think that about covers it for the night."

"Sweet."

Paige began putting her things away.

"You know..." Steven spoke. Paige turned to face him. "It's kinda wild."

"What?"

"Just that, after tomorrow we won't be doing this anymore. ...I've kinda gotten used to it."

"Yeah, I was talking about this earlier with the girls. It's gonna feel weird readjusting, isn't it?" she said, clearing her desk.

Steven nodded in agreement. "Well, on the plus side, we have our weekends to do whatever we want again."

"Yeah. That'll be nice," she said, unsure of her own words.

"Welp, I guess we can call it a night." He stood up and began packing up.

"Yeah, I guess," she agreed. "Or..." This time Steven turned to face her.

She sat there quietly for a moment before looking up at him.

"Or... it is only eight o'clock. Do you think ...maybe you'd want to ...stay a little while longer?" she proposed as shyly as she'd ever been.

Steven got a look of interest on his face.

"When you say 'stay a little while,' what exactly are you asking?"

"Just... hang out. Maybe we can... watch a movie or... s-something?"

Steven thought about it. "Um, I guess I got nothing better to do tonight."

"Really?"

"Yeah, what the hell?"

"Well, great! We have a smart TV in the living room. Just follow me."

"Fine, but not because you told me to! Just let me get the rest of my shit."

"Of course."

She walked out into the hallway and waited by the start of the staircase. She suddenly got a notification on her phone to join a group video call with the girls, remembering that Amy said she'd let them know how the competition went. She's about to answer it but stopped herself. She'd hate to bail on her friends like this, but she just agreed to hang out with Steven. This left her with a lot of thoughts running through her mind about why to answer it and why not to. After a few seconds of temptation, she erased the notification, deciding that she could just ask Amy how it went later and explain where she was then. She then stared at her lock screen for a few seconds, letting her action sink in. This was the first time she'd ever ignored them, and she couldn't help but feel guilty.

"You all right?"

She's suddenly knocked out of her daze by Steven's voice.

She nodded her head. "Yeah. I'm fine," she said, putting her phone away. "So any ideas on what to watch?" she asked.

"Hmm... how 'bout *The Fault in Our Stars*?"

"OH MY GOD!" She slapped his chest.

"I'm kidding! Come on, you know I'm kidding!" he said with a cocky grin.

"You're disgusting!" she said, trying to sound offended, but unable to stop herself from chuckling. She started walking downstairs while Steven followed.

"You asked."

"I will throw you down these stairs."

"Wouldn't be the first time I fell down a flight of stairs."

"Oh, good for you!"

Meanwhile

Jason was in his room, tuning his guitar before practicing a song: "In the End" by Linkin Park.

"It starts with—one thing, I don't know why, it doesn't even matter how hard to try. Keep that in mind, I designed this rhyme to explain in due time, all, I, know. Time is a valuable thing. Watch it fly by as the pendulum swings. Watch it count down to the end of the day, the clock ticks life away. It's so, un, real. Didn't look out below, watch the time go right out the window. Tryin' to hold—"

His rhythm was cut off by the sound of his phone vibrating.

"Son of a bitch!" He looked at his screen to see he's getting an audio call on Messenger: from Jenn. "Hmm? Son of a bitch," he repeated in a surprised tone before answering. "Y-ello?"

"Hey, Kennedy, you wouldn't happen to have my Misfits hoodie, would ya?" Jenn asked.

"You didn't pick it up when I dropped you off?"

"No, and I can't find it anywhere. I must've left it in your car."

"All right, hold up." He sat up and started walking downstairs. "So what else are you doing?"

"Don't try to start a conversation."

"Just trying to ease your mood. You sound tense," he said as he's leaving his house out to where his car's parked.

"I'll be fine. Just tell me if you have it."

"I'm on it."

147

He unlocked his doors and checked the passenger seat to find her sweatshirt lying on the floor.

"Uhh, yep." He picked it up. "You were right. It was underneath the seat." He shut the door.

She gave a sigh of relief. "Thank God."

"All right, just give me at least an hour. I'll drive over and get it to you," he said before opening the driver-side door.

"What? No no, are you nuts?"

"Really, I don't mind."

"Don't. I know you have it now. That's all I cared about."

"Well, all right. You sure?"

"Yes. Believe me, it's not worth the time. Remember earlier when you complained how rough Brooklyn traffic is?

"I recall."

"Well, if you come out here now, you'll get stuck in traffic for about an hour going back to the Island."

"Well, when you put it like that, fuck it." He slammed the door. "All right, tell you what, I'll drop by your place tomorrow and give it back."

"It's cool. Really, you don't have to do that."

"I don't, but I'm doing it anyway, and nothing you say is gonna change my mind."

Jenn rolled her eyes. "You really are stubborn, you know that?"

"You call it 'stubborn.' I call it 'dedicated.'"

"Well look, if you wanna spend your Sunday driving through snow just to bring me a sweatshirt, then by all means go for it, DiCaprio."

"I never saw that movie."

"Oh, but you saw *Jem and the Holograms*?"

"Leave me alone!"

"I will never leave that alone."

"Yeah yeah. But seriously, I can drop by tomorrow no problem. I insist."

"It would be nice to get that back sooner rather than later."

"Exactly."

"Well, in that case, I'll see you tomorrow."

"Count on it. Have a good night."

"Same. Later."

"Bye-bye."

They hung up.

Jenn slouched down on her couch, put her phone away, and started browsing through Netflix, feeling relieved.

Jason put his phone on silent, picked his guitar back up, and sat down by his bedroom window, retaining the smile he'd had since hanging up.

He continued playing "In the End" from where he left off, but with more confidence and charisma than the first time.

"Didn't look out below, watch the time go right out the window. Tryin' to hold on, didn't even know, I wasted it all just watch, you, go. I kept everything inside, and even though I tried, it all fell apart. What it meant to me will eventually be a memory of the time—"

A Few Minutes Earlier: Morgan's Bedroom

Morgan was sitting Indian style on her bed, wearing her pajama bottoms and an oversized T-shirt, humming the chorus of "In the End" to herself as she blindly scrolled through Instagram.

"God, I will never get used to this new layout."

She refreshed her feed and saw a new post from the page presenting the gymnastics competition that Amy was in, which featured a clip showing her whole routine. Morgan's attention was fully drawn to the video, and she watched her friend's incredible performance.

Amy started it off with a basic swing back and forth, then followed it up with a side-split three-sixty flip around the bar. She then went for a second and stopped halfway, holding herself up and stretching her legs upward for a handstand, then managed to spin around in a full motion as she's still holding on to the bar. She successfully flipped herself around the bar three times before swinging to the higher bar through a somersault. She grabbed the second bar and swung back to the top, releasing herself ever so briefly to turn her body around in midair and regain her grip. She split out again and oriented her body to where she's positioned south of the bar, sitting forward while still holding herself up. She pressed herself upward back to a handstand position, and she swung around forward before bringing her feet up to the side of her clenched hands and swung in the opposite direction curled up. She released her grip, propelling back to the shorter bar, pulling herself up into another handstand. She turned herself to face the taller bar, and she gracefully flipped around forward two more times before swinging to the taller bar with a backflip. She gripped the bar and swung back and forth once more before finishing her routine with a corkscrew backflip into a forward leg split.

The audience gave her a standing ovation right before the video looped, as Morgan watched with the biggest smile she can muster. She watched the video one more time, admiring how talented Amy was. It's one of the many things she found so attractive about her, on top of being beautiful, kind, supportive, loyal, and a whole list of other traits she could go on about forever. It baffled her how no guy ever realized how special she really was. If she ever gave Morgan a chance, she would treat her like a queen. But c'est la vie.

She got lost in her thoughts thinking about all of this. She could even feel her hands start to shake, not realizing that her phone was ringing. After a couple of seconds, she snapped out of her daze and realized what the sensation was. She looked at the screen and saw Amy was requesting for her to join a group call. After regaining her composure, she answered.

Amy appeared on the screen. She's wearing a bathrobe, and her hair was wet, clearly having just got out after a shower.

"Hi, Amy," she answered.

"Morgan! Finally, I got through to someone."

"Where are Paige and Jenn?"

"I don't know. I thought you would. They both declined."

"Weird. Nah, I haven't heard from them since this morning."

"All right, so it's not just me. Ah well, I'm sure they have good excuses for not picking up." Amy shrugged off.

"Or maybe they're just sick of us both."

Amy chuckled. "Well, I guess for now I could just talk to you."

"Yeah, tell me how it went! Details, bae!"

"Well . . ."

She pulled out a gold medal from her hotel bed's nightstand that read "First Place," with a big smile on the verge of squealing.

Morgan was in disbelief. "No!" she exclaimed. "No fucking way!"

"Yes fucking way!" Amy replied, full of joy.

"Hell to the yeah! I'm so proud of you!"

"Thank you!" She let out that dormant squeal. "I still can't believe it. I really thought I was gonna lose!"

"I knew from the beginning you were gonna win. Never doubted you for a second."

Amy smiled. "I definitely owe this to you all—I owe a lot of my success to you girls. Especially you."

"Nah, don't do that. You've won God knows how many trophies and medals before we ever met. You would've won that easily without me."

Amy sighed. "I mean, I won't lie. This is a tough thing to do, and sometimes I doubt my own abilities. But the support from people like you, it-it really pushes me to keep at it and to do better. So I honestly don't think I would've gotten this far without that."

Morgan blushed, touched by her words. "Well, it's nice to know I'm good for something."

"Of course, you're good for something. You're the only one who's here right now to congratulate me while those two are doing whatever. I'm glad somebody made time for me."

"I always have time for you." They both shared a laugh. "For real though, congratulations. Don't ever sell yourself short. I'd kill to be able to do a fraction of what you can."

"Thanks, Morgan. My biggest fan." She snickered as Morgan nodded. "You know what's funny?"

"What?"

"That we've known each other for about two years, and I feel like this is the first time we've ever talked this long without Paige or Jenn around."

"We've talked one-on-one before."

"Yeah, when we're at one of our houses or in class or at the movies and they leave to go get snacks, but they're always involved in some way. Think about it."

Going over her memories of Amy, Morgan realized she's right. "I . . . guess I never really thought of that."

"Like I work out with Jenn all the time, and I spent a lot of weekends with Paige when she was tutoring me, but I've never really hung out with just you."

"I guess it is funny when you put it that way."

"I love them, don't get me wrong, but this is kinda nice, chatting with just you."

"Yeah. It is." Morgan got an idea and started to mischievously smile. "You know what? What time are you coming home tomorrow?"

"Uh, probably around noon? Why?"

"Let's celebrate!"

"Huh?"

"Tomorrow. Just the two of us, nobody else. We'll hit this island where it hurts!"

"Well, that'd be nice, but didn't you say you had Christmas shopping to do?"

"Christmas ain't for another week. I got time! Come on, we'll do whatever you want."

Amy thought about it. "All right."

"Really?"

"Yeah, it'll be fun. I just gotta stop at home real quick and drop off my stuff, but as soon as I'm done, we can go to the mall."

"I like the way you think."

"Then it's a date."

Morgan was thrown off guard by her remark. "What'd you say?"

"I said 'it's a date,'" she said, bemused.

"Oh. Yeah, that's what I thought you said. It is then!" she said, forcing a smile.

"Great."

"So with that, I think I'm gonna let you go."

"Are you okay?"

"Yeah, of course. I'm really tired, that's all. Just gonna binge anime 'til I fall asleep."

"Yeah, I'm tired too. I'll see you tomorrow then."

"Count on it."

"Great. Good night, Morgan." Amy warmly smiled.

"Good night, Amy." She returned the smile.

The two girls hung up.

Morgan slouched, replaying when she said "it's a date" over and over in her head, like a broken audiocassette that's stuck repeating the same lyrics on a nonstop loop.

Morgan's wanted to hear Amy say those words to her ever since she first saw her. But now that she did, it hurt; it wasn't said in the context that she wanted to hear it. There's nothing that can be compared to the pain of being so deeply in love with somebody who doesn't love you back the same way; this was the pain she felt and hid every day.

But then she thought back to what Jenn said earlier.

"You either gotta get on with your life, or you gotta do something about it."

Morgan realized that she now had the chance that she so desperately wanted. Yeah, it was a bit of a stretch, arguably a fool's wish, but she felt a sudden surge of determination to make the most out of this one day, to give her a "date" that she would never forget. She had no idea how it would play out, but this was the closest she would ever get to what she wanted, and she was not going to waste her one chance. At the very least, she would have a taste of what it would be like to be with her, to be the one that she deserved.

Later: Paige's Living Room

Paige and Steven were sitting on opposite ends of her couch watching *Elf*.

"Wait a minute. Isn't that Tyrion Lannister?" Steven asked.

"Yeah, that's Peter Dinklage," Paige answered.

"Jesus Christ, what the hell's he doing in this?"

"Oh, this was one of his first major movie roles before he got famous."

"That's wild. Why am I now just recognizing him?"

"Probably 'cause he doesn't have the accent."

"Yeah, that's probably why. You know what it is too? That scowl he gives. It's too badass to not recognize."

"That too. I know what you're talking about."

"But yeah, that's insane."

"I know. When I realized they were the same person, it blew my mind."

"Now whenever I watch *Game of Thrones*, I'm gonna think of him being called 'an elf.'"

Paige giggled. "Side note, if they kill him off, I'm quitting that show! I am just quitting!"

"I'm afraid they're gonna kill Arya."

"No! Don't even talk to me about that! Do not, even, make me think about that happening or so help me, I will smash your head against my wall, make it look like an accident, and have you pay for it!" she vented.

Steven's eyes widened. "Wow. I think that's the second most mad I've ever seen you."

Paige calmed herself down. "Sorry. I just don't play around with that stuff."

"It's good. I'll be the same way if that happens."

Paige gave an awkward chuckle. "Anyway, I still can't believe you've never seen this."

"I mean, I kinda have. Lisa watches it every year with Samantha and Bruce, so in the background I've probably seen about ten minutes. Also, I've heard a lot of people quote it. Never understood what they were talking about until now."

"It's great, right?"

"Eh, it's all right, I guess."

"Don't act like you weren't resisting the urge to laugh when he was fighting Santa."

"Unless you caught it on video, it didn't happen."

"Nobody caught Lincoln getting shot on video, but everybody still knows it happened."

"Oh, for all I know that was some crazy government cover-up."

"Oh god," Paige said, bringing her palm to her face.

"I'm just saying, nobody can attest to that, and anybody who could've, can't do it. Because they're dead."

"You know? If I was given the chance to live in whatever world you think you're in, I would say, 'Just send me to hell. It's cheaper.'"

"Suit yourself. The real world is one step away from hell anyway."

Paige laughed. "You sound like my dad."

"Do I now?"

Paige nodded. "I mean, it's a good point. You're both kinda right."

"Hmm. Imagine that—a parent you actually think alike with."

Paige looked at him, confused. "What does that mean?"

Steven looked back at her. "Nothing. ...Nothing."

A few moments of silence were left in the room, except for the movie playing on the TV.

Paige adjusted herself to face Steven. "Hey, could I ask you a question?"

"I don't know. Is it a personal one?" he returned the question, looking at the TV.

"Actually yeah."

"Eh, lay it on me."

"How come you call your parents by their first names?"

Steven turned to her again, hesitant to answer for a few seconds. "Why does it matter what I call them?"

"Well, it just... It's almost like you don't want to acknowledge them as your parents."

"Hey, I can call 'em whatever I want. If I wanna call 'em by their first names, I will."

"But why?"

"Because."

Paige waited for him to finish.

"All right, well, let's try this one. What happened?"

"What's that supposed to mean?"

"I'm not that oblivious. Something bad obviously happened. Something that affected your relationship with them."

"You don't know that!" Steven started getting agitated.

"I do!" Paige raised her voice.

The two can feel each other getting tense and calmed themselves down.

"Believe me. I know about this kind of thing more than you realize," she assured him.

Steven was confounded. "How would you? I mean, not that there's a 'kind of thing' going on with me; but if there was, hypothetically speaking, what would you know about it?"

Paige sighed. "Let's just say I've seen this sort of thing before. I know how a relationship with a parent can affect someone—for better or worse. What I just don't understand is how you could resent your mom and dad."

Steven looked down, feeling solemn. "Who said that I resented them?"

"It seems like you do."

He looked back at her. "It's not that. They've never done anything to make me hate them."

"Then what is it?"

"It's a little more complicated than that."

"What is?" She scooted over closer to where he was. "I really wanna know."

Steven rubbed his face and groaned. He looked back at her and succumbed to her wide-eyed plea.

"How do I put this? Just—"

Suddenly, the front door opened.

"We're back!" Catherine announced, stepping into the house.

Paige jolted up, looked to the door, and froze in place, seeing that her parents were home. "Oh my god!"

Steven then looked over and stood up, shocked to see their English teacher. "The hell? Mrs. Curtis?"

"Steven?" she responded.

"Mom! You two said you wouldn't be back 'til ten!"

"We did. It's 10:02," she said, pointing to the clock on their wall.

Paige ran her hand through her hair, realizing she'd completely lost track of time. "How long have I been here?"

"Wait, hold up. 'Mom'?" Steven asked, wanting to be sure he heard Paige correctly.

Paige covered her mouth, realizing that she just said that out loud, jerking her neck back and forth between looking at her mom and Steven.

"Well, uh." Catherine gave a nervous giggle. "You see, Steven, I—"

"What's going on here?" Richard asked, entering the house behind her and spotting a boy in their living room.

"It's not what you think, Dad! I swear!"

"And just what did I think it was?" he asked, with some sternness in his voice.

"Well, I—he was just—I would never—it's not—oh god!" Paige panicked and ran past her parents to go up the stairs, completely flustered.

"Paige! Baby!" her mother called out.

Paige ran to her bedroom and locked herself in. She leaned back against the door, collecting her thoughts of what just happened. She then flopped down on her bed and started to cry, horrified that her biggest secret had just been revealed.

Meanwhile, Steven walked over to the stairs and looked up. He then turned his head to face Paige's parents.

"So you're the boy she's been tutoring these past four months?" Richard asked strictly.

"Honey, be nice."

"Yes, what you said is true, and I can tell it's way too late, so I'll just see myself out," he said as he's walking out the front door.

"Wait just a—" Richard began.

Catherine grabbed his shoulder. "This is not a good time," she whispered to him. "It's all right, Steven, just go home. Have a good night!" she said, forcing a huge smile.

"Right. You too... Mrs. Curtis..."

Steven closed the door and walked away from the house, completely shocked.

He stopped himself in his tracks to look up at Paige's bedroom window that overlooked her walkway, with so many things running through his mind.

Just when you think you know a person, you learn something about them that puts so many things into perspective. Suddenly, some questions you were having about them are answered. But often a big answer can lead to other questions:

How many other people know this?

How did he not see this sooner?

Should he have seen it sooner?

Was it that obvious and nobody paid enough attention?

How did they manage to hide this for as long as they did?

But all those were pushed aside; all Steven could think about right now was Paige's reaction. This huge secret was now out in the open, and she was mortified beyond comprehension. Steven spent the rest of his night thinking about how she was feeling, while Paige spent her night drowning in her own feelings until she fell asleep.

Chapter 17

Last Sunday Before Winter (Jason/Jenn)

As promised, Jason made his way to Jenn's house in Brooklyn to return her lost hoodie. The weather was cloudy, and the winter air was already kicking in as he made his way over the Verrazzano Bridge and down the I-278 Highway. Halfway through his trek, he tried calling Steven—for the third time since he woke up—but once again, it went straight to voicemail. He didn't respond to any of his text messages the night before, so now Jason became desperate to get through to him, sensing that something was wrong. It was normal for Steven to miss a call, but not this consistently. If he missed a call, it's either because he was in a bad mood or because he was with a girl doing some R-rated, possibly NC-17-rated things. He wasn't sure what was going on, but this time he left him a voicemail.

"Hey, Steven, just want to make sure everything's good. Uh, my phone says you're not reading my texts, and I've tried calling you three times now. I know you're not doing anyone right now, so… just thought I'd let ya know that if something's wrong, don't be afraid to share it with me. I'm in Brooklyn right now, but I'll still be here all day if you get the chance or just wanna blow off some steam. So yeah, gimme a call back whenever. All right, later, bro."

Jason ended his message and continued driving.

December 18, 1:47 PM

It's beginning to snow as he entered her neighborhood.

"Ah shit," he said to himself.

Eventually he pulled up and parked in front of her car in the driveway, which was a relief knowing he didn't have to drive around the block over and over until he found a spot. He exited his car with her sweatshirt before making his way up the stairway to her front door.

He rang the doorbell and waited for an answer.

As he began to shiver, he tapped his foot repeatedly to get some blood flowing; he then started turning his body until he started unconsciously dancing and began singing Drowning Pool's "Step Up" to himself.

"You had your chance to walk away, live to see another day. If you wanna step up (step up), you're gonna get knocked down (knocked down). You're gonna get—"

"Dude!" Jenn interrupted him.

He turned back to face her. "He-e-e-e-y, what's doing?" he casually asked.

"Well, I'm getting a free one-man show in front of my house, so there's that."

"Ah, nice," he said, embarrassed. "I guess this cold was getting to my head."

"Yeah. That was it," she said sarcastically.

"Anyway, I got your sweatshirt." He handed it to her, and she took it from him.

"Um, thanks. But seriously, you didn't have to come all the way out here for this."

"It was nothing. Granted my body still hurts from yesterday, but still, I'm happy to help."

"I mean, whatever, it's your life. Nah, for real though, thanks again."

"Welcome." The two of them smiled. "Well, it's getting pretty cold, so I'll just get going." Jason was about to leave.

"Hold up," Jenn said, and Jason stopped himself. "Since you came out here, I feel like I owe you one now."

"Oh, you don't have to repay me."

"Not even if I invited you in for a fresh pizza?"

"Perhaps. From where?"

"Ever eat from Spumoni Gardens?"

"Never heard of it."

Jenn was astonished by his answer. "Get in here," she ordered.

"Well, all right then," he obliged and entered her house, removing any winter clothing he had on. "Oh, thank God for air-conditioning!"

Jenn shut the door behind her. "Yeah, well, I don't do this for a lot of people, so don't make me regret it."

"Oh, I'm sure you won't." He gave her a brash smile.

"We'll see, and just so you know..." She walked up to him until she's up in his face. "The next time I catch you doing that on my stoop, 'you're gonna get knocked down,'" she recited before walking toward her kitchen.

"Ah, I see what you did there," he said as he's following her.

—ᴡ—

A couple minutes passed by as the two of them had pizza and talked about whatever they could, while the snow continued to fall outside.

"Why do you know all this?" Jenn asked.

"Because I used to go out with somebody who was obsessed with *Twilight*, and I was forced to watch them all," Jason answered.

"And when was all this?"

"Like, seventh through eighth grade."

"That doesn't count."

"What?"

"You can't 'go out' with someone in seventh through eighth grade."

"Why not?"

"You're twelve. Where would you 'go'?"

Jason was stumped. "You know what I mean."

"Yeah, you mean you wasted your time."

Jason shot her an exasperated look. "Yes," he replied as Jenn smirked. "I was even dragged to *Breaking Dawn Part 2* on opening night."

"Oh, you poor soul."

"Actually, I don't regret it," he said as he's chuckling. "Oh my god, the finale of that movie was one of the most amazing things I've seen in any theater."

"I'm sure it was."

"No, I'm dead serious. Okay, picture this," Jason began. "It starts out with these two armies of vampires on two different sides of the snowy field, and there's also werewolves that join in. They start running at each other while this epic choir music plays…"

He continued to explain this movie's climax while Jenn casually ate a slice of pizza, listening with great interest, like she was hearing about a fever dream.

"Then Bella rips the dude's head off and chucks it across the battlefield. Then it goes to this POV of his decapitated head. He sees all these burning corpses scattered all over the place and then watches Bella bring this fire up to his face. The entire screen fills up with flames! And *then* we see that… it wasn't real!"

Jenn was flabbergasted. "Are you fucking serious?"

"Dead fucking serious! Out of nowhere it just cuts to this one vampire who can see into the future, and she's like, 'That's what will happen to you,' and then they're all just like, 'All right, screw this. Let's go,' and it's over."

"What the fuck?! You can't do that!"

"Well, they did do that. By god, it was amazing. I never heard an audience laugh so hard in my life." He laughed to himself, remembering his experience.

"If I saw that, I probably would've chucked my soda at the screen and booed it."

"Ah man, I can't do it justice. It has to be seen for itself."

"Well, I'm gonna take that brilliant endorsement and never see it, or any of the others."

"I mean, it's your loss; but on the other hand, you are making the smart choice. Too late for me."

"Clearly."

Jason finished one last slice of pizza.

"You gonna eat any of that crust?" he asked.

"Nah, go nuts." She passed the crust over to him, which he then consumed. "I've never liked eating the crust."

"I respect that. Mmm, this is good pizza!"

"What did I tell ya?"

"They don't make it like this anywhere on the Island."

"Again, I'll take your word for it. I mean, I've had some from a few places. None of them make it this good."

"And I can confirm that theory. This is why the other boroughs don't respect us."

"Fact. Morgan always said, 'You can tell how good or bad a place is based on how they make pizza.'"

"That! That could not be any more true. That should be on a T-shirt."

"I'm sure Spencer's would sell that."

Both laughed.

Jason swallowed the rest of her crust. "Thanks again for the food."

"No problem." She nodded. "So long as I get nine bucks." She put out her hand.

"What!?"

"I paid eighteen bucks for it, and you ate about half of it."

"No fair, I only had three slices."

"And the piece of crust I gave you. So technically you ate half the pie, which technically means you owe me nine bucks." She makes a "hand it over" motion with her hand.

Jason, in defeat, took out his wallet and handed her nine dollars. "You set me up, didn't you?"

Jenn put the money in her pocket. "Maybe, maybe not, but that's for you to never find out." She gave a complacent smile.

Jason sighed. "Well, on that upsetting note, I should probably get going." He began walking into the living room.

"Uh, you sure you wanna do that?" Jenn asked, stopping him in his tracks. "The snow's coming down good."

"It's not that bad. I'll be all right."

"Trust me, the highways are rough in weather like this. The traffic takes forever. The roads are icy, so you're gonna have to drive slow anyway. Somebody's bound to get into an accident. You don't wanna brave any of that."

Jason thought about it and then looked out her window to see a major amount of snow coming down.

"Strong case. Well, any chance I can bunker here until it dies down?" he asked.

"Yeah. You can do that." She smiled kindly.

"Whoo, hardcore."

"Again, just don't make me regret this, 'cause if I feel like it, I will throw you out into the snow."

"Fair warning," he said before slouching onto her couch. "Thank God I have nowhere else to be."

Jenn rolled her eyes, quietly snickered to herself, and sat on the other end.

5:20 PM

The two waited out the snowfall by streaming whatever they could agree on. They attempted a conversation every so often, but there was still a sense of awkwardness that kept it from moving. It was the longest they'd been in the same company without any of their friends around, but this time there weren't any weights to bond with, just the sounds of the TV playing in the background.

"You ever notice how in every movie Tom Hardy does he somehow ends up with sweat on his face?"

Jenn didn't answer; her eyes were glued to her phone's screen.

"You know, *Dark Knight Rises, Black Hawk Down, Warrior*?" he listed. "I mean, he was also in *Inception.* ...I'm sure he was somehow sweaty in that too. It's been a while since I saw that." He looked over to her, seeing she's stuck on her phone. "You all right?"

"Huh?" She snapped out of her trance and looked at him.

"I asked if you were all right."

"Uh yeah, I'm fine," she answered, looking back to her screen.

"You sure? 'Cause I put on *Fury Road* like twenty minutes ago, and you've been staring at your phone for longer than that. Did another celebrity die?"

"No. I mean not that I know. If one did, then it's not a major one."

"So then what's up?"

She sighed. "I haven't heard from Paige all day, and I'm starting to get worried."

"Wait, really?"

"Yeah."

"Well..." Jason turned the volume down. "This probably won't lessen your nerves, but I haven't heard from Steven all day either."

Jenn looked up. "For real?"

"Yeah, and I get the feeling that somehow they're connected."

"No... You think that they're..."

"Hey, let's not get ahead of ourselves. We don't know that."

"What if they are? And what if something horrible comes out of it? What if he does something that throws her entire life out of whack?"

"Hey hey hey, chill out! They're both smarter than that."

"Oh bullshit!"

"Okay, she's smart enough not to do anything like that. But believe it or not, he usually comes prepared; and even if he forgets, he'll just—"

"This is literally the opposite of helping!" she cut him off.

"Just trying to be reassuring."

"Well, you're terrible at it!"

"Okay, you're right. Sorry."

"Even if that's true, as hard as it is for me to believe you're not bluffing, it doesn't mean some kind of accident won't happen!"

"Okay. Just breathe. Breathe," Jason told her, which she obliged. "There ya go. Now, don't you think you might be overreacting? I get it, but didn't she say nothing else was going on?"

"Yeah, she says that, but let's not kid around. You said it yourself. She's changed him, and he feels strongly about her. Even if nothing's going on at this moment, that could always change."

"Well, I mean, if it does, what's wrong with that? Don't you care about her happiness?"

"Dude, it's because I care about her happiness that I'm freaking out right now. I said I'd let this play out however it would; but God forbid this ends badly, she gets hurt, and I didn't do anything when I should've..." She sighed. "I'll have that on my conscience."

Jenn looked down. Silence followed.

"I can tell you've really thought a lot about this," Jason said. She didn't reply. "I'm not really sure what to say to that, except we just gotta trust them."

"I do trust Paige."

"You still don't trust Steven?"

"I wanna trust Axl. But as different as he seems now, I just can't shake this feeling that the second I let my guard down, he's gonna bounce back and hurt her like he has so many other girls."

Another few moments of silence passed.

"Look, if he was gonna do anything like that with her, it would've happened by now. Or at least, the Steven I knew a few months ago would've done that."

Jenn turned to him. "Hmm. Tell me. What is it with you two?"

"Qué pasa?"

"I let it slide at Halloweekend, but not this time. What is it about Axl that makes you all buddy-buddy with him?"

Jason didn't answer and looked away. He could sense her gaze still on him, and despite being hesitant, he eventually caved in.

"Well, when I was a kid, I used to act out a lot."

"Used to?"

"All right, I still do, but not nearly as much as I once did. Point being, I always did whatever I wanted, never thinking about any kind of consequences. And I guess I alienated a lot of other kids, 'cause I never had any friends. I always assumed people hated me because I listened to different music or that I never watched the same shows they did, or for how I dressed. I took that personally, and I always got into fights, or I pushed other kids around, or I spoke out against my teachers. I thought I was such a rebel and that I was sticking up for myself, but I look back and realize that I started all of that, and I had nothing to rebel against. I was too late to see that though, so for a good half of my life, I was on my own. But then in sixth grade, I met Steven, when I was suspended, for forgetting to take my dad's cigarettes out of my jacket. We both had to sit in the same room all day for a week, so the two of us started talking one day about Marilyn Manson, and next thing you know, we're suddenly hanging out after school every day."

"Ah, the cellmate story, always classic."

He chuckled. "Yeah. So I guess that worked out 'cause I finally met someone I could relate to and who had my back when I did something dumb."

"Hmm-hmm. So when exactly did it hit you that you were doing stupid shit? Like, the precise moment?"

166

Jason thought about it and sighed. "I guess deep down I always knew that. But when he came around, he always talked me into taking things further. We made fake IDs and started going out to clubs, buying our own beers, hooking up with plenty of chicks, getting into bar fights. We even became masters of pick-pocketing wallets and purses. I've lost count of how many times we had to outrun the cops. We always had to take refuge in this nasty-ass run-down diner by the woods until they stopped looking for us. He was way more into it than I was. I knew what we were doing was wrong, but I overlooked that because I finally had someone to hang out with, a real friend. I couldn't pass that up. So I kept rolling with it for about two years, until I got to eighth grade."

"Right, 'cause him and I were in the same freshman class, and you're a grade below."

"Yep. So for about a year we couldn't hang out as frequently as we did. I guess that time apart left me with plenty to reflect. Somewhere in between, I figured I might as well do something to occupy myself, and I always wanted to learn how to play guitar. So I started taking lessons after school, and I don't know, there was something about playing music that… made me feel good. Like, anything I was feeling, I could express them in a way that wasn't illegal or hurting anyone… or disappointing my parents. …So I kept going back, learning the methods, teaching myself how to play some songs, and eventually I started performing at any place that'd gimme a few bucks. All of that took a lot of weight off my shoulders, and it helped me see things a lot clearer. …I guess music in some way has always been my form of therapy. It's guided me towards becoming who I am now."

Jenn hung on to everything he was saying, actually feeling sympathetic for him.

"I see," she said. "So why still waste time on Axl?"

Jason sighed again. "Well, I wasn't going to just drop him by the wayside like that, especially with us both going to Meadows Forest. He was the only person that ever made any effort to be my friend, and the both of us knew how it felt for people to label you as something without even knowing you. Without him making me realize what a jerk I was, I would probably be digging deeper towards hell. He ain't just my friend, he's my brother in the pit. I . . . I feel like I owe him that. But also, I kept hanging on to faith that something would help turn his ass around, like mine did. Or someone."

Jenn thought about all of that. "You think Paige …might be the one to do that?"

"That's what it seems like. I get your skepticism; but I really think that Paige, you know, might be his music."

Jenn stared blankly at him. "You know, the way you put that sounded really corny." Jenn let out a slight laugh.

"Yeah, I guess that does sound pretty stupid."

"Well, just the way you said it, but it… kind of makes sense."

"You think so?"

"Kind of. But probably because I see where you're coming from. All that stuff about being labeled, getting into fights, pushing others around, spending most of your life alone… I know what you mean."

"Well, I get the middle two things. I've seen that firsthand, but really? You were a loner?"

"Yeah. But unlike you, I enjoyed being on my own. I never gave anybody a chance to come into my life. Most people who tried to left with something in return," she said, balling her fist during that last statement.

"Yeah, that was pretty clear. Why though? Why are you so scared of letting people in?"

"It's not that I'm scared to."

"Then what is it?"

Jenn huffed before getting up off the couch and walked over to a shelf of picture frames. She picked one of them up and walked back over to hand it to him.

"What's this?" Jason asked before he took the picture to observe it.

The picture was of Jenn and two other people. She looked slightly younger, probably fourteen or fifteen; and alongside her were a man and a woman who didn't look that much older than her, probably in their late twenties or possibly thirties.

"Siblings?"

"No." She took a deep breath before she answered. "My parents."

Jason was stupefied. He looked at the photo again and stared for a good couple of seconds with his jaw reaching for the floor.

"No. No, you're fucking with me. That's impossible. These people look like gotta be in their twenties."

"That's because they are. My dad's twenty-nine here, and my mom's just over two months older."

"Well, I guess it's not entirely impossible. But wow!" He did some quick math in his head. "So you were born when . . ."

She nodded her. "Yup."

"Whhh-whoa!" he exclaimed.

She sat back down in her spot, looking at the floor. "I was born when they were both sophomores, and as you would imagine, it was really tough for two teens to be raising a baby. Especially in a neighborhood like this. I saw that every day, how much of a toll I was taking on them."

"Hey, come on, I'm sure you're exaggerating."

"It's true. Because of me, they had to work so many long hours at a lot of dead-end jobs, while trying to get through high school, and then college—pretty much giving up their entire lives. They were lucky to have my grandparents help them through it all, but they still had to sacrifice a lot. My dad had to give up playing basketball so he could look after me while my mom was out, and vice versa with my mom who was going to be a dancer. Instead, now she sells cars while my dad works in some office building, taking calls and filing out shipping reports or whatever." She groaned. "All because of me."

Jason took in the weight of her family's situation, unable to comprehend what it'd be like to be in this scenario.

"Well, I mean, it couldn't have been all that bad. With a house like this, and the fact that they made it long enough for you to become a senior, that's gotta be pretty good, right?"

"You're missing the point! It could've been a lot better than good! They had so much more going for them, and they threw it all away like the broken condom that made me!"

Jason shivered at that thought.

"Knowing how much they gave up, every day I'm carrying guilt. There's always something that's reminding me, and no matter how hard I try, I can never shake it off. Like I've always got some bloodsucking parasite on the back of my skull, and it's so frustrating!" she exclaimed.

"Go on?"

She huffed. "I've been feeling this anger for as long as I could remember. When they started sending me to school, I only got angrier. I never wanted to be around any other kids, and none of them were respecting my personal space, never taking a hint. Eventually, they started calling me names like Ratgirl or Creepy Jenny, making fun of my oversized hand-me-downs, telling me nobody wants to be my friend. This was every day of preschool, and it followed me to kindergarten. Then one day, this one girl walked up to me and started saying that I looked like a boy—calling me Jim. Next thing I knew, there was a whole crowd around me, all chanting, 'Jim. Jim. Jim.'" The memory caused Jenn to ball her fist and clenched hard enough that her veins started becoming visible. "Then, I decided to shut her little mouth up myself. So I punched her in the face and broke her nose. She fell down, and I punched her a good couple more times before I was sent to the principal." She brought her clenched fist up higher and looked at it. "And it felt good." She smiled. "Really good."

"Sounds to me like she had it coming."

"She did. So from then on, I started giving people a choice: get off my back or fall on your ass. I even started taking boxing, judo, and hitting the gym to ensure that. Most people do this sort of thing for self-defense or to improve their health. I do it because I love giving people what they deserve."

"Yeah, well, you've definitely made that very clear."

"Good. That's what I wanted."

"Now, wait, if you were so antisocial, how exactly did you become friends with the other girls?"

"That goes back to sophomore year. I got expelled from Scholes High for dislocating some guy's shoulder."

"Jesus, how'd that happen?"

"One story at a time. I got expelled, and I ended up in Meadows. On my first day, Amy was assigned to escort me around the school and show me to my classes, which—I don't know if this was a coincidence or not—we happened to share most of. But I didn't want anybody following me, especially her. I mean, here's this beautiful girl with this huge smile and the most perfect blonde hair, who had all the guys' eyes on her, all the other girls wished they were as hot as, and she's some kind of all-star performer. It was everything I hate compounded into a single person. But whatever, I didn't have a choice. I just figured that once I was settled in, I wouldn't have to deal with her again. Then, lunch came. I chose the one table nobody else was at, and she sat across from me. I tried ignoring her, but she kept trying to stir up a conversation. After about four minutes, she asked me about my workout routine, and I caved in. Turns out she wasn't as bad as I made her out to be. We both clicked talking about our experiences as athletes, and from there, we just kept talking in between classes. Then we started going to the gym on weekends, texting each other every day, hanging out from time to time, all that shit. She even gave me a spare ticket to a Panic! at the Disco concert."

"Oof, and you took it?"

"Yes, I did. And I'm glad I did, 'cause from that day on, she's been my best friend." Her eyes panned off to the side, and she smiled reminiscing.

"You actually liked it?"

"God no. It was a terrible show, and the nonstop squealing and sing-along from the crowd made it a lot worse. I've never told her that though."

"I can see that. Don't worry, I'll be sure to take that to my cremation."

"You better or I'll be sure I'm the one who does it."

"You know? You make so many different threats. You gotta pick one."

"Well, you have many different ways of being annoying."

"I know." He smiled. "So back to business: what about the other two?"

"Oh, Amy was having trouble in science last year, so Paige ended up tutoring her. After she got her grades back up, they both stayed in touch, and eventually Amy introduced me to her and Morgan."

"I'll bet Morgan was pushing her to do that so she could get with Amy."

"You caught on to that too?"

"Well, yeah. It's pretty clear she's got it bad for her."

"Uhhh-huh. I'm amazed Amy hasn't caught on to that."

"Or maybe she has, and she just doesn't wanna let her down."

"I don't know. I feel bad for Morgan though. I can't imagine being in love with somebody who doesn't love you back."

171

Jason was silent for a second.

"Yeah. She's… in a pretty tough position, I imagine."

"Actually, the crazy thing is Morgan would be a step-up from literally any other idiot she's gone out with. At least she really cares about her."

"Ah yeah. I've heard her name-dropped by a lot of other idiots talking about what they'd 'do to her.' It's disgusting."

"Ugh! I swear, Jesus will come back to life and helicopter his dick before you meet any good guys on that Island!"

"Hey, what'd I do?"

"I said 'good guys.' At best you're …decent."

"Eh, I guess that's fair. And I guess it'd also be fair if you busted up a few lips too. Especially if they ever did anything to hurt our friends." Jason stopped and thought about what he just said and got nervous.

"Well, it turns out I'm even more dangerous when I'm inflicting pain on others' behalf. Most of those guys should consider themselves lucky," she sternly declared.

"Yeah," he said in a monotone voice. "But with that said, it wouldn't hurt if you lightened up a little more often."

"Fuck that."

"I know you—"

"I said, 'Fuck. That.' You know why that's bullshit? Because the reality is this: life throws way too much shit at you, you can't take a break even for a minute. Every second, you're being watched by somebody; and if given the chance, they'll get you! So you gotta get them first. Even if you think you've got it under control, something else comes along and fucks it all up! So now, you have to rethink everything going forward, because that one mistake, no matter how tiny, will take everything away from you, and all you'll have left is the thought of how it should've never happened in the first place!" Jenn slammed her hands on the coffee table and stood up. "Considering what you just told me, you of all people should know how dangerous it is just to be *alive*!"

Jenn started huffing and looked down on her hands that had been balled up into trembling fists. Jason didn't know what to say to all of that.

After fully processing what was just said, he stood up and walked over to where she was. Jenn looked at him. Her face was completely red, and she was short of breath. Jason slowly lifted both his arms up, inviting her in for a hug.

"What are you doing?" she asked, feeling irked.

Jason took an extra step in her direction. "I was just—"

"Don't touch me!" she spit.

Jason saw she wasn't gonna take the bait, so he put his arms down and his hands in his pockets.

"Sorry. It just sounded like you needed it," he apologized.

Jenn collected her thoughts and relaxed. "It's all right," she replied.

"Just… know that you're a good friend to those three, and …I understand how you feel. Most of all, even if you don't feel like there is one …you are here for a reason."

Jenn noticed there was some hurt in his eyes. "Thank you."

Jason nodded.

An uncomfortable silence came between them. "Um, I don't know if you need to hear this but…" Jenn slowly cracked a smile. "I'm glad you're here."

"You mean that?" he asked.

"I do. And I really appreciate everything that's happened these last two days. Especially you listening to me rant like that."

Jason let out a breath and smiled. "Well, I'm actually really happy you trust me enough to tell me all of that." Jenn nodded yes. "And about all that stuff I said… you're the first person I've ever shared all of that with …and it felt really good to get that all out there. So thank you."

"You know what? Fuck what I said earlier." Jason looked confused by her statement. "You are a great guy." she finished.

Jason went back to smiling, and the two silently shared a look.

"So you're like a legitimate fighter."

"Pretty much."

"Nice." He grinned. "So, uh, listen, shot in the dark, but do you think maybe you can teach me?"

"You wanna learn how to fight?" she asked, and Jason nodded in confirmation. "'Cause it sounds to me like you already know."

"I mean, I've won a couple of brawls, but they've all been over a bunch of drunks. You, like, actually know about defense and holds and how to throw a real punch. I'd like to know how to do more of that. You know, in the event I ever get into a real fight. With someone that could, you know, kill me. Could you show me sometime?"

Jenn thought about it. "You understand that what I do is some serious shit. If you thought yesterday in the gym was hard, then you're gonna enjoy this a lot less. I won't go soft on you. You sure you can handle it?"

His body tensed up. "I could try."

Jenn was amused by his uncertainty. "Well then, let's find out," she said while moving some of her furniture around.

"What's happening now?" he asked.

"You wanna learn something? I'll teach you something. Come here."

"Wait, we're doing this right now?"

"Yeah, right now. So come here." For the second time, she gestured him to come toward where she's standing.

"O-kay then." He moved over to where she's standing.

"Relax, this will be super simple. All right, so I'm gonna face away, and I want you to put me in a rear-naked choke."

"Umm, sure, no problem," he said, suddenly feeling very uncomfortable.

He slowly applied a rear-naked hold like she said to and held her there.

"Okay, first of all, that's not a real choke."

"It's not?"

"No, in a real fight, this won't choke anyone. You want this arm behind my head, like this…" she said as she readjusted his arms. "And this arm, your wrist should be between your bicep and forearm. Like you're trapping your own hand," she said, continuing to fix his hold.

"Like this?"

"Yeah. And then you just squeeze. …You just squeeze!"

"Oh! I didn't realize we—"

"Squeeze!"

"Okay!"

174

He started to choke her out but released the pressure once he heard her gasp.

"I'm sorry!"

"You don't apologize when you're choking someone out."

"Sorry again."

"Stop saying sorry."

"Sor—" He stopped himself from finishing. "I'm just gonna stop talking."

"Good. Now, if this were real, this is a simple counter out of it. Ready?"

"Hmm-hmm."

"All right ..."

Jenn grabbed his forearm that's on her throat with both hands, before she leaped upward, landed on both her feet, and yanked him down as she got herself into a seated position. The force of her pull caused Jason to wince and loosen his hold around her neck. She took the opening, grabbed his arm, and escaped, standing up and holding on to his wrist.

"How'd that feel?"

"Well, I felt it."

"There ya go. And from here, you can do whatever you want. You could kick 'em in the face, get 'em into an arm bar, chicken wing, hammerlock, triangle choke..." she listed, playing around with his arm. "Or my personal favorite..."

She sat back down to wrap her legs around his abdomen, and he winced even more when she completed the hold.

"The kimura lock!"

Jason immediately submitted. "All right! Tap! Tap!"

She let him out. "How 'bout that?"

"Ugh! That was horrible," he said, favoring his arm.

"That was me being nice. If I wanted to, one good jerk would've snapped your arm just now."

"Oh, that's comforting."

"You still sure about this?"

"Ugh. Yeah. I can handle this. No prob!"

"Okay." She stood up. "So you wanna try that escape yourself?"

"I do it to you now?"

"Yeah. Let's go, tough guy."

"All right, cool." He got up slowly. He already felt sore; now he was hurt. "Let's do this," he said, trying to sound amped up.

"Position yourself." She motioned him to turn around, which he did.

She went to apply a chokehold, and Jason started to wince at her touch.

"Relax, I'm not even squeezing."

"I'm anticipating."

"You'll be fine. Besides, I thought you wanted me to put you in a choke hold," she joked.

"I said I was sorry!"

"Chill out. A good fighter restrains their emotions."

"I'm going to kill Steven," Jason grumbled.

"That doesn't sound like restraining."

Jason eased up.

"Now, try to do what I just did."

"Okay."

Jenn squeezed his neck, warranting a gasp from Jason. He then grabbed her forearm like she did and jumped upward. He landed on his feet but couldn't get enough force to drag her down, so he's still stuck in the standing position.

"Dammit," he said, still being choked.

"All right, try that again. This time bring your knees up to get the extra height and pull me down on the way as you're sitting out."

"Got it."

"And after you go down, if you did it right, you'll be able to get your arm between mine and my neck to spin out and grab my wrist."

"This is a lot."

"Wanna tap out?"

"No, no, I can do it."

"I hope so."

She reapplied the pressure. Jason went for the counter again. This time he did what she said and managed to pull her down with him. He quickly sank his arm into the opening, successfully spun out of her grasp, and stood up holding on to her wrist.

"All right! There it is!" she approved.

"Yeah! I just did a thing!" he raved, still holding on to her arm.

"Pretty good for a first try. Just one little mistake."

"What'd I do?"

She slowly, deviously smirked, before she pulled him into her as she rolled backward down to the floor. She entrapped his rib cage around her legs and got him into the kimura again.

She wrenched, and he immediately screamed and tapped out again.

She let him go and maniacally laughed out loud.

"What the hell, man?" he whined.

"You never gloat—you'll only give them a chance to take advantage," she teased.

"Ugh. You set me up again," he said, rubbing his elbow.

"Look at you." She stood up and offered her hand. "You're a fast learner."

He saw her arm and flinched, before he took it and was helped off the floor.

"And I thought you didn't have a sense of humor."

"You seem to have a lot of thoughts. So how's that one about wanting to fight? Still think you're up for it?"

"I mean, if I'm still walking after what you put me through these last two days, I could do a couple more."

"Pretty confident there."

"Or if you don't wanna waste your time with me, that's fine."

"You really want me to teach you or not? Be honest."

"I would."

Jenn took a moment to consider. "It's gonna take a while, but maybe we can work something out."

"Yeah?"

"Sure, why not?"

"Awesome."

The conversation halted, and both found themselves staring at each other. They held this pause for a while before Jenn lifted her eyebrows. Jason looked confused by her expression until he realized he's still holding her hand. He snapped his head down and up before he let go.

"Well, um…" Jason looked outside and saw the snow was dying down. "I think that's a good note to end on. I should… probably get back to SI."

"Ye-yeah. Should be easier to drive by now," she replied, following him to the entranceway.

He picked up his jacket and walked toward the door. "So I'll see you at school tomorrow?"

"We'll see," she said, prompting him to chuckle.

Jason opened the door and stepped out, but Jenn stopped him when he reached the bottom of the stairs. "Wait." He turned to face her, and she stepped outside to meet him at ground level. She pulled out the nine dollars he gave her earlier and offered it to him. "Here."

"Oh, don't worry about that."

"No, seriously, I've had my fun. It's your money. Take it."

"I really don't care. Keep it."

"You don't have to be so—"

"I insist. Keep it."

"You're sure?"

"Would anybody turn away nine bucks if they weren't sure?"

"I mean, whatever you say." She put it back in her pocket.

"If you won't accept it for that pizza, think of it as a thanks for the shelter."

Jenn snickered. "Sure. Whatever. Just… drive safely."

"Yes, Coach."

She started going back up the stairs. When she opened her front door, she's now stopped by Jason's voice saying, "Hey."

She turned back around.

"Good night, Jenn."

Jenn nodded her head. "Good night, Jason," she called out before closing the door.

Jason took a few moments to stand in the light snow, rubbing his arm as he gazed at her front door, smiling as he reflected on what transpired today.

—⁓—

Slowly but surely, two people caught in the crossfires of a heated feud had found mutual ground. Jason finally had the respect and also the trust of the girl he'd had eyes for since that day in the parking lot. As for Jenn, she finally read past the lines of his less-than-subtle flirts and saw who he really was. Troubled pasts had been revealed and converged. With so much weight off their shoulders, the future of this newly established friendship seemed much more promising.

Chapter 18

Last Sunday Before Winter (Morgan/Amy)

Amy's team left the hotel they were staying at shortly after 10:00 AM. With the snowfall, the trip took longer than usual. Very shortly after departure, she decided to put her earbuds in and catch some extra z's.

She was woken up over an hour later by her phone vibrating; she checked her lock screen and saw it was a message from Morgan. She opened it and saw a selfie of her waiting outside the school's bus stop, wearing a neon-colored beanie, a big winter coat, and a scarf that was covering her face below her eyes that were wide open, while giving a thumbs-up.

Below it was text quoting Richard Marx's "Right Here Waiting": "I will be right here waiting for you lol" surrounded by music note emojis.

Amy palmed her face and mouthed "Oh my god" followed by a giggle. She looked out the window and saw that they were coming up on the Verrazzano Bridge; from there, they'll only be a few blocks away from the school.

She texted back, "I'll be there in 10 min. PS you're insane! Lmao."

To which Morgan replied with a GIF of Sideshow Bob from *The Simpsons* saying, "GUILTY AS CHARGED."

Noon

The bus stopped in front of the school where the team and staff walked off to greet their families. Amy found her parents standing with

180

Morgan and went over to hug them before she showed them her medal. She told her parents last night that she wanted to spend the afternoon with Morgan and would celebrate with them later that night, which they agreed to. Her mom even offered to drop them off and take her luggage. Before they did that, she got a couple of pictures with them wearing her medal, as well as a few shots with Morgan.

After this brief photo session, Morgan and Amy got in Amy's dad's car, and they left the school grounds.

Thirty-Seven Minutes Later

Amy and Morgan were dropped off in front of the Staten Island Mall.

"We'll pick you girls up at four," said Amy's mom.

"All right, thanks, Mom," Amy replied.

"Have fun, you two. Just remember whatever you use your debit card for, I'll know," Amy's dad said.

"I know, Daddy. I swear I won't use it without your permission."

"I know you won't," he said. "And, Morgan, for the love of God, don't get her kicked out of anywhere."

"You have my word, Mr. and Mrs. Brookes, I'll take care of your girl," she said, putting her arm around her head and pulling it down to her shoulder.

"Ow," Amy flatly said.

"Just please stay out of trouble," her mom said, cracking a smile.

"We will. We'll see you at four," Amy said as she and Morgan got out of the car.

"Atta girl," her dad said.

"All right, I love you." Amy blew a kiss.

"We love you too," her mom said, and her dad waved.

"And I love you too!" Morgan said.

"You too, Morgan." Amy's mom chuckled.

Her parents then drove off, leaving the duo.

"So what do you wanna do, champ?" Morgan asked.

"Well first, I'd love to get out of this cold," she said, walking toward the entrance.

"I love this plan so far," Morgan said, following behind.

1:52 PM

Over an hour had passed, with the two of them just going into a variety of different stores, trying on clothes, accessorizing, sampling makeup and perfumes, snooping at random products, and taking pictures as if they were models. Amy every so often bought something she liked, but Morgan didn't do much purchasing for whatever reason. It wasn't a particularly glamorous day, but it was fun for just the two of them to hang out without Paige and Jenn for a change. Getting to do a one-on-one "date" gave them a chance to really get to know each other, to be more than just mutual friends. Morgan had always wanted to have a day like this, and finally getting to have it made her happy; for her, it felt like a first date. Whereas Amy started to realize what a great friend Morgan was and how fun she was to be around; she's weird and somewhat loony, but that's what's so lovable about her.

By now, they were in the shoe department at Macy's, and Morgan was trying on a pair of black combat boots.

"How do they feel?" Amy asked.

Morgan was tapping her individual feet to get a sense of how comfortable they were. "They feel great." She stood up to walk around. "How do they look?" she asked midwalk and then turned around to pose like she's on the catwalk.

"They look really good. Except…"

"What?"

"You walk funny." She cracked a smile.

"Oh, shut up!" Morgan chortled.

"Seriously though, those look awesome on you, especially with your white pants."

"Ah yeah?" Morgan turned her body to show off the back of her pants, sticking her tongue out at Amy.

"Stop that!" Amy giggled. Morgan reoriented her body. "So you gonna get 'em?

"I don't know. How much?" Morgan asked, lifting her foot with the price tag on and placing it in Amy's hands.

Amy was startled by her sudden action but grabbed a hold of her foot. "Dear God. Uhh..." She read the price tag. "$150."

"Per shoe?"

"No. Just $150."

"Oh. Well, forget it then." She brought her foot down, sat on a bench, and started taking them off.

"Why? You can't afford them?"

"It's not that. I just... wanna save up for food, ya know?"

"How much are you really gonna spend on food?"

"As much as I can get before I have a stroke," she said, taking the boots off.

"Morgan, you're being silly. You were so excited about these, and they look great."

"I know, and I know I was excited about them, but I already have shoes. I don't... really need these," she said, holding up the box they came in.

"You don't sound so sure. Just get them."

"Forget it, Amy. I'm fine," she claimed. "Hey, lady!" she called over the same employee who brought out the pair for her to try on.

"Sorry, I was helping another customer. So should I ring these up?"

"Actually, I'm not gonna get them." She handed them back.

"You're sure? If it's the money, we do have a sale going on."

"Nah, it's all right." She turned to face Amy. Before she can speak up, Morgan cut her off. "Don't say it. Just buy your stuff and we can go. I actually really have to pee."

"Okay then. Uhh, you know what? Uh, why don't you go, and I can just meet you in the food court."

"You always have great ideas. I'll see you there," she replied. "Thanks anyway," she said to the employee before speeding off.

The employee nodded and went to bring them back. "Wait!" Amy called out to her. "Jessica," she read off her name tag. "Actually..."

Nineteen Minutes Later

Amy arrived at the food court three minutes ago. She expected Morgan would be there, but she wasn't. She had her back up against a wall looking at her phone when Morgan finally arrived.

"Hey. Sorry I kept you waiting," Morgan said.

"Hey, what happened? It took you twenty minutes to pee?"

"No. I, uh… had my period." She awkwardly smiled.

Amy's felt queasy. "Did not need to know that." She picked up her Macy's bag and walked toward the ordering counters.

"You asked," she said, following her.

—〰—

About an hour went by of just the two of them eating food and having a couple of laughs.

"I'm just trying to imagine Jenn at a Panic! at the Disco concert," Morgan said, laughing.

"Oh, you had to have been there. She just looked so dead inside. This was her face." Amy mimicked how she remembered Jenn's face, a combination of grouchy and bored. They both laughed at it.

"What did she say about the show?"

"Well, she said she liked it, but I can tell she hated it." She chuckled.

"Whatever. Not everyone can appreciate the great artists of our time and all time like we do."

"True that," she said, eating a fry.

Suddenly, two guys approached their table.

"Hey, pretty ladies," Guy 1 said.

"Uh, hi," Amy said, uneasy.

"What up?" Morgan added.

"Not much, we just couldn't help but notice you two having a good time, and I thought my buddy Johnny and I could help make it more fun," Guy 2 said.

"You know? What a great thought, Charles. Huh, I just had one myself. Why don't we take these two out for a couple of drinks?"

"God, you're a genius! Whaddaya say, girls?"

"Well, I would normally never turn down some drinks but don't swing on the side of the plate," Morgan said.

"Huh?" they both asked, looking confused.

"I'm gay," she clarified.

The two faced each other. "Ni-i-i-i-ice," they said, giving fist bumps.

"Well, hey, you don't gotta be so hesitant," Charles said.

"Yeah, how 'bout you try experimenting? We'll see how certain you are afterwards," Johnny said, giving her a wink.

"I'm pretty certain, thank you!" Morgan said in an annoyed tone.

"Come on! Ya never know—" Johnny continued.

"She said no!" Amy loudly intervened.

All six eyes were now on Amy.

"Well. What about you then? What team you on?"

"I, uh, I'm not—" Amy began.

"All right, a more open mind! Let's get out of here then?" Charles said, putting his hand out for her to take.

"I didn't say yes," Amy cleared up.

"Come on! You two are so boring! Don't you wanna have a little fun?" Charles asked.

"Listen, I just came here to be with my friend, so if you could please just leave us alone," Amy said.

"You serious right now?" Johnny said.

"You heard her. *Los vámonos,*" she said, shooing them off.

"Yeah? Well, maybe we don't wanna leave," Johnny said.

"Yeah. Maybe we'll stay here until you change your minds," Charles added.

"Seriously, please just go away!" Amy exclaimed.

"What if we don't?" Charles grabbed Amy by the chin and pinched her cheeks with his thumb and index finger. Amy flinched at the pressure, too scared to move.

Morgan shot up, fuming. "Get away from her!" She reached out to grab his face, but Johnny grabbed her wrist and jacked her toward him. "Let go of me, you sick fuck!" He wrenched her, causing Morgan to grunt.

"Whatcha gonna do? Hmm?" Johnny yelled in her face.

Morgan was suddenly freed when Johnny was tasered from behind and apprehended by a mall security guard.

"The fuck do you think you're—" Charles started to scream before he's shocked by a taser from another security guard, allowing Amy to get free.

"All right, that's enough," Security Guard 1 said as they and Security Guard 2 put them in handcuffs and removed them from the food court as the other customers there, employees, and a few bystanders applauded as they were taken away.

Amy and Morgan found themselves in each other's grasps, startled by what just happened and relieved that it didn't go any further.

The head of security turned to them both. "One of the employees alerted us, and we got here as quick as we could. I'm just sorry we didn't get here sooner," they apologized.

"It's all right. Your timing was perfect," Amy said.

"Yeah, don't beat yourselves up," Morgan added.

"I'm assuming you girls want to press charges," they suggested.

The two shared a look. "Actually, we're not going to," Amy said.

"We're not?" Morgan asked.

"No, we're not."

"You're sure?" they asked.

"Yeah, I'd rather just forget this even happened," Amy said with a little mellowness in her voice.

Morgan gave her a sympathetic look. "Yeah, just forget this whole thing. We'll be all right."

"I see. Well, I'm sorry again. Please, have a happy holidays," they wished the two before walking off.

"You do the same," Morgan replied. She turned back to Amy who looked distraught about what just happened. Morgan was distraught too but could tell she was hurting more.

They sat back down to face each other, not saying a word.

"Hey, I'm really sorry about—" Morgan broke the silence.

"Don't even say it. It's not your fault. Some people are just too pigheaded," she said, rubbing her chin. Morgan just nodded her head. "Thanks for sticking up for me."

"Thank *you*. I mean, I understand what you're feeling right now."

Another period of uncomfortable silence passed. Amy noticed how tense Morgan was as well.

"Could I... Would you mind if I asked you something... kinda intimate?"

"Sure."

"You don't have to answer if you don't want to."

"It's okay. Ask."

Amy nodded. "Were you, ever actually, umm... you know? Have you, done—or, I mean, been anything with, another..."

Morgan knew where she's going with this. "No. No, I've never actually been with a girl before." She blushed.

"Really?" she asked and was met with a nod. "So then how did you become so... so sure of it?"

Morgan took a few seconds to think of how she can answer that.

"I feel like I always knew that somehow. Like, when I was younger, I had this group of friends that I always played with during and after school. As we grew up, we started talking about stupid things, like if we had a crush on anyone in our group. Whenever they asked me if I liked one of the boys, I'd always said no. If they asked me if I liked any boy outside our circle, I'd also say no. If they were gushing over some celebrity and asked if I thought he were hot, same deal. I was just never interested in any of these guys. My parents told me that would change eventually, that when I got older, I'd start liking boys. But that never happened. I didn't know why though, so I thought something was wrong with me. Then, my friends and I all ended up going to different schools, so we lost touch. I didn't try at all to make any new friends. I just wanted to be alone and wait for something to change me. Nothing did though, so my only conclusion was I just wasn't normal. So for those first couple of days, I just stayed away from everyone. Until I met Paige."

"On her first day of school, I saw her sitting by herself in the courtyard, and I felt sorry for her. I knew how she must've felt, so I figured I might as well be lonely next to someone else. I didn't know why I did that at first, but we both clicked right away. What was really great about her is that she didn't ask any questions like my old friends did or wonder why I dressed the way I did or put any pressure on me to do something. Around her I could do whatever I wanted without being judged. As we got closer, I started to realize more and more that I wasn't becoming interested in boys because I loved hanging out with girls more. Then, I began to look at girls like Jennette McCurdy, Scarlett Johansson, Emma Stone, Tifa Lockhart in ways that I've never looked at any guy. My parents and friends made me think I was supposed to feel this way about boys, but by eighth grade, I knew that nothing was gonna change. Finally, I came to grips with what I was, and I came out to Paige. After I got through that, she made me feel comfortable enough to come out to my parents. I was so sure they were gonna hate me forever. I thought I was gonna make them cry, and they did. Then, they told me they loved me and that they were proud of me." She sniffled as she's shedding a tear, remembering both those days. "And for the first time in my life, I felt comfortable to be in my own body. That I could finally be myself. And I've never looked back." She smiled as she shed another tear of joy.

Amy grabbed a napkin from a container and handed it to her. Morgan took it and wiped it away.

"I'm sorry," Morgan said.

"Don't you dare say you're sorry," Amy said before she wiped a tear that was building. "That was really beautiful." She smiled.

Morgan returned it. "Thank you. It's always much easier to say it when you know that person supports you. Especially to idiots like that," she said, pointing in the direction they were taken in. "'Duhh, I could change that!' 'I can't wait to tell my bros I did a lesbo!' 'Make an exception. It'll be fun!' 'For once, act like a normal girl!' Like wow, did you come up with that yourself? How original! Fuck off!" Morgan smacked the table and turned her head to the right, resting her forehead on her hand.

Amy got sad seeing her friend so distraught.

"I'm sorry. That must be really hard to hear."

Morgan huffed. "It's just annoying. It always is."

"If anything, I really envy how you never give in to peer pressure. ...I wish I had that kind of willpower myself." Morgan looked back at Amy. "Anytime a cute guy shows any interest in me, I'm practically in their hands; and anytime it happens, I end up feeling like an idiot and looking like a slut to everybody else," Amy said as more tears built in her eyes.

"I just don't know how I always manage to choose these kinds of guys. The next one always seems different, and then they turn out like all the rest!" she said with some hostility in her voice.

Now she's the one not looking at Morgan.

Morgan processed this rant. "Well, I mean, you turned down those morons. That's something, right? You're not giving them that satisfaction," she said, making a half smile.

"Honestly, if you weren't here, I probably would've left with one of those jerks," she shamefully admitted. "I didn't answer right away because I didn't want to ruin our day," she said, still not looking at her, letting another tear drop. "Just once in my life, I want to date somebody who... actually cares about me." She sniffled.

Morgan was quiet for a couple of seconds; all the noise of the mall was faded out, and she could only hear Amy's soft whimpers.

"Amy, I get it. But... you don't have to hook up with every guy you meet." She sighed before begrudgingly saying, "You'll know the right one when you meet them, and ...they're gonna be the luckiest son of a bitch—in this galaxy, or any other." She said it in a solemn tone.

Amy let out a few more soft cries before she exhaled and looked up at her empty plate into Morgan's eyes to respond.

"You wanna know something?" Amy asked, wiping her eyes. "I'm tired of dealing with this."

Morgan's eyes widened.

"I think maybe I just have to get away from guys for a while. Maybe I need to focus on a couple of other things. More important things than commitment."

"Such as?"

"Well, like school. Like applying for college. My gymnastics. Looking for a job."

"Three of those things sound awful."

"Well, you know what I mean."

"I think. What you mean is you're giving up dating guys?"

Amy took a moment to consider that possibility. "Yes. Yes, I am."

"Yeah! I can get behind that!" Morgan raised her hand up, offering a high five.

Amy shook her head, cracked a smile, and lightly slapped her hand.

"You got a lifetime to date!"

"You're right. I do!" she confidently said. "Besides, I don't need a man . . . Not when I have friends like you," she admitted.

Morgan blushed. "Thank you. I'm… really glad you think of me like that."

"Of course, I do. I mean, I know when I speak it sounds like I'm talking down on the stuff you say and do, but that's honestly what I admire about you. You never put on some sort of act or hide anything. You're always so open and honest, and you're not scared or worried about what other people think about you. You're so unapologetic. You're… you're real …and I'm not just saying this: I've had more fun with you today than I've had with any guy I've ever dated," she confessed.

"You mean that?" Amy nodded. "I… I've had a really great day too. I'm happy we did this."

"Me too."

They both took a few moments to stare at each other, not saying a word.

"So, um, what should we do now?" Amy asked.

Morgan got an idea. "Come with me." She got up, grabbed Amy by her wrist, and ran off with her.

First Floor

"Morgan, where are you taking me?" Amy asked, laughing.

"You've asked me that three times."

"And you've answered none of them."

"Just bear with me, all right?"

She brought her to one of the mall's exits and triggered the automated doors.

It started snowing over an hour earlier, and the sidewalk had been covered in about ten inches.

"Jesus Christ, Morgan!" Amy broke free from Morgan's grip as she reacted to the sudden cold air. She put her winter wear on. "What are you doing?"

"We're celebrating, babe!" Morgan put her own apparel on. "That's why we're here. Come on!" she said as she walked outside, motioning for Amy to join her.

"Why would I want to go out in this weather?"

"Because why the hell not!" Morgan put her arms out and fell backward into the snow.

"Morgan!" Amy exclaimed. She ran outside and stopped in her tracks when she saw Morgan's making a snow angel. "What is the matter with you?"

"Try it. There's plenty to spare."

"I am *not* lying on the ground."

"Come on, you never did this when you were a kid?"

"I did, as a kid."

"So what's the difference now?"

"There's a big difference."

"Differences are an illusion." Morgan stood up and looked down at what she's done. "All right, so you're not a fan of snow angels. But how 'bout"—she drew a pair of horns where her head was—"snow devils?" She stuck out her tongue and made a pair of horns with her hands. Amy covered her mouth, trying to hide her laugh. "Come on, don't hold out on me. Enjoy this now because every snowfall after's gonna suck," Morgan said as she stealthily rolled up a snowball and then hit Amy with it.

"Hey!" Amy said with her jaw dropped.

Morgan waved. "Hey," she replied before throwing another one that also hit.

"Okay." She put her bag down and rolled up her own snowball. "You are so dead!" she said while smiling, before she threw it.

Morgan dodged. "Ha! You missed!" she said before pulling up her scarf to cover her mouth.

"I'll get you eventually!"

The two engaged in a full-on snowball fight.

Amy ran up and grabbed her from behind around the waist, spinning the shorter girl around. Morgan escaped and leaned up against a wall, pulling down her scarf. Amy met her there, and they both burst out laughing.

191

Amy laughed so hard that her voice cracked, and she squeaked like a chipmunk. She covered her mouth embarrassed, and Morgan stopped laughing.

Amy cleared her throat. "Oh god. Sorry."

"It's all right. I thought it was cute," Morgan said, giving her a warm smile.

"Really?" Morgan replied with a nod. "Well then." Amy surprised her with a snowball that hit her in the head. Amy laugh-squeaked and ran off.

"Hey! Get back here, Brookes!" she demanded, chasing her.

"No way, Chambers!"

The snowball fight resumed.

3:30 PM

After their little war, and finally encouraging Amy to make a snow angel right next to Morgan's, the two girls went back inside to sit on one of the benches by the exit, waiting for themselves to dry off.

"We are never doing that again," Amy declared.

"That's cool. Why ruin what was already perfect?" Morgan replied.

Amy rolled her eyes, before checking her phone. "Hey, has Paige texted you today?"

"No, why?"

"I just haven't heard from her today, or even Jenn, come to think of it."

"Oh, I'm sure they're fine. Besides, they've got other people to direct their attention towards, if you catch my drift."

"You really think there's something going on between them and the guys?"

"Well, I mean, let's not lie to ourselves, all right? You see it too. They just won't say anything, 'cause Jenn acts like a robot not programmed to love and Paige just… doesn't know how to handle it yet."

Amy pondered what was just said. "It is pretty great seeing both of them ease up the way they've been, and I'm just glad that it's gotten to a point where I don't feel any dread around them." Morgan nodded in agreement. "But I don't know. These are some pretty bizarre pairings, isn't it? I mean, Jenn and Jason makes a little bit of sense, but I never pictured Paige with anybody like Steven."

"Honestly, I could never picture Paige with anybody. In the five-plus years I've known her, she's never shown any interest in anybody. If somebody tried flirting with her, she would just look at the top of their head or off to the side of their face. Whatever Axl's got that makes her act this differently, I don't know what it is, but... he's got it." Morgan sighed. "When I was pushing her to dig deep, I didn't think she'd get *this* deep."

"I couldn't have seen this coming either. I mean, I still have my concerns, but what else is new, right?" Amy chuckled. "But with that said, I'm actually really happy for them, and ...kind of envious. I didn't think this was conceivable, but they're honestly much better than most boys—at least that I've known—more respectful too."

"I was thinking the same thing. It's wild, isn't it?"

"Seriously!"

The two shared astounded looks.

"Well, enough about other people. Let's get back to what's important." Morgan stood up.

"All right, well, we got... less than a half hour before my parents show up," Amy said, checking her phone and grabbing her bag.

"Then we better hurry."

"For wha—" Morgan cut Amy off by grabbing her wrist and pulling her to run, again.

Second Floor

Morgan dragged Amy to the outside of a small retailer store.

"Could you at least let go when we're going up to the escalator?" Amy asked, getting out of Morgan's grip again.

"No. Now, wait here for a minute."

"Why do you have to do in—" Amy started as Morgan ditched her to go into the store. "And I'm alone again," Amy said, crossing her arms.

Three Minutes Later

Amy was against the railway looking downward to watch the people walking around the first floor of the mall, when Morgan suddenly walked up behind her.

"Hey, I'm back!" Morgan exclaimed with a huge grin.

"Took you long enough. So what was so important?" She looked down at a rectangular-shaped box Morgan was holding. "What's this?"

"See for yourself." She handed the box to Amy.

Amy opened the box and found a freshly made metallic picture frame. Inside of it was a picture that her mom took of them a few hours ago at Meadows Forest High using Morgan's phone—they agreed it was the best photo of them together.

Amy's face brightened when she saw it and read the personalized engraving right underneath the picture:

> You'll always be number one to me. Merry Christmas.—Morgan <3

"Oh my gosh, Morgan," she said with a huge smile.

"You like it?"

"I love it! Where did you find time to do this?"

"Remember when I went to the bathroom and told you I had my period?"

"Yes?" she grins.

"Well, I made that up. In fact, I never even used the bathroom. I actually came here, and they said it'd take an hour and a half to make it, so I just had to keep you busy. Also, when I said I wasn't gonna buy those boots, it's 'cause I was saving it for something like this," she explained.

"Well, I think you could've come up with a better cover-up, but I don't care. This is so beautiful. This is the sweetest gift I've ever gotten," she said before pulling Morgan in for a hug. "Thank you."

It caught Morgan by surprise, but once she got over the shock, she hugged back. "You're welcome."

Amy let go. "I have something for you too."

"No, come on now, no exchanges."

Amy dug in her bag and pulled out a large shoebox with Christmas wrapping. "Just open this."

She handed the box to Morgan, who had a confused look on her face, but it quickly changed to a look of excitement. "You didn't!" Amy motioned her to open it.

She unwrapped it and opened the box. Morgan gasped and covered her mouth with her free hand when she saw the combat boots she was trying on earlier but refused to buy.

"Amy! I-I... You—really!" Morgan stuttered, trying to enunciate her words.

"Merry Christmas, Morgan."

"I don't—I'm so—but these just cost so much, and—"

"Actually, between the sale they said they were having, my dad's credit card—with his approval—and a discount my mom had in her account, they went from $150 to $90. Plus, an extra $2.99 for the wrapping paper."

"Amy, you really didn't have to."

"Oh please, it's Christmas. Also, I wanted to thank you for a fun day, and for being a great friend."

This time Morgan was the one to engulf Amy in a tight hug, which Amy immediately returned.

"Morgan?"

"Hmm?" Morgan had her eyes tight shut, savoring this warm embrace that she'd wanted to feel for a long time.

"Morgan, you're hurting me."

Morgan snapped out of it and let her go. "Oh! I'm sorry."

"It's okay."

"It's just that I really love—" Morgan stopped herself from getting in an extra word and cleared her throat. "Love... these ...these shoes. They're- they're awesome."

"It's all right. That still felt nice." Amy smiled.

Morgan mirrored the smile and nodded. The two were still within a close distance, merely inches apart, lost in each other's eyes.

"Umm, you know?" Amy checked her phone. "My parents will be here soon. Why don't we go wait for them?" Amy had an anxious laugh.

"Yeah! Yeah, let's go. Go. Let's wait for them," Morgan said as the two recollected themselves and their gifts.

"Great!" Amy said.

Morgan went to grab her wrist again, but this time she slapped her hand away and looked at her with a raised eyebrow.

"You're learning," Morgan said in an impressed tone, and the two walked off laughing.

Later That Evening

Morgan was laying on her bed with her feet in the air, wearing pajama bottoms, an oversized T-shirt, and her new pair of combat boots. She just lay there, admiring the boots and reflecting on her day with Amy. It all left her with mixed emotions; on the one hand, she had a great time with her, and it was more fun than she could've ever imagined. On the other, she wished it could've been more. She thought that this would've been enough for her to move on, but all the events that occurred today—good and bad—made their connection stronger, and her feelings for her even more undeniable. She wanted to be more thrilled about today, but in that moment, her heart was going through too many other motions.

She heard her phone going off and reoriented herself to where she's sitting on the edge of her bed. She looked at her screen and saw Amy sent her a message saying,

Incoming Photo Dump lol

She was then bombarded with a bunch of selfies they took on Amy's phone and other pictures her parents took of them. Morgan couldn't help but lovingly gaze at all of them.

She then replied,

Damn we're a good looking pair lol.

(*laughing emoji*) Well, you def make me look good lol.

BS you're hot. I'm average at best.

That's not true. You're way above "average at best."

Aww thank you.

Seriously, you're beautiful.

You really think?

Absolutely. You're a babe!

(*blush emoji*) I mean if you say it then I know it's true. Thank You. (*heart emoji*)

You're welcome. & Thank you btw. Despite what happened, today was one of the best days I had in a long time.

Me 2. I hope we can do it again

I'd love that. (*smiling face emoji*)

Morgan smiled at that last message and fell backward onto her bed to glare up at her ceiling again.

Meanwhile

Amy had been in her room, on her bed, during this whole conversation. She set her phone down after sending that last message, picked up her picture frame that she sat right beside her, and placed it on the nightstand by her bed, in the open center between some other photos she had sitting there.

She looked at it for a few seconds, staring at Morgan with a beam. As she reflected on what they did today, how much fun she was having with her, and all the intimacy that occurred, her smile changed. It became warmer. More infatuating. More... loving.

She snapped out of her hypnotized state and became surprised. Her heart started pounding, her hands were clammy, and she had a look on her face that said, "Where the hell did that come from?" She brushed off whatever state of mind she was just in and turned on the TV to distract her from those thoughts. But through some sort of pathos, they kept creeping back in her head, making her very confused...

It's one thing to learn something new about somebody. But once in a while, you start to learn something new about yourself. Whether you stumble upon it on your own or somebody else helps you discover it, there could always be a part of yourself that you might not even be aware of. Even if you already believe you know yourself, something might come along to prove whether your beliefs are true or not. Even if you live your life a certain way, it can always change course to a pathway that's much less bumpy. It just took the right person help you find that road.

Chapter 19

Last Sunday Before Winter (Paige/Steven)

Paige cried herself to sleep last night and spent the next day continuing to wallow in her own sadness. She locked herself in her room, not wanting to see or speak to anybody. When her parents tried to talk to her through the door, she only gave them a basic response, barely speaking more than a few words, or no words at all. Her phone had been going off every so often by her friends' leaving messages or trying to call her only to be met by the voicemail, until she just shut it off. Her biggest secret had been revealed against her will—exactly what she feared would happen eventually—and now that it was, she had no idea how to handle it. She just stayed in her room, sitting on her bed, with her unwashed frizzled hair done into a ponytail, her tomboy aesthetic replaced by a pair of sweatpants and a strappy tank top, and her face buried into a manga, utterly embarrassed.

Meanwhile

Steven had spent his day more or less the same. He didn't talk much to his family—not even Lisa—and isolated himself. This was typical for him, but it was different this time. He couldn't stop thinking about last night; between finding out that Mrs. Curtis was Paige's mother and the way Paige went storming upstairs, he had a lot of thoughts that he couldn't shake off. He tried doing his Sunday workout but didn't feel motivated enough to finish it; he drowned out his music, only hearing the memory of Paige crying as she slammed her door shut, and the fainter cries he could still hear after it was closed. He couldn't help but feel guilty, like it was somehow his fault, but however she was feeling was clearly a lot stronger.

Steven eventually zoned out and found himself on the living room couch, with the TV playing in front of him. He had his phone by his side and let a voicemail from Jason play out, barely paying attention to it.

"Hey, Steven, just want to make sure everything's good. Uh, my phone says you're not reading my texts, and I've tried calling you three times now. I know you're not doing anyone right now, so… just thought I'd let ya know that if something's wrong, don't be afraid to share it with me. I'm in Brooklyn right now, but I'll still be here all day if you get the chance or just wanna blow off some steam. So yeah, gimme a call back whenever. All right, later, bro."

The message ended.

"Steven? Are you okay?" Samantha asked him, entering the room.

"Yeah, I'm good," he replied, still looking at the TV.

"You sure? You seem a little less poignant than usual."

"Eh, it's probably just the weather. I'll live."

Samantha just nodded lightly. "I made hot chocolate. You want some?"

"I'll pass."

"All right." Samantha rubbed his shoulder before heading back into the kitchen.

Shortly afterward, Bruce entered the house, covered in a few snowflakes. "Ah yeah, it's starting to come down. Looks like tomorrow I'll be shoveling a good foot of this stuff, eh, Steven?"

"Fun. Too bad I got school tomorrow," he sarcastically said, not looking at him.

"I could call in for you if you want."

"No," he said in an annoyed tone.

"Smart decision." Bruce took off his jacket and was met with no reply. His smile shrank into a frown. "You all right, bud?"

"Yes, just had this talk with Samantha. I'm good. Don't worry about me," he answered sternly.

"All right, your choice." He started walking toward the kitchen and stopped in his tracks. "You know I love you, right, bud?"

"Thank you," he responded. Bruce nodded and continued walking away.

When he's out of sight, Steven mouthed to himself, "I ain't your bud," before getting up off the couch and going back upstairs to his room. He sat at his computer desk and just stared outside his window, watching the snowfall. It felt like he was looking out on the streets for hours, but he could tell by how much was on the ground that it couldn't have been more than twenty minutes at best. He just stayed there, thinking about Paige.

Steven's train of thought was interrupted by Boscoe, who rested his chin on Steven's lap and whimpered. Steven started scratching his head.

"I think he's trying ask you what's wrong."

Steven looked behind him and saw Lisa, sitting on his bed.

"How long have you been sitting there?"

"Ten minutes. I was waiting to see how long until you noticed."

He sighed. "You know, I swear there's at least six or seven of you, and they switch out shifts of eavesdropping."

"All right, you got me. I'm number 7," she replied with a smirk.

"What do you want?"

"I wanna know what's wrong with you. Or… I guess just this one thing out of all the other things."

"There's nothing wrong with me."

"That's what you always say when something's wrong. Come on, who am I gonna tell?"

"It's not about my problems."

"Then what is it?"

"Ugh. Listen, you're a little too young for this kind of shit, all right? You wouldn't understand." Steven turned away from her.

"I'm a lot smarter than you give credit, you know." Steven didn't reply. "Is something wrong with Paige?" Steven still gave no answer. "I knew it. What's wrong with her?"

"Whatever's wrong with her is none of your business. In fact, it's none of my business either."

"And since when do you care about being out of other people's business?"

"It's different this time, all right!" He raised his voice.

Lisa didn't reply. She just gave him a worried look. She could tell whatever it was, was serious.

She huffed. "Look, let's just say last night, I learned something about her. Something that I wasn't supposed to know and . . . puts a lot into retrospect."

"Oh. …Was it bad?"

"Well, it is to her. She was really upset, and I can see why she didn't want me to know. But… I kind of feel weird that she didn't want me to know."

"Huh?"

"Well, I mean, I've known her for months now; but as far as everyone is concerned, we're total strangers. I never told her family that she bailed on her job to go to Halloweekend. I even held up my end of our deal and pulled my grades up. I mean, Jesus Christ, I've gone out of my way for this girl, and she still doesn't trust me enough to tell me herself? What else am I supposed to do!" he ranted.

"Is this seriously what the problem is?"

"Exactly, you don't understand!"

"You're right. Except what I don't understand is probably different from what you don't think I understand."

"What's that supposed to mean?"

"You're the older brother. You're supposed to be wiser, so you tell me what it means!"

"Oh, well, if you got something you wanna say, then just say it!" Lisa hesitated. "Go on, just say it! See what happens!" he threatened her, causing Boscoe to move away and sit beside Lisa on the bed.

Lisa took a deep breath before speaking. "All right, I'll say it. I don't understand how you can be so selfish!"

"Selfish! How the hell am I selfish?"

"Because you always somehow find excuses to make everyone else look like the bad guy."

"Oh, is that right?"

"Yeah, that's right!"

"Okay then. Explain to me how I'm 'finding excuses.'" Steven leaned in to hear what she had to say.

"All right." She cleared her throat. "Anytime you start a fight, it's because somebody 'looked at you funny.' Anytime you get a bad grade, it's because your teachers 'hate you.' Anytime you break up with a girl, it's because they're 'a gold digger,' 'attention seekers,' or 'a slut.' Anytime you get chased by the cops, it's because 'some hipster SJW has nothing better to do than snitch.' Anytime you break one of my toys, it's because I 'shouldn't have left it there.' When you got left back, it was because of 'the broken system.' And when Paige was assigned to tutor you, it's because 'they enjoy making me look stupid.' It's always everybody else's fault."

"It is everybody else's fault. Someday you'll learn exactly what it feels like when the world has a vendetta against you."

"Well, why do you think that is, huh? I might only be eleven, but I actually pay attention in school. Like in science class, I learned about Isaac Newton's theory of relativity, which states, 'For every action, there's an equal or opposite reaction.' You know what that means?" Steven didn't answer. "Also, in social studies this month, we were learning about the Civil War, which happened because the Southern states didn't want to free the slaves. They instead seceded from the US so that they didn't have to obey the government and acknowledge that the slaves were human beings that were taken from their homes to do manual labor. They so badly didn't want to acknowledge that what they were doing was wrong that they started a war that lasted four years. You're aware of all of that, right?"

Steven didn't answer right away and regained his composure. "Yeah, I knew all of that. Paige touched on them a lot during the last four months," he remembered. "Anything else?"

"Yeah, when you found out about whatever you weren't supposed to, you got angry at her because you learned what you weren't supposed to learn. Don't you think that sounds a little sketchy?"

"Who said I was mad at her?"

"You sure sound like it."

"Well, I'm not."

"Yeah right." Lisa folded her arms and looked away from him.

"I'm not mad at her!" he stated. "I'm mad at myself." Lisa looked back at him. "I just—I feel like I haven't done enough. Like, I still haven't gained enough trust for her to tell me this herself. And that I hurt her." He put one hand to his face and let out a sigh. "Everybody I get in contact with, I somehow end up hurting, even when I don't mean to! I'm just like—" Steven stopped himself.

"Just like who?"

Steven looked into his sister's concerned eyes, and his mood became more fretful.

"Never mind. You don't know this person, but you get my point. All I ever do is ruin people's lives." Steven's head hung low, and he looked at the floor.

Lisa looked sad and walked up to him. She put her hand on his chin and tilted it back up to face him.

"That's not true."

"Yes, it is. Don't patronize me."

"No, you're wrong. I mean yeah, you definitely do a lot of dumb stuff; but when you're not, you do good stuff."

"Like what?"

Lisa thought. "Well, you helped Mom make Dad's birthday cake."

"Eh, all I did was mix it up while she was on the phone."

"It still came out really good." Steven shrugged. "You took Boscoe to the vet when he was sick."

"After about an hour of waiting in the sun for them to even see him, all for an X-ray."

"It was worth saving his life though, right?"

"Oh, I didn't do anything. The doctors got that foam cup out of his stomach. It wasn't that big a deal."

"God, you're picky."

"All right, so I do a couple of things for people time to time, but you just proved my point. Anytime I try to be decent, I still get shit on. What's the point if nobody else is gonna try to do the same to you?"

"I don't know. Why do you still try?"

Steven let out a groan. "Because I keep thinking someone will finally look at me and see me as something other than a criminal," he said, looking away from her.

"What do you mean 'finally'? I don't see you as a criminal."

"I told you to stop patronizing me."

"I'm not. When I look at you, I see you as my big brother." Steven looked back over to her. "I know everybody makes you think you're a bad guy, but I know for a fact that you're not. I know, because I've known you my entire life; and for my entire life, you've been there for me. You've always taken care of me, listened to me when I had problems, stood up to other kids picking on me. You never leave my side unless you're sure I'm okay. I always see what's beneath this 'I hate everybody, everything, and I wish I was dead' shtick, and it's a very caring boy. Anybody who calls you a criminal just doesn't know you like I do. …Like how Paige knows you."

Steven slowly cracked a smile. "You were right. You are smarter than me."

"I just said that I'm smarter than you think."

Steven stood up. "I know what you said."

He picked her up and brought her in a hug, which she returned.

Steven sat her back down on his bed and stayed hunched over to her height.

"If I'm being honest, if you weren't here, I'd probably go insane," Steven confessed.

"Probably?"

"Don't ruin it."

Lisa giggled at his remark.

"You've got a good heart, kid."

"So do you. Even if you don't feel it."

Steven thought for a second.

"I gotta go fix this." He stood straight back up and headed to the door.

"What are you gonna do?"

"I don't know. But I might be home later than usual." He opened the door and stepped out, but before he closed it behind him, he left it halfway open to face Lisa. "Just two things—"

"If Mom and Dad ask, you're being tutored, and this conversation doesn't leave the room," Lisa cut him off to list for him.

"Okay, three things." Lisa tilted her head. "Whatever happens, I'm always here for you."

Lisa smiled. "You too, big brother, and good luck."

"Thanks, baby sister." He closed the door.

A few seconds later, Lisa heard a knock.

"Four things. When I come back, I better not find you sleeping in my bed again," Steven said from behind the door.

"Roger dodger." She listened to him walk down the stairs. When the sounds of his footsteps stopped, she lay down on the bed with her arms behind her head, next to Boscoe. "He didn't say I couldn't lie on it," she told him before she picked up the remote for his TV and turned it on.

Downstairs, Steven was about to open the front door but stopped before he turned it.

"Shit. Almost forgot."

He walked toward the closet.

One Hour Later, 4:50 PM: Paige's House

Steven was sitting in his car that's parked on the outside of the driveway.

"So, uh, how are you? ...How ya feeling? ...How are you feeling? ...Look, about last night... Do you wanna talk about anything? I mean, it's fine if you don't. I just-just—sigh. ...Uh, Mrs. Curtis! Funny seeing you here. ...So-o-o is she home? ...So you're her dad? I'm here for tutoring and nothing else. No, stupid! ...Wassup? GAH! What is happening to me!?"

He looked upward toward where her window was. The blinds were shut, but he can see the lights were on. He took a second before he left his car, grabbed his baggage, and headed for her front door.

He hesitated before he knocked but shortly afterward finally did it. "Shit." He adjusted himself a couple of times before finding a pose to stick with. "Yeah, this works," he muttered.

"Hello?" The door opened, and he's met by her father, who, after realizing who it was, changed his expression to a judgmental glare, not saying anything more.

The mood became very tense before Steven finally spoke.

"Wassup?" he said, trying to break the silence, but quickly realized how dumb that sounded. "Dammit," he whispered to himself.

"You're the guy from last night."

"Uh, yeah. I am. The name's Steven, and I'm guessing you're her father."

"Correct," he sternly answered.

"Well, um, she and I are supposed to be scheduled for a tutoring session right about now, so if she's home—"

"She is, but I don't think she wants to see you or anybody else right now, so I'm only once gonna ask nicely that you leave," Richard cut him off.

"Sir, I swear I just—"

"I said I'm gonna ask once!"

"Richard, be nice!" Catherine intervened. "Steven, um, good evening!" She forced a smile.

"Hey... Mrs. Curtis."

It was at this moment where the reality finally hit him. Their teacher was her mom. As if on cue, he fully grasped how she was feeling; if the roles were switched, he would be embarrassed too.

"Would you like to come in?"

"Actually yeah."

"Catherine!" Richard began, only to be quickly shushed by her.

"Please, enter," she invited.

Steven did such. "Uh, how is she?" he asked.

"She hasn't left her room all day. She won't even come out for food."

Steven felt bad. "Yeah, I could tell she was really upset."

"I know. I understand why though. I should've given her a warning that we were coming home."

"Does anybody else know? About..."

"Just the girls, and now you. I guess somebody was bound to figure out sooner or later. Heck, I'm amazed we hid this as long as we did."

"Well, you had me fooled."

"No surprise there," Richard said in a low voice.

"What was that?" Catherine asked him.

"I wasn't talking," he covered up.

"Anyway, I'm really sorry. I never meant—"

"It's all right," Steven interrupted. "It's all right. You don't have to apologize. You don't have to explain anything. I understand completely."

Catherine nodded. While this was going on, Richard raised an eyebrow and lowered his rigidness, but just a little bit. "So she's upstairs then?"

"Yeah," she replied.

"Well, if you don't mind, I'd—"

"Not so fast, you," Richard interrupted.

"Richard, please—" Catherine started.

"Mrs. Curtis." Steven stopped her from intervening. "It's all right." Catherine backed off.

"Listen, sir, I get it. I totally get it. But I want you to know, I would never do anything to hurt your daughter."

"I've heard that a lot, from people who are all talk. Most of them look and dress exactly like you."

"I know, but I'm not like them. I mean, I used to be, but I'm not anymore, and it's all because of her." Richard didn't look like he's buying it. "I get that you don't trust me, but I assure you, once this semester's over, I'm... I'm never gonna bother her again," Steven admitted, and Richard's expression went from stern to puzzled. "But before that, I really owe her for all she's done for me. So if it's cool with you, could I at least try and convince her to come out of her room?"

Richard looked away from him and up at the top of the staircase, then to his wife, who had a look that said, "Come on, let him go." He's still uncertain but ultimately made his decision.

"You have one hour. Be sure her door stays open."

Steven nodded and began to walk upstairs. "Thank you," he said before disappearing from their sight.

Richard looked down, wondering if he's going to regret this. Catherine hugged his arm to ease his stress and walked him into the dining room.

Upstairs

Steven stepped onto the next floor and saw every door was open, except for the one to his right: Paige's.

"All right, now for the hard part," he said, below his voice.

He walked up to the door and was once again hesitant. He took a little longer than he was at the front door, but finally knocked.

208

"Einstein?" Paige heard him from the other side. Her eyes expanded, and she turned her head to face the door. She didn't respond, figuring she's just hearing things. But another knock followed. "Einstein? It's me." Now she knew she heard it right but was too embarrassed to say anything. She just ignored him and went back to reading her manga. "Come on, it's okay. You don't have to hide from me. Just open the door." She's still ignoring him. Steven sighed and didn't talk for a few seconds. "Well, if you won't open the door, could you at least say something?" he asked.

Paige fought back her tears, before she huffed. "What do you want?"

"I just want to make sure you're okay."

"Well, I'm not. You can go now."

"Come on, don't shut me out. You can talk to me. I thought we were clear on that."

"I can't talk to you about this. You'll never understand how embarrassing it is."

"You're right. I never will. But you don't have to feel embarrassed."

Paige looked up and turned her head to face the door again. "Don't you tell me how to feel, Jacobs! How dare you!" She threw her book at the door.

"All right, all right, I'm sorry! I didn't mean to say it like that."

She finally got off her bed and walked over to the door. "You don't realize what it feels like, to hide something like this for so long—something you never wanted anybody to know—and then for it to be spat out against your own will like that! If everybody else at school finds out about this, my life is over!" She pressed her back up against the door and slid downward to where she's seated.

"Well, nobody else is gonna find out."

"Don't try to make me feel secure with false promises!"

"I swear it'll be fine. You—"

"Just leave me alone, okay!?"

"I can't. I'm supposed to be getting tutored right now."

"Ugh. All right. Who was the father of the atomic bomb?"

"Robert Oppenheimer."

"Great, you've been tutored. Now go away."

Steven rubbed his eyes before he placed his backpack down on the floor and knelt to the same height where Paige was still sitting.

"Listen. I understand why you're upset. But you know? Everybody has some crazy secret that they're hiding, and you're not the first one who's had it exposed like that." Paige didn't respond. "And you know what? This isn't as embarrassing as a lot of those other secrets. Some people are hiding some things way bigger."

"Don't give me any of that."

"It's true."

"And just what would you know about anything that I'm going through? What?" she asked as her face turned vermilion.

"Because... Because..." Steven struggled to speak.

He took a deep breath and started to talk again.

"My name's not Steven," he confessed.

Paige's face cooled down, and she looked confused. "Huh?"

Steven sighed. "It's Nicholas."

He didn't get a response.

He then heard the doorknob turning and stood back up as Paige opened the door. Neither said anything.

Paige moved aside for him to come in, which he did. She left it open by a small crack.

"Last night, when you asked me why I call Samantha and Bruce by their first names, and if I resented them... it's because they... they aren't my parents."

Paige was shocked and muddled. "You mean, you're..."

"Yeah. Adopted. Both me and Lisa."

"How long?"

"Since I was six, and she was only four months... not too long after we lost our mom."

She could only gasp. "What happened?" she asked.

Steven looked into the eyes behind her glasses and saw the sincerity that's illuminating from them. She invited him to sit next to her on the edge of her bed, and he accepted it. He took a moment to breathe before he started talking.

"My real parents' names were George and Elizabeth. The first few of years of my childhood were somewhat normal. We just lived in a small apartment. My father was working in real estate while my mom would stay home with me. There were a couple of other families living in the same building. My mom would always make me play with the other kids, even though I didn't want to. She was always encouraging me to be nice, behave, and socialize. With my father always working, she was the only real role model I ever had. She taught me how to read, how to tie my shoes, how to use a fork. She even taught me how to ride a bike. No matter how many times I kept falling off, she'd talk me back on until I finally got good at it. Anytime I ever felt sad or scared, she was always by my side, to tell me, 'It's going to be okay.' She was the greatest woman I'd ever known. She was also the only one of them who knew how to raise a kid. Whenever my father had to look after me, he really sucked at it. He always just fell asleep watching the news or just sat back and let me do whatever I wanted so long as it kept me busy. He was rarely ever around."

"That was until he lost his job. He didn't take it well. He blamed us for whatever it was that got him fired, never thinking that maybe it happened because he was lazy and uninterested in people around him. Eventually, he started going to bars in his spare time, spending the money he was getting from unemployment on beer. He would always come back drunk, get angry, and take it out on both of us. And I guess being a dick crossed over to me. I started acting out, picking fights with the other kids, or just beating them up. My mom was always there to calm me down, always making sure I was okay, even if she wasn't. She did convince him to go into rehab, after about a year of putting us through hell. At first, he seemed to start changing. I thought we would finally get life back to normal, and we did. But then one night my mom had us sit on the couch, and she said, 'Things are gonna get better, starting now. I'm pregnant!'"

"And he just completely lost it. He yelled at her. He yelled at me. He threw stuff across the room, knocked over our furniture, screaming louder than I ever heard him. Then he went up in her face, and they got into an argument. I can still remember everything they said, word for word."

'You're getting rid of this!'

'What are you talking about?'

'What do you think I'm talking about? How do you plan to raise two of these little things on our income?'

'George, we can figure something out—'

'Oh, quit being so fucking naive, Elizabeth! We can barely afford to raise his ungrateful ass. I am not prepared to deal with two of these selfish creatures! Yeah! You hear me, Nicholas? I see you behind there! I know you can hear! SO I HOPE YOU'RE FUCKING LISTENING!'

'George, leave him out of this!'

'No no no, he decides to intervene in my life and cost me my job, he's gonna listen to this! You're getting rid of that thing, and we are gonna get our shit back on track together! Or you're gonna deal with this by yourself!'

'George, please...'

'It's either me and him, or him and this. You can't have all of it! What's your fucking answer?!'

'Get out.'

'What was that?'

'I said get out!'

Smack!

'So that's it then? After all I've done for you? You disrespectful bitch! Well, good fucking luck then. I hope it's worth it!'

Door slam.

"I never heard from him again after that. Now, it was just me, my mom, and my new sister. She did everything to ensure that she could support herself and two kids, while also making sure I wasn't getting into any fights, but I could see the toll it was taking on her. It was scary. ...Then the day finally came. She went into labor, and just about everything that could go wrong went wrong. I was sitting in the waiting room with some other doctors when they started running into her room. During one of her contractions, she started losing blood, and she was rushed into the emergency room. I ran alongside her all the way down the hall, looking at her, lying on the gurney, surrounded by doctors, with tubes and wires coming out of her body that was soaked in red. I kept calling out for her, but she didn't respond. When they got her into the ER, I tried following her, but the doctors wouldn't let me go in. They carried me away. No matter how much I fought, I couldn't get free. I just kept calling out to her, even after they closed the door. I just wanted her to wake up and tell me, 'It's going to be okay,' but she never did …and that was the last time I ever saw her."

"The only bright side is that she fought long enough to save Lisa. I waited two days before they finally let me see her. I can't remember anything from those two days, except them asking me for a name. I told them that she always wanted to have a daughter named Lisa. Next thing I knew, we were being sent to an orphanage, and that's how Samantha and Bruce found us. Everything else since then has just been one big blur."

Paige was stunned to silence after hearing all of this. She just sat there with her hand covering her mouth, and no idea what to say except for a barely audible "Oh my gosh."

Steven didn't say anything more. His posture and expression told the rest of the story.

"I'm… I'm sorry. I had no idea."

"I know. Nobody else does. Not even Jason," he confessed. "You're the only person I've ever told this to."

Paige tried to comprehend. "Why? Why are you telling me all of this?"

"I just thought you'd feel better knowing how much better you have it. I'd be embarrassed too if my mom was our teacher, but I'd also do anything just to have her here."

"Well, now I feel horrible."

He sighed. "I didn't mean to do that."

"No. I meant I feel horrible that I was so quick to judge you." Steven looked up at her. "For so long I thought you were some pretentious asshole with nothing to be so angry about, but now I get it. I… totally understand how you feel."

"What does that mean?" He adjusted himself where he's upward again.

"I mean…" Paige hesitated before she continued. She sighed. "I wish my dad was here too."

"What?" Steven's expression went from distraught to confused.

"Richard is my stepdad. My real dad died when I was eight."

Steven was now the shocked one.

"He was driving home from work one night and... and was hit by a drunk driver. ...My mom met Richard less than a year later, and she brought him to our house really early into their relationship. At first, I couldn't stand her for moving on that quickly, and I didn't want to give him a chance. That same night, he came up to my room; and despite how many times I talked down to him or yelled at him or told him to stay away from my mom, he just stood there and let me vent. After I calmed down, he started talking to me. He told me that he understood where I was coming from and how I wasn't wrong to feel upset. Then he told me about how he always wanted to have a daughter. He then said, 'I know I'll never replace your dad, but could you at least give me a chance? To show that I care about your mom? To help her take care of you? To be your friend?"

"So I did. He kept true to his word. We grew close and got along better than I could've ever imagined. He even asked me for permission to marry my mom before he proposed to her. He swore he wouldn't unless I was okay with it. I said yes, she said yes, then when I turned twelve, they got married, and that same day, he adopted me."

"It's been great having a whole family again, but I still miss my dad." Paige began to tear up and turned away from him."

"You must've been really close."

"We were. My dad worked a lot, but he always made time to be with me. He always made me laugh when I cried. We'd play his old video games together, watch movies cartoons and anime until we both fell asleep, and he was always encouraging me to do better in school. But that's probably because my mom was homeschooling me, and he wanted me to give her a break." She chuckled for a brief second before going right back to grieving.

"I'm sorry. I'm sure he'd be proud of the girl you grew up to be."

"Thank you."

"I just really wish you told me about this earlier."

"It's not that I didn't want to. I was just scared."

"Of what? I thought we made it clear we can trust each other."

"I did too. My problem is I've always had issues with trusting people. So many I've grown to trust either leave me"—she placed her hand on the back of her head—"or they hurt me."

"Who?" Steven asked. Paige turned to face him. "Who hurt you?" Paige tilted her head down.

"When I was little, I didn't have any friends. I was shy around other kids, too afraid to ever talk to them. If any of them ever tried talking to me, I would almost pee myself. I guess I left myself open for abuse because they all started picking on me. My parents would take me to the park, and those kids would call me Baby Alive and say things like 'Did the baby learn to talk yet?' 'Hey, baby, can you say "ugly"?' 'Are your batteries dead, Baby Alive?' and I was always too scared to speak up to them or to tell my mom and dad. But there was this one boy. He lived on the same street, and our moms always arranged playdates. He was the only kid that ever made any attempt to be nice to me. No matter how quiet I was, he still tried to be friendly. He was the one boy I ever felt safe enough to talk to. We ended up becoming best friends. We did everything together. It couldn't have been more than two years, but it felt like a lifetime. It was great. ...But then something changed in him. Suddenly, he was the quiet one. Anytime I tried to talk to him, he barely answered me back. I thought he was just in a grumpy mood that day, but the days kept coming and going, and it was the same story, except he seemed to gradually get less talkative, and more angry. Then one of those days, we went to the park, and everything just imploded. ...We were sitting on the swing set when the same kids that always picked on me came up to us. This time though, they were more interested in picking on him. I tried to tell them to leave him alone, but they didn't. One kid started pushing him, and then..."

Punch!

"That kid fell on the pavement and was spitting out his teeth. Another one got kicked in the kneecap. He wrestled the third one to the ground and choked him until he screamed 'Uncle!' I just sat there, scared to death, watching my best friend acting like some enraged animal. While he was pummeling one of them, I ran over to pull him off. That's when he grabbed me by my wrists and just glared at me. I couldn't even recognize him anymore. His eyes were bloodred, and his face looked like his head was about to explode. I told him he was hurting me, but he just screamed, 'GET OUT OF MY FACE!' Then he shoved me. I felt the back of my head collide with a metal edge of the playground's tower, and everything just went black.

"When I woke up, I was in a medical room, and I had this." She parted her hair away to reveal her scar.

"Whoa. I've seen MMA fighters with lesser cuts than that," Steven said and was met with a huff from Paige.

Realizing what he said sounded insensitive, he asked, "So whatever happened to that punk?"

"I don't know. My parents never let me see him again, not that I wanted too anyway. Frankly, I don't care where he is. That jerk took our friendship, shoved it onto a piece of sharp metal, and left me with a permanent reminder of what happens when you let people in!"

Her tears started to flow down her face, and she started to cry again. With nothing else to lean on, she buried her face in his chest and let out what had to have been a lot of pent-up sorrow. Steven didn't know what to do, so he just sat there while she sobbed on his shirt.

She sniffled. "I wanted to tell you, but I wasn't ready to go through all that hurt again!"

She continued to sob while Steven just sat there. He hadn't seen emotion emanating from her like this since the night she yelled at him. Except this was stronger. He had been with several other girls but was never in a situation with one of them that was like this, one where he actually cared about their feelings.

With no idea what to say or do, he slowly lifted his arms up and pulled her in for a warm hug. They stayed like this for a while as she cried herself dry. Halfway through, Steven tightened his grasp and held her firmly. Both found themselves able to relax in each other's space.

"You don't have to be afraid of me," he told her.

"How can I ever know that?"

"You can't. But if you don't open the door, you'll never see what's on the other side."

The two separated, and she wiped her tears. "I know that. It's just always hard for me."

"I don't think you realize how brave you are." She looked up at him. "These last few months you braved being around my dumb ass. Not to mention you have Morgan, Amy, Jenn. Hell, you were brave enough to give your stepdad a chance. Your mom could've married some deadbeat douche, but she found somebody you got along with, somebody that took you in and treated you like their own child, even though you shut them out and treated them like shit. …If that's not a strong love …I don't know what is." Steven slumped.

Paige realized what he's referring to and noticed him feeling down.

"Hey. You may never show it, but you're a really good guy." Steven just brushed it off. "Come on, you're so much nicer than people realize. Than you realize."

"You sound just like Lisa. She told me the same thing."

"Well, she's right. And if you don't believe me, I'm not the only one who thinks that. Because your parents think so too."

"I doubt that."

"It's true. They told me, and I quote, 'He's got a good heart. He takes really good care Lisa.' I didn't believe that at first, but now I see it." Steven looked at her. "Trust me, they love you."

Steven thought about what she said. "You know? For years, I've convinced myself that I never wanted to be dependent on parents, that I could take care of myself. I never thought about this 'til now, but I think all this time I've stayed so distant from them because I wanted Lisa to have all their attention. Because I didn't want her to grow up and be… like me." He hunched over again.

"Well, from what I've heard today, you could've turned out a lot worse. And you know? I think you've had more of an effect on her than you give yourself credit for. But in the best way possible." Steven sat up straight. "I mean yes, you do have noticeably different personas, but at the same time, you both share your best qualities, and your relationship is so admirably solicitous."

"Solici—what?"

"Solicitous—it means you're both caring, considerate, always looking out for each other," she clarified. "Believe me, you're a great older brother, and a great friend too."

Steven managed to crack a smile—the most genuine one Paige had ever seen from him yet. Paige smiled back with an equal sentimentality.

"So as long as we're sharing shit, you wanna know more about Nicholas Jacobs?" Steven asked.

Paige didn't answer verbally. She just brought her legs up, placed both her fists under her chin, and stared wide eyed at him, with some blinks thrown in. Steven snickered at her.

"As you can guess, Nicholas was the name my parents gave me. My last name was different from when I was younger though. Jacobs was my mom's maiden name. I took that name because I wanted to erase any trace of my father. In fact, when Lisa was born, I specifically requested them to legally make that her last name too."

"I see. So how did you settle on the new name?"

"Well, first of all, I listened to a lot of Guns N' Roses when I was a kid, so the name Axl was a no-brainer."

"Oh, I don't know. I think Duff, Adler, or Izzy would've been a better choice."

"Well, that wasn't your decision now, was it?" he replied. Paige chuckled at it. "And as for Steven, my mom would always listen to Stevie Wonder. He was her favorite artist. Every night when she put me to bed, she would sing me his song 'I Just Called to Say I Love You.' So in her memory, I had my name changed to Steven. To me, that was my way of keeping her alive—my name, Lisa"—he grabbed his gold necklace—"and this."

Paige observed it. It's the one accessory that didn't really match with the rest of his fashion, but what he always wore with every different outfit.

"Was that…?" she asked, pointing to it.

He nodded. "She used to wear this every day. She left it behind when she was taken to the hospital. I found it in her drawer, and I've kept it with me ever since. This way, I always feel like she's with me."

"Wow. I didn't think the most beautiful thing I ever heard would come out of the same mouth that told the gym teacher, 'I fucked your wife.'"

"Yeah, well, this isn't the type of thing I normally talk about."

"Well, I really admire you for being strong enough to tell me all that. Now I know I can always trust you."

"I'm glad to hear that. And just so you know, your secret's safe with me. I'll never tell anyone."

"I know you won't. I'm really sorry. This was easier to tell Morgan because she wasn't my teacher yet. And when I told Amy and Jenn, I was ready. I really did want to tell you, but I wasn't yet."

"It's okay. It isn't worth being angry about that."

"I'm also sorry I made you share all that. That couldn't have been easy."

"Honestly, it felt really good letting it all out. I've been hiding that for so long it feels good to get the weight off. Now I know what it feels like to be Chris Pratt."

Paige laughed at his comment. "Well, I'll be sure nobody knows about that either."

"Great, Steven Axl is too big of an attraction to change the marketing." Paige laughed again. "And I really appreciate you listening. A lot."

"Don't mention it. Truth is, I've actually enjoyed these last few months. It's been great seeing how much you've turned your grades around, and . . . I'm glad I got to see the real you."

"Me too. I had no idea I could actually enjoy learning something." The two shared a glance. "You know what?"

"What?"

"You've gotten to see the real me. How's about you let me see the real you?"

"Hmm?"

"Come on, you're on the honor roll. You should know what I mean."

"Uh…" Paige ran her hand through her hair; and when she touched her ponytail, followed by her adjusting her glasses, she figured out what he meant. "Oh. I-I can't."

"Yes, you can."

"No. …You're gonna laugh at me."

"Don't give me that seventies rom-com crap. I'm sure underneath those you have a face *Maximum* would kill to have on their cover."

Paige blushed in embarrassment and turned away from him. "I don't know."

"Hey." He lightly touched her chin and turned her to face him. "We agreed that nothing leaves this room. This doesn't have too either."

She pondered for a moment as she looked into his eyes, seeing the sincerity that's emanating.

"You promise you won't laugh?"

"Promise."

Paige took a deep breath and nodded her head. Her eyes moved down while she's slowly undoing her hair band. She then pulled it off but still held her hair in place. She looked back up at him who's still watching her. She closed her eyes and tilted her head down, slowly lifting her glasses off, while simultaneously letting her hair fall.

She looked back up and opened her eyes to look at him, showing him her natural beauty. She sat there trying to read his face, waiting for a comment.

Steven smiled and spoke. "I knew it."

Paige nervously asked, "Do I look okay?"

"Okay? You're… It's like I'm meeting you all over again." He smiled.

Paige smiled back after hearing that, not even trying to hide her blush.

"Thank you."

"You're welcome, Einstein—I mean… Thank you. Paige."

The both of them smiled at each other for a solid ten seconds.

Paige stood up. "You know, I haven't eaten anything all day. You think you'd wanna stay for dinner?"

"I would." Steven looked out the window to see it's still lightly snowing. "But I think it'd be a better idea if I left before the snow gets heavy again." Steven stood up.

"Yeah. Good point."

"Besides…" He looked at his phone's clock. "Wow, we've been here a while. My hour's almost up."

"Your hour?"

"Don't ask." He grabbed his backpack. "But, uh, before I leave…" He unzipped his bag and pulled out a big wrapped box. "Merry Christmas." He handed it to her.

"Oh my god, Steven." She took it from him. "You didn't have to do this." She started to unwrap it and found a black-and-white box.

"Well, I did do it."

"Yeah, but you really…"

She opened the box and pulled out a glass container with a bejeweled rose inside, like the rose from *Beauty and the Beast.*

"Oh my god. It's so beautiful!"

"Like it?"

"I love this! Where'd you get it?"

"Some antique place over by Bay Street. I saw that and remembered how you compared this whole thing with us to *Beauty and the Beast*, so it just seemed too appropriate to not get."

"Oh my god, this had to have cost a lot."

"Oh, it wasn't much. Just $99.99."

"A hundred?"

"It's all right. I can spare that. I just took it out of my motorcycle fund."

"You have a motorcycle fund?"

"Yeah, whatever money I've been making, I've been saving up for a ride. Anyway, it doesn't matter. After all the time you wasted on me, it's the least I can do."

Paige was touched by this thoughtful gesture and shed another tear, this time of joy. "Thank you so much."

"You're welcome."

Paige admired at the rose. "I have something for you too." She set it down.

"Really?"

"Yes. But you need to go downstairs first."

"Why do I—"

"Just do it! It'll make sense!"

"All right all right, I'm going."

"I'll be right down." She closed the door on him.

Steven looked at the door with a bemused look before heading down.

Downstairs

He walked downstairs and into the living room, where her parents were there to greet him again.

"Steven? Is she okay?" Catherine asked as she got up off the couch.

"Yeah. I think she's feeling a lot better. She'll be down in a little bit."

"Oh, that's wonderful!" she said, and Steven nodded.

"Hey, Steven," Richard called out. "Come here." Steven did such and sat down opposite from him on their chair. "Listen, now I know that I was pretty quick to judge you. But I had a long talk with my wife just now, and she tells me that Paige has had a little influence on you."

"I mean, I guess, a little bit."

"Well, I'm not entirely sure about that, but because I care about her, and because you came down within an hour like you said you would, I'm gonna give you an opportunity to prove that. The only thing I ask is that you treat her well."

"Oh, actually, you see, it's not like that—" he began before he's shushed.

"You don't have to lie to me, son. Just swear to me that you'll be good to her."

Steven was somewhat embarrassed by what he was implying but decided to make things easier for everyone involved. "Um, you have my word," he agreed.

Catherine rubbed Steven's shoulder, and the two shared a look. "You've really come a long way this semester, Steven. I'm proud of you," she told him.

"Thank you, Mrs. Curtis."

"Oh please, we're not in school. Call me Catherine."

"All right, Catherine." Steven gave her a friendly smile, but inside he's thinking, *This is so weird.*

Everyone's attention shifted when they heard footsteps coming down the stairs. "Hey, Mom. Hey, Dad." Paige came down with a paper shopping bag that she set down on the bottom step.

"Ooh, you're looking a lot better," her mom cheerfully said.

"Yeah. Turns out I just needed someone to talk to," Paige said.

Richard got off the couch. "Well, it's great to see you moving about again, kiddo. But if I may make a suggestion, you should come inside and eat right now while dinner's hot," he said.

"I'll be right in."

"Good. Umm, Richard, why don't we get started on dinner ourselves?" Catherine spoke.

"I'm not in any rush," he replied.

"Like you said, 'while it's hot.' Come." She started pushing him from behind toward the dining room. "See you in class tomorrow, Steven."

"You too, Catherine," Steven said right before they're out of sight.

"You call my mom by her first name now?" Paige smirked.

"Yeah, we just became besties in the"—he checked his phone—"two minutes it took you to come down."

Paige chuckled. "Well, I just needed to get this out of my closet." Paige held the bag up.

Steven took the bag and dug into it. "Ah now, isn't necess—"

He pulled out a denim vest with the name "Steven" stitched on the upper back.

"Ah man! This is so cool! Damn, check out the font!"

"You sure this is something you'd wear?"

"Yeah, I'd totally wear this! In fact…" Steven took off the leather jacket he usually wore and put the vest on. "Look at that, perfect fit!" he said, adjusting it.

"Oh, well, that's a relief."

"For real though, this is sick. Thanks."

Paige was pleased by his gratitude.

"I, uh, I know we talked about a lot of stuff; but as far as material possession goes, this is the nicest thing I've ever gotten."

"Well, my parents always rewarded me for good grades, so I figured you deserved something for shattering your F average."

"'Failure starts with an F but is followed by an A.'"

"You remembered." She smiled.

"For some reason, yes."

Paige giggled. "So since we're off for the next two weekends, I guess we'll pick this up in January."

"But we're done with this after tonight."

"I know." She grinned.

Steven did the same in return.

"So I'll see myself out." He headed to the door.

"Uh, you're gonna walk out with no sleeves?"

"I'm only going out to my car."

"Suit yourself."

He snickered. "See ya in class tomorrow."

He waited for a response, but instead, Paige wrapped her arms around his neck and pulled herself in for a hug. Steven was surprised again but was quicker to return this one. It was more warming than the first one; it felt lighter—like all the negative feelings they both felt were gone this time.

"Merry Christmas," she whispered.

She let go, but not before leaving him with a kiss on his cheek.

She walked away from him and toward her dining room, leaving him speechless, putting his hand where she kissed him.

Steven snapped out of his trance and noticed her looking back at him from the doorway with a big smile. He lightly waved goodbye with his other hand before she left behind the door.

Steven left the house and walked out to his car, with his grin still on his face.

He'd been kissed by a lot of girls, but this was different. This one had actual affection behind it. That one peck felt more wholesome than any make-out session he had ever had.

Steven got in his car and started it up. The radio started playing the next song as Steven took off, looking up at Paige's window again.

As the rest of the evening went by, Steven finally got in touch with Jason. When Jason asked where he'd been, Steven vaguely told him he was "busy doing other stuff" but felt good. When asked about Paige, he told him, "She's good. No problems at all." When he got home, he—for once—greeted his adoptive parents, even asked how they were. He then went upstairs to his room where he found the TV on and Lisa sound asleep on his bed. Normally he'd get angry and wake her up, but because he was in a good mood, he just picked her up and carried her to her own bed, not waking her.

On Paige's end, she sat down to have dinner, then finally got in touch with her friends for a Skype call. When they asked if she was all right, she assured them that she was feeling "pretty good." They shared stories about how their days were, with Paige's being mostly vague, covering up for Steven like she promised. When they hung up, Paige placed her new rose directly in front of her bedroom window to display it and marvel at how pretty it was. As she's doing this, Spotify decided to play Avril Lavigne's "Complicated."

Chill out, what ya yellin' for?
Lay back, it's all been done before.
And if, you could only let it be, you will see.
I like, you the way you are, when we're, driving in the car.
And you're, talking to me one-on-one, but you become.
Somebody else, 'round everyone else.
You're watching your back, like you can't relax. You're trying to be cool; you look like a fool to me. Tell me, why'd you have to go and make things so complicated? I see the way you're acting like you're somebody else get me frustrated.
Life's like this, you, and you fall, and you crawl, and you break, and you take, what you get, and you turn it into. Honesty and promise me I'm never gonna find you fake it.
No, no, no.

You ever had a song you've listened to a hundred times, then you hear it for the hundred and first time and it sounds different? Like the lyrics have a whole new meaning? You understand what the singer is talking about? You feel like they're singing about you? It's kind of like when you've known somebody for a while, and then you look at them differently than how you did before. Paige and Steven had certainly changed a lot since the beginning of this school year, at least from their perspectives. To them, it's almost like they were completely different people, and that's because they were. Now, they were who they really were.

Chapter 20

Just When You Think You Know Someone...

Three Months Later

Things were going well for this band of misfits. Their bonds had grown a lot stronger since they first crossed paths in September, and after December, it only got better; both of their limited social circles had become one well-rounded unit that had a noticeable effect between them.

After being snowed in with Jason, Jenn allowed herself to mellow out around Steven, and they started to get along relatively well. She even stayed true to her word and started to give Jason a couple of private sparring lessons, teaching him whatever she knew any chance they had.

Meanwhile, Jason had decided to start properly promoting himself as a musician; on weekends, he started working for parties, playing at stores and at the Staten Island Ferry station, making some pretty decent cash.

Amy had not gone on any dates during this time frame. She built a streak of rejections that boosted her morale. She felt much less stressed and was consistently upbeat among her friends, realizing how much she really loved being with them.

Morgan was still her typical self, at least around her friends. When she wasn't, she felt a numb sort of feeling that she hadn't felt before; this started back in December, but she wouldn't talk about it with anyone. She just acted like her usual whacked-out self.

But the two who changed the most—big surprise—were Paige and Steven, or… Nicholas. Paige was becoming less shy and spent more weekends hanging out with everybody else. She even continued to help Steven out with his work whenever he asked, despite their arrangement technically being over. She was finally letting her true self be more prominent around everybody.

Steven was able to keep his grades up and became more self-reliant when doing his homework and assignments. He even became more open to connecting with his foster parents, making more of an effort to be with the family and hold conversations with them.

Also, Lisa turned twelve. That's important to note.

Life for them had become significantly better. Whether directly or indirectly, they were all benefitting one another, even if it was unbeknownst to the rest of the school. Steven and Paige were still concerned with how their reputations could be shattered if word got out that they were friends, so they agreed to keep their word about staying secret. They even got the rest of their friends to take the pact: nobody knew about the *Avenger Initiative*, as Morgan put it. So as far as everybody else was concerned, these girls and these boys were complete strangers.

Months ago, Paige would've liked it to stay that way, but now she was starting to feel guilty. Steven had been stuck by a label, one she believed for two years and caused her to stay away from him at all costs. But then she met him. In her mind, Steven could bury all of that by showing everybody the sweet guy she had come to know. Until she reminded herself that she hadn't been very honest about who she was cither, which only added to her guilt. She just wished she and all her friends could be happy and accepted for who they were. But the world isn't perfect. At least, they could accept each other for who they were. That's what mattered, right?

Friday, March 17: English Homeroom, 8:42 AM

Paige's mom was reciting their latest lessons on *The Great Gatsby*.

"So when you really break it down, Jay Gatsby is an ideal of who James Gatz had always wanted to become. James was just a simple farm boy who had always wanted to become rich and famous. Gatsby is an embodiment of that dream he always had, and when he finally achieved this dream, he fully embraced that ideal he had and became it. But for your exit card today, I want you all to write a short paragraph about why he embraced this second personality as much as he did. Was it because James believed in Gatsby? Or because other people believed in Gatsby? Please take the next five minutes to write down your answers. I'm not looking for perfection. I'm only looking for an answer."

The class began to write down their answers.

While Paige was writing hers down, Morgan tapped her shoulder to get her attention and showed her phone's screen.

Morgan got a message from Steven:

> Jason wants to know if were still on for tomorrow night.
> I'm asking you cause I know she's not gonna answer til
> the end of the day.

Paige looked over at Steven who noticed her and acted completely clueless. "Tell him to tell Jason yes, *we're* still on," she whispered.

Morgan typed, "She says yes and that you're illiterate."

"Fuck You," he typed.

Morgan showed his reply.

"You or me?" Paige joked.

Morgan typed, "Me or her?"

Morgan this time peeked behind to look at him with a grin. Steven looked up from his phone and flipped her off. Morgan and Paige shared a quiet giggle. If there was anything they both enjoyed, it was making him feel stupid.

Paige was, as per usual, the first student to leave her work on her mom's desk. The rest of the students followed after.

"All right, well, since we have one minute left before bell, real quick I wanna go over your next assignment," Catherine said. Most of the students groaned after hearing that. "Oh, don't worry, you don't have to do it if you're okay with failing this marking period." The students who groaned went quiet. "Relax, this'll be fun." She moved to the next image on her smart board. "To go along with the themes of the book—specifically how Gatsby was a great inspiration to Nick—this weekend I want all of you to write an essay about someone who inspires you. Talk about who they are, what they do, how they inspire you, anything on the who, what, when, where, why, how criteria. Not only that, but throughout next week I'm going to call on you all randomly to come up here and share with everybody why this person inspires you so much." Once again, the class groaned, even louder. "Well, this counts as your final grade, so you better learn to get into it and have something prepared," she replied. "Anyway, this person can be anybody—a celebrity, historical figure, somebody in your family, a good friend, anyone who's had a really positive influence on you."

While she's talking, Morgan showed Paige another text from Steven reading, "I see where you get it from, Einstein." To which Paige shook her head and glanced back at him.

"On that note, we're about to hit dismissal time." Everybody stopped to listen. "And it's late again..." The bell rang. "There it is. Have a great weekend everyone!"

The students backed away from their desks and one by one emptied out. Paige and her mom shared a brief wink like they always did on her way out.

Steven, as usual, was the last one to hand his exit card in after everybody else left.

"Not so fast, you," Catherine said before he can leave.

"I didn't do whatever it was."

"Relax, you're not in trouble. Paige said she's having company over tomorrow, and I'm assuming that includes you?"

"What if it does?"

"Then I only want to let you know that me and her dad will be going out tomorrow, and we don't usually leave her alone like this, especially with this many other kids. It took some good convincing for her dad to agree. So we're trusting that you can all be responsible."

"I can assure you, neither of you will regret this. Your daughter's in good hands."

"I'm sure I won't. Look, I know you won't admit this, but you're a good young man, and you've shown that when you want to be responsible, you can be." Steven awkwardly shrugged at her compliments. "And just between us, you've had a really good influence on her. I've never seen her glowing the way she is now."

"What does that mean?"

"Oh, nothing. Just try to have a nice time tomorrow, all right?" Steven nodded. "Great, now you should really get to your next class. I'm done wasting your time," she said before going back to grading the exit cards.

"Allll right." Steven began to leave. "Hey, how come Morgan didn't get this same lecture?" he asked.

"I've known her much longer. She's heard this a number of times already. Hopefully someday she'll abide," she said before looking back down at her desk.

Steven left looking weirded out.

As he's walking through the hallway, he thought about what she just said and how similar it was to what Paige told him months ago.

"She really is her mother."

Later

The four girls were driving home from school in Jenn's car.

"Okay, thank you so much. ...You too. Bye-bye." Amy hung up her phone. "So three o'clock it is then."

"Guys, we really don't have to go through this much effort," Paige said.

"Paige, you only get one sweet sixteen, and we are gonna give you a great one!" Amy exclaimed. "And that begins tomorrow by getting you an amazing dress."

"We're meeting up with the guys tomorrow. Couldn't we at least do this a different day?"

"We have all day tomorrow and the rest of our lives to meet up with the guys. Your party's next Sunday. We should've done this much earlier. Why am I the only one taking this seriously?"

"Amy! You need to calm down," Jenn said from the driver's seat.

"I'm sorry. I just want this to be perfect for her."

"Shouldn't the party planners be the ones losing their minds?" Morgan asked from the passenger seat. Her seat was all the way back for her to lie down and her feet on the dashboard.

"Party planners don't pick out our dresses, so it's up to us if we all wanna look good!" Amy replied.

"Well, you don't gotta worry about me. I'm fucking beautiful," Morgan gloated.

"I swear, she just gets worse every time one of us has a party," Jenn said.

"Was she like this when you turned sixteen?" Paige asked Jenn.

"Yes. In fact, I didn't even wanna have a sweet sixteen. I only had one just so she'd shut up."

"And you said it was a nice time. You're welcome." Amy smirked. Jenn just rolled her eyes in response.

"I believe that. I mean, who could say no to a pretty face like that?" Morgan said, pointing at Amy, who then hid that she's starting to blush. "But yeah, remember how insane she went prepping us for mine? Oh my god! I remember the day of. My dress had this loose thread; and when I tried pulling it out, she came running with a scissor, slapped my hand away, and said, 'Don't do that, you dumbass!'" Morgan laughed. "And then when the hairdresser was running late, she decided to do my curls herself, and then he showed up, didn't realize the iron was plugged in, and he burned his hand and cried." Her laughter increased.

"All right! I get it! Sorry I care so much about the special occasions in my friends' lives!" Amy said.

Morgan's howling calmed down. "Chill out, bae, we're just fucking with you. We always appreciate the effort," she reassured her.

Amy fixed her hair, stressed out.

"God, can you imagine what she's gonna be like when she turns sixteen in July?" Morgan asked.

"Oh, pray for us all," Jenn answered.

Amy huffed.

"Amy, seriously, I'm not exactly crazy about having a sweet sixteen anyway. You don't have to lose your mind over me," Paige reassured her.

"Come on, Paige, lighten up. Remember how much fun Morgan's party was?" Amy reminded her.

"That was different. I don't like having all the attention on me. Besides, I've . . . never exactly had a birthday party before."

"Really?" Amy asked.

"Not even when you were a kid?" Morgan asked.

"Not really. I usually just celebrated it with my parents. The closest was when we spent a day in the park with this boy I used to know and his parents, but no, I've never had a real party," Paige confessed.

"Morgan?" Amy asked.

"Now that you mention it, I've known her since sixth grade, and I don't recall her ever going through crazy lengths to celebrate it."

"Okay, all writing's on the wall. We are going to fix that," Amy said.

"Amy—" Paige began.

"Nope! You are gonna have the best party of your life whether you want to or not, I swear it!"

"Why would you tell Amy this?" Jenn asked.

"It slipped out," Paige answered.

"All right, look, man, just take her advice and have a better attitude. You've earned it," Morgan said.

Paige sighed. "What time do we meet up for dress shopping?" she asked.

"Jenn and I can get you both around two-thirty, and don't worry, we'll have plenty of time for you to see Steven," Amy said.

Now Paige tried to hide her blush.

"This is gonna suck," Jenn said.

"Relax, Jenn, we'll get you a nice white tux and be back in time for you to see Jason too."

"Amy, shut the fuck up before I hit the brakes and make you slam your head on my seat," Jenn threatened.

Amy just giggled at her, along with the other two.

"You'll feel better tomorrow," Morgan said.

"And would you get your filthy-ass boots off my dashboard?!"

Morgan shrugged and then took her boots off, placing her socked feet back on the dashboard and putting her hands on the back of her head.

"You are such a dick."

Amy chuckled at Morgan's wiseass actions.

The Next Day

After an afternoon of fittings, the girls went back to Paige's house to get some time for themselves before Steven, Jason, and Lisa arrived. Their parents were going out that night too, so Steven asked Paige if she could join them. Of course, she said yes.

6:01 PM

Steven, Jason, and Lisa were heading to Paige's house.

"Yo, Jason, before we go inside, I don't know if she told you this, and I swore I wouldn't, but—" Steven started.

"I know. Your English teacher is her mother," Jason finished for him.

Steven was surprised. "When did you find that out?"

"Umm, today's Saturday so… two months ago."

"She told you two months ago and I've had to keep that secret from you for nothing?"

"She made me swear not to tell anybody."

"Oh my god," he said, rubbing his temple.

"Is this something I wasn't supposed to know either?" Lisa asked.

"I think you'll be fine. You don't go to our school anyway," Jason replied.

"Well, that's good. But I'll still keep it anyway. If she asked, I don't know a thing."

"You're a good kid, and a good copilot at that," Jason said.

Lisa replied with a wide smile.

"Yeah, remind me again why I'm in the back seat?" Steven asked.

"I called dibs," Lisa said.

"Sorry, bud, I just drive. I don't make my parents' rules," Jason added.

Steven groaned. "You people make me wanna kill myself," Steven replied.

Paige's House

The three of them arrived at the front door and were greeted by Paige.

"Hey, guys," she said, smiling.

"How's it goin', Paige?" Jason asked.

"I'm good. Hey, Lisa."

"Hello," Lisa replied.

"Well, come in." The three obliged and entered the house. "Everybody else is upstairs in my room."

"And we brought donuts!" Jason added, showing off the box.

"Oh, you guys didn't have to do that."

"Lisa insisted," Steven said.

"Our mom always says it's polite to bring treats when visiting someone else's house," Lisa replied.

"And any excuse I have to eat donuts is all right with me," Jason added.

"Well, thank you, all," Paige said.

"Uh, I paid for them," Steven said.

"Well, then thank you. That was very sweet of you," she teased him, pinching his cheek.

"Yeah yeah. Let it be known though, I only did because this guy left his wallet at his house."

"I didn't think taking it was necessary," Jason replied.

"You drove us!"

"Don't you keep your license in your wallet?" Lisa asked.

"Yeah," Jason answered.

"You drove here without your license?" Paige asked.

"I figured if he had his wallet, bringing mine would've been redundant," he answered.

"You're an idiot," Steven told him as Paige and Lisa chuckled.

"Steven! Great to see you." They're suddenly interrupted by Catherine.

"Hey, Catherine."

"Oh, you must be Lisa!"

"Yeah. Hi," Lisa replied, waving to her.

"Hi. You are so pretty."

"Thank you."

"And you're, Jason, right?" Catherine asked Jason.

"Uhh, yeah." Jason had seen her around school before; and seeing her for himself, even with the prior knowledge, surprised him. "Hey, Mrs. Curtis."

"Come on, when we're not in school, you can call me Catherine."

"S-Sure." Jason nodded in agreement.

"So, sweetie, your dad and I are about to leave. If there's any trouble, we're a call away."

"It's okay, Mom, we'll be fine."

"I know you will." Catherine kissed the top of her head. "We'll see you tonight." Paige nodded. "Richard, are you ready?" she called.

"I'm on my way," Richard said, entering from the kitchen. "Steven, how are you?"

"Well, aside from my friend here scheming me out of twenty bucks, fine."

"Ah yeah, been there," he replied before shifting his attention to the small preteen. "I take it you're his sister?"

She nodded. "Hmm-hmm. Hi, my name's Lisa."

"God bless you, Lisa. My name's Richard." He then turned to Jason, who's still distracted. "And you're…?"

"Wha—uh, Jason. I'm Jason," he answered, snapping out of his confused state.

"Jason," he said, shaking his hand. "God bless you."

"All righty, you kids have a good night," Catherine said.

"See you later, kiddo," Richard told his stepdaughter.

"Bye-bye," Paige said before they closed the door behind them.

"All right, we doin' this or what?" Steven asked.

"Yes. But before we do…" Paige went into her kitchen and returned with two sealed envelopes. "These are for you guys," she said, handing them to Steven and Jason.

"What are they?" Steven asked.

Paige motioned the two to open them.

Jason set the box down, opened his, and pulled out an invitation.

Jason began to read out loud, "'You're invited. Please join us Saturday, March 18th., for her sweet sixteen celebration.' Oh, say no more. I'm in!" Jason pulled her in for a one-armed hug, to which Paige laughed. Jason let go.

"Okay great, but ouch," Paige said while she rubbed her arm, still smiling.

"Sorry." Jason read more, as Steven stole a quick glance at the address. "Richfield Regency. Fancy. I've never heard of it," Jason said.

She shook her head. "Well, I also have a favor to ask you." Jason listened. "We're still looking to put a band together, and they need a bassist. You think you'd wanna do that?"

"Fuck yeah, I'll do that! Come here, you!" Jason pulled her in again, this time picking her up off the floor for a two-armed, tighter hug, hurting her again.

"Dude!" Steven exclaimed.

Jason let her go. "Sorry, sorry again. I've just never been afraid to express my feelings."

"It's fine." Paige laughed in between breaths. "Thank you. You don't know how much that means to me," Paige said.

"Aww, anything for my pal's lady friend." He put his arm around Steven, patting his chest.

"Get off me," Steven ordered, and Jason let go.

"Oh also, this invite is for your whole family, so please let them know."

"No prob. I'm sure they'd love to come."

"Great." She shifted her focus. "Steven?" she asked him.

Steven looked at her, noticing the anticipation in her face. "I mean, I don't really do this type of things…" he began, and her eyes started to widen. There was something about those eyes that could instantly soften him up, whether they were behind those glasses or not. "But after all we've been through, I'd be selfish to say no. I'll come," he answered.

"All right!" she said with much excitement. "Thank you!"

Steven nodded. "I'm sure my folks will be interested too."

"Great. I'd love them to be there too."

"Can I come?" Lisa asked.

"You'd better," Paige answered.

"Then I'm in." The girls laughed. "That means I gotta pick out a dress."

"Whatever you wear, I guarantee you'll look beautiful."

Lisa developed a large smile, which Paige returned.

"All right, as joyous as this moment is, are we actually gonna do stuff?" Steven asked.

"Sure, let's all head upstairs. Come on," Paige said, leading the way.

They made it to Paige's room where Jenn and Morgan were in the middle of a round of *Mortal Kombat X* with Amy as the lone spectator.

Jenn took a quick glance at them before looking back toward the screen. "Hey, took you guys long enough."

"Nice to see you too, Owens," Steven replied.

"Hey, Jenn, and the rest," Jason greeted them.

"Hey, guys. Hi, Lisa," Amy greeted them.

Lisa waved. "Oh, I got the winner!" she said before she ran and hopped onto Paige's bed to watch.

"Great. Now we can officially begin the night," Paige said.

"And just in time too. I'm about to kill Jenn!" Morgan said as she performed Johnny Cage's Fatality on Jenn's character. "HA! Un-touch-a-ble!"

"Whatever. Kid, do me a favor. Win the next match and shut her up," Jenn asked, handing the controller to Lisa.

"I'll do it," Lisa replied.

"All right, Lisa, show the MK goddess what you got," Morgan said.

"Bring it," Lisa said, selecting her character.

Everybody else surrounded the bed to face her TV.

"So, Paige..." Jason began. "Elephant in the room, you could've prepared me for meeting your mom."

"I told you about her."

"Yeah, but you forgot to mention she was also the hottest teacher in our school."

"Dude!" Steven slapped the back of his head.

"Ow!" Jason exclaimed before then being punched on the arm by Jenn. "Oww!"

"You don't just say that out loud, dipshit," Jenn commented.

"It was a compliment! Come on, she's not hitting me!" He then got flicked on the forehead by Paige. "OWW! Okay, I get it! I'm sorry, Paige!"

"It's fine. Just watch your words in the future," Paige told him.

"I swear on my bruising arm and migraine," he said, right before Morgan reached back to smack him on the chest. "OWWW!"

"Morgan!" Amy exclaimed.

"I didn't wanna feel left out," Morgan answered, focusing on the screen.

"Fucking hell," Jason said, annoyed.

"That's what you get for costing me money," Steven said, causing Jason to form a grumped expression.

It had been about an hour and a half to two hours of playing some games, joking around, having snacks and drinks, sharing laughs, Morgan and Amy filming Snapchat stories (making sure to exclude the boys), sharing YouTube videos on their phones, letting music play in the background, and gossiping—having a fun time all around without any concerns. Whenever this group was together, it was fun for everybody no matter what the circumstances were, and this was probably the most fun yet.

Paige and Jason were now up to play a round of *Mortal Kombat X* while the rest were spectating.

"Be careful, Paige, he likes to spam Ice Klone," Steven told her.

"He's one of those guys?" she asked.

"Yeah, just keep jumping over and go for your combos."

"Hey hey, don't give her advice!" Jason told him.

"Too late, Jason!" Paige replied.

The two had an intense match, Paige playing Erron Black, Jason playing Sub-Zero, with commentary from the rest of the party and Steven coaching her.

"Block block!" Steven told her, which she did, stopping Jason's ice blast.

"Steven, shut the fuck up!"

"Focus!" Jenn told him.

After a close final round, Paige landed the last hit as the rest of the room reacted. She performed Erron's Fatality, garnering more response.

"Bull-fucking-shit! I can't concentrate with Jiminy Cricket shouting in your ear what I'm about to do!" Jason screamed.

"Jason, calm down," Amy said.

"No! These two are cheating!" Jason ranted.

"Hey, who's the one playing as the cheapest character? I'm just evening the odds," Steven defended himself.

"You're being annoying and making me lose focus! Goddammit, everybody's trying to fuck me over because I'm so good!" Jason continued.

"Welcome to WatchMojo.com, and today we'll be counting down our picks for the Top 10 Video Game Rage Moments," Morgan said, breaking the silence and accompanied by laughs from the others.

"Shut up," Jason snapped back.

"Okay, on that very angry note, I'm gonna go get another drink," Paige said, getting up.

"Ooh, I'll join you," Steven said.

"Bring me back something?" Lisa asked.

"I got ya," Steven replied as the two headed downstairs.

"Don't take too long," Morgan whispered loud enough for the rest of them to hear, to which they chuckled, except for Jason.

"Aww, I think somebody needs a hug," Morgan teased, wrapping her arms around him.

"Don't touch me!" Jason said.

Morgan ignored his demand and hugged him. "Shhh shhh. It's okay, it's okay," she continued to tease him.

"You'll see, the sun will come out tomorrow," Amy joined, speaking in the same patronizing tone as Morgan and making it a group hug.

"We love you, Jason," Lisa said, adding herself in.

Jason's now-grumpy mood can be noticed through his frown.

The three girls turned their heads to Jenn, who's giving them an expression of cringe/judgment. She then rolled her eyes, moved closer to them, and patted Jason on the head.

"You'll be fine."

Jason retained his frown, refusing to make eye contact.

Kitchen

"Does he always get like this when he loses?" Paige asked Steven.

"If you thought that was bad, you should see him playing *Halo*."

They both laughed.

Paige opened her refrigerator. "Does iced tea work for you?"

"You sure you don't have any beer?"

"Yes, I'm sure."

"Eh, I guess so."

Paige giggled at his response.

She closed the fridge and set the pitcher on the counter. Steven observed the fridge's door and spotted the party invitation from earlier. He saw a picture of a younger blonde girl at the center of it.

"This you?"

She turned around to see him pointing at it. "Yeah. That was taken when I was three."

"Damn. You look so different here."

"I would hope so. I looked like Gollum."

"Well, some people think Gollum's cute."

"How reassuring," she sarcastically responded.

"I kid. You don't look so bad here."

"Well, it wasn't my first choice for a picture."

"Then why'd you choose it?"

"I didn't. My mom said, 'Well, if you don't want to choose the picture, then I will,' and poof."

"Ah. Seriously though, you look kinda cute here."

Paige giggled. "Thank you." She turned around to pour a drink, doubling as an excuse to hide her blush.

"Wait, so…" Steven began, and Paige turned back to face him. "This isn't natural?" he asked, referring to her brunette hair.

"Nope. I'm actually a blonde," she answered, handing him a drink.

"Wow. Why don't you go natural? You realize how many hot points you'll get?"

Paige awkwardly chuckled. "I'll pass. I don't care about attention. Besides, I like having brown hair."

"Whatever, just an idea. See if I care." He took a sip as Paige gave him a slight nod and poured her own drink.

Steven stared at the picture still sipping his cup when suddenly, something hit him.

He looked closer at her three-year-old face, feeling a sense of suspicion, and familiarity.

Paige turned back and noticed his intense focus. "What are you doing?"

Steven looked to her and quickly switched his view back and forth between Paige and Younger Paige. "Hey, did you go to PS 30?" he asked.

"No? Remember? Homeschooled?"

"Ah yeah, that's right."

"What's with you?"

"I just—I *swear*, I've seen this girl before?"

"Huh?"

"Stand right there," he said before opening the envelope she gave him.

"Steven, what are you doing?"

"Just hold still."

He took out his invite and held the photo up in a way where he can see it and Paige simultaneously. He took a long look before shifting his eyes back and forth, trying to look for any sort of similarities. But between the quality of the picture and how different Paige looked now, they may as well have been two totally different people.

"Why can't I piece this!" He aggravatingly hit himself on the head.

"All right, stop doing that." She grabbed his wrist with her free hand.

"I've seen this girl somewhere before. I know it. I just don't know where or when!"

"Steven!" Paige exclaimed, still holding on to his wrist as tight as she could. She let go when he recuperated. "There you go. Now, there are lots of girls that look like this. You're just confusing me for someone else."

"And... you're *sure* we've never met before?"

241

"I'm sure I would remember meeting somebody like you. How are you so certain about this?"

"I don't know. But when I look at this picture, it feels like some ghost from my past is looking at me. A ghost of someone I haven't seen in a long time." He stared at it for a bit, completely mystified.

Steven turned back at her.

"Look at me."

"Steven, I—"

"Just look at me. Really look me in the eye and tell me nothing seems familiar to you."

"You're thinking way too strongly about this."

"Please."

Paige was hesitant, but she could tell this was important to him, enough that he said the word "please." So she took a deep breath and did what he asked.

The two of them shared a long, intense stare, not saying a word. It felt like everything else around them just faded away into nothingness, except for each other. After a couple of seconds, Paige now started to feel bewildered. She'd looked him in his eyes several times before, but something about this time felt different. Now that she had taken a long-enough look with Steven's hypothesis in mind, she developed a similar vibe comparable to what he was talking about. Something this time was recognizable, but she wasn't sure what it was. Was he on to something?

Paige put up her glasses and looked deeper, like she was investigating his soul. She was reminiscing of her past for any sort of connection, some memory to trigger, but to no avail. As for Steven, this only raised his suspicion; he was practically lost in the bright orbs peeking out of her face, illuminating a sense of intimacy.

"Well?" Steven softly asked.

"I, I don't know what it is, but you're right. I... I do feel something. Almost like ...something locked away just escaped. But it was locked away for so long I don't recognize it. Whatever it is," Paige confessed.

"What do you think it is?"

Paige stepped in toward him; enough distance was closed to where they could practically feel each other's body heat.

"I think—"

"Yo, guys, I just wanted to apolo-o-o-o-o—what the hell did I just walk in on!" Jason interrupted, shattering the plane of existence they were stuck on.

"Nothing! Nothing!" Paige panicked as she put her glasses back on, trying to regain her composure.

"Oh, for fuck's sake, what do you want?" Steven asked.

"I was just gonna apologize for freaking out, that's all. I didn't mean to intrude on …this… personal moment." Jason said, defending himself.

"It isn't like that! I swear on my life nothing was happening! We were just, just…" Paige started to get hot and was blushing so hard she thought her glasses might fog up.

"Apology accepted. Would you just go?" Steven told him.

"All right all right, I'll just leave you two be until you're good and ready." Jason slowly backed up, with a suggestive tone of voice.

"And quit talking like that! We weren't doing anything!" Steven said, feeling embarrassed.

While this was going on, Paige set aside her embarrassment and watched their confrontation unfold.

"Relax, bro, you don't have to be so embarrassed. I've seen you do a lot of—"

"QUIET!" he cut him off. "JUST GET OUT OF MY FACE!"

Paige's eyes widened when she heard him say that.

All of a sudden, she flashed back to when she was younger:

> "Nikko, you're hurting me!"
> "GET OUT OF MY FACE!"

This memory echoed over and over, cross-fading with Steven's voice saying the same phrase. Paige then let out a large gasp, getting his attention.

"What?" Steven turned to face her.

Paige looked into his eyes again, now realizing why they looked so familiar.

She dropped her cup on the floor and immediately backed away from him toward her kitchen counter, terrified.

"YOU!"

"What? What'd I do?" Steven asked, walking toward her.

"Stay the fuck away from me!" she blurted out, moving away from him.

"Paige, what's the matter with you?"

"Okay, where'd this come from?" Jason asked.

At that moment, Jenn, Morgan, and Amy all came in.

"What the hell's going on down here?" Jenn asked, to which Jason just shrugged and gave a look of confusion.

"You're right, I have seen you before! I know exactly who you are!" Paige said.

"You do? Well, from where?" Steven asked.

"Don't act like you don't know! Nikko!" The tone of her voice turned from scared to angry.

Steven was struck. "How—wha—why did you call me that?"

Paige's expression changed, and her eyes went cold. "Look at me again and keep pretending you don't know," she said with resentment.

Steven looked deeply at her again as the rest of their friends watched on, confused and concerned.

The spiteful look on her face suddenly flashed to a vision of a smiling little blonde girl calling him Nikko, the same girl who's in the photo. At that moment, all the feelings of familiarity she brought him since the very beginning added up.

Steven's jaw dropped, and he can only utter one word.

"MIRANDA?"

Paige continued to stare at him, her face unchanged.

"Miranda?" Morgan asked.

"What is going on?" Amy reiterated.

"Miranda ...it's really you?" Steven asked, slowly walking toward her.

"I said get away from me, Nikko!" she repeated, moving away again.

"Miranda, please—"

"Shut up, you monster!" she demanded, moving closer her friends.

"What did you do to her?" Jenn aggressively asked.

"What are you guys doing?" Lisa suddenly interrupted.

"Lisa, I said to stay upstairs!" Amy told her.

"But why are Steven and Paige—"

"Lisa, stay out of this," Steven demanded, silencing her. "I can explain everything, I swear, just let me—" Steven began.

"No! You don't get to do anything anymore! After what you did to me, I never wanna see you again! Take your sister, and your apologist, and get out of my house!" she said. Her face was crimson red, tears were spilling out of her eyes, and her voice cracked.

"Please, I'm sorry!"

"No, you're not!" Paige screamed and started walking up to him. "Now get out now before I—"

"Paige, watch your feet!" Morgan warned.

Paige slipped on the iced tea she spilled on the floor and fell forward, only to be caught by Steven.

Her anger turned back into fear when she looked up and back into his eyes. She attempted to run, but Steven held on to her wrists. She began to squirm, attempting to escape his grasp, but couldn't overpower the larger boy.

"I don't wanna hurt you! Just please listen to me!" Steven begged.

"NO! LET ME GO! LET ME GO!" she screamed.

"Dude, let her go!" Jason told him.

"You have to calm down!" he shouted at her.

"YOU'RE HURTING ME!" she screamed again while everybody watched in fear or anger, excluding Lisa who looked like she was about to cry.

Finally, Paige brought her foot up and kicked him where it hurts most. Steven instantly let go to favor where she made contact, and she lost her balance, moving backward. She fell down, and the back of her head collided with the edge of her glass kitchen table, causing her to immediately hit the floor.

"Oh my god, Paige!" Morgan immediately rushed to her aid, followed by her other friends, including Lisa and Jason.

Steven looked up and immediately forgot about the pain he was feeling. All he could do was put his hands on his head, as he became overwhelmed with guilt seeing he had hurt her, again.

"Miranda?" he asked, quietly but loud enough to be heard.

Jenn turned her head to him and pounced on him, forcing him against the wall. Steven didn't make any attempt to resist.

"I'M GONNA FUCKING KILL YOU!" Jenn screamed.

Before she can land the first punch, Jason intervened, grabbing her wrist.

"Jenn Jenn Jenn, don't do it!"

She quickly wrestled him to the floor and put him in a high wrist hold. Jason quickly tapped out, writhing in pain.

"YOU'RE NOT PROTECTING THIS FUCKING BASTARD!" she shouted, attempting to break his arm.

"Jenn, stop it!" Amy shouted.

"ARE YOU FOR REAL, AMY?" Jenn replied.

"Forget them! Paige needs help!"

"SHE CAN RIDE IN AN AMBULANCE WITH HIM!" She wrenched his arm.

"Jenn! Look at you! You're not even hurting the right guy! He didn't do anything!" Morgan added.

Jenn looked down at Jason and realized what she's doing. She looked back over to Steven who's just standing there watching, completely frozen. Jenn still wanted to hurt him but then looked over to her friends, and to Paige who'd fallen unconscious and was losing blood.

She agitatedly let go of the hold and stood up.

Jenn looked over to Steven. "You're not worth it." Steven didn't reply. She then looked down to Jason and picked him off the ground. "Neither of you are worth it." She threw down his hand and shoved him to where Steven was standing. "Get her into my car. We need to get her to the hospital," she said, tossing a hand towel from the kitchen sink's counter to them, before leaving the house to start her car.

"Let me come with." Steven finally spoke up.

"No!" Morgan said. "She said get away from her, so get away from her!" She said it in a tone none of them had ever heard her speak in before. "We're done with you."

"Girls, I never meant to—"

"Steven!" Amy cut him off as she's pressing the hand towel against where Paige was bleeding. "Or Nikko, or whatever your name is. You've done enough, so just leave her alone. Please," she said with sorriness in her voice, as she and Morgan picked Paige up off the floor and began to walk toward the door.

Before he can say anything else, Jason stopped him, shaking his head no.

Defeated, Steven stayed in place.

Lisa followed the girls outside, worrying about Paige, to watch as Morgan and Jenn got her in the back seat of Jenn's car. Morgan sat on the far end of the back seat and let Paige's head rest on her lap. Amy came out of the house with an ice pack and gave Lisa a quick reassurance that she'll be okay before she got in the passenger seat up front, and they drove off, leaving Lisa where she stood.

They didn't notice Steven was watching from the front door, absolutely distraught by what just happened. By what he had destroyed.

Chapter 21

Full Circle

After Midnight

Paige woke up hours later in the emergency room. Her vision was blurry, and she could only hear the faint echo of a ringing phone. She tried sitting up but instantly became woozy, then felt a pulse where she hit her head and reached back to feel fresh stitches close to her scar, flinching upon contact.

"Here." She opened her eyes and noticed a hand in front of her offering a pill. She turned over to see Morgan's face. "Doctor said to give you this when you woke up."

Paige looked around to realize she was lying down on a bed in a plain white room, her only company being Morgan and Amy. She was confused and feeling head trauma.

She took the pill from Morgan's hand, and Amy then handed her a fresh water bottle, and she took a sip to help her swallow it.

"Your mom and dad are on their way," Amy said.

"What happened to me?" Paige asked, groaning.

"You hit your head on your dinner table," Morgan answered.

Paige groaned again. "How did I do that?"

"It wasn't your fault. You were assaulted by that hotheaded, DeviantArt-looking, dead-cow-wearing, deceiving stupid son of a—" Morgan said, raising her voice.

"Morgan! Shhh," Amy interrupted. "Paige? What's the last thing you remember?" she asked.

248

Paige laid her head back and thought. "Umm, we were all at my house. Steven was there with Jason and Lisa. Me and him went downstairs into my kitchen, and then I was looking at blurs."

"Hmm. Well, there was a little altercation that happened."

"Huh? What was it? Where's Steven?"

Amy looked over at Morgan.

"You wanna tell her? Or should I?' Morgan asked. Amy motioned her hand, telling Morgan to keep it down.

"Paige? Who's Nikko?"

Paige's eyes grew wide hearing that name. "Why—who—how did you hear that name?" she asked.

"That's what you were calling Axl before you got hurt," Morgan answered.

Paige suddenly began to recall what happened, and her mood saddened.

"That's right. Now I remember." Paige sighed and buried her face in the palms of her hands. "I thought I was rid of him forever."

"So his real name is Nikko?" Morgan asked.

Paige nodded.

"Well, I see why he chose Steven Axl, 'cause that is the dumbest name ever," Morgan spit.

"Morgan!" Amy exclaimed.

"I'm just saying. Anyway, going back to her question, who is he?"

"It's a long story," Paige answered in a melancholy tone.

"We're listening," Morgan said.

"But you don't have to say anything if you don't—" Amy said.

"No, no, it's fine. It's out in the open now, so might as well." Paige sighed. "Nikko, or Steven, he was..." She paused. "He was my best friend. My only friend." Morgan and Amy both gave off looks of shock. "When I was a kid, him and I lived in the same apartment complex. We grew up together..."

Paige went into every detail about their preexisting relationship. Everything she confessed to Steven, she was now confessing to them, but this time in a whole new context.

"And sure enough, we ended up in the same class without even knowing. You three know the rest from there," Paige finished.

"Wow. I don't believe it. I'm so sorry, Paige. Or... Miranda," Amy said, getting no response.

"So he was the one who...?" Morgan asked, touching the back of her own head.

"Yep, and now..." Paige touched the back of her head. "He's done it to me again." Paige began to get emotional and covered her face with her hands. "I'm so stupid. How could I not recognize him?" She began to sob.

"Come here." Amy got up from her chair to hug her from the edge of her bed. Paige leaned her head into Amy's shirt and released what had spilled out of her broken heart.

Morgan watched this, still seated in her chair. Amy looked to her, waiting for her to join her in comforting her best friend. But Morgan just sat there with an unreadable expression. She turned in her seat and stood up to walk out the door.

Amy continued to look at the doorway after she left, going back and forth between confused and disappointed.

Amy tightened her hug. "It's going to be okay. ...It's going to be okay," Amy tried to reassure her, even though she herself was uncertain.

Her comment, however, just caused Paige to continue crying.

After a minute of bawling, Paige released herself from Amy's arms. Her face was completely drenched with tears. "I wanna see my mom and dad," she wheezed.

"They'll be here. Soon." Amy handed her a tissue.

Paige wiped her face and sniffled. "Where's Jenn?" she asked softly.

Amy huffed. "She drove us here. But she told us she needed to get her car home before midnight."

"Did ...did she do anything?"

Earlier

Jenn managed to keep herself serene long enough to drive them to the hospital, but on her trip home—with the thought of Paige's condition occupying her mind—all that anger she felt came back. She was known for having a short temper and would even admit it, but this was a level of frustration she had never felt. Had she been given the chance, she probably would've killed Steven back there. She most definitely would've broken Jason's arm if not talked out of it. In the end, however, there was only one hospitalization tonight, the person who deserved it the least; it was what she kept telling herself. As she replayed what happened in her head again and again, all that rage came back, and her driving became more reckless. She was speeding through stop signs, going over the speed limit, slamming her brakes in barely enough time to stop herself from running red lights, or worse colliding with other vehicles. Fortunately, there weren't that many cars heading into Brooklyn at this hour, but the few that were, were endangered.

She made it home without an accident just a few minutes before midnight struck. Her parents still weren't home to hear her forcefully open and close the door before stomping her way upstairs to her room. She slammed the bedroom door shut behind her, and she pounded her fist against it as hard as it would've been if she was punching Steven, leaving a dent in it to go with the ones that were already there and causing her knuckle to start to bleed.

She picked her phone out of her pocket, hoping to see a notification from either Morgan or Amy giving an update on Paige, but there wasn't. Her anger subsided, as she then felt a sense of worry—for a brief moment—before her phone started vibrating. She quickly looked at her screen and saw it still wasn't either of them; it was instead the last person she wanted to hear from right now.

Incoming Call: Jason

Jenn, out of anger, tossed her phone across the room, which hit the wall and landed on her bed. She was in no mood to talk to him after that. Why would he even want to talk to her after she just tried to break his arm? Whatever the reason, she didn't care; she just grabbed a towel and headed for the shower, leaving her phone behind to go the voicemail.

"Hey, Jenn. It's me. I get it, you don't wanna talk. I wouldn't want to me either..."

Elsewhere

The ride home for Steven, Lisa, and Jason was as quiet as Jenn's. Nobody bothered to speak a word. They just stayed in their individual minds reflecting on the series of events that unfolded; the only sounds being heard were the ones emanating from their car or any other ones passing by.

After dropping off Steven and Lisa, Jason headed home accompanied by the same disturbed silence.

When they got inside, Steven didn't greet their parents; he just went upstairs to his room, leaving Lisa downstairs. Steven used to do this all the time, but these last three months he was saying hello consistently enough or at least was acknowledging them. At this moment, however, he didn't want to acknowledge anything. The only difference is that this time he wasn't feeling anger, resentment, or disinterest; this time, he just felt guilty. Guilty and depressed.

Minutes turned into hours as he sulked in the darkness of his room, sitting there on his bed with so many things to comprehend and reflect on. A lot was put into hindsight, as the weight of what he did became heavier with all those passing thoughts. For the first time in his life, he felt happy, and he had just sent his one source of that happiness to the hospital with a bloody skull. Again. He now felt in his heart that he would never be happy ever again, for in one night, he lost his new best friend, his old best friend, and... the girl he fell in love with.

Chapter 22

Shattered Reality

Paige's parents picked her up from the hospital late that same night and were filled in on what happened. She was diagnosed with a concussion, and the doctor recommended she'd stay home for at least five days to recover. After making it home, she immediately went to bed; her mom stayed with her overnight while her stepdad brought Amy home, who had been trying to get a hold of Morgan since she seemingly disappeared on them.

It's suggested when you receive a concussion to only sleep a certain number of hours at a time, but that wasn't going to be the case for Paige because she didn't get a second of sleep that night. All she could do was think about Steven/Nikko; the visual of him grabbing her wrists and shouting at her replayed on a loop, along with the resurged memory of when he hurt her on the playground, to a point where both those memories were converging. When it wasn't either of those, it was of every other memory she built with him over the past few months interspersed to make it more painful.

It's tragic how in the span of a few hours somebody can go from your best friend to the person you hate most, how all the great times you shared and cherish now promptly become bleak memories; it makes those happy times now feel excruciating. This marathon of thoughts haunted her all through the night, making her already aching head feel more pained. The only thing that was hurting more was her heart.

Sunday, 7:00 PM

Steven had spent the entire day in bed, listening to the next depressing song that played on Spotify; the one that spoke to him the most was "I've Given Up on You" by Real Friends.

> I've given up on you, but it still hurts to know you're not alone.
> Don't worry, I'll keep out of your life and stay awake at night.
> With just my skin and bones.
> It hurts to know you're not alone.
> I've given up on you, and my skin, and my bones.

He's listened to these kinds of songs hundreds of times, for no reason other than to just have something playing in the background while he did stuff; but for the first time, he was connecting with them. You never understand songs about a heartbreak until you experience one; it then went from sounding like something you overhear in a side conversation at a bar to feeling like somebody is talking directly to you, saying that they know what you're going through.

He felt broken. He felt lonely. He felt like he had been shrouded by a black cloud. It was something he hadn't felt since his mom died. In that same regard, he went through all the stages of confronting death: denial, anger, bargaining, sadness, eventually reaching the acceptance phase. Accepting that he'd never be loved by anybody and that everyone would only see him as a "stubborn, selfish, narcissistic, egotistical jackass." He never cared if anyone felt that way about him, but that's only because he never realized how true it was until the night Paige slapped and yelled at him using those adjectives. He wanted to change all that, but it was in vain. Ultimately, he just thought to himself, *What's the point?*

Monday, 8:45 AM, English Homeroom

Neither Paige nor Steven had showed up in class that morning. The old Steven was known for frequent cutting, but lately he had been in regularly. As for Paige, her perfect attendance record no longer stood.

Class went on as was originally planned, with students presenting their projects on who inspired them, but there was a noticeably different feeling in the environment. Mrs. Curtis didn't seem like her normal self; she did her job like usual but with a different kind of mood. She wasn't as engaging with her students as she'd normally be.

Morgan was in class as well but was so disengaged in what was going on and devoid of any wit that she always had, there might as well have been a ghost sitting at her desk. She had felt drained since that weekend's incident and sat as still as a ninja in the dark, occasionally glancing at the empty desk right beside her, or at Mrs. Curtis, trying to read her expression in hopes of getting an idea of what her best friend might be going through. She didn't dare glance backward at the empty desk in the far back of the room. Just the sight of where Axl once sat would infuriate her.

The bell rang, and Morgan made sure she was the first one out, refusing to engage with Mrs. Curtis or anybody else.

She made her way down the stairwell to her next class. When she opened the door to the second floor, she found herself bumping into Amy. Normally her face would brighten up to see hers, but now it was like taking a shank in the gut. Once she got over the surprise, she tried to walk away from her; but Amy grabbed her wrist, stopping her from doing so.

As the late bell rang and the hallways cleared out, Amy dragged her back into the stairwell. Under different circumstances, this would be one of Morgan's fantasies come to life, but now it felt like a scene out of a TV thriller.

"We need to talk," Amy started, still holding on to the other girl's wrist.

"We're late," Morgan replied.

255

"I don't care," Amy stated. Once Morgan saw the urgency in her eyes, she stopped resisting. Amy let go. "First of all, why'd you leave the hospital like that?"

"What do you mean?"

"I mean the way you just walked out on me and Paige so abruptly."

"Do we really need to talk about this here?"

"Yes. You haven't answered any of my phone calls, voicemails, or text messages. I DM'd you on everything. I even sent you an email, so now we're talking about this here," she said in an aggravated tone.

"Don't take it personally. I'm ghosting everybody."

"Why? I know a lot happened this weekend, but this isn't the time to shut us all out, especially her."

"Look, I just need to get away."

"That wasn't an answer."

"I just have to."

"Why? Just tell me!" Amy demanded.

"Because it's my fault!" Morgan snapped. "Is that an answer? Is that what you wanted to hear me say? I did this to her! She's hurt because of me!" Morgan began to huff, and her face glowed red.

Amy looked at her, confused. "How is this your fault? What are you talking about?"

Morgan was still huffing as she began to explain. "She talked to me the first night she started tutoring him. She knew going back to him was a bad idea. She knew she should've never kept taking those gigs, but I influenced her to keep going. I told her to stand up for herself, and now she's got two scars on the back of her skull. …It's all my fault." Morgan stopped for a brief time as the tears built in her eyes, not looking at her. "She was the first real friend I ever had. She encouraged me to let everybody know I'm gay, and I encouraged her to play Russian roulette. And why? Because I wanted her to get some dirt on him? Because I thought it'd be funny to discover some wild secrets he might have? Well, that happened all right, and now I wish I didn't know anything about him!" She huffed. "She should've just flipped him off, tell him to go fuck himself and leave. But I made her a pawn for my own selfish wants. It's what I always do. That's why I left. I just couldn't stand to see her like that."

A few tears rolled down her face.

"Morgan." Amy lifted her chin with her hand. "You can't blame yourself for this. I mean, how do you think I feel? I knew that this was a bad idea, and I wish I could've done something to stop her too. But it doesn't matter now. She needs all of our support. We can't blame ourselves for what someone else did," she said before sulking. "We-we shouldn't worry about what could've been. Just have to move forward until we make another mistake that'll tear us down. Wait until someone else comes along, lies to us about who they are until they inevitably hurt us, and then repeat it again and again even though we should've learned by now. It happens to all of us. It was bound to happen to her sooner or later!" Amy went off.

Morgan now looked confused. She wiped the tears away from her own face before speaking.

"I can tell that I'm really triggering something in you. I'm sorry."

"No, don't be sorry. Don't be sorry to anybody for something that isn't your fault. We weren't the ones that hurt Paige."

"Miranda. ...Her name is Miranda," Morgan said in a somber tone.

"Not the point. You wanna show you're a real friend? Well, right now, she needs us. So you can't shut us out."

Morgan sighed. "I know I shouldn't. But I just can't fathom how this is affecting her. Never mind the concussion, there's no telling how much damage Axl or Nikko or Artist Formerly Known As Whatever has done to her mentality. When she comes back—if ever—is she going to start acting different? Looking different? Treating us different? What if she shuts us out? How are we supposed to be there for her then? What can we even do to help her after all of this?"

Amy didn't reply.

"Answer!" Morgan said.

"I don't know!" There's a long moment of silence between them. "All I do know is she's a great friend and has always been there when we needed her. She was always around to help me, whether it was with geology, or to comfort me after every breakup I've gone through since I came to this school. Before then, I never had any friends who would've done that."

257

"Oh, don't talk like that. You're worshiped like a goddess around here, by everyone."

"Those aren't friends—those are peers."

"What about your gymnastics teammates?"

"You just answered your own question. Teammates. Not friends. If I wasn't such a big asset to the team, they wouldn't care about me. If I didn't look the way I did, nobody would care about me." Amy paused. "The truth is, before you girls came into my life, no amount of popularity changed how alone I was feeling. All the time." Now Amy was the one who was developing tears. "You all make me feel so loved and happy and… I don't know, I guess I just wanted to make sure you all felt that same love. The happiest I've ever seen her was whenever she was with Steven, so I put my resentment towards him away, and now she's hurt… so much worse than I ever have, by anyone."

Amy couldn't hold her feelings in any longer. She walked toward Morgan, gripped her shoulders, buried her face in her neck, and broke down.

Morgan remained silent, wanting to relieve Amy, but was still consumed by her own emotions. With being left muted, she pulled the taller girl in for a warm embrace and let her own tears drip down her face.

They stayed like this for a while before pulling away, still clinging to each other and glaring into their teared faces. "I'm sorry." Amy wiped away Morgan's tears. "I'm supposed to be the one comforting you."

"It's okay." They let go, and Amy wiped her own face. "You're right though. She needs us," Morgan said.

Amy just nodded and agreed with her.

"You feeling better?"

"Kind of. You?" Amy returned the question.

"I just hope we'll all be okay."

"Me too."

There's a tension between them following that intimate moment.

"You're also wrong," Morgan said, befuddling Amy. "The way you look isn't what makes you beautiful. That's only a coincidence. You're beautiful because you're so amazing. You're cool, you're fun, you're nice, you're caring, you're talented, you've got an adorable laugh, a great taste in movies, and I'm tired of people making you feel like you're hot and nothing more, because there's so much more to you than I can list. If anything, your beauty on the outside can't even do justice of your beauty on the inside."

Amy was taken aback by her words.

"Morgan, that's... that's really sweet of you to say."

"It's true. Anyone who can't see that is an idiot. You're the best. You're number one."

Amy bit her lower lip. "You know something? Paige really has been such a bright spot in my life. But... the best part of being her friend is... that I got to meet you too."

Morgan warmly smiled. "Really?"

Amy nodded. "Yeah," she said, matching her smile.

"Guess you owe her one then." Amy gave a light giggle. "And I guess I owe her for that too."

Amy's smile grew bigger. "Actually, I do feel a little better."

"Great. So do-so do I."

The tension increased as the two tried to read each other's faces.

Amy cleared her throat. "We should, uh, probably get back to class."

"But..." Amy waited for Morgan to continue. "Never mind, I'm being stupid. I'll... see you later."

Morgan began to leave, but before she walked through the door, she heard Amy call to her. "Wait." Morgan turned around. "One more thing."

"What is it?"

"Umm. Morgan?" She walked to her, getting as close to her as she was a minute ago. "I've... been doing a lot of thinking, and I'm beginning to think that... that maybe... I feel like I might be... or I guess I should say that I..." She moaned. "Goddammit," she said with her face buried in her trembling hands.

"You what?"

"I... Forget it. It's nothing."

"I can tell it's something. Say it."

"No, really, I'm just making this all about me. Go to class."

Before she can respond, Amy was rushing up the stairs to her next class. Morgan stood motionless, desperately wishing she heard the rest of that. The way Amy spoke and her mannerisms were familiar from experience. She swore she was about to hear her say what she'd always dreamed of hearing her say. But she brushed it off and began walking toward where she was supposed to be minutes ago. She could hear the door on the next floor open and close as her sour mood returned.

Amy stopped moving when she was in the hallway on the other side of the door. She was starting to sweat, her breathing was heavy, her face was hot, her hands were still shaking, and she felt a pain in her chest, like her bloodstream to her heart was clogging up before it entered all at once. She felt a sense of relief that was outweighed by feelings of shame, frustration, and disappointment; it made her feel like a coward. Amy had been going through this for months now, but this time—in that moment—she knew she couldn't deny it anymore...

Amy went to her second-period class and couldn't for the life of her focus on a single thing that went on. She knew whatever she was feeling she had to talk to somebody, right now.

After going to her third class, she waited a few minutes after the late bell, went to her teacher, and desperately asked them for a pass. When the teacher asked what was wrong, she was ready to abandon this plan, but managed to successfully lie and whisper as quietly as she could that it's "her time." Without hesitation, the teacher handed her the pass, and she left the room; she played it up perfectly as it looked like she was emotionally falling apart and in pain, probably because she really was, so that helped.

She went to the bathroom and locked herself inside one of the stalls. She put her earbuds in before dialing her phone, putting it to FaceTime.

She called her mom and dad. The both of them answered as quick as they could and saw that their daughter was on the brink of tears.

"Amy?" her mom asked.

"Mom? Dad? Can you hear me?" Amy asked, her voice cracking.

"Yeah, I hear you."

"Me too. Where are you?" her dad asked.

"I'm at school."

"What's going on there? Did something bad happen?" her dad asked.

"Are you all right?" Her mom panicked.

"No, no, nothing bad happened. It's fine. But no, I'm not all right. I really need you two right now."

"What is it?" her mom asked.

"Are you hurt?" her dad asked.

"No. Kind of. I don't know how to explain it."

"Well, just tell us," her mom asked.

Amy sniveled. "Just... Before I tell you guys, just promise me you won't be ashamed and that you'll still love me."

"Baby, of course we will," her mom assured her.

"Nothing you say will change that. Now what is it?" her dad said.

Amy took a deep breath. "I, uh... I think that I like Morgan, and not just as a friend. That I'm... attracted to her and ...I want to be her girlfriend."

"Amy...?" her mom asked, surprised.

Her dad looked just as surprised.

"Yeah. I think so, and I had to tell someone, but I can't tell her." Amy wept. "Please don't be mad." Her voice cracked, and she wept again, closing her eyes.

"Amy. Amy, open your eyes," her dad told her, and she did as he asked. "How could you think we'd be mad at that?"

"I just... I didn't know if you'd be—"

"Baby," her mom interrupted. "We don't care what you are or who you feel attracted to. All that matters to us is what makes you happy."

"Well, I'm not happy. So much has been going on lately. Paige is hurt, Morgan's blaming herself for what happened, I still don't know where Jenn is, it feels like all my friends are drifting apart, and now I'm just scared, depressed, confused, and not even sure who I am anymore," she whimpered.

"Aww, Amy, it's okay," her mom said. "I understand you're really upset, but I'm sure everything's going to be fine. You girls are so inseparable."

"But let's stick to the subject. Tell us, when did you start to feel like this?" her dad added.

"Back in December. The day we went to the mall. That was the first time we ever hung out together—just the two of us—and I guess, I never really knew her until then. I felt like we clicked better than I have with any guy. She just really understood me and didn't treat me like I was something to brag about, like I was a friend first. Even though it wasn't a date, to me it felt like one, and I don't want to go on a date with anybody else because nothing will compare to how I felt that day. I want to feel like that again and again."

"Well, I don't think you're confused. I think you're just realizing something about yourself that you never considered," her dad said.

"Amy, the truth is you're only fifteen, and nobody knows who they really are at that age. You're still getting older, and as you get older, you'll still have to figure stuff out. Some more complicated than others. But for now, I am just so happy for you, for realizing this now when you did." Her mom started to tear up.

"So am I. I'll admit I'm surprised, but I'm relieved that you're not in danger. When you're not home, all I want is to know that you're happy, and of course, I accept whatever makes you that. However you identify yourself, we'll always identify as your parents who love you."

Amy finally managed to smile. Though it was a light on, it was enough to show her spirits were lifted.

"Thank you, Daddy. You too, Mom. And I'm sorry for scaring you both."

"It's okay, baby. We're just glad you're safe," her mom said. "So what about Morgan?"

"I don't know."

"Does she like you? 'Cause she's made it very clear what she's about," her dad said.

Amy chuckled. "I, uh …think she and everybody else have been trying to tell me she does. If she does, then she won't say it."

"Well, then maybe you should say it to her," her dad suggested.

"I can't."

"Well, somebody has to."

"No, I mean, not right now. Not with everything that's going on …and even then, even if our friendships survive this, we might end up destroying them all by doing that."

"Amy," her mom began, "as I said, you girls are inseparable. Things will work out. And if you and Morgan feel that strong about each other, then it'll survive, and you two will make it work."

"So how do you feel?" her dad asked.

"Better. But I'm still not so sure."

"Well, how about you girls work on getting everything together first and see how you feel then?" her mom suggested.

She wiped her eyes. "I think for now I should get back to class."

"You sure you don't need anything else?" her dad asked.

"No. I'm okay. But thank you so much. I'm sorry for distracting you from work."

"Not at all," her mom said.

"Just take care of yourself," her dad added.

"We love you."

"And we're proud of you, our brave girl."

Amy sniffed. "I love you too." She blew them a kiss and waved goodbye before hanging up.

Amy stayed there for a bit before getting up and leaving the stall.

She stopped at the mirror to wipe her face and fix her makeup, the whole time thinking about Morgan. Though she's still uncertain if this should happen and what may potentially come of it, she could now at least think of her lovingly.

Wednesday Night

The last two days went at a length that felt like two weeks. Paige still didn't come into school, and despite her friends offering to come visit her, she told them that she didn't want to disrupt their lives. She just wanted to be alone and kept using her concussion as an excuse why they shouldn't do so. That, however, didn't stop them from messaging her, only to be given either vague responses or no response at all. Her parents kept checking in on her but were met by a lack of engagement. She just laid in her bed, shutting herself out from the rest of the world that seemed so much darker now than how she already perceived it. She'd been waiting for the day she could just go away to college and make something out of the life of dread she was living. But now, she didn't even want this life anymore.

Meanwhile, Steven hadn't come in for school either. Any messages sent to him would get no response whatsoever, not even a reading. He wasn't motivated to do anything, not even to work out. All he did was lock himself away in his room, disregarding his family, overwhelmed by his guilt.

Knock-knock.

"Steven?" He heard Lisa's call from the other side of the door but didn't answer.

Lisa let herself in. "Hey. Mom told me to come up here and let you know she made lasagna." She spoke in an irritated tone. He snubbed her. "I take it by your cold moody silence that you don't care?" Still no response, prompting her to sigh. "So this is it then? You're just gonna sit here for the rest of your life? Not even gonna try and fix what you did? Is that what you're gonna do?"

"There's nothing I can do. It's over," he answered aloofly.

"So then you're just gonna obsess over it? Live the rest of your life being a miserable jerk that's locked himself in his room?"

"That's the life I'm used to."

"Well, if it gives you any comfort, there's a lot of other people that feel much worse than you do right now," she stated, her voice sounding more miffed. She began to walk out the door.

"Yeah? Well, what do you want me to do about it?" he said, sounding more annoyed.

"I'm not telling you to do anything. I'm just saying you should probably stop acting like the victim whenever something bad happens. I can't believe I even have to say this for a second time."

"Oh, all right then." He finally turned around in his chair to face her. "And where did you suddenly get all this sassiness?" he asked, looking bellicose.

"What? You think I'm all just rainbows, cupcakes, smiles, and unicorns? You think I don't have the capability to get mad?"

"Well, just what the hell do you have to be so mad about?"

"I'm mad at you! You sent Paige to the hospital!"

"You think I meant to do that? I didn't even do anything. She freaked out for something that happened *years* ago! That I didn't even know I did!"

"Well, you haven't even tried making anything better. All you've done is sit up here in the dark like an owl!" She turned on the lights. "You haven't even tried apologizing to her!"

"That's because apologizing to her would be completely pointless." He turned his focus away from her. "She's never going to forgive me anyway! Now all she's ever going to see me as is some stupid little jerk boy that busted her head open!"

"Like how you're acting now?"

He turned back to her, scorning. "Look, just get out of here."

"See? This is what you always do. Anytime you do something you know is wrong, you just run away from it. Now you're running away from Paige."

"I ain't running away from anything! She pushed me away!"

"Right there! You're playing the victim again because you're so scared of your own feelings!"

"You wanna know what scared feels like?" He stood up and got closer to her, making her walk backward out the door. "You think you're better than me? You think you're tougher than me? You think you're so brave? Is that why you're backing away from me? Huh?"

Lisa didn't respond. When she felt her back against the railing, she tried to make a break for the stairs, but Steven grabbed her by the waist and shoved her aside toward her bedroom. She fell on the floor and started to move backward, still facing him.

Steven noticed she's developing tears quick. "Oh, you gonna cry now? Huh? Not so tough all of a sudden?"

"Steven, what are you doing?" Samantha screamed, coming upstairs, and rushed to Lisa's side.

Bruce followed behind and nudged Steven backward.

"Get out of my face!" Steven shouted.

"You need to back away and calm down right now!" Bruce asserted himself.

"What is the matter with you?" Samantha exclaimed, seated next to Lisa who's wrapped around her adoptive mom's arms.

"You two need to teach her to keep her mouth shut!" Steven said.

"You need to be taught to keep your hands to yourself!" Bruce replied.

"Ah yeah? Well, it's not like you two ever tried teaching me that! Where were you on that one?"

"We're always telling you that! You never listen to us!" Samantha said.

"'Cause you never say anything interesting!" Steven shot back.

"Don't you talk to her like that!" Bruce replied.

"This is America! I'll talk however I want!" Steven said.

"That's it! Go to your room!"

"I already was until she decided to burst in!"

"Then go downstairs! We'll have a serious talk with you in a bit!"

"I don't feel like talking!"

"Steven, please just stop and listen to your father!" Samantha spoke up.

"No, I'm not gonna listen! He's not my father, and you're not my mother! YOU'RE NOT OUR REAL PARENTS, SO STOP ACTING LIKE YOU ARE!"

The house went from deafening to inaudible. The only sounds being made were Steven's heavy breathing and Lisa's quiet sobs.

Both Samantha and Bruce developed expressions of shock and hurt hearing those last words.

"Just stay the hell out of my life, all of you!"

Steven began to stomp toward the stairs.

On his way down, Lisa quietly muttered, "Fuck you."

It was still loud enough for Steven to hear, who jerked his head to face her.

"What did you just say?"

"I said *fuck you!*" Lisa repeated. Samantha shushed her.

Now Steven had become completely enraged and started walking back in her direction.

"Steven, get—" Bruce began to speak as he stepped in front of him. But Steven shoved him off to the side and stomped toward Lisa who buried her face in Samantha.

Suddenly, Boscoe sprinted upstairs and got in between them, barking up at Steven.

"Shut up, Boscoe!"

He grabbed Boscoe's collar with one hand and reached to grab Lisa's hair with his other. But the loyal canine jerked his head away, pulling Steven away from them, still barking.

"SHUT UP, YOU DUMB DOG!"

He reached with his other hand to grab his collar, but out of instinct, Boscoe bit his right forearm.

"OWW! FUCK!" Steven screamed in agony as he let go and dropped to one knee, favoring his arm and wincing in pain while Boscoe continued to bark.

"Steven!" Bruce exclaimed.

"Oh my god! Boscoe!" Samantha said, getting up to calm him down.

"Let me see that," Bruce said, attempting to look at Steven's forearm.

"Don't touch me!" he said, jerking it away. "OWW!"

"Steven, settle down, settle down," Samantha followed up and glanced at the nasty bite mark. "Oh god, that looks bad. We should get you to a doctor."

"No, I don't need a damn doctor!" Steven got up and walked out of Lisa's room.

"Steven! Get back here!" Bruce said.

"No!"

He stomped down the stairs.

"Oh my god! Lisa, do not leave this room!" Samantha ordered, to which Lisa just nodded. Samantha kissed the top of her head before leaving for the door. "Bruce, come on." The two guardians followed Steven downstairs, leaving a terrified Lisa behind.

Lisa remained seated in that same spot on the floor, silently sobbing as Boscoe walked over to lie beside her.

Upon setting foot on the first floor, Steven began searching through various drawers in the kitchen.

"Where's my fucking keys?" he asked himself.

"Son, listen—" Bruce started.

"Where did you two put my keys?" He raised his voice to them.

"Steven, please stop this! You need help!" Samantha finished.

"I don't want help! From you two or anybody else! I just need my car keys, so where are they?"

"We don't know! And you shouldn't drive with that anyway!" Bruce said.

"FINE!" he said before slamming the drawer closed. Forcing his way through his adoptive parents, he headed for the front door, attempting to open it, but the glass exterior door was locked. "ARE YOU FUCKING KIDDING ME?" He attempted to unlock it with his good arms, but the handle was stuck again. As he's aggressively jiggling the handle, Samantha and Bruce hopelessly tried talking him down.

Steven growled and kicked the door, shattering most of the glass and leaving the house.

"STEVEN!" Samantha screamed.

They both followed him outside and saw him walking down the street.

"Steven! Stop!" Bruce called out.

The two of them chased after him, but Steven picked up his pace and started to run.

He easily gave them the slip and was now out of sight. A good couple of minutes of searching went by, but—despite splitting up—neither of them could find him.

Half Hour Later

Steven had been walking around incessantly with no direction, still favoring his arm, until eventually, he found himself in the middle of a rural area of the Island.

He stumbled upon a local bar and made his way inside. He observed his surroundings and noticed there were a lot of sketchy-looking people occupying the establishment: bikers, frat boys, rednecks, drug dealers presumably in the middle of business, people with tattoos or piercings—or both—some were likely carrying guns or knives. He wasn't intimidated in the slightest though; he'd seen plenty of crowds like this and knew enough to just act tough and not look at any of them funny.

He sat down in an empty bar seat.

"Yo!" he said, getting the attention of the bartender. "Get me something strong!"

The bartender walked over to him, giving him the stink eye.

"ID?"

Steven handed her a driver's license. After observing it, she took out her own to compare it.

"Yeah, nice try, kid. We don't take fakes."

"Fuck are you talking about?" he said with a straight face.

"Well, let's see. First, it's not laminated, and it's too thin, and you chose Florida, the most common state used for false IDs. Not all bartenders are as dumb or as desperate for profit as you may think they are, but I'd suggest finding one who is, and being more polite to them."

"Am I really gonna have a problem with you too? Just give me a drink. Nobody's ever gonna find out!"

"Save it and get out of here before I call the cops," she said before sliding the fake ID back to him and walking away.

Steven clenched his good hand and pounded it on the counter, exasperated.

He got up gripping his head and looked around to see a lone glass of beer at an unattended table. He made sure nobody was looking before he picked it up and downed the whole drink. He placed it down and walked away acting casual.

He found himself in a room with a pool table, where he saw four scrawny-looking men with tattoos playing a game. Acting without thought, he walked up behind one of them and deliberately bumped into him.

"Hey!" the man exclaimed. "What's your problem, creep?"

"I slipped," Steven answered, not looking at him.

"Bullshit, you better apologize to me right now!"

"I'm so so sorry," he patronized, still not looking at him.

The man was about to walk up to him, but another one held his shoulder.

"Dude, chill. Don't waste your time," Pool Player 2 said.

"What was that?" Steven said, turning his attention to this group.

"Forget about it. Just go," Pool Player 2 said.

"I'm a waste of your time?"

"Are you deaf, boy? Beat it," Pool Player 3 responded.

"If I were deaf, I wouldn't have heard that," Steven shot back. "You wanna repeat that to my face?" he said to Pool Player 2.

"You better shut your mouth right now, you little shit." Pool Player 1 spoke up, still being restrained.

Steven raised his hands up, looking at Pool Player 1. "I was just asking him a question."

"Kid, we're only gonna give you one last chance. I don't care how old you are. Get out of here now or you aren't getting any older!" Pool Player 3 said, getting up in his face.

Steven stood there, unfazed. "Fine."

The pool player backed away to let him leave. Steven turned around halfway before picking up a beer sitting on the table and took a gulp of it, pissing him off further.

"Are you fucking playing with me right now?" Pool Player 3 asked, getting back into his face.

Steven emptied out half of the glass before looking at him. "Oh sorry, was this yours? Here." Steven splashed it in his face.

Pool Player 3 turned around, reacting to the splash, and quickly turned back to beat on him. But Steven picked up one of the pool balls and threw it at his face, knocking him down.

"Fucking shithead! Get him!" Pool Player 2 instructed and released Pool Player 1 who launched at him like a wildcat.

Steven managed to fend the two of them off, though only briefly. He got in a few strikes and used any foreign object he could grab, managing to knock the two of them down at a time. The chaos attracted the rest of the bar's attention, and the owner of the joint—the same woman at the counter—called the police.

Eventually, Pool Player 4, who had to have been over six and a half feet tall and wasn't nearly as scrawny as he appeared, intervened. After a brief stare down, Steven picked up a pool cue and broke it over his shoulder, barely fazing the large man. Out of instinct, he threw a punch with his right hand and was grabbed by the forearm. Pool Player 4 squeezed it, causing Steven to let out an excruciating scream. Pool

Players 1 and 2 took the opening and began an assault, forcing him on the ground where they proceeded to stomp him down.

"Out of my way!" Pool Player 1 knelt down and started to bombard his face with punches. "You wanna apologize now, you piece of shit? You sorry YET?! ANSWER ME, YOU FUCKING BITCH!" he shouted in between punches.

Steven's face was busted open, and his vision went blurry; he's in too much pain to reply.

"Stand his ass up!" Pool Player 3 demanded, back on his feet.

Pool Players 1 and 2 grabbed him by both arms to force him up and shoved him back into Pool Player 4, who trapped his torso and arms in a bear hug.

Pool Player 3 looked at the defenseless teen. He touched where the ball hit him to feel a bump starting to swell up. He looked back at him and pulled something out of his pocket.

"You got balls, boy. But you aimed for the wrong set of pins, and now..." He revealed the item was a switchblade. "God's gonna strike you down."

Despite his struggling, Steven was too weak to fight back.

"If it weren't for your squirming, I would've assumed you came here to die. Could've fooled me," Pool Player 3 said, slowly walking toward him.

Everybody else in the bar just stood there, whether it's out of their own safety or apathy, ready to watch him die.

"See you in hell."

As he prepared to dig the knife into his neck, the sounds of thuds and smacks can be heard. The three turned their attention to it and saw Pool Players 1 and 2 had been incapacitated by someone.

It was Jason.

"Oh what, you wanna die too?" Pool Player 3 turned himself around, pointing his knife at him.

Steven took this opening and kicked him in the crotch, making him drop his knife.

Jason then ran up and delivered a roundhouse kick to knock him out.

271

Pool Player 4 started to squeeze Steven, making him scream again. Jason tried to save him but was pushed back by the large man's foot, knocking him to the floor.

Jason found the pool ball that Steven threw before, picked it up, and threw it at the large man's head, causing him to loosen his grip. Steven then stomped on his foot. He escaped and stumbled into the pool table. Pool Player 4 went after him, but Steven picked up the empty beer glass he threw into Pool Player 3's face and shattered it over Pool Player 4's, making him fall backward.

Steven, gasping for breath, looked over at Jason standing above him.

"Let's go!" Jason demanded. They then heard police sirens in the distance. "Now!"

Steven got up, and the duo made a break for the door.

"Hey! You two stop right there!" the bartender protested, but they were already out the door.

The police arrived shortly after, and they both ran for it.

Steven was in too much pain to run at a regular pace but stayed behind Jason.

"Get in the car!" Jason ordered.

"Will you slow down?" Steven asked.

"Shut up and get in the fucking car!"

They ran across the street, avoiding oncoming vehicles toward Jason's car that's parked on the sidewalk.

Steven jumped in the passenger seat; and Jason started the car up and stomped on the gas pedal, nearly ramming another car on the way out, onto the road.

They drove around until they were far enough from the police and certain they were no longer in pursuit, the entire time not making conversation.

11:30 PM

Jason drove them to their old hideout, the old, abandoned diner on the edge of the woods. It must've gone out of business as long as over a decade ago. The windows were boarded up, and there was graffiti on the walls. It's covered in cobwebs, dirt dust, and debris on the tabletops.

272

Cushioned seats in the booths had been ripped up overtime, wooden flooring was chipping away, and most of what was metal had started to rust. It's no wonder why this space wasn't bought out for another business.

Jason and Steven parked behind the building and entered through a back door. Jason illuminated the only room with no windows—the kitchen—with a lantern light. They were both on opposite sides of the room and still hadn't spoken a word to each other since their escape from being arrested. Or killed.

"Isn't this nice? Being back in our old hideout, laying low from the cops, hoping they don't burst through the door and shoot us? Really makes you feel nostalgic, don't it?" Jason spoke sarcastically.

"I'm not in a mood for your wit." Steven replied.

"Aww, no need to thank me for saving your ass. I'm always more than happy to do it, and just a few days after I almost had my arm broken sticking up for your dumb ass. You know? I was thinking we'd finally moved past all this, but honestly, I was starting to miss it. God, it's just such a thrill!" he ranted, maintaining his tone of voice.

"I get it! You're pissed. Welcome to my world. Now cut it out with the attitude."

"Fine. Fine. I'll stop. But I do have one more question. No sarcasm, no jokes, just give me an honest answer. WHAT WERE YOU THINKING?" he shouted. "And I know for a fact you started that, so don't fucking lie to me!"

"That whole thing could've been easily avoided if that bitch bartender took my fake ID."

"Fuck off with that! You were this close to being killed!"

"I wasn't though!"

"Thanks to me risking my life for yours!"

"I didn't ask for your help! I could've dealt with those crackheads myself!"

"That's not what I saw. I saw you covered in blood, squirming in a three-hundred-pound man's grasp, about to have your throat opened by a pocketknife!"

"Okay, how did you even know I was there?"

"Well, first, your parents called me and said you ran away after you yelled at them and Lisa and that you were injured, so they asked me to help them find you. Of course, being the good friend that I am, I said yes; and from there, all I had to do was think, 'Hmm, what's the stupidest thing he could be doing right now?' Since you were on foot, I knew you'd be close by and most likely in a bar, which brought me exactly to where you were. I would've brought you home by now, but you can guess why I didn't." He gestured toward the outside.

"Well, yippee for you. Ever think of becoming a detective?" he shot back.

"Let's just keep talking about you, all right?"

"It's over, dude. Done. Finished. Concluded. Let's just move on with our meaningless lives. Shit happens. Can't change it!"

Jason folded his arms. "I knew this was about Paige."

"No, it isn't."

"I said don't lie to me."

"I didn't lie."

"You're still lying."

"Stop fucking with me."

"Then why did you go out and start a bar fight with four guys?"

"Because."

"Because?"

"Yeah, because."

Jason kept listening for him to give an actual answer.

"Because I felt like it."

"You 'felt like it.'"

"Yeah."

"So you decided, even though you were horribly outnumbered and had limited mobility of your right arm, that you were just 'in the mood.'"

"That's what happened."

Jason shook his head. "Dude. I know you're upset. Lots of bad things happened this weekend. But you don't gotta fake this. I know you still care about her—"

"Shut up! I don't need a therapy session from you."

"I'm just trying to help."

"I said I didn't ask for help, from you or anybody else, so shut up!" Steven stood up to shout.

"Well, you clearly need help after the shit you've pulled the last few days! Scratch that, the shit you've been pulling since we were kids!"

"Oh and suddenly you're such a saint? Who went along with all that shit? All the times we cut school, stole from convenience stores, threw smoke bombs into our seventh-grade teacher's house, burn our childhood toys with matches. If you were afraid to do all that, you sure tricked me into believing you were having fun! Or what about all the times you swiped money from your father's wallet to buy us concert tickets from scalpers? To get the tattoos all over your arms and abs? Hell, how many of those fights did you start? When we were getting our fake IDs done, who came up with the name Vincent Kalthoff?" Steven ranted.

Jason got more angry listening to this. "Anything else you wanna say?"

"Yeah! You are so delusional that you're the more responsible one of us, that all the bad things that have ever happened to you is because of me! And why do you do that? Really, tell me why! Is it because you're scared it'll hurt your music career? Or is it because you think if you sound convincing enough, that you may have a chance with Jenn? Well, I hate to be the one to tell you this, but you never will!"

Jason began to get fed up with how he's talking and got up into his face. "I know you're hurt, but you better take that back right now," he said silently but aggressively.

"No. 'Cause you need to hear this. Jenn. Will. Never. Love you!"

Jason stared him down with an intense scowl.

Punch!

Jason knocked him down with a single blow.

He got down to pummel him with all his fury. Steven blocked one punch and delivered a headbutt. Jason staggered, and Steven took this chance and pushed him off. Jason got back to his feet and stepped away.

Steven got back up and came up from behind to get him into a rear-naked choke.

But Jason jumped up to a horizontal position and pulled Steven down with him, aggravating his arm and making him release his grip as he screeched. Jason, now in a seated position, with Steven crouched down and against his back, took this opening by grabbing Steven's injured arm, turning his own body and putting him in a kimura lock.

Jason wrenched his arm around, applying pressure to the forearm, and Steven started writhing in pain before immediately tapping out.

"NOT GOOD ENOUGH!" Jason shouted and continued to wrench.

"AUGHHH! I'M SORRY I'M SORRY!" Steven screamed.

"WHAT'D YOU SAY?"

"I'M SORRY!" he screamed louder, still tapping out.

Jason let him go and stood back up, staring down at Steven who's lying on the dirty floor.

Steven sat up and looked up at Jason, holding on to his now-exacerbated injured forearm.

"Jenn taught you that, didn't she?"

"As a matter of fact, she did. She's been teaching me a couple moves like that on the side. Including that high wrist hold I was put in, when she tried to break my arm for protecting you." Steven didn't reply. "Yeah, every time we got in trouble for something, whether it was your idea or my idea, how minor or how major it was, I have always had your back, even when it seemed entirely indefensible. And why did I do that? Because you're like a brother to me. You were the only person who didn't immediately judge me at first glance. I thought that everybody else were just a bunch of conformist douchebags and the two of us were the outlaws with free will. But I was wrong. It wasn't that we were wearing different clothes, listened to different music, liked watching more 'edgy' movies. It was because we were the douchebags! All of our problems arose because of what we did! Yeah, I'll admit that I've come up with stupid ideas. I've been as equally responsible for getting us in trouble. But you know what the difference is? I'm not afraid to admit it. I'm ashamed, but not afraid. I recognize that I've screwed up quite a few times in my life, and I'll acknowledge that. You, on the other hand, you screw up with such pride; and yet you're terrified to admit that! You instead just try to make other people feel worse than you do! Even if they've been unapologetically loyal to you! If they've stuck their neck out for you when nobody would! Even after they devoted themselves to fix your miserable existence, sacrificing their precious time on you when you didn't deserve it!" Jason took a moment to catch his breath. "I may be a screwup, but I'm trying to get better. No matter how futile it might be, whether or not Jenn will ever talk to me again, I will still take responsibilities for my shortcomings, and I won't blame anybody else except myself. Not even you."

Jason walked through the back door, slamming it shut, exiting the diner.

Steven, still grounded, took in everything he just said. He recollected those comments as he flashed back to months ago. The night when Paige slapped him and what she said to him interspersed with the parallel event that happened when they were kids and last Saturday, accompanied by every terrible thing he'd ever done.

"For once in your life, shut the fuck up!"

"I thought there was something more to you."

"I almost felt sorry for you. I felt like maybe you weren't a complete ass..."

"YOU'RE HURTING ME!"

"...you are the most stubborn, selfish, narcissistic, egotistical jackass I have ever had the misfortune of associating with!"

"For once in your life, shut the fuck up!"

"...compensate for your lack of self-esteem!"

"...shut the fuck up!"

"YOU'RE HURTING ME!"

"I am done with you!"

"...shut the fuck up!"

"...you'll just be a distant memory to me!"

"...shut the fuck up! ...shut the fuck up! ...shut the fuck up! ...shut the fuck up!"

"...memory to me!"

"YOU'RE HURTING ME!"

"YOU'RE HURTING ME!"

"YOU'RE HURTING ME!"

That last one, he was remembering as if both of those moments were happening at the same time.

Only a minute had passed, but it felt like an hour before he snapped back into the present.

He struggled but managed to stand up and limp his way out of the diner through the same door, where he saw Jason standing against his car, staring a hole into his face.

Steven slowly walked up to him to speak.

"Before you showed up back there… one of those guys was saying that …I wanted to die." Steven exhaled and slumped. "He was right." Jason's eyes widened, and he now gave him his full, genuine attention. "Back there, and right now, I wish they did kill me. That they would've just put an end to my suffering …and that I could stop hurting people. My friends. My family. Everybody," he admitted. "Honestly …you should've just let them slit my throat."

"I don't like hearing this."

"No, I mean it. My soul is pretty much just sitting in vessel on the verge of blowing up. Except it's like autopilot. I'm moving, but there's no direction, or destination. That's what it feels like, every freakin' day, and these last few months proved it. I thought this would be the end of all that. It felt like it was. I thought Paige came into my life for a good reason, that she could help me forget about all the bad things I've ever done and move on. Now I realize that she was just a reminder of all those things. Of how… irredeemable I am." He leaned forward onto the hood of the car. "My past was looking me in the face all this time, disguised as the only thing that's ever made me happy. I mean really, what are the odds the girl I knew when I was a kid comes back, just for me to repeat the same stupid mistake? It's like this universe just loves to fuck me in the ass!" Steven began to huff. "I just… I can't take it anymore."

Jason remained quiet for a few moments as he processed what was just said to him.

"I wasn't going to let you die. You're my brother in the pit," he began. "And I never said you were irredeemable. Back in September, when you went up to Paige, and you told her that you wanted to make things up to her, the Steven I knew would've just shouted in her face. But you didn't. You really committed to that gig and stuck to your guns. …So maybe I don't know you as well as I thought I did, and maybe you're more capable than I think you are."

Steven sighed. "Even if I am, what reason do I have to even bother? How am I supposed to live when I'm never happy?"

"I guess you just gotta look for a reason. Find something that makes you happy. Maybe something will find you," he suggested. "But hey, what do I know, right? I don't even have a reason myself." Jason suddenly began to feel down himself.

Steven noticed this change in his morale.

"I mean, I'm trying to get better, but I can't help but feel like it's all in vain. In the back of my head, I always have this combination of guilt and… fear. Fear that no matter what I do, somehow my past will catch up to me, that it'll affect any chance I have for a career, or at a relationship …Like, like a real one. That …that you're right," Jason confessed. "Why would Jenn ever wanna be with someone like me? What have I ever done to deserve her? I'm just some creep who looks like he got turned down by Korn. Why am I even still alive?"

Jason was now the one who slumped, before he turned his back on Steven. "Get in the car. We should both get home," he said before getting into the driver's seat and shutting the door.

Steven took a minute to soak up Jason's words.

He looked at his bite wound, thinking about his family and what he had done to them.

He joined Jason in the car, and the two sat there in silence.

"You," Steven began, "have way too much talent and loyalty to die." Jason turned his head. "You're going to connect with a lot of people and change lives, and for real, you're not the same punk kid I met in sixth grade. You're not even the same dude I knew six months ago. You're a lot smarter. A lot more …solicitous."

"Paige teach you that word?"

"Yes." Jason chuckled. "Point being, you're a goddamn G, Jason. You're awesome. You're a good person with a shitload of talent. You're gonna sell out MSG one day," Steven said.

Jason only let out an "Eh."

"And I don't know what your odds with Jenn are… but they're a lot better than mine," Steven somberly assured him.

Jason can only sigh at that statement.

"And listen, I'm sorry, man. For real, I'm sorry," Steven said, extending his left arm.

After a few seconds, Jason grinned and accepted a bro high five. The two friends then shared an embrace unlike any other they'd had before.

As they drove back, Steven caught Jason up to speed with all the unanswered questions—about his name, his family, his past friendship with Paige/Miranda, anything that he kept hidden from him for all these years. Knowing all this gave Jason a much better understanding as to why Steven was so screwed up. Even with all this information, he still couldn't grasp how torn up these last few days made him. But he wasn't going to quit on his best friend; he was going to be there for him and help him see this thing through to the end. They were and would always be brothers in the pit.

1:00 AM

Samantha and Bruce were still up, seated at their kitchen table in complete silence, worrying about their adopted son.

They were alarmed by the sound of footsteps on the floor and looked to the front door that was still open.

Steven walked in, and his parents immediately moved to his position. They noticed he's hurt even worse than before and checked on his wounds.

They both asked him the barest of questions: "Where were you?" "Are you all right?" "What happened to you?"

Steven didn't give them any answers; he instead sat on the floor, broke into tears, and apologized to them over and over again.

His parents joined him where he's seated and comforted him, both in tears as well.

When Steven's vision cleared, he saw Lisa standing at the top of the stairs. Before their parents told her to go back to bed, Steven let them know it's okay.

Lisa slowly descended the stairs with Boscoe behind, and they're given a clear pathway to him. She stopped when she reached the first step.

Steven flinched as Boscoe continued to walk up to him. Boscoe stopped in front to sniff him out, and stared directly at him. He moved to the bite mark he left and began to lick it. Steven grinned as he started to scratch under his chin, and Boscoe started to lick his face, either to clean his wounds or to show affection. Maybe both.

Steven then gently dismissed Boscoe and returned his attention to Lisa.

Without either of them saying a word, Steven lifted his good arm upward. Lisa, without hesitation, hugged her elder brother and was entrapped by his arms.

Lisa began to bawl as Steven lost control of his own tears, as their parents let the two have their moment.

Steven had a lot of making up to do but being immediately accepted by his family—especially after all the years of neglecting them—made him feel recuperated. He felt a sense of love that he hadn't felt in a long time, and all the dark emotions he felt started to drift away, even if only temporarily.

This gave him a sense of hope. Maybe things could get better. Maybe he could get better. Maybe things weren't as bad as he convinced himself. Maybe there was still a chance for him...

Chapter 23

Beautiful Little Fool

Thursday Morning

Steven was brought to the emergency room to get patched up. His bite wound wasn't as serious as it looked. However, he was diagnosed with some broken skin and minor internal bleeding. They wrapped his forearm and hand up in bandages and prescribed him some pain medications, and he was advised not to do any sort of heavy lifting or put unnecessary pressure on the arm for a few days.

Paige had still been missing from school and practically ghosted herself from her friends. Both of their absences now had people talking. It didn't take long before rumors started to spread. They even went as far to say that "they fled the country together" or "they're dead." A week ago, nobody suspected a thing about them, but their long truancies caused a lot of them to connect the dots on a blank sheet of paper. Paige always believed she was the last thing on anybody's mind, but now she was the most popular topic of interest.

Meadows Forest High School, 9:00 AM

Jason had fallen asleep during his first-period class: gym. His class went out to the track to run laps, which he was too tired to deal with, so he snuck off and lay down on the footing of the bleachers between two sections. He dozed off and remained that way, until he felt a backpack come down on his face.

"OWW! The fuck, dude!"

282

He sat up and looked around to see Morgan standing there, wearing her gym uniform.

"I'm sorry. I didn't see—" she began to apologize, and then she realized who it was. "Oh. Jason, hey," she said awkwardly.

"Morgan." Jason wiped his eyes. "Sorry."

"Why are you apologizing?"

"I don't know."

"What are you doing out here?"

"I, uh, I have gym this period. Wait, what time is it?"

"Nine something."

"Jesus Christ! I slept through the whole period!"

"And apparently the first ten minutes of this one."

"God-fucking-dammit, I'm missing Spanish."

"You have a test?"

"No."

"Then who gives a shit?" She sat down beside him.

"What are you doing here?"

"Well, this is my gym class."

"Right. Right of course, you got the uniform and . . ."

"Oh this? Nah, this is just my usual style."

"Oh, is it now?"

"Yeah, it's practically my aesthetic. You never noticed?"

"Ah, well, it's cute."

"I'd hope so. They charge twenty bucks for it, plus an extra ten for a lock, and hey, not bad on you either."

"You think?"

"Well, not as good as me, but it's honestly refreshing to see you in something not black."

"Thanks for the backhanded compliment, Coco Chanel."

"I don't know what that is." Jason rolled his eyes. "So why were you sleeping in the bleachers and unintentionally cutting Spanish?"

"What does it matter?"

"Come onnnn, I don't wanna do aerobics. Talk to meee."

"Well, I didn't get a lot of sleep last night."

"How come?"

"I... I had to deal with an emergency."

"Emergency?"

"Yeah."

"Did this, by any chance, have anything to do with Axl?"

"Yes."

"What happened?"

"I'd rather not tell, and why do you care? I thought you girls hated him. And me."

"You're right. I don't like him. As far as you go though, I can't speak on everyone else's behalf, but I know you didn't do anything."

"Thanks."

"So what happened last night?"

Jason sighed. "Let's just say he hasn't exactly been the same since Saturday."

"Yeah, neither has Paige."

"I'm sure of it. How is she?"

"I wish I knew. The doctor said she had a concussion, but I haven't talked to her since."

"How come?"

"She won't talk to anyone. Now I'm hearing all these rumors going around, and I just want to shut them up and say what really happened, but I can't 'cause then they'll know about what was going on, and I swore I wouldn't say anything."

"I feel ya. The last two days I've been hounded by questions about if 'what we heard is true' no matter how many times I've said I don't know anything."

"Oh my god, it's ridiculous. Some actually think she's dead, like, what the fuck!"

"Relax, these morons will believe anything."

"I know. But on the other hand, she probably wishes she was dead."

Jason thought about what Steven told him last night. With how distraught he felt, he didn't want to imagine how somebody as innocent and fragile as Paige felt right now. It scared him.

"You need to go talk to her."

"Huh?"

"All of you, even if she doesn't want to, you have to talk to her."

"I know, and we would, except… Amy and I haven't seen Jenn all week."

"Jenn's not here?"

"I don't know. She drove us to the hospital, and then it's like she just disappeared."

"You're sure she isn't here?"

"If she is, then she's been avoiding us."

"Oh god, is this the rapture? Everybody's just going off the grid!" Jason agitatedly held his head. "Look, go find Amy, and tell her you're going to check on Paige today. Don't matter when, but it's happening today."

"Okay, you can't just make demands after all that's happened!"

"Fine. *Please*, go check on her today."

"We can't do this without Jenn. It'd feel wrong."

"I'll …I'll take care of that."

"How?"

He exhaled. "I swore I wouldn't go this far, but I'll make sure she's there."

"Again, how?"

"After school, I'm going to Brooklyn."

"You're going to her house?"

"Yeah."

"Dude, you know that nobody will be there to talk her out of what she's gonna do."

"I do know, but she can dodge you girls here fine, and I'm the only one with a car and nothing better to do. Plus, I really need to talk to her too."

"What makes you certain she'll listen?"

"I'm not." He started to leave.

"Hey."

Jason turned around. "What?"

"If I may say so, it's sweet how much you still care about her. Even after she tried to turn you into the Winter Soldier. That's some hardcore loyalty."

Jason nodded with a look of sorrow. "Thanks."

285

"And Jenn might not act like it, but she sees that too," she spilled. "Just in case you needed some reassurance."

"Appreciate it." He gave her a mini smile. "You've got a great deal of loyalty yourself. You're absolutely insane, but that's a good thing. That means you've got character, and you're confident in that. A lot of people don't have that kind of security, and part of me …admires that." Morgan gave him a wholehearted smile. "And I'm sure Amy sees that too."

"Wha-what does—what does—what does that mean?" She put on a baffled expression and started to blush.

Jason snickered. "It's all right. I get it. Everybody gets it. Except Amy." Morgan didn't answer; she just got redder. "Just in case you needed some reassurance," he said before leaving Morgan hotter than Mount Saint Helens' core.

"Chambers! Get back on the field now!" her gym teacher called out, snapping her out of her trance.

"Shit!" She got up and ran back to where she should've been that whole time.

Later

Jason kept true to his word and drove to Jenn's house as soon as dismissal hit. He knew this was bad idea, but he's carried out more than enough of those in his life, so why not one more?

He parked his car by the curb a few houses down and walked down the street toward hers. He arrived only to see that her car wasn't there, so he took a seat on the stairway and waited/hoped for her to make it home. Ready for the worst.

Jenn eventually pulled up and noticed him sitting there. Without a second thought, she hit the brake in the middle of the road and got out, leaving the car still running.

"The fuck are you doing here?" Jenn walked toward him.

Jason stood and put his hands up. "Before you—"

"Shut up! You stalking me now, you creep?"

"I just need to talk to y—"

"Oh, you really are stupid if you thought I'd talk to you!"

"Jenn—"

"Get out of here now!"

"I will. I'll go." He walked around her.

"Bye!"

"But first—"

"No! Get out of here before I have you arrested!"

"Please. Please. I just need to ask you one question."

"No!"

"Just one. Then I'll go."

Jenn growled. "Fine. One question!"

Jason put his hands down. "Where've you been all week?"

"I've been at school."

"So you've been avoiding Morgan and Amy."

"Who said I'm avoiding them?"

"Morgan did."

"What? When did you speak to Morgan?"

"This morning."

"Why the hell was she even talking to you?"

"It's a long, not really that long story, but she and Amy said you haven't talked to them all week."

"I've... been busy."

"Well, if you're not busy right now, they're going to see Paige."

"They are?" Jason nodded. "So she sent you up here to tell me that?"

"No."

Jenn looked confused. "Well, I can't go." She turned away from him.

"If you think she's mad at you, I seriously doubt it."

"It's not that. I ...I can't face her, not after all that," Jenn confessed, not looking at him. "I knew this was all a bad idea, and I did nothing. If I just stepped in earlier, she wouldn't have gotten hurt, she would've never gotten attached to that bastard, and none of this would be happening." She turned back to him. "I don't know what I would say. Hell, I don't even know what I should call her anymore. Paige? Miranda? But it doesn't matter, 'cause even if she's not mad at me, I'm still gonna be mad at myself! Because if I'm not mad, then I'm scared!"

Jenn sat down on the steps of her house, moping.

Jason was taken aback and diligently sat beside her.

"Never expected those words to come from you."

Jenn sighed. "Well, they just did... I'm always scaring people away from me, but the truth is ...you were right. I am scared to get close to them. Because I knew something like this would happen. Somehow, either directly or indirectly, I'm responsible for someone's pain. I know I'm not supposed to be here anyway, but since I am, could I at least do something, anything that I don't have to feel ashamed of?" Jenn slowly turned her head to look at him. "That I could make somebody's life better?"

Jenn looked down at her feet with a sorrowed expression.

Jason thought about how he could reassure her, but blanks. He could only speak what his heart said.

"Please, don't say you shouldn't be here."

"Why?"

"Just don't. Please," he begged. "It's not true."

"Yeah yeah."

"Yeah yeah!" He got up. "Because you do make people's lives better."

"How? How do I make people's lives better, Jason?"

"By being here!" Jenn didn't reply. "You say you don't want anybody getting near you, and yet you built an unbreakable bond with Amy, and when she let Morgan and Paige into your life, you didn't push them away either. Now I know I agreed to only one question, but sorry, I'm breaking that deal: why do you think you did that if you were so afraid?"

Jenn looked for an answer. "I don't know. But I should've scared them off when I had the chance. They're all too good for somebody of my rep."

"Or maybe it's because you're tired of feeling the way you do. That your friendship with them makes you feel happy. That even though you might make mistakes, it gives you comfort knowing someone accepts you for you, and they can look past those mistakes to see the incredible person you are. Probably because you make them happy too ...and maybe because, no matter what happens, you can't imagine your life without them in it." Jason sat back down to brood. "I get why you might feel that way, but just, please don't say you shouldn't be here. Without you here ...the world would be incomplete."

The conversation went silent. The only thing heard was a light breeze.

"Jason…"

"I promise, they won't be mad. Paige really needs you right now. They all do," he said, not looking at her.

"Actually, what I was gonna say was…" Jason looked at her. "I'm sorry for almost breaking your arm."

"It's all right."

"No, it's not. I took my anger out on you for something that wasn't your fault, and as annoying as you can get, you've never done anything to deserve that."

"It's fine, really. I was never mad."

They stopped talking again.

"You really meant all those things you said?" Jenn broke the tension.

"Of course. And I know everybody else thinks it too—Paige, Morgan, Amy, and your parents."

Jenn finally managed to crack a smile. "Well …thanks. For listening to me say all that …I've never told this to anyone."

"Really?" Jenn nodded in response. "I wish you told me this before."

"Well, before …you weren't my friend."

Jason was surprised to hear her call him that. He wanted to smile but felt angst looking at Jenn's afflicted expression.

"I'm still happy you did though. You're welcome."

Jenn slightly nodded at him.

"I should probably get out of here." Jason stood on his feet. "Sorry for surprising you like this."

"It-it's cool."

"I just hope things look up for all of you. …Good night." Jason walked off.

Jenn remained seated and thought hard to herself. She pulled out her phone and went into her voicemails. She only has one listed: from Jason.

She clicked on it, put it up to her ear, and began to listen.

"Hey, Jenn. It's me. I get it, you don't wanna talk. I wouldn't want to me either, but I just want to make sure Paige is okay. Or Miranda, I guess. Uh, that was just a really crappy situation, and I hope you guys got to the hospital and that it's not that serious, uhh… But yeah, I'm just really sorry about that whole thing. It shouldn't have happened, and

I swear, I had no idea about any of that. I know you're mad, and you're probably not gonna believe me, but I really didn't. That was just as much a surprise to me, and—" He sighed. "Honestly, I… I don't know why I'm leaving this. You probably won't even listen to it. But if you are, I just… I just want you to know I'm sorry, and I don't blame you if you never talk to me again. I mean, why would you? Besides, you said that once they cut ties, we cut ties, and, well, you saw that. …Anyway, I, I guess I should just use this time to say …to tell you that you're a great friend to all of them. No matter what you think of yourself, you're a good person, with a strong heart. Whoever you let into your life, you'll make theirs a lot better. I know because you've done that to mine. And also, I, I really… Ah man, listen, I'm not trying to make this about me, just …I hope everything's okay. …Goodbye, Jenn."

The message ended.

Jenn lowered her arm with the phone still in hand, as a single tear ran down her face.

5:30 PM

Knock-knock.

"Miranda?" Catherine called from behind the door but was met by silence. "Miranda? Your friends want to see you. Should I let them in?"

Paige sat up in her bed. Her hair was a mess, and she's still in her pajamas from the night before. "Sure," she said, disinterested.

Catherine opened the door, allowing for Morgan and Amy to move inside. She took a glance at her daughter's appearance and felt her heart sink before slowly closing the door.

"Hi," Amy said.

Paige weakly waved her hand.

"How are you feeling?"

"As great as I look," she replied.

"Well, as far as bedridden goes, you look great." Morgan awkwardly chuckled, but Paige didn't react. "So how much longer until you can come back to school?" Morgan asked her.

"Today."

"Hmm?" Morgan replied.

"I technically could've gone back today, but I don't care if I ever go to that school again. I'd rather just go back to being homeschooled for the rest of my life." Paige flopped down on her bed.

"Paige..." Amy sat on the edge of Paige's bed. "I understand how you feel, all right? I've been down this path a lot more times than I've told you girls."

Morgan sat on the other side, across from Amy. "But you've got way too much to live for. You can't waste it away dwelling over this."

"I know," Paige said, looking at the ceiling. "I know I shouldn't but..."

"Paige, I promise, it's gonna hurt for a while; but after enough time, you'll feel even better having went through it," Amy told her.

"Amy, stop!" Paige sat up. "Stop talking to me like that, okay?"

"All right, I just—"

"No, you don't! All right? You don't know how it feels! This isn't like anything you've ever gone through—it just isn't!" She raised her voice.

"Paige, Paige—" Morgan tried to speak to her.

"I can't even explain how much this hurts! It's like my heart's been frozen to exact zero and there's no structural density anymore. It's just empty, hollow, and just the slightest bit of contact will shatter whatever is left! You ever felt that? Of all the times you've broken up with somebody, all the times you've been dumped, have any of those guys left you just completely broken? Have you ever actually given them a chance to enter the deepest part of your soul and just drain the life out of you?"

Amy stayed there still, shaken by Paige's assertion. As did Morgan.

"Have you?" Paige cried out.

Amy shook her head. "No. No, I haven't."

"Well, that's what I did! TWICE! And it's not something that'll just go away. The cuts on the back of my skull may heal, but there's nothing in the world that'll stop the pain I feel in my chest!"

Paige brought her legs to her chest, buried her head into her knees, and started bawling.

Morgan and Amy looked at each other, waiting for the other to say something to her.

Amy sighed. "I'm sorry," she said to Paige. Paige looked up with her soaked face. "You're right. I... I don't know how that feels. ...As many times as I've experienced a heartache, what you've gone through must've been a thousand times more painful," Amy said as tears were building in her eyes. "I'm sorry."

"I'm sorry too." Morgan spoke up as her own eyes got wet.

Paige sniffed. "Why are you sorry?" she asked.

"'Cause you could've backed out of this thing earlier, and we wouldn't be doing this right now. But I pushed you to dig deeper into the hole, and now you've got a broken heart." Morgan wiped her eyes. "All for my own stupid ego!" Morgan punched the bed and sighed. "I'm such a shitty friend."

"Morgan, it wasn't your fault," Paige said.

"Yes, it was."

"No, it wasn't. It's mine. I'm the one who gave him a second chance. I'm the one who opened up to him, and I'm the one who…" Paige hesitated, before she confessed. "Who fell in love with him."

Both Amy and Morgan simultaneously got shocked looks on their faces and glanced at each other.

"And even though he hurt me, and I never wanna see his face again," Paige whimpered, "I still am." Her voice cracked. "And I know that's insane. I know you all think he's a monster, but you don't know him like I do. He shared so many things with me, personal things, and I shared a lot with him too. And I saw this, this side of him that I connected with. Something about it felt familiar. It felt …comforting. Like, when I was around that side of him, I could be myself. I didn't know why, but now I do. And now, every time I look at him, I won't be able to see that side of him. I'm only gonna see the face of the boy who betrayed my friendship and scarred me for life." She put her hands to her face. "I'm sorry, guys. I didn't mean to yell. I just don't know what to do."

Morgan and Amy shared another extended look while Paige quietly wept.

"However you're feeling right now, it's all right," Morgan told her. "You're not the only one who's dealing with an… unobtainable love. But I want you to know there's nothing wrong with it. Love can be magical, and poisonous."

Amy gave Morgan a look of sympathy and bewilderment.

"But… if you really feel this strongly, then the best thing to do would be …something. I know you're scared and conflicted, but you should at least admit how you feel. Say what you have to say and then you'll at least know where to go from there." Amy looked to Morgan. "Right?"

Morgan blushed. "Ye-ye-yeah. You should definitely tell… Axl that you feel that way. About him."

Paige brought her head back up. "How? I'm scared to even look at him. Shouldn't you be talking me out of it? You guys hate him."

"Screw what we think. Worry about what you want," Morgan said.

"We love you, and we want you to be happy. We agreed from the start, whatever you think is best, we'll always have your back when nobody else does," Amy said.

Morgan thought back to what Jason said earlier. "And while this contradicts what I just said, I think you and this whole thing have had a strong effect on him as well. Like, the whole thing. I'm still very indifferent to him, but same with what Amy said. If he makes you happy, then I'll be happy."

Amy took a deep breath and cracked a smile. "Me too."

Paige barely mustered a smile and pulled her friends in for a group hug.

Her attention then turned toward the door, and she pulled away. Morgan and Amy looked in the same direction.

"Sorry I didn't get here sooner," Jenn said.

"How much did you hear?" Paige asked.

"Like, 90 percent of it," Jenn answered. "Whatever you decide to do, I hope it's the best decision," she said, stepping inside. "Also, um, I haven't been the greatest friend lately, and I've been deliberately ducking all of you when I should've been close by. I let my guilt get the better of me, and I wasn't thinking of you, Paige. Or at least I was thinking about you in a wrong way, and I—" She sighed. "Anyway, I'm sor—"

"Jenn," Paige cut her off.

She then gestured her to join in their group hug.

Jenn turned her head away; she felt awkward and reluctant. But she looked at her friends again, made a heartfelt smile, and joined them on the bed.

She gradually lifted her hands and let herself into this huddle. Jenn's shoulders felt much lighter as she tightened her hold around them all, and her smile grew.

All four shared the long, warm embrace.

"I suppose this would be a bad time to mention everybody thinks you're dead." Morgan spoke up.

"What?" Paige asked, and they all split apart.

"It's just some stupid rumor going around," Amy said.

"Yeah. Let's just say that everybody's noticed how both of you have been absent a lot lately," Jenn added.

"He hasn't been in either?" Paige asked.

"Nope. I haven't seen him in English class all week," Morgan said.

"English class! Oh my fucking god, my essay!" Paige freaked out.

"What about it?"

"I completely forgot!"

"What's happening now?" Jenn asked.

"We have an essay assignment about who our biggest inspiration is, and the deadline is tomorrow," Morgan explained.

"And I haven't even started! Grr, I let my stupid broken heart distract me!" Paige panicked.

"Okay, okay, calm down. Is there anything we can do?" Amy asked.

"No. I just—I just need some time to think," Paige said, getting out of bed.

"You sure you don't want help?" Amy asked.

"I can handle this myself. Just you guys go home. Do whatever you gotta do. Thank you for your love and support. I very much appreciate it." Paige talked at a rate equivalent to if someone just drank a lot of caffeine.

"Okay, she's on the verge of a panic attack. We should go," Jenn said.

"All right. Just call if you need anything else," Amy said.

"Sure sure. Goodbye now!" Paige continued to panic.

The three began to leave. Amy and Jenn exited the room while Morgan stopped at the door.

"I finished mine two days ago if you need any pointers."

"Bye, Morgan!"

"Love you," she said, shutting the door.

Paige grabbed one of her small pillows and screamed into it.

One Hour Later

Paige was sitting at her personal workspace, staring at a blank sheet of paper with a pen in one hand and her head leaning on the other.

"Hey." Catherine came in carrying a laundry hamper. "You're finally out of bed. That's good to see."

Paige didn't respond.

"Sooo what are you working on?"

"Nothing, 'cause I'm completely blank trying to write this stupid essay you gave us!"

"I see. Well, anything in particular that's staggering you?" she asked while she put Paige's laundry in her drawers.

"Yeah, I put it off all week, haven't given it any thought, and now I don't know where to begin!"

"Well, all you gotta do is write about your greatest inspiration. You're a fast writer. You'll get this done quick."

"Can't I get an extension and hand it in on Monday?"

"I'm sorry. The deadline is tomorrow or it's a zero. No exceptions. Even for nepotism."

"Dammit."

"Of all the work you've been given, this is the one that's breaking you?"

"Yes. I have no idea what to say. I don't even know if I have an inspiration."

"Oh, come on now."

"No, I'm serious. There's no one that makes me wanna be a better person or encourage me to do this thing, that I want to be like, or anything. And on top of that, I've barely slept all week, my head still hurts, and all this thinking is making me feel like I have another concussion." She leaned her head on both hands. "I've become everybody I ever pitied."

Catherine saw she's struggling, put the hamper down on the bed, and walked over to her daughter's side.

"You know? I always choose to read *The Great Gatsby* for my classes because it's such a great story. But more important than that, I think

295

it's a very important piece of literature. The one thing that I personally always took away from it was how James Gatz became so good at convincing people that he was somebody else that it seemed like the person he was before never existed. And how all that reinventing of himself was just to earn the love of somebody else. When the truth is, Daisy loved him for who he was. She never cared about riches. It really makes you think about how this story could've gone if he just accepted that he was a poor farm boy and stayed with Daisy, instead of getting rich off illegally selling liquor. …But hey, that's love, right? People will do whatever they have to for it."

Paige hung on to every word she said.

"But even though Gatsby's story was fabricated, it still inspired people. People like Nick Carraway. It inspired him to pursue riches and make something special of himself, and along the way, he formed a strong friendship with that same man who got him there. So some good did come from that. But in the end, Gatsby never got that one thing he really wanted. Then he left the world as somebody he wasn't, and only a handful of people knew who he really was."

"Why are you telling me all of this?"

"I don't know. Maybe because I really love talking about this kind of stuff. I do have a tendency to overthink things, but that's the beautiful thing about art. It gets your mind thinking, and the best part is that you can interpret it however you'd like. Maybe you didn't see it like that, but that's always what I took away from it, and that's why I assigned the class this project. Because there's always something that's driving all of us. Sometimes to a point where you're no longer steering yourself in the direction you want to go, and along the way, you might forget why you're on that road to begin with. Or even who you were when you started."

Paige looked away from her mom. Catherine leaned forward and grabbed both her shoulders.

"But the important thing is whoever you want to be, or what you want people to call you, that's fine. As long as you never forget who you really are and that people see who you really are. Not everybody will accept that, but the right ones will, and they'll always be there on that long, tedious, perilous road with you. Even if you're apart for a long time, those same people will always find their way back." Paige looked back at her mom. "You might not be thinking about it now, but I'm sure in your heart, there's someone you always want in your passenger seat."

Paige continued to stare at her mom.

Catherine kissed the top of her daughter's head before leaving with the laundry hamper.

Paige got lost in her thoughts as she stared at that blank piece of paper again. She then glanced over to look at her bejeweled rose by the window and let out a deep sigh.

She pushed her messy hair out of her sight, thought about what her mom just said, and got a resolute look on her face.

She marched into her bathroom, opened the sink's drawer, and took out two unopened, differently sized boxes.

She stared at herself in the mirror before opening a second drawer to pick up a pair of scissors…

The Next Day, 8:01 AM: Meadows Forest High School

Steven had finally returned to school for the first time in a week. His presence was noticed more than usual, especially with the bandaged arm and the healing cuts and bruises on his face. A few other students attempted to ask him some questions—about him, about Paige, all of which he ignored.

He walked into homeroom and caught the attention of the class. There were audible whispers among the students and eyes glaring in his direction. On the way to his seat in the back room, he met Morgan's face in the front. Her expression was hard to make out. He then stopped to turn to Catherine who's seated at her desk.

"Steven. Welcome back," Catherine said with a genial smile, but in a hushed tone.

Steven nodded without saying anything and went to sit down at his desk.

"What happened to you?" one of the students sitting next to him asked.

Steven told them to "shut up" through a hand gesture, which they obliged.

"Is it true? Are you—" another student sitting in front of him began to ask, but stopped when Steven shot them a cold glare. "It's... not important," they said before turning back around.

The bell rang.

"All right, guys, this is our last day of presentations and to hand in your essays. I trust that everybody who hasn't yet is ready to do so now?" Catherine spoke and was met by silence from the class. "I'll just assume you're all thinking yes. So who'd like to go—"

She was interrupted by the door opening. All attention shifted to it, and the class got talking again about who they saw.

It's Paige. Except she didn't have her glasses on, and instead of having her trademark ponytail, her hair had been cut to shoulder length, but most striking of all, she dyed it back to her natural blonde. Some students were questioning if that was really her.

Steven's head looked up from his desk, and his heart skipped a beat when he saw her. He wasn't sure if he'd see her at all today, let alone looking like this. She looked exactly how he remembered her when they were kids, which just drove the knife deeper into his heart. Now his past literally did come back to haunt him.

"Paige. It's such a relief to have you back," her mother said, trying to be casual.

"Thank you," Paige faintly said and went to her seat next to Morgan.

Morgan was as shocked as everybody else was; her jaw was practically hanging from her skull.

Paige turned her head to face her.

"Dude! What did you do?" Morgan mouthed, but Paige simply shrugged.

Meanwhile, Catherine spoke to the class. "So as I was saying, who'd like to start our last batch of presentations?"

A Few Minutes Later

"So to make a long story short, she's not only one of the most beautiful women on the planet, but also one of the best actors of all time. Whether it's *Easy A*, *La La Land*, *Spider-Man*, *Bird Man*, *Irrational Man*, other things with 'Man' in the title, or *Movie 43*, Emma Stone's just amazing in everything she does, and she gives me a lot of encouragement to just be true to myself, to never be afraid to crack a joke, and that's why she's my biggest inspiration. Morgan Chambers, out!"

She was met with an applause from her class.

"Excellent job, Morgan. I could tell you put a lot of thought into it," Catherine congratulated her. "So with that, we only have two left. Umm, Steven?"

Steven looked toward her as all other eyes were drawn to him, except for Paige whose eyes just expanded.

"Would you like to go next?" Catherine asked.

Steven hesitated for a second before agreeing. He walked to the front, and Paige immediately noticed his face was damaged. She examined him further and saw that his arm was bandaged. She grew concerned seeing him like this. Concerned and hurt. She lowered her head so she didn't have to look at him.

Morgan noticed where her friend's attention was at and was very conflicted herself about how to feel. She faced her own head forward but glanced off to the side, not looking at him.

Steven began to read.

"For most of my life, the things that have left the biggest impressions on me have been music, action movies, or video games. But I've never had any one person that's inspired me in a strong way. I've mostly just done things however I wanted, whenever I wanted, not caring about the circumstances, with nobody to deviate me. I'm sure you can all tell. Which I now realize is something I badly needed, and this last year, I found somebody who did. Their name is . . . Albert Einstein."

This sparked some varied reactions among the rest of the class, some whispers and puzzled looks.

He had all their attention, and Paige was no exception. Her heart skipped a beat, and she turned to face him with a mystified look, as did Morgan who's now just as engrossed.

"I know. Just hear me out."

He continued to present.

"Not only was Einstein one of the greatest minds of modern time, but he was also one of the hardest working and most compassionate. He was most famous for coining the equation $E=mc^2$, or energy equals mass times the speed of light squared. As well as his own twist on the theory of relativity, both of which have respectively been practiced by other scientists at his time, and to this day. But he wasn't just a genius. He was also somebody who was passionate about his work and wanted to pass along his knowledge to others, despite how some of them treated him. ...Many other scientists laughed at his theory of relativity. Nazi Germany was calling for his execution, and the American government wanted to throw him out of the country. But he still believed in the best of humanity. He advocated for peace, was a civil rights activist, and his research helped lead to the end of World War II. So while I'm sure he might've lived to regret a lot of things, and even working with a lot of the people that he did, he ultimately did a lot of great things for the world, even if it didn't deserve them." He released a deep exhale. "Einstein had a lot of passion for what he did and loved sharing his knowledge with anyone he could, regardless of how disrespectful, obnoxious, hardheaded, or cruel many of them could be to him. And I wish I saw that earlier than I should've, because if I had, maybe I would've turned out better than I am. I guess it just goes to show that once you take time to get to know somebody, you might find something that... you've been missing for a long time. Somebody who will... save your life."

He finished his presentation and went back to sit at his desk, to an atmosphere of stunned silence from the class, with Paige being the most stunned. She was blown away further by every next thing he was saying, and by the end, she had no idea what to make of it.

"Wow. I have to admit that was pleasantly unexpected of you, Steven. Wonderful job," Catherine praised him. "And then there was one. Paige? Are you ready?"

"Huh? Oh! Yes. ...Yes, I am." She hesitated before going up. "But before I start..." Paige took a deep breath. "I can tell you all have questions about why I look like this. Well, this ties into why this person is my greatest inspiration. That person in question being"—Paige looked over to Catherine—"Mrs. Hetfield."

Catherine wasn't sure how to react to this; she's as puzzled as everyone else.

"What is happening?" Morgan mouthed to herself.

Steven, who was afraid to look at her, now gave his undivided attention, wondering what she was doing.

Paige started reading.

"I know to all of you, she's just our homeroom English teacher. But she's a lot more than that to me. She is incredibly caring, always pushing us to do our best, and daring us to take on new challenges, even ones that seemed terrifying. Whether those challenges are the tests she gives us or just for us… to get along with people that we don't like. No matter how scared I can get, I always feel a sense of comfort whenever she's around, and it doesn't matter how big or small my problems are—she'll always be the first one I go to. Without her …I don't know what I would do or where I would be right now." She started to second-guess herself but kept going. "And because of her influence, I've discovered, and rediscovered, so many things about myself. As I'm writing this, the thought is finally settling in for me. For as long as I can remember, I've wanted to be just like her; and anytime I would tell her that, she would say, 'Sweetie, that really means a lot. But don't worry about being like me. Focus on being you. Be the first… Be the first Miranda.'"

Another wave of surprise arose from just about everyone.

Paige stopped reading to address her class.

"Yes. My first name is Miranda. For years I've gone by Paige Hetfield, because I was so afraid of what people would think about me. But I'm tired of pretending to be somebody I'm not. I'm sick of lying to everybody, and to myself. I just want to live my life without a care about judgment. …So I've never asked anybody for their attention, and I still won't. But if I do have it, then you can start calling me by my real name: Miranda. Miranda Paige"—she turned to her mother—"Curtis."

A variety of reactions erupted from this revelation; most students were shocked or confused, with a few indistinctly talking or even gasping. Morgan felt stupefied and covered her face, knowing that people might start asking her questions. Steven wasn't sure how he should feel about what she'd just done.

Meanwhile, Catherine was completely thrown off. She felt genuinely touched by her daughter's essay as she was reading it, and now she's trying to comprehend what's happening. She spent years keeping Miranda's secret for her, and suddenly it was all publicly exposed without warning. The questions that arose from her students weren't helping much.

She stood up from her desk, and the room went quiet.

"Wow. ...I don't think anybody was ready for that. ...I wasn't." Catherine let out a nervous chuckle. "Umm..." She turned to Miranda. "Sweetheart, I thought that. Where... Why all of... Miranda—Paige— no, I-I don't under—"

"Mom!" Miranda cut her off. "It's okay." She smiled.

Catherine let go off her confusion and smiled back at her little girl.

She stepped forward and put her hand on her shoulder. "I love you, Miranda," she said, unable to hold back her tears.

"I love you too, Mom," she replied with tears in her own eyes before she hugged her mom, no longer caring about how many people saw it.

However, they heard the class was applauding this moment. Morgan uncovered her face prior and, after seeing this embrace, set aside all her worries and clapped along, even taking it a step further by rooting.

Steven grinned when he saw her having this sweet moment with her mom and how warmly she was accepted by everyone else. He knew instinctively that from here on out, she was going to be all right. ...She was going to be all right.

After first period ended, word quickly spread around about Miranda and Mrs. Curtis being mother and daughter. People seemed to have forgotten about those other rumors rather quickly as now a somehow crazier piece of gossip came to light, straight from the source.

Miranda was used to being transparent for as long as she'd been going to public school, so it was a bit overwhelming to suddenly be such a hot topic, especially with her change in appearance. She had gained a lot of newfound attention after trying to avoid it for so long all at once, but it didn't bother her. Despite being bombarded like a movie star would be by TMZ, she still felt free. She felt like for the first time in her life, she wasn't hiding. She didn't think it'd be possible, but she loved finally being seen. Not as Paige—as Miranda.

Sixth Period, 12:06 PM

Miranda went to her usual spot in the library for lunch. Even though she no longer felt a need to avoid people on principle, she just needed to escape the attention for a little bit. Besides, she liked going to the library.

When she got to the table she'd normally sat at in the back room, she found a *Fullmetal Alchemist* manga on it, unattended. She looked around to make sure no one was looking for it, then looked in it to make sure it wasn't currently checked out, which it wasn't.

After deducing that it didn't belong to anybody, she decided to read it for fun. But after turning the first page, she found something inside it: a note signed "Miranda".

Naturally curious, she flipped over the note, which read, "Look under the table."

She immediately recognized the handwriting that she had seen multiple times; it was written by Steven. Her instinct was to ignore it, but she was too inquisitive and followed the instruction. After finding nothing on the floor, she then checked the underside and found a small cardboard box with a bow, which was attached to a letter and was taped to the table. She pulled it off and observed it, completely befuddled. She saw the words "I'm sorry" written on the back of the folded-up paper and carefully detached the other piece of tape, placing the box down. She reluctantly opened it and noticed that this letter was written from back to front, like a manga.

She then read it.

> What you did back there was really brave. Knowing how long you've been hiding all of that, it couldn't have been easy. I'm really proud of you. And I'm excited for the world to finally see the real you. The one that I got to know. The one who made me realize how badly I needed to turn my life around. The person that I idiotically pushed away long ago and hurt again when I got her back. I said a lot in there myself, but I know that wasn't good enough. I don't believe anything I say

here will be enough either, but this is just something I need to say. For years, I thought my life was destroyed when my father left me and my mom, but I was wrong. I never needed him. It was destroyed when I lost you. Deep down I knew something was missing, but I was too blinded by my own rage to see it, or even bother looking for it. Now I know what that was, and I know now why Mrs. Curtis sent you to me. Even though I hated it then, I'm happy she did. Because of you, I felt things that I forgot how to feel, and I realized how much more fortunate I am than I took for granted, with the people I have with me. Samantha and Bruce, Jason, Lisa, and my Mom. I've had the Devil whispering in my ear for so long, but you became my Guardian Angel. And as hard as this is going to be for me, I'm writing this note to say Goodbye. When I came here today, I was hoping you would be here so I could give you this gift and beg you to give me one more chance. But then I saw you up there. You looked happier than I've ever seen you, and that made me happy to watch. Now, I realize that you don't need me. You have so much potential, so much talent, and everything you do, you do with such finesse. You're gonna go on to do amazing things, and I wish I could be there to see you do all those amazing things, but all I would be doing is slowing you down. You've done everything you could've done for me, and I'll always be grateful for that, especially after how I treated you. But I guess that's the thing, you deserve better than me. I want to be that guy, but I can never be him. I hurt you more than once, and I don't want too again. So I'm not gonna make you take that risk. But I just want you to know, I'm Sorry. For everything. I know you'll never forgive me, but please at least accept this birthday gift, even if just to remind you to never trust someone like me again. And to remember this:

No matter who comes into my life, or what happens to me, you will always be the most special person I've ever known. You're the best friend I've ever had, and my greatest inspiration. Miranda or Paige, you'll always be a part of my heart.

I Love You.

—Nicholas Calaway

Paige's heart pounded as she read that letter, and by the time she finished it, her tears had fallen onto it. It was the most beautiful and most devastating thing she'd ever read. Everybody wonders what it will feel like when somebody tells you they love you and how it would feel for them to leave you; she just experienced both. She wanted to desperately go look for him and tell him what she thought and how she felt, but she knew he had made up his mind, and accepted that there was nothing left. That they just weren't meant to be.

With that, she turned her attention to the box. She took the bow off and removed the cover. What she found knocked all the air out of her.

It was his mother's gold necklace.

Her heart went from beating rapidly to stopping dead in its track. The one accessory that he wore every day regardless of what outfit he had on, the last remnant of his mom that he had and held close to him, and he just gave it to her. She had felt so unsure about her feelings for him this past week, if what she felt before was still alive or if they were even real at all. But all those negative ones had just gone away. She knew right then and there, without a single doubt in her mind.

She was in love with him.

This revelation that should've been an amazing feeling instead left her feeling distressed. With his written words in the back of her mind, she clasped the necklace in her hand and held it close to her heart, not caring if the entire world was watching her cry.

Chapter 24

Sweet Sixteen

Saturday, March 25: Miranda's House

It's the afternoon. Miranda was in the center of her kitchen having her hair done. As her mom was making conversation with the hairdresser, she was lost in her thoughts.

"Got three more for you," Richard said, coming into the room being followed by Morgan, Amy, and Jenn.

"Bam!" Morgan said, pointing toward Miranda. "I told you she went blonde, but y'all didn't wanna listen," she told the other two.

"What are you talking about? I told them in the group chat. I sent a picture," Miranda said.

"I had to see it for myself. Hot damn," Jenn said.

"I love it. This color looks great on you!" Amy complimented her.

"I mean, it's all right. Hopefully it'll look better in a minute," Miranda said.

"Not even. Just another second and…" The hairdresser applied hair spray on her last curl. "Beautiful." They handed Miranda a mirror.

Miranda stared at herself for a few seconds.

"Well?" the hairdresser asked.

"Something wrong, sweetie?" Catherine asked.

"No. No, it looks great. It really does. I'm just… not used to seeing myself looking like this," she said, touching her hair.

"Just wait. Once we get everything else on you, you're gonna look amazing," Amy said.

"Yeah, you're gonna look so hot we won't be able to post pictures 'cause it'll make people go blind for staring at you too long," Morgan said.

"Oh my god," Jenn said, rubbing her forehead.

"Thank you, Morgan," Amy said, patting her shoulder.

Miranda lightly chuckled. "Thank you," she said to the hairdresser.

"My pleasure. So who's next?"

"Jenn," Amy and Morgan said in unison.

"What? Why?" she asked.

"Oh, come on, Jenn," Amy said.

"Besides, your half-shaved head will take the least work," Morgan added.

"Wow. You really have a way with compliments," Jenn sarcastically replied.

"You're welcome," Morgan said.

"All right, are we doing this? Or are we doing this?" the hairdresser asked.

"Come on, Jenn. Sit down," Miranda said, standing from the chair.

"Goddammit. Whatever. Move," she said, pushing Morgan out of her way—into Amy—before sitting down.

"Don't worry, I know just what to do with you," the hairdresser said, putting a sundry cape around her.

"Goodie," Jenn said. She then looked over to Miranda. "So contacts?" she asked her.

"Yep," she answered, not looking at her. "I've had them for a while. Just never bothered to try them on."

"Hmm. And this is natural?" Jenn asked, referring to her hair.

"Yep. This is the real me," Miranda uncomfortably answered.

"When did you even find time to do it?" Morgan asked.

"I just did it while I wrote my essay. Wasn't that hard."

"So you got that done then?" Amy asked.

"She did, and it was excellent," Catherine answered for her.

"Ha. Ego much, Mrs. Curtis?" Morgan asked, and Catherine laughed while Miranda shied away.

"So now everybody knows you're related? After all this time, you came out and confessed it"—Jenn snapped her fingers—"just like that?"

"Yeah. You had to have been there. It was like the ending of *Iron Man*. She was all like 'You all know me as Paige Hetfield, but I'm Miranda Curtis now, bitches!' Oh, I wish I could've filmed it. It was incredible," Morgan raved.

"All right all right, I think you're overselling it a bit, Morgan," Catherine said.

"Not as much as everyone else."

"It's true. Everybody's talking about you two," Jenn said.

"I'm aware. All day yesterday I had students asking me about her," Catherine said as Miranda continued to feel bashful.

"So have all of us," Amy said.

"At least they're all off the 'Is she dead?' stuff," Morgan said.

"Yeah, but…" Amy turned to Miranda. "Okay, I am proud of you for revealing that, but what changed all of a sudden?" she asked.

"I just got tired of keeping that secret. I… I wanted to stop lying and start being truer to myself, I guess. I don't know how to explain it," Miranda answered.

"I think I know," Amy said.

"I was there. I saw where you were coming from," Morgan added, to which Miranda nodded.

"So what are you gonna do now?" Jenn asked.

Miranda shook her head. "I don't know."

"Do you want to talk about anything?" Catherine asked.

"I think I should," Miranda agreed.

"Actually," Richard interrupted to ask Catherine, "would you mind if I take this one?"

"Miranda?" Catherine looked to her for an answer.

Miranda looked at her stepdad. "Sure," she said, following him upstairs to talk in private.

"So should we all just get used to calling her that? 'Cause it's gonna be hard for me," Morgan said.

Upstairs

Richard let Miranda into his and Catherine's bedroom and closed the door.

"You know? You don't seem very chipper for a girl about to celebrate turning sixteen," he began.

"Well, I've had a really hard week."

"Yeah, a concussion will do that. But I don't think that's entirely it. What's really got you down that's made you alter your whole appearance?"

"I don't know."

"All right, let's try another question. How exactly did you hit your head? Your friends said you were pushed. Is that true?"

"Well, it's not entirely. …It's-it's like… What happened was uh—" she stuttered.

"Miranda. Angel. Chrysalis. Just tell me what happened."

Miranda sighed. "Last weekend when I had my friends over… I was in the kitchen with Steven. And I kind of …found out something about him that… threw me off guard."

"What?"

"His real name is Nicholas. Or Nikko. And he's actually someone I used to know when I was little." Miranda tightened her eyes closed and breathed out. She reopened them and continued, "I'm not sure if Mom ever told you about him, but he was my best friend, until his dad left him and his mom. He started taking his anger out on other kids, and …I kind of got in his way when I shouldn't have," she said, touching her scar.

"So he's the same boy who did that to you?" he said, surprised.

"Well, technically yes. And when I recognized him, I kind of lost control of my emotions, and I don't remember all of it, but I started pushing him away. So I know you don't really like him, and now that I've told you all this, you're only gonna hate him more, but my point is, in hindsight, what happened last week was really kind of my fault." She touched her fresher scar.

Richard thought about what she just said.

"So, then he never actually pushed you?"

The memory came back to her, enough that she can recall striking him below the belt, losing her balance, and falling backward. "No."

Richard sighed into his hands. "You really care about this guy, do you?"

"I do." Her voice cracked. "He doesn't look like it, but he's the sweetest guy I've ever met. He listens to me. He remembers little things. He understands me, how I'm feeling, and makes me feel safe, like I can talk to him without having to hide anything. I didn't see that at first, but now—despite everything that's happened—that's all I see now." She sat on the edge of her parents' bed. "And even after how I treated him …he still loves me. I know this is hard to understand."

He sat by her side and wrapped his arm around her. "Not as hard as you think." Miranda leaned her head into his neck. "So… what's stopping you?"

"He… thinks that he'd be slowing me down. That I deserve better, and he'll never be that kind of guy. …It's over before it ever even started."

Richard saw how despondent she was. "Miranda, ever since I married your mom, my biggest priority has always been to make sure you were safe and happy. Now, I admit I've been a little on edge about whatever you and Nicholas have. But I can't deny that these past few months… you've been the happiest I've ever seen you. Your mom says that she's never seen you beaming with so much joy, and we could tell that it comes from him. I'm always going to have concerns about you, but you're only a couple of birthdays away from becoming a woman. Every choice made from then on is going to come down to you, and all we can do is hope that you're doing what makes you happy." He leaned away to look her in the face. "So forget about how I feel and what everybody else is saying. What do you want?"

Miranda took a couple of seconds to muster up her courage.

"I just want to be with him," she confessed.

Richard smiled. "Well, then you need to tell him that."

"Even if I do, how will I know it'll work out? What if we do risk it and everything falls apart again?"

"That's what a relationship is. One big risk."

"You think he'll be there tonight?"

"If he is, then that's the perfect time to take that risk."

"And if he's not?"

"Then maybe he isn't the one for you."

He kissed her cheek before leaving her alone to think.

She reached into her shirt's collar and pulled out Nikko's mom's necklace that she was wearing.

"That's what I'm afraid of," she whispered to herself.

6:00 PM: Nikko's House

Nikko was on the end of his living room couch glued to his TV playing video games—if you consider walking around an open world's hub not doing any objectives playing a game.

"Hey, we're... about to head out to the party," Samantha informed him, with Bruce beside her.

Nikko briefly glanced toward them. "All right. You guys have fun." He turned back to the TV.

"Last chance to change your mind. You're sure you don't want to come?" Bruce asked him.

"Don't worry about me. I can survive on my own," he said, not looking at them.

Samantha sat on his left side. "Nick? We know you're upset. But we also know how important Paige—Miranda—is to you."

"And we know you didn't ask for advice, but tonight would be the perfect time to let her know that. Before somebody else does," Bruce said, walking up to his right side by the armrest.

Nikko sighed, putting his controller down. "I know it would be. But what would be the point? No matter what I'd say, she wouldn't listen, let alone believe me."

"Do you know that for sure?" Bruce asked.

"Yeah, I do, and who could blame her? I hurt her too many times. I put her in the hospital when we were kids, I treated her like garbage when she was trying to help me, and then when I let her help me, I put her in the hospital again. Just one big cycle of shit that keeps repeating."

"You know, Lisa told us that what happened last week wasn't really your fault," Bruce told him.

"Yes, it was."

"Well, from what she's told us, it sounds like you're putting too much blame on yourself for a freak accident," Samantha said.

Nikko didn't reply.

"Look, you didn't mean to hurt her, did you?" Samantha asked.

"No. Of course, I didn't. I would never hurt her ...not on purpose."

"We know you wouldn't," Bruce said. "I'll admit, you can be a bit difficult to reach. At times you can be irritable, and I can't deny that you've done some bad things."

"But just because you do bad things, it doesn't make you a bad person," Samantha added. "You're not a bad person. We know you would never intentionally hurt the people you love. You may not say it, but we know you feel it."

"It's not that I don't wanna go ...I just can't," Nikko said. "I don't want her to get hurt again. So I need to just let her go. ...Besides, she wouldn't even want me there. Just go without me."

"That's your final decision?" Bruce asked.

"Yeah."

"Well, just know that whatever people say about you, your mom and dad will always have your back." Samantha paused after realizing she used the *M* and *D* words. "Sorry, could we still call ourselves that?"

Nikko lightly chuckled. "Yes. You can both say that."

"That's our boy," Bruce said, and both hugged their son from the side.

Samantha kissed his cheek, and the two slowly left.

They looked back at him from the doorway. "Nicholas?" Samantha said. He turned his head back to them. "We love you."

Nikko deeply breathed in and out. "I love you guys too," he admitted.

They both gave him sympathetic smiles before leaving the house.

Nikko lay back against the couch, despondent.

Forty Minutes Later

Nikko was still seated in the same spot. He just finished an online Team Deathmatch in *Call of Duty: Black Ops III* and was listening to children who were clearly under ten years old shouting profanities at him. He was in no mood to deal with them this time. He just took off his headset, closed the software, and scratched Boscoe's head that was lying on his lap.

He heard Lisa's footsteps coming down the stairs into the living room and turned to face her.

"Hi," she said, walking around the couch to the other end, and sat down.

"You're still here?"

"Yeah. You didn't notice me not leave with Mom and Dad?"

"Oh, Jesus Christ." He rubbed his eyes. "Well, why are you still here?"

"I didn't want to go."

"How come?"

"I'm not really in the mood."

"Ah come on, she really wants you to be there. You can't let her down."

"How am I supposed to have fun knowing that you're here all alone and completely miserable?" Nikko didn't answer her question. "She wanted you to be there too, and you're just going to stay here because of something you didn't even do. That's not fair."

"It's a lot more complicated than that." Lisa looked at him, waiting for a reasoning. "It's more like. ...Listen, there're some things you'll never be able to really understand until you've experienced it."

"I don't have to be in love with somebody to know when somebody else is," she said, throwing him off guard. "You're not fooling me, big brother."

"I'm not trying to fool anyone," he defended himself. "But it doesn't matter."

Lisa scoffed. "You're right. I don't understand."

"Someday you will. You'll meet a boy or a girl, and your entire world will change, because they'll become it."

"It's still not fair," she repeated. "It's not fair that you're just going to give up on her and be sad for the rest of your life because you can't move on."

"It's what I have to do. If my misery means she's happy, then I can live with that."

"And what if it doesn't make her happy?"

"It will eventually. She'll find someone else a lot better for her than me."

"So you're not even gonna tell her?" Nikko didn't answer.

Lisa then noticed something different about him. "Hmm. Where's your necklace?"

"Oh, I, uhh…" Lisa stared at him with her chin leaning on her fist. "I… left it in a box at school." Lisa's still listening, with a raised eyebrow. "As a gift. …For her." He picked up his controller and casually scrolled through his Xbox One menu screen while she maintained her focus. "With a note telling her that I love her!" he said, speeding up his voice. "Ya happy now?"

"So she knows!" she excitedly uttered.

"I left it in the library. For all I know somebody else found it and sold Mom's necklace to buy a karaoke machine."

"Or she found it, read your note, and is praying that she'll see you tonight!"

"Okay, you know what? We've completely lost track of this whole thing. Why don't you just go to her party? I'm sure she's praying you'll be there."

"Well, I would, bu-u-u-u-t Mom and Dad already left, and I can't drive." She smirked, while Nikko was dumbstruck. "Your keys are in your vest," she said, walking toward the staircase.

"What?"

She turned her head in his direction. "The ones you couldn't find a few nights ago, they're in the pocket of your vest. I think it's still lying on the floor in your room," she said, pointing upward.

Nikko moved past her to go upstairs to his room. He spotted his vest on the floor as she said and dug into his pocket to find his lost keys. He got a vexed look on his face and looked back to Lisa who's standing at the door with her hands on her hips.

"Just go put your dress on," he directed her.

"Yay!" she expressed with glee, before going back to her room.

Nikko held the vest up—the gift Miranda gave him for Christmas. He turned it around to read the "Steven" stitching on the back of it.

He stared at it for a couple of minutes, reminiscing on all the memories they shared, which for the first time in a week looked bright and not desaturated.

He walked out of the room still looking at it, lost in his thoughts, when Boscoe walked past his legs and into Lisa's room. Nikko noticed that he's looking under her bed, trying to crawl underneath but can't. He went over to look under her bed and saw one of his toys got stuck underneath. Nikko reached in and pulled it out.

"Here ya go, boy," he said, handing it to his now-happy dog.

He glanced back under her bed and noticed something off to the side. He pulled it out to make out what it was.

He had found a finished drawing Lisa had done.

It was a clean, beautifully illustrated, manga-styled piece with caricatures of him and Miranda. They were holding hands, their foreheads and noses touching, both of their cheeks blushing, and the two of them looking into each other's eyes with loving smiles. It was during nighttime, and they're standing against the New York City skyline as it can be seen from St. George, with the Freedom Tower and Downtown Manhattan in the background. The city was illuminated along with the stars in the sky, and the two were shrouded in the light of the moon in contrast to the dark foreground. The moon itself was surrounded by clouds that were shrouding it, leaving only its center exposed to appear as if it were in the shape of the heart that directly hit them both to cast a same-shaped spotlight on the wooden walkway, accompanying their silhouettes.

Between the amount of attention to detail she put into this piece, from the line work, color scheme, lighting contrasts, textures, everything drawn in the background, to how well she captured their likenesses—their clothes, hair, eye color, skin tones, her glasses, and his tattoos—it made for a beautiful sketch that he became entranced by. Once he got over his amazement of his sister's talent, it added more conflict among his emotions.

He turned to see Lisa at the door wearing her baby-blue dress, frozen in an awkward state, stuck looking for some sort of response.

"You did this?"

She responded with a slow stiff nod of her head, with a timorous look.

"Hmm-hmm," she mustered to say.

"When did you—"

315

"I've been working on it since January. I finished it about a week ago, and I was going to give it to her as a birthday gift, but then this all happened, and I didn't want you to see it until—" She groaned. "I'm sorry. I'm not trying to trigger you. I swore I moved that. I don't know how I forgot—"

"Hey!" He stopped her rambling and pointed to it. "This is really good," he complimented her.

Lisa was silenced for a second. "You think so?" She walked over to him.

"Yeah. I knew you had an arm, but this, this is really something."

Lisa wasn't sure what to think of his response. "Well, thank you. I'm glad you like it," she said.

Nikko nodded, again engaging with the piece.

"Nick? What are you thinking about?"

Richfield Regency, Verona, New Jersey

It was 7:00 PM, and Miranda's party was just beginning. She was outside the main hall, in her royal-blue dress complemented by her tiara bejeweled with an aquamarine in the center, alongside her trio of friends. Morgan and Amy were wearing different-colored blue dresses that suited their styles, while Jenn was wearing a black suit with another distinctly blue-shaded vest.

All their respective parents were with them gushing over how their children looked, getting a few quick pictures in before their entrance. Miranda did her best to look brave and excited among all the attention, but she couldn't help herself from constantly looking at the door wondering, *Where's Nikko?*

After a few minutes and photos were taken, Miranda's parents went up to her.

"All right, this is it. Are you ready?" Catherine asked her.

Miranda looked around at everyone and took another glance at the door. She felt queasy but wasn't going to let her feelings ruin everybody else's night. So she put on a smile and answered, "Yes."

"In that case, let's do this!" Richard exclaimed.

Their parents left them outside to go into the main hall and let the host know they're ready. Miranda took a deep breath. Her friends comforted her to ease the tension she felt.

The lights in the hall went dim and lit up blue as the host began to speak.

"All right! At this time, I ask if everybody could please take your seats and clear the entranceway, for it is time to introduce the reason we've all come out here tonight. That's right, everybody, join me in welcoming our beautiful girl of the hour, who as of now would be old enough to drink except this isn't Germany, Denmark, or Switzerland. Being accompanied by her own personal 'Charlie's Angels'—Morgan, Amy, and Jennifer—ladies and gentlemen, family and friends: Miranda Paige Curtis!" the host announced.

The band started playing her favorite song, "Breakaway" by Kelly Clarkson.

Miranda and her friends made their way out to a roaring applause from the party, which consisted of Miranda's grandparents, aunts and uncles, cousins—older and younger, close and distant—and even a few guests from her friends' families. Miranda wasn't ready for as many people as there were that night. She saw Jason was playing bass with the band and noticed that Nikko's parents were there as well, but still no sign of him, or even Lisa. She felt the pit in her stomach come back but was still overwhelmed by everything else going on, so she kept on smiling as best as she could while she greeted her guests and got some pictures taken with her cousins and other relatives.

At one point shortly after her entrance, Paige was escorted outside the hall to do a photo shoot with the professional photographer, starting with her mom and stepdad, as her friends watched, waiting for their turns.

Meanwhile, Jenn was watching and saw how happy she looked with them, and thought about how much they loved their daughter, between throwing her this big party and being attentive when she needed it most. She then turned her attention to her own parents who were also watching the photo op as they're having their own side conversation.

Jenn excused herself from Amy and Morgan to go over to her folks.

"Mom? Dad?" She got their attention.

"Yes, Jenn?" her dad said.

"Are you okay?" her mom asked.

"Yeah, umm, can I talk to you guys for a sec?" Jenn asked.

"Absolutely," her mom answered. "What do you wanna talk about?"

"Well…" She glanced back to Miranda who's still posing with Catherine and Richard. "Do you guys ever think about… what could've been?"

"What do you mean?" her dad asked.

"I, I've been talking to some people and…" She looked back to the stage in the main hall where Jason's playing with the band to entertain the guests still in there. "I'll just come right out and ask. Are you both happy with your lives?"

"What? Of course, we are," her mom said.

"Why wouldn't we be?" her dad said.

Jenn sighed. "Because I know I wasn't really supposed to be here, that you two made a mistake when you were around my age, and it forced you to rethink your lives. Knowing all that makes me feel, I don't know, guilty," she said. "You two had so much going for yourselves and gave up all of it to raise me, and all I ever really do is beat people up and cause trouble." She sniffed. "I just, I just wanted to make sure you two didn't… that you didn't regret me." Her voice cracked.

"Jenn, that couldn't be further from the truth," her dad said, touching her face.

"We don't regret you at all. You're the best thing that's ever happened to us," her mom added.

"Sure, we weren't planning for it to play out like this, but the truth is…"

"We were still planning on it."

Jenn looked surprised.

"I knew I wanted to be with your mom for the rest of my life…"

"And I loved your dad well before we, well, took that leap of faith."

"And when she told me she was pregnant, I won't lie, I was terrified."

"So was I. But we both had a long talk that same night, and after going over all our options, we ultimately decided…"

"We were going to drop everything else and devote our lives to you."

"You were the sign that we were meant to be."

Jenn started to develop tears.

"So you never think about what might've been? About what you both could've accomplished?" Jenn asked.

"Not nearly as much as we think about how gracious we are for what is," her mom assured her, kissing her cheek.

"Nothing we ever could've accomplished would compare to what we did accomplish—being your parents," her dad said.

A single tear rolled down Jenn's face. "You really mean that?"

"Damn right we do," her mom said, while her dad wiped her tear away.

"And no matter what you do, nothing will change that," her dad said.

"Even with that said though, you have been noticeably tranquil lately."

"How so?" Jenn asked her.

"Well, you come home with a lot less bruises."

"As in none."

"You're not having as many outbursts."

"You converse with us a lot more."

"Not to mention, you haven't cried since you were a baby." She wiped her daughter's eyes.

"I'm not crying," Jenn bluffed.

"Hmm-hmm. But she's right, you seem a lot more at ease lately."

"Your friends seem to think so."

"Huh?" Jenn was startled and quickly glanced to where her friends were. "What did they tell you?"

"Nothing, just that you're not 'on edge' as you normally are," her mom said.

"They must finally be rubbing off on you."

"Well… they're certainly a part of it," Jenn said.

"Jenn? I know we don't have the most luxurious life," her dad said. "But you're luckier than you think you are. Especially with friends like them." He gestured to her friends.

Jenn looked over to see Miranda taking pictures with Morgan who was doing a silly pose that's making Amy laugh.

"Which is especially great, considering you never had anybody to play with when you were a kid," her mom recollected.

"Yeah, well, they wouldn't have been my first choice," Jenn admitted.

"But you chose them anyway," her mom said.

"And that's the great thing about life …at least in this country. You always have a choice on where it goes."

"But other times, the best things that happen in life are the ones you don't expect."

Jenn sighed.

"Yo, Jenn!" Morgan screamed to get her attention. "We need you for a group shot!"

"Yeah, get over here, JO!" Amy told her, as Miranda gestured her toward them, giggling.

Jenn turned back to her parents, who motioned her to go over to her friends. Jenn smiled and nodded her head and then embraced both of her parents for a group hug, which they immediately returned.

As she's hugging them, she looked up to see Jason still playing his guitar; and her smile grew, making her tighten her hug.

Jenn let go of them.

She turned to walk toward her friends; but she stopped, looked back at her parents, and smiled.

"I love you," she said before walking away.

Her parents smiled and clutched at each other, and they watched her join her friends for pictures.

The first portion of the night went by as scheduled. Dinner was served. Miranda shared dances with her mom and stepdad. The dance floor was opened up and occupied. There was a photo booth that was being used on the side. The band was hot. Everybody was just having a good time, making for a beautiful ceremony and celebration.

Miranda most importantly found herself having fun, despite how much her anxiety grew as the night went by. She slowly but painfully started to accept that Nikko wasn't coming. That what they had …really was over.

8:55 PM

Miranda was outside the hall with her parents. In just a few minutes, she would have to go up to the front of the room for the lighting of her candles. Right now she was going over her speeches for all sixteen.

"Okay, I think I'm ready," Miranda said nervously.

"You want us to be up there with you?" Richard asked her.

"No. I'll be fine."

"All right, we're just gonna go grab a drink, so just go back to your table and we'll give them the word in a bit," Catherine said.

She nodded, before heading back to the room.

They went over to the bar counter for some wine. They shared a toast and had a sip when suddenly, Richard noticed the door open.

Catherine turned to see what he's looking at and saw none other than Nikko and Lisa arriving.

Nikko immediately caught them standing there. "Shit," he murmured.

To make things even more awkward and daunting, Catherine walked over to them.

"Nikko?" Catherine said. "Or I'm sorry, what would you prefer I call you?"

"Nikko. Nikko's fine," he answered.

"Okay then. This is a surprise. We weren't sure if we'd see you tonight."

"Yeah, well, here I am," he awkwardly responded.

"Hi." She then looked down to the little girl. "And, Lisa, you made it too. Wonderful!"

"Hi, Miranda's mom," Lisa greeted her. "We hit traffic. So sorry we're late."

"No problem at all. This is actually perfect. You both showed up just in time for her to light the candles," she informed them.

"Ah. That's ...awesome," Nikko said.

"Hello, Nikko," Richard greeted him.

"Mr. Hetfield," Nikko returned.

"Hello, Lisa."

"Hello." Lisa waved.

"So you made it."

"Yeah, and, uh ...Lisa, why don't you go in and see her?"

"All right. But first, I gotta use the bathroom."

"Right over there." Catherine pointed her in the direction.

"Thank you." She ran off through the door.

"All right, now that she's away for a minute, I just want to reassure you two," Nikko began. "I'm only here because she really wanted to come, and I'm her ride. I'm not here to start anything, and as much as I would love to patch things up, I know Miranda doesn't, and that's okay. But I want you both to know that I am so, so sorry about what happened to her. I really do care about your daughter, and I never meant to hurt her. It was an accident, and after tonight, you don't have to worry about me doing that again, because I'm gonna leave her alone. I'll get out of your lives. In fact, I'll just... hang out here and wait for the party to end, take Lisa home, and that's it. So again, I'm really sorry." He turned to Catherine. "And, Mrs. Curtis ...I also want to thank you, for setting up those tutoring sessions," he told her. "You have such an amazing daughter, and she helped me a lot. With so much more than schoolwork ...and I'll never forget that," he told them.

Nikko started to walk out but was interrupted before he can open the door.

"Nikko, wait," Richard called him. Nikko turned back around. "Before you do whatever you decide to do, we'd appreciate it if you came in to watch her light her candles."

Nikko stalled. "You think that's a good idea?"

"Yes, I do," he told him.

Catherine smiled, as Nikko agreed to come inside.

Main Hall

Miranda was seated at her table at the front of the room with her friends. Her nerves were running wild as she prepared for the ceremony. But her mood lightened when she saw a small waving blonde girl coming her way. Lisa.

"Lisa!" Miranda excitedly called out.

"Hi!" Lisa ran around the table, as Miranda stood up and gave her a big hug.

"Hey! You made it!" She let go of the hug, and Lisa went to hug the rest of the girls. "When did you get here?"

"Just now. Nikko drove me."

"Nikko's here?"

"Yeah. He should be." Lisa looked around to spot him.

Miranda searched, until her friends pointed him out in the farthest part of the room. It's dark but just lit enough that he could be made out. She saw that he was wearing the vest she gave him. The nerves she'd been experiencing all night were now hijacking her whole body. She was hoping he'd be here, but now that he was, she didn't know how to feel. Should she feel joy? Sadness? Fear? Relief? Should she go talk to him? Should she wait for him to come to her? How was this going to affect her party? Did her parents see him? What was she supposed to do?

"Hey. Are you all right?" Lisa said, shaking her.

"Lisa?" she responded. "Did he tell you anything at all before you came here? Like, why he came here?"

"He just said he'd drive me here. I'm not really sure where his head is at tonight."

"Well, did he say—"

Before she could finish, the host of the party cut her off.

"All right, everyone, it is now nine o'clock, so please clear the dance floor as tempting as it may be. Find your seats and break out the tissues because it is now time to commemorate this night with the lighting of the sixteen candles. So, Miranda, please come up to where I'm standing. You may have my microphone and take on the role of Molly Ringwald."

Miranda was given a loud applause but remained seated, still stuck on Nikko's presence. She snapped out of her trance amidst the ovation, cautiously stood up, and walked on over to where her candle display was.

"It's okay to be nervous. Playing with fire can be scary," the host said. "Just take all the time you need, birthday girl; and if you feel like crying, that's okay too."

Miranda took the microphone and turned her focus to her audience. She took a deep breath before starting to talk.

"Well, first of all, I just want to thank you all for coming here tonight. I, uh, wasn't really so sure about having a party; but I guess there was no talking my parents out of this." She awkwardly giggled. Her guests laughed along with her.

"Which brings me to my first two candles…" She pulled out her phone and began to read her speeches. Before she started reading, she looked up, scanned the room, and locked onto Nikko's location. She thought for a few seconds, before beginning to read.

"My first candle is for the most important, strong, patient, and above all loving woman that I will ever know. She has been with me since literally the very beginning. She worked so hard to become a teacher, because she loves working with kids and teens, and by some crazy faith, I have gotten to be one of those many lucky students. She always encourages me and everybody she's ever taught to take chances, and to never give up, because the answer is always looking right at you. And even if you come up short, to always remember: 'Failure starts with an F but is followed by an A.' Mom, you won't be my teacher forever, but I'll always be your daughter. Will you please come up and light my first candle?"

The party applauded Catherine as she made her way to where her daughter stood, as the band played a verse from ABBA's "Slipping through My Fingers."

Catherine helped Miranda light the candle. The two shared a long hug before Catherine left the stage, parting with a kiss on each other's cheeks.

"My second candle I want to believe will be illuminated by two people. I feel blessed enough to have a loving mom who has looked out for me my entire life, but she isn't the only one that's been looking after me. When I was younger, she met a very kind, very caring man, who I admittedly was skeptical about meeting, for I convinced myself that nobody could ever replace my dad . . . But he never tried to replace him. He just wanted to be a father and husband in his own right, to be what me and my mom needed. It's one thing getting to have one dad who loves you, but I have been blessed enough to have two, who are always watching over me." Miranda sniffled before she looked up to the ceiling. "Daddy, I miss you every day, but I know you're here with us tonight, and I'm happy that I got to be your daughter." Her voice started to crack. "And, Richard, I'm happy that out of all the men my mom ever dated, she chose you. You're more than my stepfather—you're my third parent. So will you please come up here and help my dad light my second candle?"

Another applause occurred, slightly louder than the previous one, as the band played a verse of Tim McGraw's "My Little Girl."

Richard went up; they lit the candle together and hugged. They touched foreheads before Richard kissed hers and left the stage.

Miranda continued her speeches, calling up guests to light candles three through eleven. Nikko stayed the whole time and couldn't help but smile seeing all the love she's surrounded with.

"For my twelfth candle, this person's really going to hate me for putting her on the spot like this, but I have to let her know how much of an integral part of my life she's become. On the surface, she looked like someone who could easily beat you up if you look at her funny, and she definitely would; but if you're brave enough to get close to her, you'll discover that she's a very funny, strong-spirited, and above all loyal woman who will always have your back. I always feel secured when she's with me and my friends, and I mean this with all due respect— she looked better in a suit than anybody here." The crowd laughed. "Jenn, you can kill me after this; but for now, will you please come light my twelfth candle?"

The crowd applauded. Jenn smiled and put her head down, as Amy and Morgan pestered her to go up. She reluctantly stood up as the band played the chorus of Breaking Benjamin's "Blow Me Away."

She lit the candle with Miranda and wrapped one arm around the smaller girl and side-hugged her. Jenn went to sit back down at her group's table, catching a glimpse of Jason, and they both locked eyes. Jason raised his hand to wave at her. Jenn quickly did the same before going back to her seat.

"For my thirteenth candle, I turn my attention to the person whom I met Jenn through. Sophomore year, I was asked to tutor this girl who was having trouble in geoscience, and little did I know that same girl would become one of my best friends. She is recognized as the most beautiful girl in our school, and she certainly lives up to that alias. But as beautiful as she is physically, her soul is even more beautiful. In movies, people who look like her are always portrayed as some stuck-up bratty bully who talks down to everybody else, but she's nothing like that. She's modest, kindhearted, and, despite how much she's achieved in athletics, never considers anybody to be below her level. Every day, she dresses like a homecoming queen while carrying the heart of a Disney princess, and I'm glad Morgan pushed me into being her friend." Amy looked over at Morgan. Morgan shrugged, embarrassed. "Amy, will you please come light my thirteenth candle?"

The crowd applauded while the band played Panic! at the Disco's "House of Memories." Amy went up to light the candle, while Morgan was pumping her fist doing a "whoo" chant.

After lighting it, Amy hugged her tight before sitting back down.

"For my fourteenth candle, this one is for two very special people that I've come to know this last year. They've become like an older brother and little sister that I've never had. They are two incredible artists, and someday I know for a fact that they're going to touch the hearts of millions of people around the world with their talents, the same way they've touched my heart with their friendship. Now, only one of them I can call up here because the other is on the stage right now but, Lisa…" Miranda looked at the table she's sitting at with her parents, looking surprised. "On behalf of you and Jason, will you please come light my fourteenth candle?"

The crowd applauded. Lisa's parents encouraged her to go up there, but she's taken aback as she wasn't ready to be called. She turned to look at Nikko who's still standing in the same spot. He motioned her to go up there, which she finally did. The whole time the band was playing "Sanctuary" from *Kingdom Hearts II*.

Miranda looked toward Jason. She shot him a heart shape with her hands, to which Jason smiled and gave her a salute with a free hand before going back to playing. Lisa went up and was nervous about handling the fire, but Miranda reassured her that it's safe. She slowly gripped the candle, and Miranda helped her lower it to light the candle.

The crowd applauded again, and Miranda gave Lisa a long hug. They let go, and Miranda looked in Nikko's direction; despite being far away, she could see that he was also applauding. Lisa walked off and headed to where Nikko was, and he embraced her, proud of his baby sister.

Miranda got deep into her thoughts again and became resolute. She looked to where the band was.

"Excuse me for just one second." She spoke into the microphone.

She ran toward the band, up to Jason, and whispered something in his ear. The crowd looked puzzled, especially Nikko.

Jason looked at her and agreed to whatever she just told him with a thumbs-up and wink. Miranda nodded and stepped away from them.

The band asked him what she just said, but he told them to "wait for it."

Miranda went back to where she was standing.

"Sorry about that. Moving on," she awkwardly addressed the crowd.

She picked up her phone and resumed reading.

"For my penultimate candle, this person has had such a huge influence in my life, for better or worse." *She giggled.* "But no, this girl has been my best friend ever since I started going to public school. She was the first person who ever talked to me, that I ever had a sleepover with, who I could share secrets with, and who taught me a few bad words." The party laughed. "And I'm sure my mom was hesitant about me hanging out with her, but I'm really happy she let me on the off chance that I could make a real friend. Except I ended up making a lot more than a friend. I found a sister. A sister who makes me laugh, who's always had a shoulder I could cry on and is so unapologetic about saying whatever she's thinking out loud."

"Damn straight!" Morgan blurted out loud.

Miranda laughed, as did the party. "To a fault. But that's all the more reason to love her. Morgan, I do love you. There really is nobody else in this world or any other like you, and unlike me, I know how much you love having all eyes on you, so would you please come light my fifteenth candle?"

The crowd applauded.

"You bet your ass I will!" Morgan shouted.

Morgan walked over to her, as the band played Weezer's "My Best Friend." She and Miranda lit the candle, while Morgan chanted, "Fire! Fire! Fire!" like on *Beavis and Butt-Head*.

They lit it, and the two best friends shared a long hug.

"I love you too… Miranda," Morgan said.

After ten seconds passed, they finally let go, and Morgan sat back down.

"You're crazy," Amy told her, laughing.

"I know." Morgan grinned.

Okay, Miranda said to herself into the microphone, getting anxious. She took a deep breath before she talked.

"So for my final candle, I actually don't have a speech written …because I didn't know if this person was going to be here tonight. But they are. So this caused me to rework my listings on the spot and to actually blur two of them together into one. So I'm really sorry to my cousins." She waved to a combined group of cousins who waved back, letting her know it was okay. "And also to the band for practicing a song that didn't even get played." The band also assured her. "Anyway, even though I don't have a speech ready, this is fine because… what I need to tell them will now be coming directly from my heart."

Nikko wondered what she's doing. Was she really doing what he thought she was about to do? What he was hoping she was about to do?

Jason then got in between the rest of the band. "Hey, guys?" They all looked at him. "Why don't you all take five on this one?" They all questioned him. "Just trust me." They all looked confused but agreed and left their posts. Jason went up to the microphone the singer was using.

"All right." Miranda cleared her throat. "This final person…"

Her anxiety grew, but she held on to her mentality, telling herself that she could do it. Her eyes turned to the back of the room, looking in a very specific direction. She stared for a bit, before she turned off her brain and let her heart do the talking, like she said.

"This final person is somebody who I met only a couple of months ago. ...Or I thought it was a couple of months ago. Somebody who I would've never talked to in a million years, except that I was asked to help them. I agreed, much to my own objection, because I was open minded enough to give them a chance. At first, they didn't want that chance, but they came back around, and they took it and ran with it. I've been tutoring for a couple of years now, but I've never seen anybody turn things around as fluently as they did. And I don't just mean in school. I mean as a person. Suddenly, I was able to look past their looks and how they presented themselves, and I saw a different person. Somebody who's sweet, somebody who listens to my problems, somebody who gave me the courage to do things I never would've done, somebody who ...made me feel things that I've never felt before. Somebody who helped me discover things about myself that I had no idea were even there and gave me the courage to show the world things only I knew were there but never wanted to be seen. ...All this time, I thought I was tutoring him. But really, he was tutoring me. He was the one teaching me, to enjoy life, to live for the moment that we have right now. That there needs to be a fine line between looking at books and looking at the world right in front of you. Through being with him, I rediscovered who I really am, and along the way... I also discovered who he really was." Miranda took a deep breath and looked back in that specific direction.

Nikko's eyes grew large as he's keeping his concentration.

Both of their hearts were racing fast, as Miranda continued to talk.

"It turned out that he was actually an old friend. Somebody who I lost through a series of really bad events that drove us apart, and for a long time, I hated him. I felt hurt. But no amount of pain I felt could possibly compare to what he went through, and when I found out they were the same person, I went right back to hating him, and I felt pained again. I blamed him for hurting me, but the reality is I hurt him. Because I saw the same boy that I wrongfully judged. ...He's really changed, for the better, and now, I just want to let the past go. I want to move forward, and I want to cherish the time I have, with my family, with my friends... and with him." She paused. "I'm sure down the line, I'll make friends that I'll lose touch with. It happens. We lose people we care about. But the right ones will always stay by your side, and even if they wind up light-years apart, they will always find their way back to you." Her eyes watered up. "And I know that I found my way back to him for a reason. Now that I have... I want him by my side right now, and I never want to let him go again. So..." She turned her head to the back area and grew a warm, passionate, intimate smile. "Nicholas Steven Calaway Jacobs..."

Nikko's heart skipped a beat hearing his full name, and every person in the room turned to face him.

"Will you please come light my last candle?"

The loudest applause yet erupted. Nikko looked to his family who persuaded him, as if they're saying, "Go get her."

The applause died down when they heard the music playing. Jason was playing his guitar and singing the last song by himself.

That song was Stevie Wonder's "I Just Called to Say I Love You."

Nikko was overwhelmed by all of this, not yet taking a step forward. But when he looked back at Miranda smiling at him, he grew a smile himself and finally started to walk toward the stage. It wasn't a long walk, but they were so lost in the moment that to them, it felt like an eternity.

He finally got to the stage, and Miranda offered him the candle. He looked deep into her eyes and wrapped his hand around hers. Together they completed the candelabra as a thunderous applause occurred.

Miranda looked up to him, still locked on that smile.

"Hi," she said softly.

"Hi," Nikko responded at the same volume.

"I'm really happy you're here."

"Me too," he replied. "Uh, are you sure about this?"

"Hmm-hmm."

"Well, I'll just say it. Everything you just said up here, that's exactly how I feel about you too. It's just that... I don't know if, if I ...if I could be the guy you deserve." He frowned.

"I don't care about what I deserve. ...For once, I'm gonna go after what I want."

She touched his bandaged hand.

Nikko returned to smiling.

"This isn't gonna be easy."

"You've never been, big boy." she said, making him chuckle. "But don't worry."

She reached for her neck and tugged at his mother's necklace that she's still wearing. He looked down at the necklace and can't help but get teared up, as his smile grew bigger, happier—the sincerest one she'd ever seen on his face.

She softly said to him, "It's going to be okay."

A lone tear dropped down from his face.

She used her free hand to touch the side of his face where his bruise was still healing, while he wrapped his arm around her waist to pull her in and put his free hand to stroke the back of her hair. They were entranced in each other's eyes, forgetting that they had dozens more on them at that moment.

They leaned into each other in sequence and finally shared the kiss they'd both been yearning for a long time. Their lips fit seamlessly together as if they were specifically made to connect with each other's, like lost puzzle pieces that completed the picture. It was Miranda's first kiss, and it felt more magical than she could've ever imagined it would be. It was far from Nikko's first; but it was so soft, so pure, and so loving, to him it felt like a first kiss. It couldn't have been any more perfect.

Some party guests clapped loud for the two, while others expressed their jubilation in their own ways.

Both of their respective parents were happy to see that their children had found true love. Lisa reacted like how a shipper would react watching their OTP get together. Jenn had her arms crossed with a big grin on her face. Morgan and Amy had their hands clenched to each other's; Amy used her free hand to film this on her phone as Morgan said, "Took 'em long enough," with a triumphant smirk. Jason spoke into the microphone in the middle of an acoustic portion of the song to scream, "Yeah! That's my boy! And my girl!"

Miranda and Nikko broke away from their kiss and stared at each other as their faces stayed connected. The party was still applauding, but they had blocked out all background noise; their senses were locked only on each other. The two eventually turned to face the crowd, noticing that the photographer was capturing this special moment, so Nikko pulled her in for a hug that she returned instantly, and they smiled for the camera.

"Wow," the host said into the microphone that was left on the table. "I think I speak on behalf of all of us when I say that was a beautiful moment we all just witnessed here. And hey, you know what? So long as we can still feel the love tonight, I say we should take advantage of it. So how's about our band resumes action? Except we play something a little slower, but appropriate, while these two savor this fairy-tale ending?"

The applause picked up again while the new couple intertwined their hands and slowly walked to the center floor.

While this was going on, Miranda's parents went over to Nikko's, and they engaged them.

"Hi," Catherine began.

"Hello," Samantha replied with a welcoming smile.

"Hi. We're Nikko's parents," Bruce introduced themselves.

"Well, adopted parents, but still parents," Samantha added.

"That's right. I've seen you at a few parent-teacher conferences. We've just never really spoke," Catherine addressed them.

"Yeah, you're Mrs. Curtis," Samantha said.

"Oh please, call me Catherine."

"Okay. Catherine, I'm Samantha."

"Bruce."

"And I'm Richard."

They all shook hands.

"It's great to finally meet you both," Richard added.

"Hear, hear," Bruce agreed.

"Sorry about butting in like this," Catherine apologized.

"Oh, not at all," Samantha said.

"Yeah, it's good you introduced yourselves now..." Bruce looked over to Miranda and Nikko. "'Cause it looks like we're gonna be seeing each other a lot more from here on out."

"Sure looks that way, so best start getting along now, right?" Richard said, and all four shared a chuckle.

"And hey, if anybody else has a special someone with them, don't be afraid to get in the love," the host added.

The band got back into their positions, and Jason stepped aside for their regular singer. Jason was about to resume his old spot when suddenly…

"Hey, Jason." He heard Jenn call his name and looked at her. "Come over here," she commanded with a suggestive smirk.

"Huh?" he responded, dumbfounded. She instructed him again using hand gestures. "Uh, I-I would, but I got to do …this, uh—"

"Yo, Jason!" He heard Nikko call him. "Get off the stage, man!" he jokingly coaxed him.

"Yeah, Jason, get over there!" Miranda added.

The rest of the crowd started to cheer and chant his name.

"Hey," the lead singer intervened. "Why don't you take five on this one, dude? We got it from here."

Jason looked over to Jenn, who's still summoning him. He smiled, shrugged, and took off his guitar strap before walking over to where she was as the crowd clapped.

"Don't worry, we're gonna play something that everybody knows," the singer said before they began playing said song.

The song was "Beauty and the Beast" from the Disney movie's soundtrack.

Miranda became so excited to hear this song being played and quickly turned her attention back to Nikko who's amused by her delight. They assumed the position and started to slow-dance together in front of everybody, without saying a word. They just listened to the music and gazed at each other with love and passion in their eyes. It felt like a fairy tale come true.

Soon, other couples in the room ranging from her grandparents, aunts and uncles, cousins and friends who brought dates, and their parents started filling up the floor.

Jenn looked over to Jason, who's standing right beside her.

"Say, Jenn?"

"Yes?" Jenn asked, playing dumb.

"Umm, feel free to say no to this…" he began, making Jenn start to chuckle, "would you like to—"

"Why do you think I called you over here?" she said, extending her hand and shaking her head as she was smiling.

333

"Makes sense."

He smiled as he took her hand, following her to the dance floor. The two of them started to casually slow-dance.

Morgan and Amy were still seated at the table; Amy was enchanted by what's going on, and Morgan was full of glee. She turned her attention to Amy and realized that they were both still holding hands. She let it go, stood up, and stepped away to stare off onto the dance floor.

Amy felt the release and looked over at her. She then stood up and moved to where Morgan was.

"Morgan? Are you okay?" she asked her.

"I'm fine," Morgan answered, not looking at her.

Amy didn't believe her. She then stood alongside her, looked onto the dance floor with her, and got an idea.

"You wanna dance?"

Morgan was surprised, and she turned to her with a staggered look.

"You mean, like how those two, and those two …and those two are?" she asked, pointing to Nikko and Miranda, then Jenn and Jason, and then another random couple she didn't recognize.

Amy giggled. "Yes."

"All right."

Amy offered her a hand. Morgan became so nervous and confused by what's going on but took it anyway. Amy guided her to an open spot among everybody else, next to where Miranda and Nikko were.

"I should probably point out that I don't know how to dance," Morgan told her.

"Yes, you do. Just follow my lead."

Amy placed Morgan's hands on her waist and wrapped her arms around Morgan's neck. She helped her move around, slowly guiding her step by step until she started to pick up on the rhythm. Soon enough, they were both moving in sequence.

"How do you feel now?" Amy asked.

"I… actually feel good."

"Good enough to tell me what you were just thinking?"

Morgan became nervous again; she looked down at their feet and then back up at her. "You really want to know?"

"Yeah. I really do. Please, no more games. Just tell me."

Morgan was still uncertain, but she nodded her head and consciously thought, *Fuck it.* "All right, I'll say it. ...The only thing is... I don't really know how to. I've thought about numerous ways to tell you, a lot of different scenarios, and all the words I could use. But... now that I'm here, right in front of you ...I don't have those words," she admitted.

Amy smiled coyly at her. "Then, don't use words..."

Amy leaned forward, and she kissed her.

Morgan was so shocked she can't react.

Amy finished the kiss and opened her eyes to smile at her. Morgan was still frozen, but once she got over the disbelief, she returned a much cheekier smile.

Amy leaned in again, and this time Morgan did the same. They kissed again, with both putting in an equal amount of energy and desire. This one lasted twice as long as the previous and sent a shock wave through both of their bodies.

The two let go and gazed at each other.

"This is real," Morgan said.

"Yeah. Yeah, it is," Amy said, fully realizing what they were doing and how much she liked it.

They both noticed that Nikko and Miranda were watching them. Miranda was overjoyed for them as conveyed by her bright grin, while Nikko was giving them a thumbs-up with his own grin.

They shifted their focus back to each other and closed the gap between them, resuming their dance.

Jason and Jenn continued to dance themselves. "So just to be clear, are we actually going to, you know, give this a shot?" Jason asked.

"Isn't that what you want?" Jenn asked.

"Well, yeah. But only if you're good with that."

Jenn shook her head and rolled her eyes amused. "Just don't ever dump me."

Jason chuckled. "That much I can promise."

"Good." Jenn leaned in and kissed him on the cheek.

Jason can't stop himself from blushing, nor could Jenn.

Nikko and Miranda remained lost in the moment, without a care in the world or an ounce of pain on their faces.

"By the way," Nikko started, "happy birthday."

Miranda smiled. "By the way," she began, "I love you too."

Nikko mirrored her smile. "I love you."

They both leaned in to share another kiss. It was brief, only a second long, but it had just as much affection to it.

Miranda leaned her head in to nuzzle his chest, and Nikko brought his arm from her waist to her back and gingerly clutched the back of her head. They shut their eyes and savored every second of this moment with each other as the rest of song played out.

Love can be beautiful, and it can also be tragic. It can feel amazing, and it can feel painful. For better or worse, Cupid will leave you differently than how he found you. There's never any guarantee it can lead you to a lifetime of happiness or if it can deliver grief for you to carry the rest of your life. But the risk is better than the regret of knowing you didn't take it.

Heartbreaks are a part of life, but it can always be repaired. It's easy to feel hopeless, but there's someone out there for everyone. They could be miles apart, or they could be right beside you. They are out there. So don't stop searching, because when you find them, all those heartaches will be worth it. If you're feeling one right now, just know: *It's going to be okay.*

EPILOGUE

Paige and Steven, or Miranda and Nikko, had come a long way since the beginning of the school year, and even further from where this all started. Their relationship went through many different phases: playmates, childhood friends, best friends, ex–best friends, strangers who went to the same school, classmates, study partners, enemies, bitter enemies, acquaintances, frenemies, friends, best friends again, back to ex–best friends, and now, they were a couple. They both brought out something in each other that no one else could and overcame their insecurities together. Despite how impossible it seemed at first to even be friends, and even after their dark—intertwined—pasts were revealed, they could now see the world with more color.

On the night of Miranda's sweet sixteen, Amy had recorded the moment they shared together at the candelabra, including their confessions and their first kiss. She asked Miranda and Nikko if they wanted her to post them on Instagram as part of a "Happy Birthday, Miranda" post she was making, if they were ready to go public with their relationship. She had the biggest social media following of them all, so if she shared them, everyone at school would know by the time they got there Monday. They spent all this time hiding that they were even friends, but the last week had made people suspicious of something between the two of them—none of which were true—and this would be a giant bombshell, generating even more attention on them. But no longer wanting to hide anything, especially their love, they both—in sync—gave Amy the cue: "Do it."

By 10:00 PM, their love story was available for the whole Internet to see:

> **amybrookesxoxo** WHAT A NIGHT! Thank you for having me & my family Miranda, & for letting me be a part of such a beautiful ceremony. Because of you I never have to read a romance novel again, I feel like I was just in one! I can't wait to have my #SweetSixteen with you. Happy Birthday, I love you. #TrueLoveIsReal

The post she shared had a selfie she took of the two of them together; a picture her mom took of her in her dress; a group picture of the four girls standing side by side with Miranda standing in front of them; a short selfie video of her and Morgan singing and dancing to Big Time Rush; a picture where Jenn was smirking as she's carrying her bridal style while she had a big goofy smile; two more pictures her mom took, one where she was helping her light the candle and then one of them hugging afterward; another group photo taken at the end of the night that included the boys and Lisa; a shot she got of Miranda and Nikko standing by her cake hugging each other; Miranda and Nikko's slow dance; and finally a minute-long video she took of their first kiss.

Before long, the gossip spread, and they were the talk of the school through DMs and group chats. But that wasn't the only post Amy made that weekend that blew up her notifications. The next day, she posted another one simply saying:

> **amybrookesxoxo** @morgans_chamber2k (A rainbow of heart emojis)

It was a picture taken of the two of them where Morgan was cupping her cheeks as they kissed.

This post was the only other one she ever shared that could contend with her previous one in terms of likes and was by far her most commented one ever.

Morgan also posted the same picture with the following caption:

morgans_chamber2k This still doesn't feel real. @ amybrookesxoxo (*heart eyes emoji*)

It blew up just as much.

Elsewhere, Jason made his own post, sharing some highlights with the band from the party and his solo performance:

j.kennedy_redeemer My first Sweet Sixteen. My first real performance. My first time with an actual band. My first time doing something right. #Redeemer

imjennowensstfu @j.kennedy_redeemer you sounded good. Maybe you can give me lessons sometime. (*wink emoji*)

Monday, March 27

Nikko and Miranda drove to school together for the first time that day. They drove into the parking lot where they first met after over ten years—even parking the car in the same spot—about to face the music.

Before getting out of the car, he turned to her and asked if she was ready to do this, to which she said yes.

Nikko got out of his seat as Miranda put on her book bag, walked around to the other side, and opened the door for her. Before stepping out, she offered him her hand with a smile. He quickly returned it and took her hand in his. She stepped out and took another step toward him to look up into his eyes. He in turn leaned down so their noses and foreheads could touch.

They strolled hand in hand through the parking lot toward Meadows Forest High, immediately catching the eyes of anyone else who was there; and as they entered the school, the attention grew exponentially. There were whispers, stares, hanging jaws, giggles, gasps, and even some fawning; it was as if they were walking the red carpet.

Nikko had heard a lot of people talk about him under their breath or behind his back—sometimes both—but this time he could tell they were coming from a good place. Even the few senses of judgment and resentment didn't get to him for once; he was just happy to have Miranda back in his life and to be able to say that he was hers. He no longer felt like he had to act like the imposing Steven "Axl" Calaway anymore; he could just be Nicholas "Nikko" Calaway Jacobs.

And Miranda, if she thought she couldn't feel any more visible than on Friday, or even Saturday, for once she would have made a miscalculation. On top of the new sporadic change in appearance and her identity reveal, she knew these students had a million new questions alone about what she was doing with "this guy." Some were looking at her as if she had gone insane; she knew her reputation would change drastically, and it seemed that this calculation was correct. But it didn't bother her. At least if people saw her, they were seeing her. Besides, she felt comfortable as long as she was by Nikko's side.

They walked into English class on time, ignoring anyone who looked at them. Miranda took her seat up front next to Morgan, and before Nikko left to take his, he kissed the top of her head and took a brief look at her.

He fixed a stray hair that was in front of her face before parting to sit at his desk, leaving her enchanted. Morgan, meanwhile, sat beside her and patted her shoulder with a huge grin, claiming that she "always shipped it."

Throughout the rest of their high school experiences, these love stories continued, only getting stronger:

Jason kept his word to Jenn and taught her how to play the guitar as she continued teaching him how to fight. Just about every weekend they were in the gym together or learning how to play a new song. After going from a one-sided crush to forming somewhat a connection in between their friend's growing relationship, they were now at the point where it was mutual. Jason proved to her he was serious when he said he'd back off. Jenn saw that and appreciated it. He didn't try nearly as hard as he did when he was flirting with her, but it proved that less means more. She saw that he had a good heart underneath all that ink occupying his pectorals, and he in turn exposed the caring soul that was hiding behind her cold attitude and spiteful outlook on the world. She felt like she could learn to trust people again and not barricade herself, whereas he saw his future looking brighter than he had in a long time; if she could learn to like him, then maybe others could too.

In April, Jason turned seventeen and celebrated by going out with Jenn to see Motionless in White, their first of many concerts together. Later that same month, Jenn turned eighteen; as a gift, her parents gave Jenn the keys to their old car that she grew so accustomed to & they bought themselves a new car from her mom's dealership job. They ended up officially meeting each other's parents that same month, and it took no time for them to fit right in with the other's family. So, they had now passed the most stressful part of a fresh relationship. In June, they graduated high school and celebrated it with their friends; it wasn't anything fancy, just another gaming night, but anytime they all spent together was enough. This was especially important though as it marked the final time they could have a night without a care, for very soon they would be leaving teenhood behind. They wasted so much of their young lives in isolation, and both knew they wanted to have as much time with their friends as they could, to make up for whatever they lost.

Jason continued learning guitar and taking whatever gigs he could get, all the while he was applying to go to community college in town. This way he could stay close to Jenn and everybody else for a while longer before those four would have to graduate too, and from there, things would be drastically different. Meanwhile, Jenn got an offer by her judo instructors to become an assistant trainer, and she took it. For three days a week, she was now teaching other people besides Jason how to fight, and she found out she really loved doing it. Perhaps it was the thought that she could help others fend for themselves, or it was just a good-paying gig, but it seemed she had found her calling.

After a couple of months just doing their casual schtick, they decided to go on an actual date. Taking Jenn's new car, they went to a coffee shop that was thrash metal themed. It happened to be a karaoke night, and Jason managed to convince her to do a duet by agreeing to let her choose the song: "Step Up" by Drowning Pool. That night, he saw her laughing her heart out from joy. He had never heard her laugh like that before, and it only made his feelings for her stronger. And it seemed his willingness to act like an idiot around her, even recreating that dumb dance he did on her porch back in winter, made her fully realize what a great guy he really was.

Throughout the course of six months—leading into September—Jason never made a move on her; he didn't want to do anything unless she was cool with it. Even on their prom night, nothing happened, not even a kiss. Eventually, Jenn got tired of waiting. So one date night, they were at his house watching *Twilight: Breaking Dawn Part 2* (on Blu-ray) and laughing at it. By the time they got to the film's final act, she was cracking up at the absurdity of what was happening, and Jason was laughing—probably just as hard as when he saw it in theaters. When the movie was over and the credits began to roll, Jenn told him that it was the worst thing she's ever seen, but she loved it, and watching it with him made it a lot more fun. That everything was a lot more fun when it's with him. She moved over to him on the couch and gave him a coy look. Jason wasn't sure if she was testing him or not and felt bashful, until Jenn finally just came straightforward and asked if he wanted to kiss her or not. To which he asked her if she was sure that she wanted it, making her chuckle and saying nothing more before she leaned in and gave him what he'd wanted from the start. After one short kiss, they opened their eyes and stared at each other. She playfully mocked how naive he was, and he just agreed with her like he usually did. They shared another light laugh before they went back to it, continuing for a good couple of minutes. Ironic that two people who listened exclusively to heavy metal would share their first kisses to Christina Perri's "A Thousand Years."

On the day after Amy came out online, she went to school as nervous as she could be, ready to now face the world of being LGBTQ. She walked into the cafeteria through the back entrance with her nerves out of whack, and before she knew it, she heard something that blew her away: applause. All the students who were there waiting for the first-period bell were welcoming her into the school with a warm reception, including her gymnastic teammates who were piling around to give her hugs, cover her in glitter confetti, put a rainbow floral lei around her neck, and present her with a box full of homemade cupcakes that spelled "WE <3 U AMY" spelled in rainbow colors. She smiled bright, comprehending what was going on while trying to contain her emotions, then she looked over to where the other half of her teammates were and saw they were crowding around Morgan, causing her to immediately burst into tears. Morgan walked up to Amy with a bouquet of flowers and gave her a hug as the crowd of students and even some faculty cheered them on. Amy immediately returned her hug, crying tears of joy as she pulled away and kissed her new girlfriend in front of everybody. All of this was being recorded by one of her teammates.

It turned out her gymnastics team secretly hit up Morgan on Instagram to arrange this whole surprise welcoming for Amy. They offered to bake the cupcakes for her, buy all these other miscellaneous things, and get Morgan to school early so she could surprise her. The flowers, however, came from herself. She even wrote her a note with them that said, "I don't do romance well. But for you, I'll do my best."

The thought alone that her teammates cared about her enough to celebrate her sexuality and new romance felt great. It made her realize that she was wrong about what she said. They really were her friends all along, not just something to help elevate one another's careers. She felt relieved to know that people didn't see her as just someone to be admired, to be lusted over, or to be bragged about for hooking up with; she was seen as a real person. And the people who still saw her like that—the guys whom she'd dated once or twice if lucky—their thoughts didn't matter anymore, because now they can all stand aside and feel envious that she now found someone who's better than all of them: Morgan Chambers.

For Morgan, she couldn't stop smiling since Saturday. This was like a dream she couldn't wake up from even if she wanted to. She finally had her first girlfriend, and she was the only girl she ever fell in love with. What seemed impossible was now really happening, and she already kept true to her word of treating her like a queen. In only a minute, before the day even began, despite her note saying otherwise, she did the most romantic thing she'd ever experienced and eradicated all her fears. She only wished that Morgan told her a long time ago.

> amybrookesxoxo Not how I expected to start school today. I still don't have the words to explain how I feel right now. Thank you everyone who made me feel belonged, accepted, & so loved. Especially you @ morgans_chamber2k. I love you. (*heart emoji*)

> morgans_chamber2k Best 48 hrs of my life. I can listen to you call me your girlfriend 4ever.

> amybrookesxoxo @morgans_chamber2k I'll be sure to do it more then. Whatever makes my GIRLFRIEND happy. (*kiss emoji*)

> morgans_chamber2k @amybrookesxoxo your killing meee!!! (*skull emoji*)

When July came, Amy had her own sweet sixteen down in New Jersey, where her family rented a vacation house one week every year. You can only imagine how stressed out she was in the preparation stage of her own party, but it all came together in the end. What made it even more special was that her parents invited Morgan to stay with them at the house all week, so as if turning sixteen wasn't exciting enough, she got to spend a week on the beach with her girlfriend. This helped distract her from all her pre-party stress. Whether they were sitting on the beach, swimming in the ocean, walking on boardwalk as Morgan playfully tried to lick smeared ice cream off of Amy's face, playing games in an arcade, chilling in the house cracking wise with her parents, or going down to the pier to watch the sunset, she enjoyed every moment she shared with her. It turned out she really knew how to mellow her out.

They celebrated her birthday that Friday morning and had the party later the same night. Everybody came: Miranda, Nikko, Lisa, Jenn,

Jason, her family, her friends' families, her team, other friends she had, and of course Morgan. While it wasn't as "cinematic" (Morgan's words) as Miranda's, it was still just as fun and felt just as special for different reasons. Amy couldn't have been any happier than she was.

After the party, she went back to the house with her parents and Morgan. Her parents crashed for the night, leaving them alone in their nightwear. Shortly after, Morgan got the idea for the both of them to eat whatever was left of her birthday cake, so they took it out of the fridge and started to do just that. Except Morgan decided she was just going to eat it with her bare hands. Amy at first just laughed watching her get cake all over her mouth, but Morgan told her to take some before she ate it all. Amy went to pick some up, but Morgan took the fork out of her hand and waited for her to "do it right." Amy finally caved in and took a handful for herself. Morgan cheered her on, until Amy decided to poke her forehead with her frosting-covered finger. Amy winked at her, still chewing some cake, prompting Morgan to scrap some more frosting off and wipe it on the side of her face. This escalated to a play fight where they smeared as much cake as they could all over each other's face, some of which got into strands of their hair. They laughed the whole time until they practically ran out of actual cake, leaving nothing but a plate of frosting. Morgan then went to touch Amy's hair directly, but she fought her off and ran from the kitchen table. She warned her not to do that, but Morgan tried to do it anyway, which made Amy go behind her to lift her from around the waist. Morgan struggled and kicked around until Amy lost her balance, and they both fell backward. Morgan rolled off her; and they both lay on the floor, covered in cake and frosting, laughing hysterically. Amy even let out a chipmunk squeak that Morgan found so adorable. They sat up and stopped laughing to look at each other's messy faces.

They remained like this for a couple of seconds before Morgan scraped off some cake from Amy's face and licked it off her fingers. Amy chuckled and then took this a step further by licking some frosting right off Morgan's face. All she could do was bite her own lower lip in response. Amy shifted away from her face, but not by much; she was still right up in her face, giving her bedroom eyes. Morgan saw the signs, cupped her cheeks, and, like a magnet, pulled herself into her lips. It started off soft and got more heated with every next kiss. Amy grabbed the bottom of Morgan's shirt to insinuate something Morgan asked her if she was afraid of waking up her parents, but Amy suggested they wouldn't, so long as they were quiet. She knew she couldn't fight her temptations anymore and started kissing her again. They wrapped their arms around each other to stand back up and—after wiping the cake off their faces and anywhere else it got on their bodies—went into Amy's room.

After a late night of celebration and passion, Amy's birthday ended with her lying in some random person's bed, sound asleep against her girlfriend. Morgan was still awake, lovingly watching her sleep as she stroked her perfect blonde her. Even after all this time had passed, and this happened, she couldn't believe this was real; it still felt like a dream. But it wasn't. She was with her one true love and just had a magical night with her. She didn't want this moment to end. She wanted the world to go on ice just so they could stay like this forever. But she was fine that it couldn't, because tomorrow she was gonna wake up, and this would still be real. She wished her a happy birthday one more time and kissed her lips once more before she drifted off to sleep. It was the best she had ever slept up to that point. She now understood how it felt to sleep beside your girlfriend. Something she will never get tired of calling Amy: her girlfriend.

On the Friday after her party, Miranda and her parents celebrated her actual birthday with Nikko; her parents took them out for dinner where for the first time, she saw him wearing a dress shirt, a suit vest, dress pants, and penny loafers, none of which had any black. Now she understood how he must've felt the first time he saw her hair down and without her glasses, like she was falling in love all over again. He hated dressing up like this, but she was the only girl he would ever do it for. For her, he would do anything just to see her happy. (He also felt this would make up for not dressing up for her party.) When he saw her wearing the same dress she wore to her party, including her tiara, and wearing his mom's necklace, all he could so was tell her how beautiful she looked. They went to dinner, and he acted more like a gentleman than he ever had in his life; if there was any doubt from her parents—particularly her stepdad—that he was a good fit for her, all those skepticisms were denounced. They may have been official for only a week, but it was clear this was the point of no return. They couldn't go back to how it was when they were kids. They couldn't even go back to just being friends. By now, the most unlikely of couples had proven they were inseparable.

When August came, Nikko turned eighteen, and now it was time for him to celebrate it with his parents he could now refer to as "Mom and Dad," his baby sister, and his girlfriend. For some people, eighteen is either the most alarming birthday of your life or the most exciting. For him, it was the latter. This was the first time since he was five that he felt happy celebrating his birthday. Before Miranda came back into his life, he considered every birthday to just be a reminder that he was closer to death, but this one felt like a celebration for surviving all the hard times he endured to find that light in the dark that never went dim: her.

For a present, she gave him something very special to remind him of all that. It was a gold chain necklace that had a heart-shaped locket. He opened it up and saw a double-sided picture frame: on one side was a picture the photographer took of their first kiss at her sweet sixteen (his favorite picture of them), and on the other side was a picture taken of an older photo that her mom found of them when they were kids on the playground. He couldn't help but tear up as he put it on, looked at her, and said he loved her, that he was glad he found her and will never let her go again. "Ever." She immediately returned the "I love you" and kissed him, neither caring that his parents watched the whole thing or that Lisa was filming it on their mom's phone.

More hard times were certainly on the horizon, but now he wasn't going to face that wave alone. He had parents, a sister, friends, and his soulmate.

They made it to being together for over a year, but whenever it seemed like they were gonna take that big next step to show their love, Miranda got cold feet. Nikko didn't ever get mad though; he would never pressure her into doing something she didn't want to. She made it clear to him the first time that she wanted to, but she wasn't ready yet; he promised her that he'd wait until she was, if ever.

But then the night of their prom came. They went together along with Morgan and Amy. They even had a pre-party send-off with Jason and Jenn, where they had their most romantic night together since her sweet sixteen. Fortunately, there wasn't any incident that ruined it like last year. (Don't ask.) It was the second time they ever slow-danced, and by now, everybody was so used to seeing them as a couple it wasn't worth recognizing anymore; they could just enjoy this evening in each other's embrace without a single damn given.

After it was over, they went back to Miranda's empty house (her parents left for her aunt's house in Long Island to spend the night). Nikko told her this night couldn't have been more perfect, but she suggested it could. She then started kissing him and unbuttoning his suit jacket. He stopped her to make sure she was ready for that, and she told him yes, that she wanted that right there and now. But not before she pulled one out of his playbook; she called her mom on FaceTime from under her bedsheets. Her mom was lying beside Richard in her sister's guest bed. They both waited up for this moment when she called. Miranda told them prom was fun, that Nikko had gone home, and she was ready to fall asleep right now but wanted to wish them good night, sounding as groggy as she could portray. They wished her good night; she faked like she was dozing off as they hung up and then got out from under her sheets, turned on her lights, sat on the edge of her bed, and told Nikko—whom she told to wait outside her door—that she was ready now. He came into her room, amused by the fact that she lied to her parents, again. He questioned when she became "such a bad girl," and she replied, "I learned from the best," uncharacteristically seductive. He chuckled in a flirtatious way before closing the door behind him, and they finally took that big step. Over a year of love and passion played out in a much shorter amount of time.

Nikko had had sex plenty of times before with plenty of other girls, but this was the first time he ever "made love," and it felt better than any of those prior times. It wasn't rough. It wasn't intense. It wasn't heated; it was soft, slow, and sweet. He knew he would much rather do this a million times for the rest of his life, but only if it was with her.

For Miranda, just like her first kiss, she shared this first with him too, and it was enchanting. She was glad they waited this long. She knew he was dying for the moment she was ready, and when it finally happened, he still made her feel comfortable and safe. He was gentle with her. He stayed cautious in case she said "stop" and looked into her eyes the entire time. He showed her he was more attracted to her soul than he was her body, and all that meant the world to her. After years of trying to be invisible, someone saw and looked at her like there was nothing else or anybody else in the world. Miranda never thought she'd ever fall in love; she had envisioned herself achieving great things on an academic level, and none of those futures included having a husband or being a mom. But as she peacefully drifted off to sleep that night, she saw the future looking different. She saw the same goals, but a new endgame; with her old friend and her new love.

—⁂—

In June, graduation finally came for Morgan, Amy, Nikko, and class valedictorian Miranda, who gave a great farewell speech. All four were happy to share this moment together, and their respective families were happy for their children. Even Jason and Jenn came to show support. They celebrated back at Miranda's house, in what would be the last time they'd all be able to hang out together, for now at least.

Lisa also graduated from middle school around the same time; Miranda went to the ceremony with her and Nikko's family. She was just as proud as they were to see her boyfriend's sister now ready for high school. Both Nikko and Miranda hoped that it'd go more smoothly for her than it went for them, and if she hypothetically met someone she liked, that they wouldn't have to go through the obstacles they did. Little did they suspect, however, on the day of her ceremony, she bumped into a boy. Literally. His cap fell off, and she picked it up for him, apologizing. He saw her and seemed to stop functioning; he didn't talk or even take the cap. So very confused, she put the cap back on his head for him. She started to walk away when he finally spoke to her to ask for her name. She told him, and he told her his, and then he asked what high school she was going to. It turned out they would both be going to Meadows Forest High, and she ended the very short, awkward introduction by saying maybe she'll see him around. They finally parted, and as she walked away, he kept looking at her. She noticed and turned her head to look back at him.

School was over, as was a major part of their lives. The past was now where it needed to be. But the future was still a blank page, waiting to be encrypted on. You never know what it will say next, but what fun is hearing a story if you know what's gonna happen?

EPILOGUE

(For real this time)

Monday, September 3, 2018, 8:30 AM: Miranda's House

Miranda was in her bedroom with Morgan, packing up anything else she needed or wanted to take. In a little bit, her dad's car would be loaded with luggage, and she and Nikko would follow behind her parents enroute to Princeton, New Jersey. There, she and Nikko would be moving into their first apartment. Miranda would be ready to go to college while Nikko would stay home to work and do classes online. Before then, she, her parents, and Nikko did one last inspection before departure.

"All right, just be gentle."

"When am I ever not gentle?" Morgan asked, helping her take down the portrait of her and Nikko that Lisa drew last year from her wall.

They got it down and laid it down on her bed with her suitcase.

"All right. That's it. …I'm ready now," Miranda said, looking around her room as the reality set in. She was leaving home.

"I still can't believe you're leaving me," Morgan joked.

"Don't try to make me cry now."

"I kid, I kid. I'm excited for you. I really am. You're getting to live on your own, with your boyfriend, finally escaping this hellhole of a borough."

"All right, you don't have to pretend you're not sad either." Miranda chuckled.

"I'm not sad. …I'm not. I'm just—I never prepared for life without my best friend. But hey, I never prepared for life in general, I guess. You know me, always making shit up as I go."

351

"Morgan, I'll only be an hour away. I'll come home for breaks and during summer. The first thing I'll do is come see you."

"I know. But… it feels like we've been together every single second since sixth grade, and now just like that, it's over. I know I'm overselling, but it won't be the same."

"No. Not entirely. But our friendship will always be the same. We can at least promise that. Right?"

"Hell yeah." Morgan smiled.

"And look on the bright side. If I'm not around, that means Amy can have a lot more of you." She winked.

Morgan awkwardly chuckled. "Good point."

"Especially now that you're both working in the mall, you practically see each other every day now."

"Hmm, two good points. Now I see how you got accepted to such a good college." Both girls laughed. "You know what? I'll be strong and let you go, but… I want to be regularly updated on how you and Nick are." She smirked.

"Yeah, I'm not promising that."

"Come on, you owe me. If I didn't lean against his car two years ago, he would've never talked to you in the first place."

"If you wanna interpret it that way, sure, but I'm not doing that."

"Can't fault a girl for trying."

They laughed again.

"In all honesty, I don't know if I could credit you for that, but the truth is, I don't know if I would be where I am now without you. …You were the first person who talked to me when no one else would, you're the reason I made friends with Amy and Jenn, you encouraged me to keep tutoring Nick, you showed me that it's okay to laugh when things look bad, and you helped me …learn to appreciate life again. So if you want credit for anything… thanks for being my best friend."

"I see how it is. I can't make you cry, but you can make me." Her voice cracked.

The two girls then shared a warm hug, with both shedding some tears.

"I love you," Miranda said.

"I love you," Morgan responded.

Downstairs

Steven was helping Miranda's parents lift a couple of boxes to bring outside the house to beside their car. Shortly after coming back in to pick up another one, the door opened.

"Sup, man?" Jason made his presence known.

"Ah hey, where's Jenn?"

"Outside with Amy waiting to say goodbye."

"Ah. Well, I think we're pretty much done. My parents' car has all my shit. Just gotta get Miranda's in hers, and we're out."

"Sweet. Gotta admit, man, the idea of you going away to college with your girlfriend, I feel like I'm in some weird alternate universe."

"Well, she's really the one who's going. Online courses don't matter as much."

"Geez, even after she mellowed you out, you're still pessimistic. I'm proud of you, bro. Two years ago, you said, 'College is for losers.'"

"Well, I guess now I'm a loser."

"Nah, man. Both of us used to be losers. Now, we've got good things going. Especially you."

"You definitely ain't the dude I once knew. But it's cool. I like this dude."

"Amen."

"Speaking of which, what are you two gonna do?"

"Well, for now it looks like we're gonna keep doing our regular thing. My gigs, her instructing, not really planning much."

"That's not what I meant. I mean, when are you two gonna move in together?"

"Oh. Shit, um. We haven't exactly spoken about that yet."

"For real? Dude, it's been over two years. Not once has that ever come up?"

"I don't wanna rush anything. I'm lucky enough to be dating her. If I bring that up, I don't know what she'd say."

"So you admit you want to do that?"

"Maybe. I don't know. ...Yes. But not if she doesn't want to."

"Hmm, that's interesting," Nikko teased.

"Don't fuck with me, man."

"Dude, relax. I get it. Agreeing to move to Jersey with Miranda was a scary decision too, but it's happening. Even now I'm close to pissing myself. I'm so nervous. But I love her, and I want to make this work. Whatever it takes, we'll do it, and I know you and Jenn love each other too. So get on that!"

Jason got nervous. "This was always so much easier when I was still a flirtatious idiot. How'd I lose my edge so bad?"

"I know what you mean. But you've got this. If Miranda's patient enough to live with me, she can deal with you. Hell, she still stayed with you after that incident at your prom."

Jason sighed. "Yeah. We don't talk about that incident."

"My point exactly. Dude, trust me, she'll say yes.

He huffed. "I'll see. Appreciate, man." Jason offered his hand.

"Hey, you're my brother in the pit. I'm always rooting for ya."

Nikko gave him a bro high five.

"I'm rooting for you guys too. Hope y'all have a great life out there."

"Same." They maintained their grips. "Thanks for putting up with me all this time."

"Thanks for never leaving me behind."

They both hugged it out and patted each other's backs.

Outside Miranda's House

Jason helped Nikko carry a big box of Miranda's stuff to the car.

Amy and Jenn were talking as they saw them coming.

"Oh, here he comes," Amy told her.

"I can't bring this up now," Jenn replied.

"You don't have to. Just initiate it."

"Amy, I can't just—"

"Jenn, he's already crazy about you. Just tell him you wanna go out tonight to talk, and so help me if you don't tell him you wanna move in by tomorrow, I'm gonna scream."

"All right, jeez. Your girlfriend's over there. Go pressure her." She pointed to the door where Miranda and Morgan were walking out with her luggage.

"You won't be sorry," Amy said before doing what Jenn said and went to where Morgan and Miranda were to hug them both back to back.

Jenn took a deep breath before walking over to Jason. *Just get it over with*, she said to herself.

Jason and Nikko began helping Richard and Bruce load one of the cars.

"Hey," Jenn said, getting the boys' attention.

"What up, Jenn?" Nikko greeted her.

"Not much. Congrats to you guys."

"Thank you."

"Imagine that. The once Steven Axl, going away to college. That's some *Twilight Zone* shit."

"That's what I'm saying," Jason intervened.

"Yeah yeah, it's mind-boggling. All right, well, I'm gonna go find Lisa. Jenn, you mind helping Jason out with this box? Thank you." He started to walk away from them.

"HEY!" Jenn and Jason said at the same time.

Jason looked to her. "This is actually pretty heavy."

"Oh, for god's sake."

She helped him lift the box into the trunk of the car.

"Yeah! That's some good teamwork!" Jason said, and Jenn chuckled.

"Whatever. ...Hey, Jason?"

"Ye-yeah?"

"When this is over, you wanna do something tonight?"

"Sure. Actually... I really want to talk to you. About something."

Jenn grinned. "All right. We can discuss it over dinner."

"Good plan!"

Jenn chuckled again and kissed him.

She walked over to the rest of her friends to say goodbye, leaving him to smirk.

After a lot of packing, both of their parents' cars were loaded and closed, leaving the front seats of both empty, with one seat in the back of Samantha and Bruce's car still upward for Lisa to sit in.

"All right, guys... this is it," Catherine said.

"Whenever you two are ready," Samantha said with tissues already in hand.

Miranda nodded her head, and Steven quickly joined her side.

Jason walked over to stand alongside the trio.

She let Nikko go first to say whatever he wanted to her friends.

"I know things didn't start off so great between us all. But you're all, for one reason or another, incredible people. You all picked her off the ground while I was off being a bastard, and you gave me a chance when I didn't deserve it. Two actually. So thank you all for that, and thank you for taking care of her."

He looked to Jenn. "Jenn... you've got a really good guy here, and he's lucky to have someone like you. Hold on to him like your life depends on it."

Jenn looked to Jason, and they shared a smile while she patted his chest. "I'll do my best."

He offered Jenn a handshake. She accepted it, and they shared a hug for the very first time.

He turned to Amy. "Amy, I know how tough it was for you especially to trust me, and justifiably so, but I'm glad you did anyway. You got a great heart, and as popular as you were in Meadows Forest, you're gonna become a lot more popular someday. For all the right reasons."

Amy was touched by his words. "Thank you, and you're a really sweet guy. I'm so happy for you both."

Steven thanked her with a nod. "Same with you two. I know you're gonna make it work."

He extended his hand. Rather than taking it, Amy instead gave him a hug, and he returned it.

Finally, he addressed Morgan. "And, Morgan... don't ever change."

Morgan snickered. "Promise," she joked. "And you, take care of my girl."

"Promise."

Morgan didn't even give him a chance to offer his hand and instantly hugged him. He hugged her back after registering the sudden action.

He finished up, and now it was Miranda's turn. She started with Jason.

"Jason, you're such an amazing person. You're an amazing musician, with so much talent; and if people can't see that, it's 'cause they don't know you like we all do. That's what I've learned through all this." She looked to Nikko. "Most important, you're an amazing friend. You really are like a big brother to me, and I'm excited to see what you do."

"Thanks, Miranda. That all means a lot to me." His eyes got misty.

"And thanks for all you've done for him. Everything."

"Just kept him warm for ya."

She giggled. "And also, if you're ever performing in town, let us know."

"Absolutely. …Have a great time. I'll miss you."

"I'll miss you too."

He picked her up off the ground, and they hugged.

He put her down; and Miranda now looked to her group of friends, unable to contain her emotions, and started to cry.

Amy made the first move and pulled her in for a hug. Morgan immediately joined in, and Jenn shortly after wrapped them all around her. They stayed like this for a good couple of seconds, and all let out some tears.

"Don't forget about me," Miranda said.

"Never ever ever," Amy said.

"We'll be here when you come back," Morgan said.

"Count on it," Jenn said.

They continued to hug as Catherine was now shedding tears and clenching to Richard. Meanwhile, Lisa hugged her brother from the side, and he wrapped his one arm around her.

They all let go at the same time.

"Hey?" Morgan intervened. "One more for the road?" She raised her arms and looked around in this circle of friends.

Miranda smiled with tears in her eyes and hugged her best friend one more time. The other girls joined in, then Jason wrapped around everyone, and then Lisa went up to hug Miranda up front, and finally Nikko completed it.

After a long, bittersweet moment, they all released. Miranda looked up at Nikko and grabbed a hold of his hand. They put on brave faces, before looking at their parents.

"Okay. We're ready," she said.

"All right. Lisa?" Bruce called.

"I'm coming." Lisa walked over to get into the back seat of the car.

"You two sure you're gonna be fine?" Samantha asked.

"What do you think?" Nikko asked Miranda.

"Yeah, we'll be right behind you," she answered.

Their parents got into the front of their cars and started up the engines.

Before leaving, they both took one look back at their friends standing with their respective partners.

"See y'all soon," Nikko said.

"We love you guys," Miranda said.

Everybody stood there and waved goodbye as Nikko and Miranda walked off.

They walked behind Nikko's family's car, where they prepared for departure on their mode of transportation: Nikko's new 2017 Honda Rebel that he got for his eighteenth birthday.

He lifted Miranda to sit on the back of the seat and handed her a helmet before he got onto the seat and put his own on with a pair of sunglasses.

He started up the engine. "It's gonna be a long ride."

"And I'm ready for it." She put on a pair of goggles and wrapped her arms around his body, clasping her hands.

"You feel safe?"

"With you? Always."

She kissed his cheek and embraced him, warranting a smile.

Both cars left the curbside and started driving down the road.

Nikko started to drive himself and Miranda behind the trail, as their friends waved them off one last time.

After a couple of miles, they were now off Staten Island heading for Princeton, toward a new beginning—the next chapter in this story of childhood friends who were torn apart by tragedy, found each other again, and became soulmates. A love story that will continue to grow. For even when it seems it's all been told, it never truly ends. There will always be "more to it."